ACCESS
All Areas

JOANNA MURDOCH

Author's Note

For authenticity, this book has been written to reflect the prevalent
attitudes, prejudices and views held by some people
within the mid-1980s.
This is especially true in terms of attitudes
towards mental health and women.

Thankfully, we know so much better today.

For the *real* Izzy
(When she's grown up enough to read it)

1

GLASGOW, SCOTLAND

'Mum! Have you and Betty been at the sherry again during one of your marathon telephone conversations?'

Izzy was trying her best to suppress a grin but—predictably—she caught one of her Mum's 'I'm not amused' looks from the corner of her eye.

'Don't be so ridiculous, Isabelle.'

Her mother always reverted to using Izzy's full baptismal name when she disapproved of something her daughter had said. It happened all *too* frequently.

'That was once, Isabelle, as well you know. I'm not a drinker.'

Mary Anderson was much more a tee-total-one-sherry-at-Christmas kind of gal.

Izzy shot another quick glance at her mother, who was seated alongside her and clutching the seatbelt between anxious hands, her sapphire blue eyes glued on the busy motorway ahead.

'Then you've got to be kidding me, right? Please tell me this is a joke?'

Izzy couldn't believe what her usually strait-laced mother had just asked her to do. It was too unbelievable, too over-the-top, and—

more to the point—knowing her Dad, he'd never agree to it; not in a proverbial month of Sundays.

'Izzy, can you please keep your eyes on the road? And watch your speed, young lady. You're not some Formula One driver, you know!' her mum reprimanded. 'We don't want to be upside down in a ditch, just six weeks after passing you're driving test.'

It was obvious to Izzy—by her mother's agitated expression—that's exactly where Mrs Anderson thought they'd end up any second now.

'Mum, we won't end up in a ditch,' Izzy soothed, but all the same she eased her stiletto-clad foot off the car's accelerator—maybe her mum had a point— it was raining cats and dogs this morning.

'And you do realise what you're asking me to do is probably illegal?' She reconsidered the proposition her mum had just relayed to her for a few more seconds, 'In fact, it sounds most definitely illegal.'

'Betty would never have suggested it if she wasn't desperate,' her mother emphasised, 'she's worried sick, Izzy. She hardly sees him these days. He's making so much money he's become one of those tax exile people. Apparently the rules limit how much time he can spend in this country.'

Her mum's lip curled. 'According to Betty, when she does get to see him, he looks awful. Death warmed up was her latest description. Whenever she asks what's wrong, he just says he's a wee bit tired, and not to worry.'

Mary sucked in a breath. 'And then last week, Betty found a bottle of *sleeping tablets* in his suitcase.'

Izzy cocked an eyebrow. There would be no 'just found' about it. Not if she knew Betty Hambro. Those tablets would have been sniffed out with the accuracy of a Saint Bernard seeking casualties in a Swiss avalanche.

'Going through his suitcase "accidently on purpose" by any chance, Mum?'

'Well, yes,' her mum admitted, colouring slightly. 'She did feel a bit of snooping was required, but only as a last resort, mind. Betty's always been adamant that he doesn't do drugs per-se. He might have the odd dodgy cigarette occasionally, but that's all. That's why she was so shocked. It's completely out-of-character. And according to Betty once you start *popping* these kinds of pills, you're on the slippery slope to God knows what. And she should know, working in a Doctor's surgery.'

'Well, Mum, he sounds like every other rock star I've ever heard of,' Izzy replied, not failing to be impressed by her mum's correct use of the term "popping". 'They all succumb to temptation eventually and, before you know it, they're doped to the eyeballs. His cousin Jonny's got a serious cocaine habit. The Sunday papers were full of it a few weeks ago. Don't you remember?'

Izzy did a mirror check for any hazards. 'Anyway, we're drifting from the point; I'm an Economics Graduate, hopefully a full-time lecturer in the not-too-distant future. Are you seriously asking me to deviate from my proposed career path to step-in as Eclectic Deviation's new PA?'

As expected, her mother failed—on purpose—to register Izzy's subtle play on words.

'Really, Izzy, you make it sound as though it's going to be forever. It would be five months out of your life—six at the very most. Just enough time to find out if Betty's suspicions are correct about him using those tablets.'

Izzy knew the hard sell was just moments away.

'You're such a smart girl,' Mary went on. 'You typed up your final year dissertation and were commended for its presentation. I've taught you to do shorthand as good as any secretary, and you're always super organised. You could do that job standing on your head, and you know it! Anyway, only last week, you mentioned taking time out before applying for your teaching post. This would be a wonderful opportunity to travel, see the world and have some fun!'

'But I was only talking about taking a few weeks, at most,' Izzy murmured, rolling her eyes.

Most surprisingly, her mother ignored the eye roll, instead laying a gentle hand on Izzy's arm and giving it a comforting squeeze. 'And it gives you a chance to re-think the "Alex" situation.'

Great, Alex. Again!

Izzy had wondered how long it would take for Alex to rear his head in their conversation. Her mum was nothing if not predictable, desperate for them to stage the full hearts and flowers reconciliation. Alex Fairbairn had been classified by her parents as one hundred per cent son-in-law material.

'I don't need to re-think Alex.' Izzy kept her tone clipped, before muttering the mantra "Mirror, signal, mirror, and manoeuvre" to herself, as she flicked her indicator, changed down gears and moved out into the overtaking lane behind a sporty *Volkswagen Golf*.

She gave its cherry red top-of-the-range chassis a wistful once-over. She'd been desperate for that kind of car, but her dad—who'd been holding the purse strings—had replied with an emphatic 'NO', hence the Mini Metro they were currently sitting in. 'Mum, they'd see through me straightaway. I'd never get away with it. And, even if I did, I'm not totally comfortable keeping tabs—no, let's be honest here—spying on some poor guy twenty-four-seven.'

She placed the car back into fourth gear, trying to ignore the clench in the pit of her stomach when she conjured up an image of the "poor guy" in question; Richard 'Rick' Hambro, Betty's son and Eclectic Deviation's drummer. Now, he definitely wouldn't be her parents' idea of suitable son-in-law material. Not that she'd classify herself as a "fan" of his rock band. She was way past the stage of mooning over pop stars like some hormonal teenager, but she had eyes, and the guy was seriously—face-fanningly—gorgeous.

Last week, she'd caught their latest video on *Top of the Pops*, Rick lying naked on a rumpled bed, sheet strategically placed at hip level, and leaving nothing to the imagination as to what *he wasn't* wearing underneath. The scene implying he'd just enjoyed a steamy romp with the video's sultry female lead. His collar-length ebony hair suitably dishevelled, those angular features relaxed into a knowing smile. And his eyes! Wow, their brown depths had been sending out a message alright. Telling the love interest to get back under the duvet pronto and indulge in Round Two.

No, neither Rick—nor his four bandmates for that matter—could be described as lightweight bubblegum pop stars; they were bona-fide rockers. Men who enjoyed the full sex, drugs and rock'n'roll lifestyle and wanted the rest of the world to know it. And that smouldering look he'd directed at the camera. She still couldn't shift it from her brain no matter how hard she tried. Definitely not the kind of look she'd ever received from Alex.

In fact, Alex had been more inclined to drop the immortal line, "let's debate the pros and cons of Malthusian Economics, Izzy" than cock an eyebrow and suggest they hightail it to the bedroom and indulge in hot steamy sex. In Alex's world, Malthusian Economics constituted serious foreplay that no girl could resist.

Rick, however, looked to be the type of guy who enjoyed hot steamy sex at the drop of a hat and didn't need to spout an outdated theory in order to get a woman to share his bed. In fact, his idea of foreplay would probably involve a very different take on the old "supply-and-demand" equation entirely. Not that she was ever likely to find out; more's the pity.

With a determined shake of the head, Izzy finally managed—for now—to dispel the arousing image of Rick reclining in that bed. Fantasising about rock stars wasn't recommended while hurtling along a motorway, dodging puddles that would have given Noah and his ark serious headaches.

'Let's not call it spying exactly.' Her mother's voice pulled Izzy reluctantly back to the here and now. 'Betty isn't too comfortable with that word. She prefers "keeping an eye on". Richard has suffered from bouts of insomnia since he was a child and always when he's worried about something. Betty wants to know why it's reared its ugly head again. He's never had to resort to taking sleeping tablets before. In fact…'

Her mother adopted hushed tones, although for whom Izzy didn't know; it was only them in the car. 'The words "heading for a nervous-breakdown" were mentioned.'

Izzy let her jaw drop, making sure she appeared suitably shocked at the weight of her mum's disclosure. Her mum expected a reaction.

'According to Betty, he's always jetting off here, there and everywhere, and as for the racy lifestyle these people lead…'

Disapproval could be heard a mile off. Rock stars were—most definitely—not Mary Anderson's genteel cup of *Earl Gray*.

'You know, Izzy, lots of heavy drinking, drug taking, and going to those orgy things every night. It's enough to make a woman's hair turn grey overnight.'

Izzy took careful note of her mum's steely curls, but decided not to state the obvious. Anyway, Rick's racy lifestyle was par for the course, as far as the average rock star was concerned.

'And Betty doesn't trust that fiancée of his. Says Francesca's too busy spending Richard's money on their new flat and forthcoming wedding to notice what's happening under her very nose.'

'Mum, listen to yourself. This is a really stupid idea. It won't work.'

It was time to be the voice of reason.

'What do you mean, love?'

'Well, for a start, if I turn up as their PA, won't Rick recognise me? I know he meets a lot of women in his line of work,'—understatement of the century—'but he can't have come across too many "Mary Isabelle Andersons" hailing from bonnie Scotland.'

'But he hasn't seen you for fifteen years.' Mary gave a sharp intake of breath as Izzy's foot depressed on the accelerator. 'Isabelle, please watch your speed!'

Her mum's eyes—so like Izzy's own—were still super-glued to the speedometer. The needle had now made it to the wrong side of sixty. 'And, anyway, you look nothing like you did when you were eight.'

'No, I don't suppose I do,' Izzy answered, taking the hint and easing off the accelerator once more.

Mum was right. Just as Rick had transformed himself into a smouldering Rock God, she'd undergone a bit of a metamorphosis too. Gone were the heavy-framed *National Health* spectacles, replaced by discreet contact lenses. Her glossy chestnut brown hair, once sporting the in-vogue 'Page Boy' haircut, was now permed and styled into a softly curling French bob that reached to her shoulders. More importantly, she'd shed the puppy fat she'd carried about in those days; her curvy figure a trim eight stone six. She might not be an *ugly duckling* anymore, but a swan was still pushing the envelope when it came to matching up to the type of women Rick regularly rubbed shoulders with.

'I still think he's bound to recognise the name, Mum.'

'Mmmmm, maybe you might be right there, Izzy.'

Great! Mary Anderson was finally seeing sense.

'And Betty did say she wants all this to be kept very hush-hush…..' Deep lines filled Mary's brow.

Silence followed for a few more moments, but Izzy could almost hear her mother ramping up the old brain cells. Like Betty, Mary was not to be thwarted when the old bee was firmly lodged in her bonnet.

'I've got it! How about using my maiden name, Stevenson? Yes, that could be your alias, Izzy Stevenson!'

Izzy let out a low groan. Her mum had obviously been watching too many of her beloved spy thrillers again. This was real life, not some silly *James Bond* movie.

'Betty always refers to you as Isabelle and never Izzy. He'll never twig Izzy Stevenson is really Isabelle Anderson.'

'But what about the fact my real name appears on my passport?' Izzy's hands gripped the steering wheel tighter. 'I hope you're not asking me to doctor that! Sorry, Mum, but I don't fancy a holiday at Her Majesty's expense because I've passed myself off as someone else on official documentation.'

'I'm sure you can come up with an excuse not to show them your passport.' Izzy received an impatient tut. 'You could even use Aunt Maggie's address if they require sending you any correspondence.'

'Great. So my godmother will be embroiled in the subterfuge, too. Somehow, I still think, as potential employers, the band might need to see proof of my identity.'

Her mum could be so naïve sometimes.

'And what about producing a reference? Where do I magic that up from? I'm currently working in *'Chelsea Girl'*. Not quite the same as churning out sixty words per minute on a Word Processer for some Company Director.'

Izzy changed down the gears. A large queue of traffic was backing up, nose to tail, ahead.

'Don't worry, darling. I'm way ahead of you, there!'

Great, what Machiavellian twist was Mary Anderson about to throw into the mix now?

'We can re-hash some of my old ones. I've still got a couple kicking about somewhere at home. Remember, I was a personal secretary before I married your dad.'

'Yes, Mum, but that was twenty five years ago. We'll need to do some pretty major *re-hashing* to cover the skills they're looking for today. And no matter how you dress it up, I'd still be deceiving them!'

There was a screech of tyres in front.

'*Shit!*' Izzy hastily jumped on the brakes.

The *Volkswagen Golf* had ground to a halt in front of her; all three lanes of traffic now at a virtual standstill for some unknown reason.

'Language, Isabelle'

Izzy exhaled with relief, ignoring the sharpness of her mother's reprimand. She'd missed the other car by a good six inches.

'Nor is there any guarantee I'd get an interview, Mum; never mind the actual job'.

As she waited for the cars to move off, Izzy's eyes rested momentarily on the hypnotic swish of the windscreen wipers. Against her better judgement, part of her was becoming interested in Betty's proposition. It certainly sounded much more exciting than her current three-days-a-week stint behind a cash desk taking the flak from grumpy customers. Her permanently aching feet would probably thank her, too.

But so much could potentially go wrong.

'I still think this idea has disaster written all over it, in big letters.' she muttered, half to herself.

'Don't be so melodramatic. You're beginning to sound like your father,' Mary dismissed. 'Betty said they're desperate for someone to start straightaway. It's unlikely any references will be chased up. Apparently their previous PA left under a bit of a cloud. Betty doesn't know the full story.'

'And talking of Dad, what does Mr Anderson say about Betty's plans? No doubt, quite a lot if I know him.'

There was no way her dad would want his daughter mixed-up with some hard-living rock band. Keeping his only child away from malign influences was Andrew Anderson's raison d'être in life. And Rick Hambro—and his four bandmates—would be classified as extremely malign in *CAPITAL LETTERS*.

'Stop trying to throw obstacles in the way of a great idea, Izzy. They urgently need a PA for the final months of their world tour— starting First December—and you'd be perfect. You know you would?'

Izzy slipped the car from neutral into first gear, releasing the handbrake as the tailback of vehicles began to crawl forward.

'In other words, Dad doesn't know yet.'

She could tell her Mum was being deliberately cagey, a mile off.

'There is only one snag; you need to get your application in by next Tuesday.'

'*Next* Tuesday!' Izzy's eyes were back on her mother. 'Mum, that's only three days away. It doesn't give me much time.'

'Isabelle, for goodness' sake, will you please watch what you are doing! You were nearly into the back of that car again. How you ever passed your driving test, I'll never know?'

'*Shit!*' The word slipped out before Izzy could stop herself, and more evasive action had to be taken to avoid an accident.

'And I despair of your language. You weren't brought up to use those sorts of words. University and today's permissive society has a lot to answer for.' Mary gave a frustrated shake of the head, before continuing, 'If you're successful, all Betty wants is regular updates on what's happening with Richard.'

'Like what kinds of drugs he takes; how many times a week he gets pissed… sorry, I mean gets drunk.' Izzy caught the censorious glint in her mum's eye. 'If he sleeps with a different groupie every night, even though he's supposedly loved-up with the beautiful Francesca. Yup, Mum, that definitely constitutes spying to me.'

'Honestly, it's not as if we're asking *you* to jump into bed with him like some modern-day Mata Hari.'

'Mum!'

Had that comment really made it past her mother's lips? According to her mother and father, nice girls didn't do sex before marriage. Consequently, Izzy was still awaiting the full "birds and the bees" chat. Thank God, her mum didn't know she no longer constituted her definition of a 'nice girl'.

'So, what about Rick's dad and his sister—Michelle isn't it? Are they on board with Betty's crazy idea?'

'Well, let's just say, Jim's not completely sold on it. Michelle doesn't know yet.

Izzy let out a bark of laughter; she wasn't daft. 'Tell the truth. Her husband thinks it's a non-starter. You do realise that if Rick finds out, he'll never trust his parents again. He's got Fleet Street constantly digging dirt on his private life, without his own mum getting in on the act.'

In Izzy's opinion, no soon-to-be twenty-eight-year-old would welcome his mother prying into his private life, especially the one he led as a member of Eclectic Deviation. According to the tabloids, the band's hedonistic exploits read like the pages of a racy Jackie Collins's novel on steroids.

'He's not going to find out, Izzy. And we're not digging for dirt per-se, yours will be purely a watching brief,' Mary said. 'You'll be with them from the beginning of December to the end of April. All you have to do is keep your head down, play the part of their indispensable PA, and send regular updates back to Betty on what's happening. Richard will never suspect a thing. Simple!'

'Simple, she says.'

'And it will give you more time to think about Alex too.'

Typical! Her Mum wasn't letting up on the Alex front, either.

'Alex's such a lovely boy, Izzy,' Mary's face had taken on an altogether dreamy look, 'one of life's true "knights in shining armour", if you ask me. Is there really no chance—?'

'No mum.' Her mother would never understand what had gone wrong between her and Alex. 'Anyway, modern women don't need all that "knights-in-shining-armour" nonsense anymore. This *is* 1984.'

Did she sound convincing? That image of a half-naked Rick had popped up once more.

'Don't be ridiculous, Izzy! You're spouting that feminist claptrap again, every woman needs a man who makes her go weak at the knees.' her mum retorted. 'Look at me; I've got your father'

This time, Izzy couldn't stifle a chuckle at the thought of her portly father dressed as a white knight. Now Rick, on the other hand…..

'And you need one too, Isabelle.'

'Mum, I don't want to argue with you about Alex. Not today…'

'Yes, okay, point taken' Mary hurried on, 'Where were we? Oh yes, at the end of the tour you'll pack your bags, Richard will be none the wiser, and Betty will be a whole lot clearer on what she and Jim might be dealing with.'

Izzy changed up another gear since the traffic had begun to move faster, and she carefully moved out to the motorway's centre lane.

'Izzy, look at it this way. Once this is over, what are the chances of you ever bumping into him again? Non-existent! Our only link to him is through Betty, and while I'm in regular contact by telephone and letter, I'm up here and she's down in Reading. Looking the way you do now, together with a change of name, he'll never suss its little Isabelle Anderson from all those years ago.'

'Mmmm, I suppose so…'

This was crazy. Was she really contemplating becoming involved in Betty's hare-brained scheme? And if she got the job, would she be capable of pulling off the deception for *six* months without Richard Hambro suspecting?

'Mum, aren't you the tiniest bit concerned about my moral welfare in all this? You're fully aware of their reputation. Dad's bound to have a coronary at the very thought of me going anywhere near them. They might try to—God forbid—corrupt his precious Izzy.'

That would be the crux of her father's argument. In fact, if he could lock Izzy up in an ivory tower for the next fifty years, he wouldn't hesitate, and he'd probably insist she wore a chastity belt into the bargain.

'We brought you up to know the difference between right and wrong, Isabelle. I have no concerns about you on that score.' Her mother gave a large sniff.

They passed under a large gantry proclaiming the *'Glasgow's Miles Better'* slogan in gaudy, neon yellow letters.

'And what if I still say no?'

Although the words— "yes please and where do I sign"—were beginning to flash like Belisha beacons in her brain.

'It's entirely your choice.'

'And Dad *really* doesn't know anything, yet?' Izzy re-checked.

'No, I'm waiting for the right moment to broach it. Get him in a good mood, but only once you've said yes, of course.'

Izzy slipped the car into third gear, flicked the indicator, and accelerated out into the lane signposted for the city centre.

The rain had started to ease off; the first glimmer of sunlight peeping through the storm clouds. Could she take the glimpse of autumnal sunshine as a good omen?

'He won't be happy, Mum. If anyone can put a spanner in the works it's Andrew Anderson.'

'Don't worry, love. If you decide to take the job, just leave your father to me.'

2

LONDON, ENGLAND

'Izzy, do you actually understand what a fucking band rider is?'

Izzy tried not to roll her eyes at the use of Davey Eastman's favourite expletive. Every word he uttered was usually prefixed with another one, and always starting with the letter 'f'. She was also being glared at from his beady hazel eyes. She'd been here since Monday, but every time he'd dispatched one of those malevolent glowers in her direction, it'd felt like five years—hard labour. Somehow, from Day One, they'd got off on the wrong foot and stayed there.

'Or have we just hired another PA who's as thick as two fucking planks?'

Don't let him provoke you. Bite your tongue. The little git's called you worse already!

'Yeah,' Steve Gilbert, the Eclectic Deviation's front man, cut-in, deliberately blowing a cloud of cigarette smoke into Izzy's face.

On principle, she refused to cough. She loathed cigarette smoking and, much to her horror, everyone around here smoked like industrial chimneys. Except Rick—thankfully—his bad habit of choice appeared to be chewing gum.

'When we specify something on our rider, the idea is we fucking get it, not be palmed off with cheap-as-shit alternatives. Got that, Lizzy?' Steve rapped out.

'It's Izzy,' she corrected him through gritted teeth.

The git was trying to intimidate her with those fishy eyes of his. And he'd called her Lizzy, *again*. Twice today hadn't been enough for him, he was going for the bloody hat trick. Like Davey, he'd discovered the knack of rubbing her up the wrong way, with his confrontational manner and constant use of the F-word.

Yesterday, in one brief conversation he'd used it ten times—she'd counted. For a man responsible for some of the most beautiful lyrics in the British Charts, together with a voice that trumped Simon Le Bon, George Michael and the rest of the *Top 40* put together, his everyday use of the Queen's English left a *lot* to be desired.

Since her arrival, he and Davey had taken perverse delight on pouncing on everything she'd said and done—with one aim in mind— to belittle her. Izzy suspected it might be some weird initiation test they'd dreamed up to see how far her buttons could be pushed before she'd quit on them too.

And to be fair, only Davey and Steve had been responsible for serious feather ruffling. The sole reason for her presence—Rick— hadn't paid her much attention at all. That is, if she wasn't counting the number of ice-cream melting smiles he'd shot in her direction over the last few days.

Is it ten or eleven now? No, it's definitely eleven.

She gave the four members of the band seated before her—Rick was currently holed up in the bathroom throwing up after last night's party—what she hoped was one of her most appealing smiles. This job was proving to be a steep learning curve, and their manager, Jack Clayton, hadn't provided any safety harness. The last five days had been a baptism of fire, and she was feeling decidedly singed by the whole experience. Where were the charming young men she'd met at her interview?

'I understand perfectly what a rider is,' she pointed out, engaging her extra-polite tone; the one that really pissed Davey off big time. She'd heard him say so.

Yep, time to lay it on with a trowel, Izzy!

'But Jack has tasked me to make savings to the catering budget for your American tour...'

She caught Davey roll his eyes at Steve, but ignored him. No wonder their previous PA, Angie had voted with her feet. 'And from my research, changing champagne brands, particularly those which are difficult to source in certain states, would help reduce our initial outlay.'

She ventured another smile but, predictably, got zilch in reply. Jonathan 'Jonny' Hambro, their lead guitarist sitting to her left, just yawned loudly and contemplated his cuticles. His elder cousin, Marc Hambro—their keyboardist—made no eye contact either; too busy scribbling more instructions on a large A4 notepad. Clearly, he was working on yet another list she would be asked to tackle—urgently— before the day was out. Everything Marc asked her to do was classified 'URGENT'.

'Surely, making savings is a good thing?'

Am I really arguing over the price of champagne?

To someone who was a bit of a lightweight as far as alcohol was concerned—two glasses of white wine was generally her limit—she expected one brand of Champagne tasted like any other. And from what she'd witnessed last night, she'd be surprised if this lot even tasted it anyway. It just seemed to go straight over their throats without touching the sides.

'And we're telling you,' Davey jabbed his index finger at her, 'make your fucking savings elsewhere. We supposedly hired you because you've got brains, with your fucking degree in God knows what.' She received a withering look. 'Start fucking using them, and make whatever fucking savings you want, but my fucking *Bollinger's* non-fucking-negotiable. Got it?'

Six times in the one sentence; not one of Davey's more restrained afternoons. But her politeness had succeeded in annoying the shit out of him. Thank God her mum wasn't here. With all the expletives flying around, she'd have keeled over days ago.

Great! Savings to Jack's Catering Budget equated to precisely nil!

'I'll see what I can do.' She answered.

'No, don't *see* what you can do!' Davey threw up his hands in despair. 'Just *do it, Izzy,*' he let out a bellow that would have awakened the dead. '*Have you fucking got that, woman?*'

She was pretty sure steam was leaking from her ears. The bloody man was impossible!

'Here, take this.' Marc tore a page from his notepad, flapping it under her nose.

As she'd predicted, it was crammed with yet more instructions and in practically illegible red writing.

'I need you to do this—'

'Urgently?' she finished for him, aiming for a touch of levity, but earning a frosty-eyed rebuke instead for perceived impertinence.

Izzy turned away. Now she had another bloody list to tackle, as well as tracking down a cheap consignment of *Bollinger.* Why had she said "yes" to Betty's scheme, again?

'Owwwff!'

Her face made contact with a hard wall of masculine chest covered in a faded black *Grateful Dead* T-shirt. Rick had surfaced.

'Sorry,' Izzy apologised, as Rick's hands went out to steady her.

An unexpected tingle shot up her forearm; his long slim fingers making contact with the bare skin of her wrist. Blood rushed to her cheeks, and she swallowed, lifting her eyes to take in the five-foot-ten ebony-haired Adonis standing before her. She received yet another of those thigh-clenching smiles. At least this part of Betty's plan was working a treat. Since her arrival, there had been no inkling of recognition on Rick's part, whatsoever.

'Sorry, that was entirely my fault, Izzy.'

Rick's pallor might still have been a little green, but hung-over or not, he still looked sexy as hell in t-shirt and ripped jeans, his damp hair brushing against collar of his T-shirt. In fact, those dark tousled locks were just asking for a girl to run her fingers through them…

Then, she caught the familiar whiff of his aftershave. As usual, it didn't disappoint. He smelt totally amazing. Fresh and tangy, just like the sea on an early summer's morning.

Alex hadn't been into after-shave.

'How are you feeling?' she asked, recovering both her balance and her sensibilities at their unexpectedly close encounter.

'Like shit,' he admitted, delivering another knee-trembling smile, and showing perfectly even white teeth. 'By the way, sorry I'm late for the meeting, Izzy. Did I miss anything important?'

Her stomach turned a cartwheel. His voice, all sexy and husky, made her feel all kinds of hot and bothered, in all kinds of places due south.

'Nah, it's just Miss Goody Two Shoes trying to turn us into a bunch of tea-total mummy's boys!' Davey interjected with a sneer, killing the moment stone dead.

'Well, given how crap I'm feeling, maybe I should consider it. What do you think, Izzy?' Rick winked at her, before collapsing down onto the seat she'd just vacated next to his cousin Jonny.

Her stomach reprised its cartwheel. That was the first time he'd winked at her.

Jeez, it's getting decidedly warm in here!

'Would you like me to rustle up some tea or coffee from Room Service?' she asked instead, hoping she sounded calmer—and way more efficient—than she actually felt with those chocolate brown eyes resting upon her.

Rick shook his head. 'No thanks, I'd never keep it down.'

'Well, if you change your mind…' She let her offer hang in the air for a second. 'Just buzz downstairs and I can organise. I'll be in my room if you need me.'

The smile he delivered ensured cartwheel number three was a mere formality.

Izzy headed for the door. It was time to get back to work. Do something constructive before she was tempted to tell *TweedleDee* Eastman and *TweedleDum* Gilbert exactly what she thought of them and their take on her cost-cutting exercise.

'And leave that fucking door open, will you!' Davey called out after her. 'It's stifling in here. In fact, call that posh bird down in reception that fancies Steve. Tell her to send up Hotel Maintenance to look at the bloody radiators. And don't take no for an answer. I'm not paying to live in a fucking sauna for the next week.'

With a curt nod, she let herself out, leaving the door ajar as Davey had requested, all the time bristling at the way he referred to women as 'birds'. Didn't he realise how demeaning that expression was nowadays?

Waiting in the corridor for the lift to arrive, she was treated to another burst of his non-stop whinging and—no surprise—she was still the target of his ire.

'I wish you'd stop encouraging that one, Rick. Cut the fucking gentleman routine for once. Too bloody nice that's your trouble. She needs to know her fucking place and fast!' Davey launched into a bad impression of Rick's middle class Berkshire accent. "No thanks, Izzy, I'd never keep it down…."'

The band's amused laughter filtered out into the corridor.

'Anyone would think you wanted to shag her,' Davey continued. 'Is that it? Fancy getting inside her knickers while we're on tour, do you?' He then added something extremely offensive about a part of her anatomy which elicited explosive sniggers from Jonny and Steve.

Izzy flinched, hating being the butt of their dirty jokes.

'Well, I'd steer clear, if I were you,' Davey hadn't finished with her yet. 'That one's a troublemaker. Could tell the moment I laid eyes on her. But as per fucking usual, no one around here listens to me. That bird, Kelly what's-her-name was a way better fit. She toured with *Black Sabbath* and the *Rolling Stones*. Jeez, she even took coke with Mick and Keith. And what have *we* ended up with? Miss Goody Fucking Two Shoes offering to make us a mug of bloody *Ovaltine*, and tuck us in at bedtime, that's what.'

The lift doors pinged, but Izzy remained frozen to the spot, her ears still straining to overhear more of their conversation. Against her better judgement, she wondered what Rick's reply might be. Her mother always said eavesdroppers never heard any good of themselves. Was he about to prove her mum right? Make some cutting remark and shatter all Izzy's illusions for good?

'Yeah, she's a good-looking girl, but not exactly my type, Davey.' Rick replied. 'Her knickers are perfectly safe from me.'

No surprise there, but at least he'd said she was good-looking. Her heart gave a little jig of pleasure. That was something—at the very least.

'And she does have a great pair of tits on her.' Jonny cut in. 'Could do worse than rest your weary head there when Francesca's 32E beauties aren't available?'

Izzy scowled at the "tits" comment. She wasn't some *Friesian Cow*. But then, should she really be surprised that Jonny Hambro had checked out her figure? After all, he checked out any female with a pulse.

'Yeah, and we know you're not into the sweet wholesome look that Izzy's got going.' Steve commented. 'Anyway, given the girls we can take our pick from, who would want a run-of-the-mill hamburger, when you can sink your teeth in a juicy fillet steak every night of the week.'

Thanks, Steve, for that vote of confidence.

Izzy could almost see their lead singer rubbing his hands together in glee at the thought of all the "fresh meat" he'd encounter while on tour.

'Yeah, our Ricky only likes the really dirty girls like my sister-in-law,' Davey guffawed.

'Six months and counting until Francesca's slips on the ball and chain; isn't that right, Ricky?' Jonny intoned.

'Fuck off. You won't be far behind me. Not if Jilly has her way.' Rick retorted.

'No fear! I might have given her the engagement ring to shut her up, but she'll have to drag me up that aisle, kicking and screaming. I intend to be single for a good few years yet.'

There was more raucous laughter, before Rick spoke again. 'But can't you just lay off Izzy for five minutes, Davey? You've been on her case from the moment she arrived. At least, she's trying to get to grips with things around here…'

'Yeah,' Marc interjected, 'which is more than Angie ever did.'

With those unexpected—but nevertheless welcome—endorsements ringing in her ears, Izzy stepped inside the lift compartment, punching the button for her floor with renewed determination, imagining it was Davey and Steve's collective noses. Time to rise above their collective put downs, Betty was depending on her, and there was no way she was going to throw in the towel after a mere five days.

Run-of-the-mill hamburger indeed!

3

MANCHESTER, ENGLAND

'You mean you and Jonny were an item?' Izzy set her milk-shake down on the floor, intrigued by unexpected and rather startling admission her new friend, Kathy Davies—the band's wardrobe mistress—had just disclosed.

'When was that?'

They were sitting in Izzy's makeshift office within the Manchester Apollo, grabbing a late lunch. This was the first time Kathy had admitted to having any past romantic entanglement with a member of the band.

'Ages before I got together with Scottie. And I wouldn't call Jonny and I an "item".' Kathy gave a snort of derisive laughter. 'We were never "officially" boyfriend/girlfriend. Just had sex a few times, and went on precisely two disastrous dates.' She rolled her eyes. 'Put it this way, I certainly wasn't taken home and introduced to the parents.'

Reaching over, Kathy helped herself to a copious handful of *cheese & onion* crisps from the packet they'd been sharing.

'We'd got totally rat-arsed one night, and it lasted about a fortnight at most. Then it just fizzled out. You know what Jonny's like, always looking for the next notch on the old bedpost. Anyway, I wasn't too bothered. My eyes had started wandering too.'

'So how do you feel about him now?' Izzy hurriedly retrieved more crisps for herself before Kathy scoffed the lot.

'To be honest I don't feel anything.' Kathy proffered a one-shouldered shrug. 'Am I supposed to? As I told you, we were never the romance of the century. We realised pretty quick, mates was our best bet.'

'But you still work with him? Isn't it a little awkward? After all, he's with Jilly.'

'Why does it have to be awkward? We're both mature adults. Well I am. Knowing Jonny, I doubt he could even spell the word "mature".' Kathy laughed 'At the end of the day, it was just sex—and not very good—sex. It never crossed my mind that I should quit my job over him. Jonny Hambro didn't break my heart, and I certainly didn't break his.'

She wiped some stray crumbs from her jeans now with a dismissive flick. 'But enough about my love life, I'd much rather hear about yours.' She fixed Izzy with a penetrating stare.

'What do you mean, mine?'

It was time to be discreet and not disclose too much. Up till now, Kathy—like everyone else around here—had only been privy to the bare minimum about Izzy's back-story.

'Well, you've been with us for a few weeks now,' Kathy said, tightening her blonde ponytail, 'and I know you've turned down several *invitations* from the guys on the road crew.' That comment elicited a suggestive waggle of both eyebrows. 'But I haven't heard you speak about any boyfriend pining away back home, so what gives, Miss Stevenson? Is there a special someone you're not telling me about?'

'I broke up with my fiancé just before I started this job.' Izzy moistened her lips. 'I'm really not ready to jump back into any kind of relationship.'

Conducting a romance around here would be out of the question, especially as she trying to pass herself off as someone else entirely.

'Wow, you were engaged?'Kathy's amber eyes were now the size of dinner plates, 'Didn't see that coming. So, what happened?'

'It just wasn't working.' Izzy debated how much more to say before settling on, 'we'd been together a few years, but I came to realise he wasn't my Happy Ever After, so I finished it. I'm still looking for Mr Right'.

Not strictly true, given her increasing 'crush' on Rick, but then realistically, he was never going to occupy that role, either.

For something to do, she picked up her milkshake, and took a slurp.

'Do you regret it?' Kathy probed. 'Splitting up with your ex?'

Izzy shook head. 'Not in the slightest. Looking back, we were totally wrong for each other; in so many ways.'

'But surely you miss the sex!' Kathy delivered a teasing dig to Izzy's ribs.

Wincing, Izzy chose a non-committal 'Mmmm' instead. She definitely wasn't ready to tell Kathy the truth about that side of her relationship.

'Well, in that case, it's confession time.' Kathy's eyes sparkled with mischief. 'If you had the chance, which one of the band would *you* like to take to bed, for a night?'

'What?' Izzy almost choked, mid swallow.

Now what did she say? Knowing, Kathy, she wasn't going to settle for a polite 'no comment'.

'Well, you must have developed the hots for one of them, what with everyone living in each other's pockets. Plus, you see them practically naked all the time, and they're good-looking guys!' Kathy clicked her tongue. 'Well, maybe not Davey. Not exactly an oil painting, that one. But I've a feeling that a classy lady like Miss Izzy Stevenson has more taste than the 'Davey Eastmans' of this world. Not yours truly, unfortunately. Been there, done that and bought the T-shirt, after a tequila session that got completely out of hand. And believe me, the rumours are all true! It ended much too prematurely, if you know what I mean?'

That naughty confession made them both burst into fits of laughter.

'But there must be one of them surely…' Kathy continued at length. 'Although I get the feeling it's not Marc either. So, that leaves Steve, Jonny or Rick.'

Izzy pretended to flick an imaginary piece of fluff from her blouse.

Damn! At the very thought of Rick, a blush began creeping up her neck. He was one of life's nice guys and the time she'd spent with him to date had only reinforced that belief. Worse, by the knowing look on Kathy's face, she'd spotted the blush too.

'I knew it.' Kathy let out a triumphant whoop of delight. 'I'm getting warmer—literally so! Let's see, don't think it's Steve, our resident Dr Jekyll and Mr Hyde. Charming one minute, spoilt git the next. Only your best friend if he wants something, otherwise he wouldn't piss on you if you were on fire.'

Kathy leaned forward, hands placed on Izzy's knees, their faces inches apart. 'Okay, Miss Stevenson, it is time to make a decision—Jonny or Rick? If I was to twist your arm, which one would you drop your knickers for?'

Izzy's cheeks were positively on fire now.

What the hell did she say? She certainly couldn't admit her ever-deepening attraction to Rick. But then, she didn't want to say she'd the hots for Jonny either.

'Okay.' It was time for some quick thinking. 'I'll concede—of the two—Rick's the better looking, but as to sex, sorry to disappoint you Kathy, but neither floats this girl's boat.'

What a liar! Pinocchio and that ever-expanding nose better watch out!

'Stop telling porkies, Miss Stevenson.'

Great! Kathy had seen through her denial straightaway. But why didn't that surprise her? Kathy was one perceptive cookie.

'I already know its Rick you fancy. It's been so fucking obvious from the very start. I've seen all those sneaky little glances in his direction. I just needed to hear you admit it.' Kathy clapped her hands together in delight.

Shit! Kathy had seen her keeping an eye on Rick; strike that, keeping an eye on had quickly deteriorated to serious ogling. And if Kathy had noticed, who else had put two and two together?

Please not Rick.

She'd have to be more careful.

'Kathy, I really don't fancy him.' A bit of back-pedalling was required here. 'Yes, he's good-looking. I'd have to be blind not to acknowledge that fact. After all, millions of teenage girls can't be wrong! But as to sex, let's just say I'm more into the studious type. You know; guys with glasses. The professor type,' she added as an after-thought.

It was time to paint a picture. And it *had* been her type, once upon a time. More importantly, she didn't need was Kathy dropping hints around Rick that Izzy was attracted to him. Kathy was about as subtle as the Berlin Wall when she got hold of a titbit of gossip.

'As Will Shakespeare said, "me think the lady doth protest too much"?' Kathy's quote only confirmed Izzy's worst fears. 'So stop trying to bullshit me, Miss Stevenson! You've got very discerning taste.'

'What's that supposed to mean?'

'Earlier this year, before I got together with Scottie, Rick and I had a bit of a thing going.' Kathy confessed.

Izzy goggled at the admission. Rick too? It sounded as though Kathy had been sleeping her way through the entire band. Did she have the full set?

Kathy was now lying back in her chair, growing distinctly misty-eyed as she recounted her tale. 'He'd fallen out with that cow of a fiancée over something—wouldn't tell me what—and I provided a shoulder to cry on. Well, one thing led to another. You can guess the rest.' She gave a slightly bitter laugh. 'And I really thought we might go somewhere. He's such a sweet guy. Shows real potential in the "Happy Ever After" stakes. But something tells me you've worked that out already?'

Kathy grinned at Izzy's still rosy cheeks. 'Then barely a fortnight later, Miss Francesca Reiss snaps her fingers, and off he trots, tail between his legs, and they're back together and getting fucking engaged. I was gutted.' She sighed. 'Trust me; Francesca has got Rick well and truly by the short and curlies.

'But my point is this. Not only is Rick one of life's "good' guys" he's also *red hot* between the sheets. Apart from Scottie, he's probably given me the best orgasms I've ever had.'

That comment was accompanied by a theatrical eye roll, and lots of face fanning. 'Davey and Jonny were very much your "wham bam thank-you ma'am" types. But Rick was a total gentleman, likes to find out what a woman wants in bed.' A swoony smile filled her face. 'You know; likes to make sure the lady comes first, every time...'

Yes, Izzy knew the 'wham bam' type from bitter experience.

'Not that any of them would be seen dead with girls like us nowadays; not even Rick. He's sold out to the whole Rock Star Cliché. ' Kathy drew out an orange from her bag and began peeling it. 'Girls like us are well and truly relegated to the 'subs' bench.'

'What do you mean?' Izzy declined Kathy's offer of an orange segment.

'Because, if you're seriously loaded and living as a tax exile before your thirty, you've got to be seen marrying the right type of dolly bird. A standard requirement of the job, you might say. And we don't make the grade. We're much too ordinary for their Happy Ever After! Rock stars have to be seen marrying women that other men can only lust after. You know how competitive men are. It's all "my car's faster than yours; my wallet's bigger than yours; my wife's sexier than yours", which all boils down to the only comparison that men really care about — "my dick's bigger than yours; so fuck off."'

It was hamburger and fillet steak—just as Steve said.

Kathy fired the orange peel into the waste bin. 'And it's not just Rick. They're all the same. A Wardrobe Mistress or humble PA wouldn't cut it in their world. Don't get me wrong, we're still totally shaggable if there's no alternative available. Just don't expect any wedding ring to go with it. Not going to happening, Izzy.'

4

LONDON, ENGLAND

'And relax!' Kathy collapsed into the faded leather banquette beside Izzy, and reached for her vodka and Coke. 'Jeez, when you said you liked a dance, Izzy, you weren't wrong. I'm bloody knackered trying to keep up with you.'

'You oldies just can't take the pace.' Izzy tsked before taking a well-earned sip of her white wine *spritzer* and glancing around the dimly lit Soho club, the venue for tonight's Christmas party.

The tiny dance floor they'd just left was still packed with members of the band, their families and road crew. With only three days until Christmas, everyone was taking the opportunity to let their hair down after the intensity of the last few months on the road.

Tonight, the band had played their final concert of the fourteen-date British leg of their world tour at London's Wembley Arena, and now there would be a three-week, well-deserved hiatus before everyone met up once more and headed out to Japan.

'Less of the old, if you don't mind Miss Stevenson, I've only got three years on you.' Kathy fished out her cigarettes and lit up, letting out a sigh of satisfaction.

'That's better.' She blew out the match, and dropped it in a nearby ashtray 'What time are you departing for home tomorrow morning? Or should I say, later today.'

'I'm getting the eight 'o'clock train from London Euston,' Izzy confirmed, undoing another button on her blouse; the heat becoming ever so slightly oppressive after all that dancing. Beads of sweat had begun trickle down between her breasts.

'Looking forward to going home?' Kathy asked, picking up her glass.

'Yes. I can't wait.' Izzy's face broke into a genuine smile as she thought of home. 'It'll be good to see Mum and Dad. The whole family tends to get together for Christmas. You know, all my aunts, uncles and cousins. Mum's cooking for over twenty this year. God knows what size the turkey will be.'

Her mum cooked for that number most years. It was the highlight of the year; the Andersons and Stevensons all getting together under the one roof. Izzy loved it.

'What about you?'

'It'll just be me and Scottie, and a pre-roasted chicken courtesy of *Tesco*.' Kathy frowned. 'Well, let's just say he's been invited, and he's indicated he'll come. But I'm not holding my breath. It could still be Christmas dinner and a cracker for one. You know how on-and-off we still are.'

'I'm sure he'll come.' Izzy patted her arm. 'You said things were getting back on track after Angie.'

'And we are, but sometimes…' Kathy gave a little shrug, her eyes distant for a second, and then she seemed to snap out of it. 'Nah, it's nothing.' She lifted her glass and thrust it towards Izzy. 'Here's to a good Christmas, Miss Stevenson, and an even better 1985.'

'You said it! Cheers!'

They clinked glasses, before Kathy reached down and drew out a small package from her jeans pocket, done up in Christmas wrap.

'Here, forgot to hand it over, earlier.' She placed it on the table, in front of Izzy. 'It's not much,' she added with a sheepish grin.

Izzy's eyes had widened in surprise, touched by the other girl's generosity. 'Kathy. That's so kind. You really shouldn't have…' She paused, before coming clean, 'but I've not got anything for you.'

She'd thought about it but hadn't been sure it was the "done" thing around here.

'I didn't expect you to,' Kathy gave a dismissive wave. 'You've been real mate from the word "go", Izzy. And after the shitty few months I've had…'

'And the fact I'm not remotely interested in Scottie,' Izzy reminded her with a grin, as she began opening her gift.

'Yeah, there is that.' Kathy laughed. 'Anyway, I hope you like them?'

'Like them… I love them.' Izzy was now holding up the silver helix-shaped earrings for inspection. 'Thank you so much, they're beautiful, Kathy.'

Immediately, she swapped out her own pearl studs, and replaced them with the new earrings.

'How do they look?' she asked, pushing her hair back to show them off to full effect.

'Perfect!'

'I adore them. Thank-you' Leaning over, Izzy hugged her. 'Right, I'm going to the ladies to inspect them more closely, and try and cool down a bit before we get back on that dance floor. Are you coming with me?'

'Nah, I'm going to sit here and finish my drink. Rest these ancient legs of mine…..'

12.55 AM

Once Izzy had braved the less than salubrious ladies loo, with its unique aroma of cigarettes, urine and cheap perfume, she decided she needed a welcome blast of *fresh* air.

A little way down the corridor, a set of fire doors were standing open, leading to an alleyway beyond. Two bouncers were standing on guard outside.

She'd just taken a determined step in that direction when Jonny stuck his head out of the gents' toilet opposite.

'Oh thank God it's *just* you, Izzy!' He exhaled a long breath, relieved blue eyes meeting Izzy's.

'Gee thanks, you really know how to boost a girl's ego!'

For once, he didn't react to her dry comment. 'Do you know if Scottie has got rid of her yet?'

'Has got rid of whom, Jonny?' Izzy enquired; her brow furrowing.

'Stacey, that flaming nutter Terry landed me with tonight.'

He and his model fiancée, Jilly Fletcher, *The Sun's* favourite Page 3 Girl and rival to Linda Lusardi and Sam Fox, were currently on one of their frequent 'breaks'. Stacey was obviously tonight's "bit of skirt", which Terry Costello—the band's Head of Security—had thoughtfully provided him with.

Jonny's mouth was now set into a firm line, and he tapped his forehead meaningfully. 'I'm convinced she's got a fucking screw loose. Kept talking about how she had a fascination with knives and big game hunting. It got so bad I told her I needed a piss, had a quick word with Scottie and insisted that he got rid of her before I came back.'

He shook his head in exasperation. 'There was no way that bird was big game-hunting me, thanks very much. I could have had my wedding tackle missing by the morning; all ready to be stuffed and hung up as some kind of trophy.'

'Sorry, I really don't know,' Izzy replied trying strenuously not to giggle at the picture he'd so eloquently sketched out. 'Want me to check, while you hide out in there?'

But before Jonny could reply, there was a commotion at the other end of the corridor, Scottie suddenly appearing with the said Stacey, and she clearly wasn't amused at being asked to leave; protesting loudly as she was frog-marched towards them.

'Fuck! You haven't seen me, Izzy. Got it?' Jonny muttered, ducking back into the gents and slamming the door hard.

Izzy gave a nervous smile as Scottie passed by, the band's senior minder finally managing to push the girl outside, and instructing the Bouncers not to let her back in while the band remained in residence.

Job done, he headed back into the club without a backward glance in Izzy's direction.

Izzy rapped on the toilet door. 'She's gone,' she called out.

There was no reply from within.

'I said she's gone, Jonny'

There was still no answer.

Izzy pushed the door open an inch, quickly averting her eyes from the urinals—just in case! The sight of Jonny relieving himself wasn't one she wished to behold, any time soon.

'Jonny? Are you in here?'

She could now hear distinct female giggling and a lot of heavy breathing emanating from the furthest away cubicle.

Typical Jonny! A replacement had already been lined up, while Scottie was dispatching Bed Mate number one.

Izzy rolled her eyes in disbelief. 'Can you hear me, Jonny?' she called again.

There was major creaking from the flimsy walls of the toilet cubicle.

'Oh God more… Yeah, just like that my little baby…Sooo fucking good……

There was a pause then she heard a 'whatever you say, Izzy,' tagged on for her benefit, before more seriously heavy breathing.

Izzy retreated back outside hurriedly. It sounded as though Jonny would be otherwise engaged for quite some time yet.

'There you are, pretty lady.'

Izzy turned to see Rick striding towards her now; clutching what looked to be a piece of mistletoe in his hand.

Her face broke into an easy smile as their eyes met. She was getting 'pretty lady' again. For some reason, he'd started teasing her with this moniker over the last fortnight; so much so it had become a bit of a standing joke between them.

He drew level, nodding towards the closed door of the gents. 'Loitering out here with intent, Miss Stevenson?'

She laughed. 'Nope, I was just taking a breather and, somehow, got myself involved in a bit of a *ménage a trois* with Jonny.'

'Sound intriguing. Are you going to enlighten me, further?' Dark eyebrows were wiggled suggestively.

'Believe me; I'm sure you can guess what's going on in there.' She replied, nodding towards the Gents toilet, heat warming her cheeks. 'I'm just heading back to join Kathy on the dance floor; much safer.'

'Yeah, I saw you up there, earlier. Very impressive moves, I must say.' He winked at her. 'Was going to come over and ask for a dance, but by then you'd disappeared. I thought you'd maybe called it a night and left without saying goodbye.'

She was treated to a reproachful pout, and heat flooded the pit of her stomach.

'Nope, not yet, but I'll have to leave soon.' she replied, glancing at her watch. 'I need to be up early.'

'Heading back to bonnie Scotland, tomorrow?'

'Yep, you said it.'

'Then I'd better be quick. Claim my Christmas kiss before you run out on me?' He held up the clump of snowy-white berries above her head, and gave an exaggerated pucker to his lips.

Izzy couldn't help but burst out giggling. 'Really, how could a girl refuse that offer, Mr Hambro?'

As she inclined the apple of her right cheek towards him, she knew her feelings for him had definitely crossed a line. This wasn't a crush anymore; far from it. She'd allowed herself to fall for the kind and gentle man behind the rock-star persona—as the old cliché ran—hook, line and sinker.

'Merry Christmas, pretty lady, I hope you have a good one.' Rick's lips brushed softly against her skin.

'Merry Christmas, Rick' Izzy's breath hitched in her throat; all her senses on alert.

If only she could turn her head just a little to the right, their lips might touch…

'Rick, your parents and Michelle are leaving,' Francesca's voice cut in, making Izzy leap backwards guiltily, her cheeks flushing even redder.

They'd been caught in the act by his bitch of a fiancée. Francesca was standing there, hands on hips, and if looks could kill, Izzy would have been pushing up a field of daisies right about now.

'And you know Betty; always has to have a word with *her son* before she goes,' Francesca stepped forward and pointedly removed the mistletoe from Rick's hand, only to dangle it above her own head.

'I think it's my *turn* for the Christmas kisses, don't you, Rick?' Izzy received another turbo-charged glower. 'And, Izzy, go fetch my fur jacket from the cloakroom. Rick and I will be leaving shortly, too?' Francesca instructed.

'We are?' That was clearly news to Rick, his eyes widening in surprise.

'And make sure you don't handle the fur too much, Izzy. I've just had it dry-cleaned. I don't want any one's sweaty paws all over it.'

With those final orders given, Francesca reached up and planted a possessive kiss on her fiancé's mouth.

Izzy pursed her lips together in annoyance.

Sweaty paws indeed!

It had been like that for the last two and a half weeks, Francesca clinging onto Rick like some rabid limpet, endlessly issuing snotty demands to Izzy.

'Yes, of course, *Miss* Reiss.'

Whatever you say, Miss Reiss, Three bloody bags full, Miss Reiss!

God the woman made her blood boil. How on earth had someone as wonderful as Rick ended up with a total She-bitch-from-Hell like that one? Couldn't he see what she was really like? A final glance backwards confirmed the kiss was still happening, Rick's arms wrapped tightly around his fiancée's waist, Francesca eating him with her mouth.

Yes, it was time for her unrequited feelings to be placed in a box and ignored as much as possible. There was not a hope in hell of Rick ever feeling that way about her. Izzy Anderson just wasn't his kind of girl. A pneumatic *Barbie* Doll, in dire need of a personality upgrade, was clearly more to his liking.

5

SOMEWHERE OVER EUROPE

The 'Please fasten your seatbelt' sign had finally clicked off, and Izzy undid the constricting belt from around her waist.

The worst part of the evening was over! While she quite enjoyed flying—not that she'd done much, family holidays to the continent the sum total to date—actually getting off the ground was an altogether different proposition. She always found take-off stomach churning in the extreme. But, thankfully, tonight's—from an icy Heathrow Airport—had proved slightly less nerve wracking than usual.

Her whispered prayers of deliverance had obviously been answered by The Man Upstairs. Their jet-liner was cruising at the required altitude, all engines still in tack, and she hadn't had to reach for the complimentary sick bag once.

It had also helped that Rick, who'd grabbed the window seat alongside her, had noticed her obvious discomfort early on. But then, her gripping both arm rests—until the whites of her knuckles showed—had probably been the dead giveaway.

What she hadn't expected was him taking her trembling hands into his; doing everything he could to reassure her as they'd taxied along the ground. So much so Izzy—lost in the intensity of his brown eyes and soothing words—had been airborne before she'd known it. And then, only once she'd finally shown signs of returning to her usual unflappable-self, had he deposited a kiss to the back of each hand, and settled down to sleep at her side.

Izzy glanced down at the two spots he'd kissed; they were still tingling from the gentle brush from those wonderful lips. But, much as she might want to, she knew she couldn't dwell on those meaningless kisses all night; she'd work to get on with.

Retrieving her notepad and pen from her handbag, she scanned the first page, ticking off what she'd already achieved. Her pen hovered over the fourth entry and she pulled a face: Samurai Photo-shoot. A last-minute addition from Lindsay, the band's Press Officer, but no one had mentioned it to the band. No one had felt brave enough.

According to Lindsay, Japan's answer to *Smash Hits* magazine, had asked the band dress up as Samurai warriors and grace their March Front Cover. Like that was going to happen. This lot were super-fussy about image, and the 'Samurai' look wasn't 'in' this year. Purely from a timing perspective, a photo-shoot two-hours before their final Japanese show wasn't ideal, but the publicity machine had to be fed.

However, there was no way she'd be broaching the subject. She'd sidestep that poisoned chalice and Lindsay could have the privilege of getting his head chewed off instead. She could just hear Marc's reaction. The phrase 'over my dead body' sprang to mind. Or 'not quite the aesthetic we're trying to portray, Izzy'. For a so-called hardened rock star, he was full of 'arty farty' phrases like that.

More importantly, Lindsay would have to come up with a watertight reason for the band not complying with the Magazine's request. There was absolutely no way they could disrespect their hordes of Japanese fans. Maybe posing with a bona-fide Samurai might do the trick, or possibly substitute a couple of Geishas instead? That second option would probably be much more up the band's street….

Immaculately dressed stewardesses had begun moving round the first-class cabin, dispensing drinks and snacks to its occupants. Dinner wasn't scheduled for another two hours.

'Excuse me, would you like a glass of Champagne, Miss?'

A blonde stewardess paused at Izzy's side, but her attention was firmly focused on Jonny's dyed locks where he was sitting across the aisle. He was gazing up at her through his fringe, a flirty smile playing on his cherubic lips.

Jonathan Hambro was on the 'pull' again.

'No thanks,' Izzy replied, used to being ignored whenever members of the band were around. 'I'll just have a *Pepsi* please.'

She glanced between the stewardess and Jonny and smiled. As ever, women were like putty in that man's hands. One look at those baby-blue eyes, firm jaw, and mullet of long fair hair and female brains disintegrated into blancmange.

Predictably, the stewardess hadn't responded to her request. And no wonder. Jonny had effortlessly switched into his trademark 'little boy lost' pose. Izzy knew his routine off by heart. Once the megawatt smile ensnared the helpless victim, this second 'look' was deployed to slay them completely. It worked every time.

For a long moment, the stewardess's gaze remained resolutely on Jonny, and then, as if remembering she'd a job to do, a switch was flipped and she swung back to face Izzy.

'I'm terribly sorry, what was that you said?'

'I'd like a *Pepsi*, please.' Izzy repeated.

Yep, another poor female had bitten the dust. Really, it was starting to get boring, now.

The stewardess moved away to retrieve Izzy's drink, but not before she'd sashayed past Jonny yet again, leaning in—just a bit too close and for a bit too long—to confirm if there was anything else he needed.

Izzy didn't hear Jonny's whispered reply, but then, she didn't have to. She'd a pretty good idea what was coming next.

Only once the pretty blonde had finally departed five minutes later, with Izzy in receipt of her requested *Pepsi*, did she catch the guitarist's eye.

'Don't you get fed up with them falling at your feet?'

Jonny shrugged. 'Fed up? Why would a guy *ever* get fed up with female attention, Izzy?'

Those blue eyes twinkled with barely disguised glee, as he polished his nails against the lapel of his very expensive leather jerkin. 'When you're voted Most Fanciable Male in the UK for three years running, beating that bloke Taylor from *Duran* into a cocked hat, it's a cross a guy learns to bear.'

Not that bearing it looked any hardship whatsoever to the six-foot-four rock star. And Jonny believed all his publicity. But strangely, his good looks and permanent charm offensive still hadn't won Izzy over. It was much too calculated for her liking.

'So, what time is tonight's hot date?'

She'd watched Jonny adopt this routine on a flight up to their Aberdeen Gig just before Christmas; the flight attendant on that occasion had been just as susceptible to his charms.

Jonny consulted the heavy gold *Rolex* on his wrist. 'Zero hour is eight thirty. That's her tea break.'

He gave a conspiratorial tap on the nose, Izzy understanding the subtext perfectly. This tea break wouldn't involve any actual tea drinking; no *PG TIPS* for that particular girl tonight.

'But we only got on the flight *twenty* minutes ago!'

Even by Jonny's standards, he'd made fast work of this one. It had taken him a whole fifty-five minutes to cultivate his previous conquest, before getting his leg over in the galley kitchen.

'What can I say, it's just a gift the angels bestowed on me at birth,' was his breezy reply.

The phrase 'cat that got the cream' could have been coined for him at this precise moment; smug just didn't cover it.

'Or it might have something to do with the bet we made earlier,' Davey butted in, seated beside Jonny, beer bottle hovering at his lips and looking decidedly miffed. 'That not even our resident Sex God could get laid within thirty minutes of take-off. Five hundred quid, this little exercise is going to cost me!'

'And where will the grand seduction take place tonight?' Izzy asked, her lips twitching in amusement. 'Don't tell me it's the galley kitchen again?'

'Huh.' Davey tossed his straggly ponytail over his shoulder. 'Nope, he's going all upmarket. Just make sure you don't need the first-class bog at half-past eight. It could be a bit crowded in there.'

Izzy couldn't contain her laughter. Jonny was priceless. His metamorphosis from university drop-out— reading English Literature at Reading University—to international Sex God—reading *Playboy*—had come quickly, and he milked it for all it was worth.

At length, silence descended on their part of the cabin, and Izzy let her eyes wander back to Rick at her side. He was still out for the count. His dark head snuggled up to his complimentary pillow, mouth slightly open—catching flies her mum would have said.

But was he really asleep or had he been downing those horrible sleeping tablets? A niggle in her gut told her the tablets had probably won out again. Not that she was any the wiser as to the underlying reason for Rick's insomnia, and his dependence on sleeping tablets. From conversations she'd overheard to date, she knew he'd been resorting to them occasionally throughout the British tour, and tonight, just as they'd taken their seats, she'd witnessed him swallow down what looked like another tablet with a large glug from the water bottle in his hand.

But the tablets were no longer having quite the desired effect. Their ability to induce sleep was becoming decidedly hit or miss; Rick disclosing that piece of information to Jonny only this morning. Worse, Jonny's next words on the subject had filled her with total dread. The lead guitarist suggesting that Rick sound out Terry about laying his hands on a stronger alternative.

Izzy allowed her eyes to sweep over Rick's broad shoulders, catching a tantalising glimpse of those cute little tufts of chest hair peeping through his half-unbuttoned shirt, before continuing lower, lingering momentarily on the bulge in his tight Levi jeans. One thing was certain; this Rick had filled considerably from the gangly teen she'd followed around like a lovesick puppy fifteen years ago.

An impatient sigh from Jonny brought Izzy out of her reverie, and she glanced across at him now. He was making an exaggerated play of flicking through a copy of *Vogue* on his lap, while checking his watch every ten seconds.

To his right, Davey was replacing the batteries in his *Sony Walkman*, a discarded *Rubik's Cube* on his lap.

In the row behind, Marc was reading; ploughing through a weighty tomb on a Canadian artist by the name of Vince Osborne. His ever-present and high-maintenance girlfriend— Sabrina Warren— was resting her chin on his shoulder, nodding whenever he imparted a choice quote from the book. As Izzy watched, Sabrina let out a discreet sideways yawn; clearly bored stiff at Marc's attempts to educate her on the finer points of surrealist art.

A quick glance down at her own watch told Izzy it was almost quarter past eight; just time to nip to the loo before the 'out of order' sign went up, and it became Jonny's latest love nest.

And sure enough, when 8.30pm arrived, the galley curtain was pulled back with a theatrical swish, and Jonny's conquest appeared, fixing him with a suitably 'come hither' smile, and off Jonny swaggered, smirking at Izzy like the *Cheshire Cat*, ready to sample the delights of the Mile High Club courtesy of British Asiatic Airlines. *'We'll take care of your every need getting from A-to-B"* proclaimed their latest advertising slogan, and clearly this employee was about to obey its sentiment to the letter.

Ten minutes later, Steve stirred in his seat, casting a bleary eye around the cabin.

'Okay, Davey, where's Jonny gone?' He gave an exaggerated yawn, rubbing his eyes and pulling himself into an upright position.

'Attending to a bit of business; shouldn't be much longer,' Davey answered, fiddling with the *Walkman's* headphones, and managing to dislodge the protective foam from around the right earpiece. 'Shit!'

Steve gave a snort of laughter, reaching over to pick up the *Rubik's Cube* on Davey's lap and giving it a few cursory twists. 'In other words, he's shagging a stewardess, and you've just lost today's bet!'

Izzy grinned to herself; there were no flies on Steve.

'You've got it in fucking one!' Davey had reattached the foam, only for it to fall off once more, as soon as he tried to settle the headphones on his ears. 'Shit!'

'Well, it's good to know our boy hasn't lost his touch. So, how much is tonight's little wager costing you?' Steve asked, two sides of the cube had been completed in double quick time, and he was well on the way to a third.

'You really don't want to know.' Davey, head to the side, was openly gaping at Steve. 'How the hell do you manage to do that so fucking quickly?'

Steve tossed the half-solved puzzle back to him with a nonchalant shrug. 'Dunno. Just got the knack, I guess.'

Watching them, Izzy tapped her pen against her teeth, wondering if Steve would be up for a bit of leg-pulling; he always enjoyed a good laugh.

'Thought I'd run something past you, Mr Gilbert. Given the cramped conditions in the First Class Toilet, do you think I should book Jonny an appointment with a chiropractor when we land?'

She made sure she channelled a 'butter wouldn't melt' expression for all she was worth, but from the answering grin beginning to spread across Steve's face, she could tell he'd already tapped into her wavelength. Even Davey was smirking, albeit reluctantly.

'After all, if we have to cancel shows,' she continued, 'I doubt the insurance company would pay out. Technically, it might be considered a self-inflicted injury.'

Steve burst out laughing. 'Like it, Izzy!'

Marc poked his head out from behind his book. As always, he had one ear opened to any conversation going on around him.

'Yes!' His face was the picture of gravity. 'As I've told you before, Izzy, it's always best to plan for every eventuality. But, word of advice, don't book a female one; knowing Jonny, and his over-active libido that would defeat the whole purpose of the exercise.'

His deadpan punch-line was delivered just as the subject of their discussion reappeared, looking even more self-satisfied than before.

Jonny certainly hadn't wasted any time with the stewardess, and by the definite spring to his step, there was no need for a chiropractor either. Jonathan Hambro remained in full working order.

Retaking his seat, Jonny held out his palm towards Davey, and without uttering a word Davey reached into his breast pocket, drew out his wallet and settled the score.

'It's a pleasure doing business with you, sir.' The guitarist parodied a salute, before stuffing the winnings into his inside pocket, not even bothering to count the cash. Clearly, the fact he'd won the bet was enough.

'Right, it's time to recharge the old Hambro batteries.' He leaned across to Izzy, raking a hand through his blond hair. 'Need to make sure I'm firing on all cylinders for later,' he explained, not bothering to lower his voice, 'says she'll bring along a friend!'

6

OSAKA, JAPAN

Izzy hovered beside the Arena's Emergency Exit, watching as the band—together with tonight's dates—piled into three stretch limousines. Apart from the permanently super-glued Sabrina, none of the said 'dates' were on the official 'girlfriend' list. This lot were purely of the one-night-only variety.

Three concerts of the Japanese Tour under their belt, and Eclectic Deviation was due some down-time. Although, knowing the band's definition of 'down-time', there would be precious little rest and relaxation involved. Izzy was all-too familiar with the devastation wrought by these types of nights. Would she see any of them at tomorrow's breakfast meeting? She might see two of them she estimated, but only if she was *very* lucky.

The first two limos accelerated down the OUT ramp of the Service Yard before disappearing into the darkness. As the final one passed by, Izzy received regal waves courtesy of its backseat occupants; Jonny and Marc. Sabrina and Jonny's date, Niroko, were sat wedged between them, Sabrina's nose pointing skywards, cutting Izzy dead as usual.

And from what Izzy could make out, they started making serious inroads into the vintage champagne she'd left in the car's mini-fridge; a bottle being freely passed back and forth between Jonny and Niroko, while the more refined Marc and Sabrina sipped their drinks from champagne flutes.

Only once their car had disappeared after the others, could she allow herself a sigh of genuine relief. 'And relax, Izzy.'

She hurried back inside to her office, flashing her Access-all-Areas pass to the arena's security guards. Just her diary to check over and then she could head back to the hotel, kick off her shoes, have a bath and maybe—just maybe—hit the sack before midnight. Now that was *her* definition of rest and relaxation.

Sitting down at her desk, she gave tomorrow's schedule a quick perusal, appending notes to several entries. With nothing too taxing pencilled in over the next seventy-two hours—three newspaper interviews, a couple of TV appearances and two concerts—she allowed her mind to drift back over the last nine weeks of her life.

What a rollercoaster ride! Whatever initiation test Davey and Steve had set her on arrival, she'd passed with flying colours and four of the band members—including the extremely hard-to-please Steve—were now firmly on her team. But not Davey; he tolerated her at best, and the feeling was entirely mutual. But, on the plus side, at least Jack hadn't chased up any of those fictitious references her mum had cooked up.

Long may that continue! Although, she was still debating whether suing Jack—for his loose interpretation of the Trade Descriptions Act—might be a possibility. Her job was nothing like the one he'd sold to her at interview. Personal Slave—constantly at the band's beck and call—was an altogether more accurate reflection of her current status, and as for an '8-hour' shift, sometimes it felt more like twenty-plus.

As their PA, she had—as her lanyard proudly proclaimed— access to all areas of their crazy lives, whether she liked or not. As well as being the ever present 'gatekeeper' between the band and the outside world, she dealt with all their correspondence, diaries, and tour schedules—the latter in tandem with Lindsay—as well as being expected to resolve the band's day-today problems.

Only this morning, she'd been summoned up to Marc's Suite, Marc complaining loudly he didn't like the art work hanging above his bed. Apparently, the colours weren't "aesthetically conducive to a good night's sleep". Once she'd stopped laughing long enough to realise he wasn't joking—"I want the bloody picture removed ASAP, Izzy," he'd barked at her—she'd spent the next ten minutes discussing the vagaries of hotel guests with the Hotel Manager. But Marc, being the piper and calling the tune, had got his own way; the painting replaced with something "much more visually soothing" to his artistic temperament.

At every gig, she stood stage-side for the first fifteen minutes, ensuring they had everything needed to get through the show, and she was the first person they saw at its end, supplying a warm fluffy towel, and effusive congratulations on another successful gig firmly under their collective belts. Her ever-ready magic wand primed to grant their next wish, however ludicrous.

In the last few weeks, her to-do list had included—amongst other things—taking Steve's *BMW* for an MOT; organising a plumber to repair a leaky pipe in Rick's new Chelsea flat; walking Marc and Sabrina's Pekinese Lulu; and removing—via a convenient fire escape— an over-enthusiastic groupie from Jonny's hotel room, while his fiancée Jilly cooled her four-inch stilettos downstairs.

And having got to grips with the formal aspects of her job, she adored it. Organisation was her forte, tracking the band's movements with military precision on a daily basis. All their engagements timed to the minute on her colour-coded schedule. She even had a tiny stopwatch to ensure flights were caught on time.

But it was the less glamorous aspects of their lives that had taken longer to reconcile. She'd read enough of the seedy stories to know they'd never be 'choir boys', but she'd still been unprepared for the blatant level of drug taking and promiscuity which took place at their 'anything-goes-and-usually-did' parties. She'd seen more naked body parts—both male and female—than any woman wanted or needed since the beginning of December.

Time to get out of here, Izzy.

Her final job would be completed back at the hotel, and involved a quick phone call home—early afternoon in the UK—updating Betty on this week's developments. Not that Rick's mum would be ecstatic by what Izzy had to impart. She'd just overheard the word *'Teraxapen'* being bandied about the dressing room. Not something she'd ever heard of before, but if Terry Costello was to be believed, it was the magic bullet as far as Rick's insomnia was concerned.

7

NAGOYA, JAPAN

They were in the process of checking out of Nagoya's Plaza Hotel. Izzy had just completed the paperwork for their bill with reception, but had still to make final payment of the eye-wateringly large amount, much of it courtesy of Davey and Marc's extravagant use of room service.

Time was marching on. In another hour, the band and their entourage should be safely aboard the 10.45am bullet train, hurtling at speeds of over two hundred mph towards Tokyo. And trains always ran on time over here, which meant—according to Izzy's calculations—they had exactly one hour and fifteen minutes to make the connection.

There was a discreet cough.

Looking up, Izzy was confronted by the Duty Manager across the desk, hovering anxiously. The receptionist she'd been dealing with nowhere in sight.

'*Ohayō gozaimasu*, Miss Stevenson *San*,' he wished her good morning with a respectful little bow.

Everyone bowed in Japan, and Izzy found herself reciprocating in polite acknowledgment.

'*Ohayō gozaimasu.*' she replied with a warm smile.

'May we speak, please?' He indicated with a finger that Izzy should move further along the desk beside him.

Immediately on alert, Izzy followed suit. What on earth did he want? They had to be out of here shortly, or today's schedule would be in danger of slipping, big time.

Thankfully he came straight to the point. 'Unfortunately, Lady in Housekeeping say there is big problem with suite occupied by member of band.'

Izzy frowned, picking up the meaning behind his slightly disjointed delivery. This was news to her. Nobody had mentioned a problem with their palatial accommodation over the last two days.

'I'm very sorry to hear that,' she answered. 'Which member of the band are we talking about?'

She just hoped Marc hadn't taken to re-arranging the furniture again. Since his arrival in Japan, he'd become fascinated by the art of Feng Shui, and feeling bored at their last stop-off, he and Sabrina had decided to indulge in a little interior design challenge. Their efforts hadn't gone down well with Hotel Management.

'Suite occupied by Mr Jonny Hambro *San*,' the Manager informed her.

Izzy sneaked a glance at her watch, hoping this wouldn't take long. What on earth had Jonny done now? And did she really want to know?

'What appears to be the problem?' she enquired; conscious that she mustn't appear rude. Courtesy was extremely important to the Japanese, and Izzy didn't want to offend anybody. She left that particular 'talent' to Davey. She'd already had to apologise for his churlish behaviour—including letting rip with the F-word three times on primetime TV—in the last seventy two hours.

'If you accompany me upstairs, Miss Stevenson *San*,' he advised. 'I show you'

With another respectful bow, he moved from the desk, and strode off across the lobby towards a bank of lifts, clearly expecting Izzy to follow him.

That was it, she thought, forced to break into a trot to catch up, her schedule had now officially gone for a Burton.

9.43 AM

The door of Jonny's suite was open and a housemaid was waiting patiently beside her fully stacked laundry trolley.

The Duty Manager exchanged a few words with her, the woman immediately standing aside to allow Izzy access to the room.

With a brief smile, acknowledging the housemaid, Izzy stepped inside. Instantly the remnants of that smile vanished. 'What on earth….?'

What had once been an immaculate Five-Star hotel suite—tastefully decorated in re-production *Art Deco* Style—had now been transformed into a post-apocalyptic war-zone.

Everything that had occupied the lounge area—chairs, tables, lamps, mirrors, pictures, TV and even the blinds and curtains—had been systematically destroyed in a rampage worthy of the latest *Rambo* movie. For some reason, known only to Jonathan Hambro, he'd decided to trash the entire room.

As Izzy swivelled on the heels of her stiletto boots, her eyes widened in consternation as she took in the full extent of the wreckage before her. Nothing had been left untouched. It was going to take more than fresh towels and a change of bed linen to fix this lot.

The Duty Manager remained patiently silent at Izzy's side.

'I'm terribly sorry.'

Jeez! Those three words were totally inadequate for the devastation Jonny had wrought in here. Part of her still couldn't believe that he'd actually been the perpetrator, yet evidence to the contrary was staring her right between the eyes. It was Jonny's room and not one stick of

58

furniture in its lounge area had made it out alive. And was that actually sick on the carpet? She swallowed in distaste, deciding not to venture too closely to find out.

He'd been completely normal at breakfast too—or as normal as Jonny could ever be—a bit hung-over, but he was always hung-over in the mornings. And, needless to say, he hadn't mentioned a word about this little 'escapade'.

The shit had well and truly hit the fan, and it was now down to Izzy to roll up her sleeves and sort it out.

'What about the bedroom? Is there anything else I ought to see?' she asked.

Was this just the tip of a very large and potentially expensive iceberg?

'Bedroom is perfect. Miss Stevenson *San*'

Well, that's relief!

She knew Jonny had a worrying tendency to violence if he overindulged in too many drugs, especially if the pressure cooker existence of his rock-star life was getting too much. But that normally involved him whacking some poor unfortunate bystander. He'd done just that staggering out of "Tramp" at New Year; the paparazzi, on hand outside the nightclub to witness the whole sorry episode. But she'd never encountered this degree of violent behaviour before.

Plus, as far as she knew, no drugs had been smuggled into Japan. The drug laws were notoriously strict here. The risk of being caught, jailed or ignominiously deported like Paul McCartney was a step too far, even for a member of Eclectic Deviation. Last night's little effort must have been done under the influence of vodka, Jonny's tipple of choice.

Turning to the Duty Manager, she knew it was time to deploy some good old British diplomacy, as well as parting with a large wad of cash. Hopefully, that would sweep today's little problem under the shag pile carpet, once all the vomit stains had been successfully removed.

'We will, of course, pay for all the damage.'

The band's *AMEX* Card would be begging for mercy when it came to settling this little lot. A full-scale redecoration job looked to be on the cards.

'And in order to deal with this quickly, would you be able to fax me over a detailed inventory of everything that's been damaged, together with any projected costings?'

Izzy hoped she was giving the impression she dealt with these situations every day, but she needn't have worried. Now that she was clearly talking the Duty Manager's language, she received another deferential bow, together with an unexpectedly accommodating smile. They understood each other perfectly.

'Of course, I place matter in hand, straightaway Miss Stevenson *San*.'

'We're leaving for your sister hotel in Tokyo,' Izzy continued, 'and if you have the information faxed there and marked for my attention, I can authorise the release of the necessary funds when I check in. No questions asked. Again, I can't apologise enough for the inconvenience this has caused, both to you, and your staff.'

She took one final incredulous look around '*Apocalypse Now*' half expecting Martin Sheen to stumble out of the bedroom brandishing an *AK47* rifle at her.

It was also time to address the more delicate issue of reputational damage limitation. A little extra cash would have to be brought into play to make sure Jonny came out of this debacle smelling of roses.

'In return, we would, of course, appreciate your absolute discretion. As you can imagine, not all publicity is good publicity and if this incident should leak to the press…'

She left the rest unsaid, hoping he'd read between the lines. If the British tabloids got wind of this, they'd have a field day. She'd love to hear Lindsay try to explain away Jonny's latest indiscretion; getting to grips with the Japanese art of Jujutsu perhaps and failing miserably?

'Of course, Miss Stevenson *San*, I understand.'

The Duty Manager remained completely on her wavelength.

'And there are definitely no problems with any of the other suites?'

'All are most satisfactory.'

Great! At least Marc had behaved himself for once!

10.19 AM

By the time Izzy had made her way back down to reception, all band members were outside in the limousines, impatient to leave.

Given the crush of hysterical teenagers surrounding the cars, thumping the reinforced glass windows and screeching at the top of their lungs, things were getting tense both inside—and outside—the vehicles.

Scottie was waiting for her as the lift doors slid apart. Izzy's stomach sank at the thunderous scowl on his face. He'd be blaming her for the delay to the schedule. She just knew it.

'What the hell is going on, Izzy?'

He made an over-dramatic play of checking the crumpled itinerary in his hand as Izzy stepped out towards him.

'According to *your* paperwork, departure time was ten fucking minutes ago,' he snapped, waving it at her now. 'We should be on the road by now.'

He took a long drag from his ever-present cigarette before he continued, 'And it's a bloody zoo out there. You know what teenagers are like, the longer the limos are at a standstill, and the crush continues, the more chance of some silly bitch getting hurt. And Security always gets the sodding blame.'

'Yes, I appreciate that, Scottie. Sorry.' Izzy tried to remain patient. Scottie had a notoriously short fuse. 'But unfortunately, there are still a couple things I need to address here.

She'd need to actually make payment of their ludicrously large bill, for a start. The furrow in Scottie's already lined brow only deepened when she imparted that piece of news. But, given the circumstances, she'd no option but to give him the green light for departure. It was time to get the show on the road for another day.

'You go ahead with the band. I'll get a taxi and meet you at the railway station. If I don't get there on time just leave without me. I'll find my own way to Tokyo.'

Somehow! Now that the initial shock had worn off, Izzy was feeling more than a little annoyed. Typical Jonny, leaving her to take the flack, and worse, she'd have to dream up an extremely creative expense claim for the band's accountants. Find a perfectly acceptable excuse as to why their client had deliberately trashed his hotel suite.

8

TOKYO, JAPAN

'So, the delectable Miss Stevenson has finally graced us with her presence!' Jonny treated Izzy to an exaggerated bow, every inch the louche lounge lizard, obligatory drink in hand.

'What the hell kept you?'

His megawatt smile—so beloved of the fans—had been switched on to full effect.

'You do realise Marc was seriously pissed that you missed the train, and he'd no one to run after him doing the full 'Yes Marc, No Marc, Three bags full Marc routine'.

Izzy could tell he was trying to get her on-side, deploying the old 'Jonny Hambro' charm offensive in spades. Well tough, she wasn't playing ball today. Not after his spectacular fall from grace, last night.

Refusing to make eye contact, Izzy strode inside his suite.

'And *konnichiwa* to you too, Jonathan.' She remained stony faced. 'Unfortunately, it's not been a good day. I had a few unexpected things to deal with at our last hotel.' Her arms were folded. 'And to add insult to injury, my taxi got stuck in traffic, and then the bloody train I caught decided to break down, one hundred yards outside the station.'

She gave a sigh. Pleasantries over, it was time to tackle this situation head on. He was a big boy. But would Jonny Hambro decide to act his age, or would she get his shoe size, as usual?

'And you'll never guess what held me up in the first place? Discussing the quite unbelievable state of your hotel suite with the Duty Manager?'

Jonny's smile was switched off instantly.

Good, he'd realised Little Boy Lost wasn't going to cut it.

'I have never seen anything like it.' Izzy fixed him with her best no-nonsense expression, but it was Jonny's turn to avoid making eye contact.

He put down his glass next to a half-empty bottle of *Stolichnaya* Vodka on the nightstand and then returned to the business of unpacking.

'You know what us rock stars are like, Izzy.' There was an annoyingly casual shrug of the shoulders. 'So, I let off some steam, and things got a bit out of hand. No real harm done! You're just lucky I didn't decide to drive a car into their swimming pool, or chuck the TV out the window.'

The massive ego of Jonathan Hambro had entered the building. There was no chance of him acting his age.

'No real harm done!'Izzy was aghast that he was making light of the situation. 'You must be joking! Are you seriously telling me you just fancied emulating Keith Moon and Jimmy Page to let off a bit of "steam"? Great! Some warning to yours truly would have been nice!'

Izzy rolled her eyes ceiling-wards. 'Before I was allowed to check-in downstairs I had to give all sorts of assurances as to your future behaviour, as well as ensuring the astronomical repair bill was paid—in full!'

Jonny continued to ignore her as he unpacked, the contents of his suitcase taking up an inordinate amount of his attention.

'Not to mention adding a little sweetener to make sure your name wasn't leaked to the press as this week's "Rock Star from Hell". And, from the veiled comments I got, we're very lucky they're willing to overlook your 'juvenile delinquency' act, provided it doesn't happen again! What on earth got into you last night?'

The blond head lifted, Jonny finally catching the full effect of Izzy's 'don't give me any more of your bull-shit' glower.

'Just feeling a bit pissed off.'

'That must be the understatement of the century.' Izzy flared back. 'Right now, I'm feeling more than a bit "pissed off" as you put it, but I don't intend going back to my room and weld a sledgehammer.'

There was no attempt to disguise his smirk at that comment.

'So, let me get this straight' Izzy began to pace, her temper simmering, 'just because you were feeling a wee bit annoyed about something, you decided that beating the crap out of your entire hotel suite might—just *might*—make you feel better?' She flung her hands in the air in despair. 'I've heard it all now!'

'Don't exaggerate, Izzy. It wasn't the entire suite, just the lounge. A chap has to have somewhere to rest his weary head, especially when he's got guests staying over!'

Jeez, he'd witnesses to his behaviour.

'Anyway,' Jonny went on, 'what I really wanted to do was smash Marc's sodding face in. He'd been getting on my nerves all through dinner. You know what a pretentious prick he can be, sometimes.'

Yes she did, but that wasn't the point.

He glanced at her through his fringe. 'It came down to a choice, Marc or room?'

Honestly, he made it sound like an entirely reasonable choice to make.

After plopping a couple of shirts into a drawer, Jonny closed it with a neat swivel of the hips. 'Given the current circumstances, I figured everyone would prefer me to opt for the latter.'

He paused at the mirror, checking out his appearance and pulling a few stray strands of fringe back into place, winking at her in the glass. 'What's the big deal, Izzy? These things happen.'

But Izzy was in no mood to soften her stance. His behaviour was completely unacceptable.

'Okay, maybe I overstepped the mark a little.' He finally backtracked.

A tingle shot through Izzy's palm. His display of arrogance was asking for a slap. Wiping that bloody great smirk off his face would be altogether *too* satisfying for words.

'A little bit?' She shoved her hands in her pockets, just in case the urge to let fly got too much. Marc had been very lucky last night. Given the grievous bodily harm Jonny had meted out to his hotel suite, Marc could have been lying in Intensive Care at this very minute.

'Anyway, we can afford it. Replacing a few sticks of cheap reproduction furniture and a quick paint job is a drop in the ocean compared to what we're raking in at the moment. You've bunged them a few quid and they've said they'll keep their mouth shut; look the other way. And I took care of the two hookers,' he wiggled his eyebrows, 'in more ways than one. Everything's cool. Stop getting your pretty little g-string in a twist.'

'That's not the point, and you know it. You've put both me, and the hotel, to a great deal of inconvenience, and if this ever leaks out, your reputation will be seriously compromised.'

Not that Jonny had much of a reputation to lose, but that was beside the point. There were days when she got totally fed up looking after a bunch of grown men who should know better; this was one of them.

Izzy was stopped from saying anything more by a knock on the Jonny's still open door, Rick's head poking through the gap. His face broke into a smile as his eyes alighted upon Izzy.

'Hey! Our pretty lady's made it at last. I was getting ready to send out a search party.'

For once, Izzy couldn't bring herself to return that butterfly-inducing smile, still too riled by Jonny and the day's events.

'Yes, I've arrived.' she replied, her tone decidedly dry.

'Is something wrong?' Rick's eyebrows shot up in surprise, glancing between her and Jonny.

'Ask your cousin!' Izzy's index finger was jabbed towards at a seemingly unrepentant Jonny, before delivering her coup-de-grace. 'And another thing, Jonny, from now on, I'm checking everyone's hotel rooms before we check out. Make sure I receive no more surprises like this morning's. And guess what, sunshine? Yours has just leapfrogged to the top of my list.'

9

TOKYO, JAPAN

Izzy's eyes were on the clock again. She consulted her watch for the third time.

Rick was late, which wasn't like him. Jonny, Davey and Steve—par for the course whenever they were entertaining night-time 'guests'—and Marc, well Marc was always late, regardless of circumstances. In fact, being on time appeared to be a pathological impossibility for the middle Hambro cousin. But Rick was *always* packed, in reception and ready to leave.

Except this morning—for some reason—he wasn't.

Where was he? Out of nowhere, her over-active imagination kicked in. Could he have been reckless with the sleeping tablets? Maybe taken one too many, and accidently overdosed? Her stomach began to work itself into painful knots as panic took hold. The papers were full of rock stars overdosing on prescription drugs. Was Rick about to become yet another grim statistic of the infamous *"Twenty-Seven'* Club like Jim Morrison and Jimmy Hendrix?

Vivid images of Rick lying naked in bed, unconscious—or worse—invaded her brain and her heart began to bang uncomfortably in her chest.

He'll be fine, he has to be. Please God!

She hurried over to the reception desk, and asked the girl on duty to buzz up to his room.

No reply.

Now what?

Thanking the girl, and with that sick feeling of panic only increasing with each passing second, Izzy headed towards the bank of lifts. It was time to get up there. Find out for certain what was going on within Suite number Five-two-eight.

Stepping inside the lift compartment and reaching for the control panel, she noted that Marc and Sabrina had finally made an appearance downstairs, a porter hauling an over-stuffed baggage trolley in their wake. As ever, neither Marc, nor his girlfriend, believed in travelling light, or carrying their own luggage. Then she spotted a brand-new suitcase lobbed on top. Its presence meant only one thing. Sabrina had been hitting the shops again— with Marc's credit card. This would be more 'excess' luggage to pay for at Airport check-in.

She stabbed the number of the band's floor. Keeping her finger pressed there until the doors finally closed over, and she was shooting upwards. To hell with Sabrina's out-of-control shopping habit; she really couldn't give a shit how much she had to pay. Her only priority was making sure Rick was still alive.

'Come on, move.' She urged, watching helplessly as the floor numbers flicked past oh-so-slowly. 'He has to be okay. Please God; he just has to be….'

9.38 AM

'Rick!' Izzy's fist made contact with the door's panelling for a third time.

There was still stubborn silence from the room beyond.

Damn! Answer me Rick! Those horrible images of Rick unconscious continued to wreck havoc in her head; playing to her worst fears. Why didn't she have a master key to their rooms for times like these?

She was about to hammer on the door for a fourth time—maybe administer a few well placed kicks for good measure—when she heard the unmistakeable rattle of the internal door chain being released, and seconds later the door swung open.

Izzy was confronted by a very much alive Rick, his hand resting against the door jamb, a white towel hugging narrow hips, clearly just out the shower, with water dribbling everywhere.

The breath she'd been holding escaped her lungs with a loud whoosh.

Thank-you God! Resisting the urge to sink to her knees and offer up a prayer of thanks-giving, she somehow managed to eradicate all traces of blind panic from her expression, painting on a suitably bland smile.

'Good morning Rick. This is your nine thirty-eight alarm call!'

It was time to call on her acting skills; pretend she was totally unimpressed by the sight of him standing there in all his semi-naked glory. Ignore those pesky little water droplets that were dripping from his hair onto that expanse of magnificent chest, and remain totally detached, as though this man—so deliciously wet all over and just asking to be dried off—didn't affect her senses in the slightest.

Licking her lips, she dragged her treacherous eyes upwards to his face.

He was grinning at her. 'Good morning, Izzy.'

Shit! Had he noticed the way she'd been looking at him? Correction, make that word "devouring"; she'd been practically salivating over every glorious inch.

'I was concerned there might be something wrong. You're usually down by now. And you didn't answer the telephone.' Yes, she sounded suitably cool and PA-like. 'And everyone is ready to leave, *even* Marc!'

At the mention of Marc's name, Rick had the grace to colour slightly.

'Shit! Sorry, I'm afraid …we… lost track of time.'

He tugged a hand through his damp hair, and glanced backwards in the direction of the bathroom door. On cue, a dark-haired female, clad in a white bathrobe appeared, smiling shyly at Izzy.

So he'd had a visitor last night! A burst of righteous indignation flared to angry life in her gut. She'd been going out of her mind with worry, imagining all sorts of horrible scenarios, and he had been having shower sex with his latest conquest.

She swallowed, her lips pursing. But then, should she really be surprised? Rick, like the rest of the band, didn't subscribe to the conventional meaning of 'being faithful'. In fact, Izzy doubted Eclectic Deviation's loose interpretation of a 'committed relationship' would find its way into the *Oxford* Dictionary any time soon. Worse, their permanent girlfriends back home apparently accepted the situation without a bat of their false eyelashes.

'We've only got an hour until check-in, and we can't afford to miss our scheduled flight. You're cutting it extremely fine.' Her tone was clipped. 'I'll make sure a taxi is waiting for your guest.'

She hoped that bit of information might make the girl hurry up. But no such luck. All she got was another shy smile as the girl padded over to the chair by the bed, picked up her evening bag and removed a hairbrush.

'Is Rick *San*, your Boss Man?' she enquired of Izzy, her head cocked to the side as she began to stroke the brush through its long length, frustratingly slowly.

Izzy gave her briefest of nods and turned back to Rick. 'I need you both downstairs in less than ten minutes. Okay?'

'Yeah, no problem, Izzy,' Rick confirmed, a hand massaging the back of his neck. She was treated to another of those apologetic and completely bone melting smiles.

9.47 AM

Rick and his companion made it down with minutes to spare.

And, to avoid any hysterical goodbyes—Izzy having been witness to a belly-full of those over the last few months—she'd deftly took the girl by the arm, wheeling her away from Rick before she could utter a word of farewell, practically shoving her out of the main entrance, down the front steps, and into the waiting taxi.

With that little problem addressed, the band's security detail took over, escorting each member of the band through the throngs of screaming teenagers milling around outside. Dark glasses firmly in place, it was time for Eclectic Deviation to run the gauntlet to the relative safety of their waiting limos, a brief 'Hi' directed towards the screaming onlookers, then they were bundled inside the blacked-out vehicles, and whisked onto the next stop on today's itinerary; the Airport, for their onward flight to Canada.

10

CALGARY, ALBERTA

'If someone asks me one more time when Jonny and Jilly are tying the knot, I'll explode.' Marc removed his headphones, dumping them on the desk with a loud thump. 'For God's sake, will your people get their act together, and remove all the "getting married" questions?'

He fixed the radio presenter with his best frigid glare to emphasise his annoyance. Izzy called it his 'Darth Vader stare', guaranteed to floor any unsuspecting victim at twenty paces.

It worked again; the poor man was visibly quaking.

Given the determined set of Marc's jaw, he wasn't in any mood to continue with the phone-in until he'd received assurances that all offending questions—of the matrimonial variety—had been stripped out. Beside him, Steve looked equally put-out by the direction of today's interview.

So far, they'd been asked—several times—when every single member of the band was getting married; their Canadian fans clearly overlooking the fact Davey was the only one of them who'd actually made it down the aisle with his beloved Caron; two years previously.

'Please don't worry, Marc, we're already on it,' the presenter reassured him, frantically signalling to his production team, visible through the glass next door, to do just that, before any more callers were put through live on air.

"

The temperature in the studio was growing chillier by the second.

'In case you'd forgotten, the whole point of today is to discuss our tour,' Marc grumbled. 'Not give the lowdown on our sex lives.' Those headphones were still not back in place.

What does he expect? Izzy gave little shake of the head. Adolescent girls, raging hormones, pulsating rock music and handsome men; of course, the band's availability was going to be uppermost in the minds of their fans. Back in the day, Izzy had been the same about Bryan Ferry of *Roxy Music*. In fact— not that she'd admit it now—but Donny Osmond had caused a few heart-stopping moments, too.

'Izzy?' Marc's flinty gaze had swivelled in her direction, and she immediately jumped to attention, making sure a pleasant smile was firmly in place.

It didn't work.

'I thought I told you to provide a *detailed* list of the questions we're happy to answer?'Marc rapped out.

He was making sure she hadn't cut any corners. Any second now, this would be down to her, she could tell by his tone of voice. He was fishing around for someone to blame.

'And I did, Marc, but please remember none of us can legislate for any supplementary questions once the fans are on air. We're not mind readers.'

Her attempt at injecting some levity—and overdue common sense—fell flat.

'You really must learn to be much more explicit.' Marc went on, lighting up a cigarette, and letting out a long sigh of satisfaction as the nicotine kicked-in. 'It's essential that you emphasise—in black and white—the subjects we're willing to talk about and those which are *strictly* off limits. Surely you've learnt the basics by now. Then their people,' he waved his hand in the vague direction of the radio presenter, 'can do the necessary weeding out.'

Izzy bristled. How dare he suggest she didn't know how to do her job by now?

'I did ask them to remove the "marriage" questions. But you know what kids are like, Marc. Once they're on air and got your undivided attention, they'll take the chance to throw in something else, before they get cut off. They just want to find out everything about you, especially who you're dating. Rick's engagement was front page news back home.'

'That was only because Francesca got drunk at *Stringfellows*, and blabbed to an undercover journalist. As I recall, Rick was furious when it was plastered all over *The Sun*, next morning. His parents' hadn't even been told. When, and to whom we get married, is nobody's business but ours.'

Marc smoothed down his immaculate shoulder-length strawberry blond hair, which had been rendered almost rock solid by hours of back combing and copious amounts of hairspray.

'I'm more than happy to talk about the music, the band's artistic direction, or our plans for the future.' More nicotine was sucked in. 'Even what I ate for breakfast or my favourite movie. Not who Jonny happens to be screwing this week. Do I make myself clear, Izzy?'

As crystal, Marc!

'And given that revolving bedroom door of his, it's impossible to keep track, anyway.' Marc's glower dared anyone to even raise a titter.

He puffed a large cloud of cigarette smoke in her direction, resorting to chastisement by suffocation. 'I don't want to sit through another afternoon like this, Izzy. Make sure this doesn't happen again!'

A scowling Steve nodded his agreement at Marc's side, and then, with one final glower in her direction, Marc replaced his cigarette in the ashtray, and clamped the headphones back onto his ears.

11

CALGARY, ALBERTA

'Izzy, stop what you're doing!' Jonny's voice cut into her thoughts. 'I need your help. I've got myself in a bit of a tricky situation with Jilly.'

Great! What's he done now?

Jonny was standing in the open doorway of her office, not yet changed back into his civvies—band code for non-stage clothing—a towel dangling from his right hand, a frown puckering his handsome brow.

'Okay, hit me with it!' Izzy sat back, waiting for today's calamity. It had to be 'other-women' trouble again! Would the man ever learn?

'I should've said something earlier.' He came fully into the room, rubbing dry his damp hair. 'But I need you to send her some flowers, *urgently*. In fact, send her the whole fucking shop. That might—just *might*—get her talking to me again.'

Like Marc, *'urgent'* in Jonny-speak meant it was time for Izzy to drop everything, take out her magic wand, swish it around and sprinkle the fairy dust. All with the requirement of extracting him from the shit in double quick time.

He'd taken up residence on the edge of her desk, definite glimmers of "Little Boy Lost" showing, as he slung the towel about his neck.

'We've had another row. She's threatening to walk out on me. '

No doubt, she'd read some newspaper report about Jonny misbehaving with one of his floozies, thrown a 'strop' and demanded an explanation. Like the others, Jilly accepted his on-tour dalliances through gritted teeth, provided he made an effort to keep it out of the public eye. What she did object to was having his sex life printed in black and white for everyone—and especially her—to digest with their cornflakes. Unfortunately—for Jilly—Jonny didn't know the meaning of the word discretion.

And Izzy could guess that Jonny, caught in the eye of the hurricane, had resorted to some serious grovelling. But when that hadn't worked, he'd had no choice but to send for the cavalry.

Step forward Izzy!

'Don't you think sending a shop full of flowers is a bit excessive? She might not have enough vases.'

The look she received was eloquence itself. Humour hadn't been helpful. It was time to give his predicament some thought. And, it just so happened, she had a possible solution in mind. A custom she'd heard about while in Japan.

'How about I organise a large bouquet of red roses with a single yellow rose at its centre?' She reached for her notepad, jotting down a quick note to herself. 'According to Japanese tradition, red roses signify true love, and the single yellow rose means "I miss you".'

She looked up expectantly. 'And quality always trumps quantity. With Valentine's Day only a few weeks away, it's bound to win you major brownie points. Let her know you're really missing her.'

The tension in Jonny's face had eased somewhat. In fact, Izzy could make out definite glimmers of a smile tugging at his lips.

'Yep that might just do it. If she asks, I'll tell her I read about it while I was over there. She'll never twig it was really your idea.'

'Perish the thought, Jonny.'

Jilly wasn't some dumb blonde—far from it. She'd put two and two together, and recognise Izzy's hand in this. After all, Jonny didn't have much imagination when it came to romance.

A thank-you kiss was bestowed on Izzy's cheek. Jonny was happy.

'Oh, and make sure she gets them by tomorrow; first thing?' Satisfied that everything in the garden was now literally coming up roses, Jonny stood up. 'You know, get old *Interflora* on the job pronto!' He clicked his tongue meaningfully.

'As a matter of interest, what are you apologising for this time?' Izzy asked, keen to satisfy her curiosity.

'I guarantee you'll not believe it, Izzy.'

Izzy rolled her eyes. Somehow she probably could.

'Those two Stewardesses only sold their story to the *Daily Star*. Apparently they're saying I'm the best they've ever had.'

As usual, he didn't look too unhappy about the content of the actual article itself. Not when his sexual prowess was being proclaimed in such glowing terms. He viewed all his 'Kiss'n'tells' as badges of honour.

Izzy decided to feign innocence for a beat, and then let him have it. 'Honestly, Jonny, you know what these women are like. It's like Warhol said, some people will do anything to get their fifteen minutes of fame —and make a fast buck in the process. You need to be more discreet. Then Jilly won't find out.'

'Look, Jilly knows these girls don't mean anything! As I keep telling her, she's the one with the engagement ring,' his brow furrowed, 'although, that comment didn't go down too well this afternoon.'

'I'm not surprised,' Izzy tried not to laugh. 'Maybe she feels that by wearing the engagement ring, you shouldn't be looking at anyone else—full stop.'

'That's what she said.' He gave an impatient shake of the head. 'But what's a guy to do? Live like a bloody monk while I'm on tour? She's over there and I'm stuck here. A man has needs you know.'

From his pained expression, Izzy could tell it was yet another cross the poor lamb had to bear.

'If sex is constantly being offered on a plate, a guy can only say no, so many times, Izzy.'

Could he hear himself? Jonny Hambro had never said no to sex in his life.

'And, anyway, she knows the rules while we're on the road. If the girls aren't here, we're free to make other arrangements. But we always know where to draw the line. Feelings never come into it.'

Izzy shot him a sceptical look.

'Look, it's just a bit of fun between two consenting adults and nothing more.' He emphasised, giving himself a leisurely stretch, 'It relieves some of the stress and boredom we're up against. Jilly knows she's got nothing to worry about. None of them have.'

'And are Jilly and the others allowed to follow the same rules back home? You know when they're feeling lonely and stressed?'

Izzy knew the answer to her question, but she couldn't resist seeing his reaction.

'Stop taking the piss, Izzy. You know as well as I do, women are naturally monogamous creatures. It's in your genes; something to do with evolution and child bearing.' He waved a hand. 'I read it somewhere, only last week.'

And where had Jonny read that piece of utter bullshit? No doubt, from the enlightened pages of the latest edition of *Playboy*, his personal *Encyclopaedia Britannica* on the female species.

'So, any particular message you'd like me to put on Jilly's card?' Izzy asked.

Time to get back to basics; she knew what she'd like to write, but she'd lose her job in 10 seconds flat.

'Just tell her what you told me. But dress it up a bit. Give her some of the old 'Izzy' flannel. You're good with words.'

As if she hadn't enough to do, she'd now have to compose another lovey-dovey epistle to Jilly begging forgiveness on Jonny's behalf.

Jonny headed for the door. 'Oh, and, while you're at it, Izzy, send some flowers to my mother She's been on my case about not flying back to attend Uncle Stan's funeral next week. Considering we're in the middle of a fucking world tour and I haven't seen him in donkey's years, I don't think he'll be caring much, do you?'

Yes, Jonathan Hambro really was all heart.

10.31 PM

'Hey, pretty lady! I've finally got you to myself, at last.'

Izzy looked up to find Rick grinning at her from the doorway; her heart giving that familiar little jolt.

He'd discarded the vest he'd been wearing on stage, giving her another tantalising view of that muscular torso with its generous sprinkling of dark hair.

'What does a poor guy have to do to get a minute with you? It's been like Piccadilly Circus in here. I was debating whether I'd need to resort to kidnapping just to get some undivided attention.' His brown eyes sparkled with fun. 'But instead, I brought you this. Hoped it might earn me some brownie points?'

From behind his back, he drew out a single red rose, presenting it to her with an exaggerated flourish, bending low at the waist.

Heat burned through Izzy's cheeks as she accepted his gift. Hopefully, he'd put their redness down to the central heating blasting in here.

She buried her nose in its petals, breathing in the bloom's fresh delicate scent.

'Thanks. It's beautiful.'

And while she knew he'd probably had it thrust at him by a fan—less than five minutes previously—she wasn't about to complain; his thoughtfulness making her go all gooey inside.

He'd come to lean on the edge of her desk, barely eighteen inches away now, his chest directly at her eye level.

She swallowed. She was becoming ever so slightly obsessed with that part of his anatomy. Wanting nothing more than to snuggle her face into it, breathe in his heady male scent. Maybe let her hands do a bit of wandering to those pert nipples, stroke her thumbs over their tips, hear him groan as her mouth followed suit…

Then she remembered where she was. Chest snuggling and nipple sucking were categorically off-limits. Worse, he had that grin on his face again. Hopefully, he hadn't developed a talent for telepathy in the last five minutes.

Serious face, Izzy.

'Yes, for some reason it's been mayhem in here, tonight.' To collect herself, she popped the rose stem into a nearby glass of water on the desk. 'Please don't ask me to do anything urgently. It might take a while. Thanks to Lindsay and Marc, my to-do list is currently running to three pages. And, according to Jonny, his relationship is hanging by a thread—*again*—and he needs this Fairy Godmother to wave the old magic wand.'

Rick threw back his head, giving an unexpected burst of sexy laughter. In Izzy's opinion, he didn't laugh nearly enough these days.

'Okay, why don't you tell your Uncle Rick everything?' His arms folded, Rick leaned back against the wall; those bewitching brown eyes pinned on her. 'What's our Jonny done now? Got *his magic wand* out and left another mess—of the female variety—for you to clean up, by any chance?'

'Pretty much spot on,' Izzy giggled, 'you have a wonderfully filthy, but extremely perceptive mind, Mr Hambro.'

'I believe the expression says "it takes one to know one", pretty lady,' he countered, winking back at her.

Izzy's insides officially turned to water.

'So, what's the story?' he probed.

Taking a deep breath, Izzy filled him on Jonny's latest 'kiss'n'tell debacle and the fact Jilly was on the warpath. 'I'm trying my best to keep their romance on track, but he's making it extremely difficult. If only he'd learn to keep it in his trousers.'

'It's never going to happen. Our Jonny's incapable,' Rick lamented with a comical roll of the eyes. 'He's been like that since he discovered girls at thirteen; very early starter my cousin, unlike yours truly. I had the decency to wait until it was legal—just—two minutes after midnight on my sixteenth birthday, with Julie Watkins from next door.'

His eyes held hers for a long moment, and Izzy knew her whole face had gone another shade pinker. He was utterly beautiful sitting there, but leaping on him was completely out of the question. She had to get the old pulse under control. Try not to dwell too much on what he might have got up to with Julie Watkins.

Lucky girl!

'Don't think I really needed to know that, do you, Mr Hambro?'

'Funny, I got a feeling you might be interested.' He gave her another flirtatious wink.

As always, he was winding her up. With an exasperated shake of the head, Izzy opened a new page in her note pad, determined to move the conversation on.

'Getting back to business, what can I do for *you*, tonight, Mr Hambro?'

'Jeez, there's another loaded question, Miss Stevenson! What is it with you and all this innuendo, suddenly?' He waggled his eyebrows. 'Ask any red-blooded male that sort of question and a girl might end up hearing more than she bargained for.'

Shit, her cheeks were officially on fire now. She'd self-combust at this rate.

'Will you please stop teasing me, Rick? Be serious for once?' she rebuked, trying desperately to channel one of her firm "no more bullshit" looks.

'Okay, okay. I'll behave, but only if you really want me to.' His hands were held up in surrender, but his eyes still sparkled with fun.

And that was the problem with all this constant joking around, she thought, wistfully. His words were only ever said to her in jest; to make her laugh.

'Just wanted to let you know it's only Mum and Dad coming out to New York.' He went on, 'Spoke to Mum this morning and, unfortunately, Michelle won't make it. The ward is seriously understaffed, and holidays aren't being authorised, except in dire emergencies.'

'And your big brother headlining three nights at Madison Square Garden isn't considered a dire emergency,' Izzy filled in, pretending his disclosure was news to her.

In reality, Betty had already confirmed the 'Michelle' situation the week before.

'Nope, and I was so looking forward to catching up with her. I really needed to…'

For a moment, his expression was strangely forlorn and then his lips creased into one of his familiar bone-melting smiles.

'But hey, these things happen.' He gave a one-shouldered shrug.

'I'm sure she's just as disappointed as you are.' Izzy consoled.

She knew the closeness he shared with Michelle, five years Rick's junior. Fifteen years ago, and with no siblings of her own, Izzy had been more than a little jealous of their tight brother/sister bond.

'When I spoke to her at Christmas she was so excited to see you playing there,' she went on. 'Well that, and hitting all the shops on Fifth Avenue.'

'Yeah, that's our Michelle.' Rick let out a low chuckle. 'You'd think she was a bloody model, not a frigging staff nurse. She's got more clothes than Francesca, and believe me, that's no exaggeration! Says she can't wait for me to move into the flat properly, so she can take over my room at home. She wants to use it as her bloody walk-in wardrobe.' He gave an exaggerated sigh. 'How *Saks* will ever survive her no-show is beyond me?'

'Yes, sounds like this quarter's profits might be heading for a serious nosedive,' Izzy agreed, pleased to see his mood lightening once more. 'Well, I'll book your parents' flights and get all their paperwork processed. If you happen to be speaking to your mum, let her know it's on its way.'

She felt a pang of guilt at how easy the fib tripped off her tongue.

Rick gave her a quick salute. 'Will do, pretty lady.'

But now to the question Izzy had to ask. 'You mentioned last week that Francesca might be coming out to Chicago? Is that still on the cards?'

She hoped not. She'd only just recovered from her presence before Christmas...

Rick stifled a yawn with the back of his hand, suddenly looking weary, lines of strain appearing around his eyes and mouth. The band was due to head out 'nightclubbing' in the next twenty minutes but in Izzy's opinion an early night would be a better option for their drummer.

'Nope, there's been a change of plan. She's heading to Marbella—a last-minute photo-shoot she couldn't pass up. She won't be coming out until March, now.'

She-Bitch-from-Hell wouldn't be appearing until New York.

Hallelujah and hang out the bunting!

But still, Chicago wasn't going to be a barrel of laughs. She'd still be juggling Jilly—providing the flowers did the trick—the Honourable Caroline Lansing, Steve's latest blue-blood squeeze, and the ever-present Sabrina.

'Izzy?' Rick's hand had crept up to grip the nape of his neck.

Izzy frowned, realising he'd been doing that rather a lot lately. She detected a slight wince as she watched his fingers working over the tanned skin. Was it just a habit, or did he have some kind of neck pain going on?

'I've been meaning to ask, would you—?' He didn't get to finish.

A shadow had fallen across the doorway.

'Hey guys!' Terry Costello was grinning broadly at them.

Straightaway, Izzy's eyes were drawn downwards to the large black attaché case clamped in his fist, and she shuddered. After Francesca, the coarse Liverpudlian was her least favourite person around here. And, given the presence of the suitcase, clearly the latest batch of recreational drugs had—unlike Elvis—just entered the building. Within the next ten minutes, he'd be flogging its contents like *Dolly Mixtures* to all and sundry.

'Either of you seen Jonny or Davey? I've got a little present for them.' He tapped the case meaningfully, all the while his snake-like green eyes darting with undisguised interest between Izzy and Rick.

'Jonny's next door in the dressing room,' Rick answered, still gripping his neck. 'Not sure about Davey; probably chatting up some poor unsuspecting female as we speak. Cherchez les femme and you'll find our Davey.'

Terry's hand flexed around the handle of the attaché case and his eyes swivelled back to Izzy. 'And how's our gorgeous Miss Stevenson, tonight?' He clicked his tongue suggestively.

Worse, Izzy noted, it was accompanied by one of his customary lecherous winks. While Rick's were always playful and decidedly sexy, Terry's variety had the ability to make her flesh creep.

She forced a fake smile to her lips. 'I'm fine thanks, Terry.'

Here we go again! He was always hanging around, dropping less than subtle hints that maybe they should get together sometime. In fact, his entirely unwarranted advances were beginning to rattle her, big time!

Reaching over, she picked up today's schedule and pretended to check its contents, willing him to leave. Thankfully, he appeared to pick up on her vibes, turning his attention back to Rick.

'And, no offence, Rick, mate, but you look like shit, tonight. What the fuck is wrong with you? We're supposed to be partying in the next twenty minutes.'

Rick pulled a face as he slid off Izzy's desk, before beginning to roll his shoulders.

'Gee thanks for the compliment. Make me feel even better, why don't you?' His tone became distinctly dry. 'It's just the fucking insomnia; driving me up the bloody wall as usual.'

'Then, isn't it about time you bit the bullet and switched to the old *Teraxapen*.' Terry's grin had grown wider. 'Everyone can see the shit you're taking isn't doing the trick.'

He snaked an arm around Rick's shoulders. '*Teraxapen* will make all your problems disappear—just like that.' He snapped his fingers in Rick's face. 'Say the word, Ricky. Flash me the cash and we're good to go.'

Izzy resisted the urge to throw up at Terry's wheedling tone. From what she'd picked up to date, the enterprising Mr Costello made it his business to know the band's personal weaknesses and whether they could be exploited for his personal gain. So far, they'd provided rich pickings, and in her book that made him nothing but a vulture, ready to swoop in and take advantage when they were at their most vulnerable. And Rick looked extremely vulnerable now. That haunted look was back. Was he wavering, about to give in to Terry's suggestion?

Please don't do it, Rick.

'And you've known me long enough, Rick. I only supply the best for my mates. No sub-standard shit from this outfit.' The quality assurance spiel continued. 'All sourced from totally legit suppliers.' Terry tapped at the side of his nose. 'I've got a few guys on the inside who turn a blind eye. If you know what I mean?'

Rick's brow puckered and he let out a long sigh.

To Izzy, he looked to be fighting some kind of inner battle; struggling against the urge to give into Terry's offer; say 'yes' to the promise of a good night's sleep. Betty had had a fit when Izzy had dropped the word *"Teraxapen"* into their last conversation.

Her thoughts were interrupted by Davey's voice echoing the down the corridor. 'Terry! Where the hell are you, man? Have you got that fucking gear I ordered?'

'And talk of the devil, here's Davey, ready to transact a bit of business.'

Fielding his first genuine grin of the last five minutes, and no doubt thinking of the wad of cash winging its way to his hip pocket, Terry ducked out of the office; Rick's sleep problems apparently forgotten for now. A 'See you later' floated back to them.

Izzy let go the breath she'd been holding. Thank God, Rick hadn't succumbed to Terry's urging—this time.

'Why do I get the impression you're not keen on our Terry?'

Izzy looked up to find Rick studying her closely.

Perceptive man, but she wasn't about to start bad mouthing Terry Costello; not even to someone as lovely as Rick. She wasn't that stupid, and while being within ten feet of the loathsome cockroach and his portable chemist's shop scared the living daylights out of her, she didn't want to get on Terry's wrong side. And she'd a feeling that if she started saying anything less than complimentary about the Band's Mr Fix-it, that's exactly where she'd end up.

'I don't really know him.'

'But I can tell he makes you feel uncomfortable.'

Damn! Rick's dark eyes were at their most penetrating, and Izzy shifted uncomfortably beneath their unwavering gaze.

Under-statement of the bloody century!

'Look, tell me to piss off and mind my own business,' Rick continued, 'but I've noticed he's been making a bit of a nuisance of himself around you. I can have a word if you want me to? Tell him to back off.'

So he'd been aware of Terry's unwanted attentions, but how? Terry usually approached her when none of the band was around but, obviously at some point, Rick had clearly witnessed his none-too-subtle chat-ups.

'Thanks, that's really sweet of you, Rick!' she emphasised, giving him an overly-bright smile, her inner feminist asserting herself. 'But I can handle the "Terrys" of this world.'

'Hey, I'm not implying you can't,' Rick replied with a frown, 'but just remember, the offer stands. Sometimes he doesn't know when to take "no" for an answer. He tried it on with Michelle a few years back. I had to step in and remind him of his manners around my kid sister.'

He flexed his hand. 'And it bloody hurt, too. But if you need me to do the same, just say the word, pretty lady.'

'Thanks.' Momentarily, Izzy luxuriated in the mental image of Rick landing a flattening punch on Terry on her behalf. 'But I can look after myself as far as Terry is concerned,' she reassured him. 'Now, you wanted to ask me something else?'

'Yeah— '

'Rick, aren't you ready yet?' Davey appeared, already changed into his civvies, with a stunning brunette hanging off each arm, neither woman wearing anything that could be described as clothing. In fact, squinting closer, Izzy had seen more fabric on her mother's lounge curtain pelmet.

'Jeez, what's keeping you, man?' he challenged Rick. 'I want to be out of here in the next fifteen minutes and you're keeping me and— more importantly—these two beautiful young ladies waiting. Get a bloody move on, Hambro!'

Izzy recognised the two women from earlier. They'd been hanging around backstage all night. On cue, Rick received reproachful pouts from both women, accompanied by lots of flirty hair-tossing.

Izzy turned her face away.

Talk about being obvious.

'Shit!' The smile Rick flashed in their direction was instantly apologetic. 'Give me five minutes, ladies, I won't be long!'

He turned back to Izzy. 'Yeah, I need a plaster, Izzy. Got this bloody great blister on my finger; occupational hazard of the job, I guess.'

He showed her the red fluid-filled blemish, which had developed along the inner length of his index finger. Giving a grimace, Izzy dug out her first-aid kit from the desk drawer and handed over the requested plaster.

'Thanks, pretty lady.' He said, in a low voice. 'What would I do without you?'

As he departed, Izzy allowed herself one final pulse-spiking perusal of that chest and those well-muscled shoulders. What would it feel like to be held in those arms?

'So, ladies, let me introduce you to our PA, Izzy.' It was Davey who spoke, breaking the awkward silence that had descended on the room.

Izzy could sense something snide was about to be directed straight at her. Snide was still Davey's default setting whenever she was concerned.

'Izzy does all our day-to-day stuff around here,' he explained. 'Makes sure my life runs like a fucking military campaign. Isn't that right, Izzy?' He fired off a totally insincere smile in her direction.

Izzy made sure to return it with interest.

'But, thank God, she's not responsible for anything too *personal*, if you get my drift? We wouldn't want to be kept to a rigid schedule for that now, would we?' His exaggerated wink set off peels of raucous screeching from both his companions.

'Hi, it's nice to meet you.' Izzy ignored his tasteless remark. 'So, where are you off to tonight?'

Her question was asked out of mere politeness. She'd absolutely no interest whatsoever as to what dive he'd be frequenting tonight or with whom. Her only concern was that Rick was being dragged along for the ride—she winced inwardly at the accurate but unintentional pun—when he looked so done in.

'Nowhere, you'd approve of.' Davey's grin didn't reach his eyes. 'So we're guaranteed to have a bloody good time, right ladies?'

On cue, his two hand puppets delivered more cackles of amusement. The sound was beginning to set Izzy's teeth on edge.

'Our Izzy's a real Miss Goody Two Shoes,' Davey continued. 'Doesn't drink, smoke or do drugs. She likes nothing better than a cup of *Ovaltine* and heading off to bed early with a fucking book. Isn't that right, Izzy?' He cocked an eyebrow in Izzy's direction. 'But in my *book*, any woman who's into that sort of thing is no bloody fun, whatsoever!'

There was more laughter from the two bimbos, and Izzy let out an irritated sigh. It was time to get rid of them. If there was any more of that mindless squawking, she wouldn't be responsible for her actions. Not that the lucky lady who ended up in Davey's bed would be giggling quite so hard later on. Not once she'd discovered Mr Eastman's rumoured problem.

'Davey, just before you go…'

Izzy lifted an over-stuffed folder from her in-tray, quickly flicking through its contents to retrieve the required information. It was 'Age-of-consent' time. She held a list of State laws on that sort of thing. Just so no one got caught out with a minor. It was a band rule never to sleep with any of their fans, but the rest of the female population was fair game, provided they were legal. Most surprisingly, even Jonny had got the memo on that one.

'Should you happen to change your mind later on, it's eighteen, remember?' She said dryly. 'And make sure Rick knows that, too.'

12

CALGARY, ALBERTA

'Hey, Izzy, it's Rick. Look, sorry to bother you, but I've got a bit of a problem. Can you come up to my room?' There was a pause at the other end of the line, before he added in a low voice. 'It's kind of urgent.'

Izzy's senses were immediately on high alert. Rick never used the word 'urgent'.

'What do you mean, 'urgent'?'

Reaching over, she picked up today's schedule from the nightstand, and cast a hasty eye down its considerable length. Their flight took off at 11.00am, then an eight-hour turnaround in Vancouver, and onto Seattle by midnight. Hopefully, at some point, she might be able to squeeze in a quick call home too — if she was lucky. A catch up with Mum and Dad was long overdue.

'Eh, you remember that girl I left with last night?'

How could Izzy forget? By the time Izzy had escorted the band from the Dressing Room to the limos; his date had been all over him like a bad case of chicken-pox.

'She's locked herself in the bathroom, and is refusing to come out.'

'She's done what?'

The sheet of paper fell from Izzy's hand; all thoughts of phoning home evaporating instantly.

Great! She appeared to have a hysterical girl on her hands; just what she didn't need this morning.

'Please tell me you're joking?'

'No joke,' he confirmed. 'Believe me I've tried everything—short of breaking down the door—to get her out of here. Maybe you might have better luck, woman to woman. I didn't want to resort to calling in Terry and the lads.'

Izzy silently agreed. Involving Terry and his band of heavies would be a recipe for disaster.

'Okay, give me a couple of minutes, and I'll be right with you.'

8.39 AM

Within five minutes, they were both standing outside the locked bathroom door. There was an ominous silence from within.

'This has never happened to me before,' he confessed. 'I just said the usual about how we had to leave, and she totally went off on one. Started crying, telling me she loved me. That we were made for each other and that I had to take her to Vancouver.'

He reached for his white shirt which was lying on the bed, and slipped a hand down the sleeve. 'When I said that wasn't possible, the screaming started. I'm surprised you didn't hear her. She was threatening all sorts if I didn't change my mind.'

Izzy cast a concerned glance at the locked door and chewed her lip, all the time doing her best to avoid staring at his chest. He was too close for comfort.

'Did you explain to her about Francesca?'

She knew—off by heart—all the lines they trotted out the 'morning after' to justify their bed-hopping behaviour. She'd even been called on to use them herself—on their bloody behalf!

'Yes, I was totally up front with her. Told her last night had been fun, but it was time for her to go,' he answered. 'That's when she decided to hit me; whacked me across the face, here.'

He pointed to an angry red mark, which was developing nicely along his left cheekbone.

'Called me every name under the sun, said I'd be sorry and then she locked herself in the bathroom. She's been in there ever since, sobbing loudly until a few minutes ago. Then it all went quiet. That's when I freaked and thought I'd better phone you. She won't say a word to me.'

Izzy knew this had to be dealt with as quickly—and discreetly—as possible, before any word leaked out and it exploded across the front pages, which it would, if the poor girl had done something silly.

'Okay, I'll phone down to reception. Ask for a doctor; just in case. What's her name?'

'Em, Shelley, I think.' Rick shifted uneasily, not meeting Izzy's eyes. 'Davey introduced her as Shell, so I presumed it was Shelley. That's what I've been calling her ever since and she's never corrected me.'

'You just think?' Izzy ran her hands through her hair in frustration, before stepping forward and knocking on the door. 'Hello, Shelley.'

No answer.

'Shelley, it's Izzy, I'm the band's PA. We met briefly after the show, last night. Is everything okay in there?'

Still no answer forthcoming, although Izzy thought she heard a muffled sniff.

'Shelley, I'm starting to get worried. Rick says you're really upset about something. Why don't you come out and we can talk?'

For a moment there was no response, and then an irate voice piped up within, 'I don't care if you're the god-damn Pope, you patronising bitch, I don't want to talk to you. And my name's not Shelley, its Shelby.'

Izzy rolled her eyes and mentally counted to ten. 'Do you know if she's taken anything?'

Rick scratched his chin for a second. 'Yeah, she did a couple of lines of coke with Davey while we were out. Then we shared a joint back here.' He nodded towards the two empty champagne bottles lying on the nightstand. 'We managed to get through those, too.'

In other words, just another regular night of excess as far as Eclectic Deviation was concerned. The girl was probably still drunk or stoned—or both!

Lifting the telephone, Izzy depressed zero and connected with reception. As tactfully as possible, she requested that a doctor, together with Hotel Security, attend Rick's suite immediately.

'Look, you'd better finish getting dressed in Jonny's room, next door,' she instructed, replacing the handset. 'Take your bags with you, and I'll fix this.'

It was always better to remove the band from the firing line as soon as possible. Plus, his continued close proximity, half-undone shirt, and the intoxicating scent of his aftershave, was making her feel decidedly distracted from the job at hand.

'Thanks, Izzy.' He looked just as shattered as he had the previous night. His right hand had crept upwards, and was now pulling on his neck. 'I'm really sorry to drag you into this, but I didn't know what else to do. Terry usually has them checked out; ensures they know the score beforehand. And she was perfectly normal until an hour ago.'

'When you delivered the sad news that she wasn't coming along on an all-expenses-paid jaunt courtesy of Richard Hambro.'

Rick's eyes finally met hers, and Izzy could read the genuine regret written there.

'I've just about had it with this whole fucked-up one-night-stand shit and our crazy rules!' He shook his head. 'More to the point, I've succeeded in totally fucking up my pretty lady's morning, too.'

Unable to stop herself, she gave him a long overdue smile. He looked as though he needed one. 'Never mind, these things happen. Let's see if the doctor has better luck?'

13

VANCOUVER, BRITISH COLUMBIA

'When we *eventually* get inside the Arena,' Marc muttered, 'I want you to make a formal complaint about their security people. They've clearly got no idea about effective crowd control. They shouldn't be letting fans get this close. Someone will be squashed under the wheels any second now.'

He lit up another cigarette, ignoring the female faces pressed up against the glass, planting lipstick kisses and shrieking his name at the top of their lungs.

'And, believe me, that's a shedload of publicity, and a potential lawsuit, we can do without. They'd take us to the bloody cleaners.' He directed an ill-timed wiggle of his fingers towards the window, which only succeeded in setting off more screaming and another surge of female bodies flattening themselves against the car.

The limos were now lining up to access the rear entrance of tonight's venue, teenagers closing in on all sides. Hands were hammering on the Lincoln's windows in a bid to gain the band's attention, the fans only knowing one level to pitch their adoration—ear splitting!

'Mmmm.' Izzy was trying not to breathe in too deeply as more cigarette smoke filled the cramped confines of their car. 'If it happens, I'll make sure we send flowers.'

She wafted away the smoke with her hand irritably. It was making the back of her throat itch, but given the proximity of the fans, opening a window wasn't an option. Someone was guaranteed to try to climb inside. It had happened before. She'd just have to hope that by the end of the tour, she didn't have a cough worthy of a forty-a-day habit.

'Someone get out of bed on the wrong side this morning? It's not like you to be snitchy,' Marc enquired, 'or is it just your time of the month?'

Izzy resisted the urge to slap him. 'In case you've forgotten, I've had a rather an eventful day.'

'Oh yeah, the girl who decided it'd be cool to barricade herself in Rick's bathroom. So how did you finally get her to vacate the premises?'

'With the help of a doctor, four guys from Hotel Security and a locksmith.' Izzy rhymed off.

Marc exchanged an exasperated look with Sabrina snuggled up by his side. 'And what did the doctor say?'

'Not much,' Izzy confirmed. 'Gave her a quick check over, and pronounced her fit and healthy apart from the after-effects of too much booze, and a large dose of unrequited love. She was threatening to sell her story to the highest bidder as Security shoved her into a taxi. The *National Enquirer* was mentioned.'

The North American gossip magazine was as ruthless as any of them when it came to printing salacious stories.

'In other words, just another fruitcake,' Marc dismissed. 'All Jonny's conquests roll straight out of his bed, hail a cab, and leg it to Fleet Street with pound signs in their eyes. Why should one of Rick's tarts be any different?'

A particularly piercing scream permeated the interior of the limousine, making Marc wince. 'Anyway, Izzy, onto more urgent matters, and given we're *still* waiting….'

The limo had moved barely six inches in the last ten minutes.

'We really need to discuss Items Four and Five on tomorrow's schedule,' he began. 'I'm really not happy…'

Here comes today's complaint!

'I appreciate you have a job to do…'

Subtext—he didn't appreciate it one bit—he was just employing the soft soap again and expecting her to perform miracles.

'But—as ever—the itinerary is too heavy. Things need to be cut. We're all struggling, and you've seen the state of Rick, lately. He's so bloody tired, he looks ready to crash and burn any second. We've still seven more weeks of this bedlam to endure and I'm seriously wondering if he's going to make it in one piece. You need to do something fast…'

5.37 PM

Izzy pushed back from her desk, stretching her arms above her head.

The schedule had been revised and photocopied; the document now reflecting all the cuts Marc had insisted upon. Not that Lindsay had welcomed those changes with open arms. When Izzy had briefed him, he'd promptly had a real toys-out-the-pram moment himself, complaining loudly he'd get it in the neck when he brought the Record Company up to speed.

The band was out on stage, immersed in this afternoon's sound check, and the dressing room was empty except for Sabrina lounging on the sofa, browsing the latest edition of *Vogue*, and sipping coffee.

Izzy consulted the next item on her to-do list. Twenty entries for today and she'd only got as far as Item six. She reached for a fresh sheet of paper and fed it through the rollers of her trusty Smith Corona typewriter. There had better be no more interruptions, or she'd be on nightshift.

'For fuck's sake, I don't believe it. Where the hell have you come from?' Sabrina yelled out, 'Izzy, get in here quick!'

'Obviously I spoke to soon,' Izzy muttered to the four walls, before answering back. 'What is it, Sabrina…I mean, Miss Warren?'

Shit! Hopefully, Sabrina hadn't noticed her slip of the tongue. One thing the girlfriends didn't tolerate was *staff* calling them by their first names. And Izzy was most definitely considered *staff*.

'Don't just sit there, Izzy. Get your arse in here, *NOW!*

Yeah, but *they* could speak to *her* any way they pleased, and *frequently* did.

Izzy poked her head through the interconnecting door between her office and the dressing room, only to be confronted by Sabrina holding up a tablecloth, revealing four teenage girls crouched under a table in the far corner; clinging to each other, absolutely petrified.

'Izzy, they'd better not be here when I come back. Do you hear me?' Sabrina cut Izzy a sharp look. 'If they are, I'll be speaking to Marc.'

With that threat left hanging heavy in the air, she dropped the tablecloth, turned on her sky-scraper heels and flounced from the room. Sabrina was always good for a dramatic flounce.

Izzy let out a weary sigh. Knowing how much Marc's beloved fiancée liked to stir things, she'd probably carry out that threat too. But for now, it was time to get a better look at their uninvited guests. She pulled back the cloth and crouched down.

'Hi, I'm Izzy.' She gave the four teenagers what she hoped was her best reassuring smile. 'Can I ask what you're doing under the table?'

There was a moment's silence.

'Eh, we sneaked in when no one was around.' the girl closest to her stammered, visibly shaking as she exchanged a sideways glance with her three companions. 'One of the arena security guards let us into the Arena.'

'But does he know you got as far as here?' Izzy prompted, with raised eyebrows.

The girl shook her head, before offering Izzy a tentative smile.

'Was that Marc's fiancée? She looks real mad.'

'Yes, she does tend to be a bit highly strung.' Izzy gave an ironic roll of the eyes. 'Look, you're not allowed inside the arena before the doors officially open at six pm. Your friend could lose his job over this.' Her expression became firm. 'In fact, he probably will. This is the band's dressing room, and I'm duty bound to report any security breaches by unauthorised personnel to their Tour Manager.'

That was, if he hadn't been briefed already, courtesy of Sabrina's mile-wide mouth.

'Please don't tell,' the girl—clearly their designated spokeswoman—replied, her lip trembling. 'He's my dad.' She wiped away a stray tear. 'He really needs this job.'

Well, maybe her Daddy should have thought more about job security, before smuggling said daughter and her mates inside.

'What's your Dad's name?' Izzy asked, kindly.

Against her better judgement, she felt sorry for them. They clearly hadn't thought through the consequences of today's little escapade.

'Gary… Gary Landsberg; I'm Sharon.'

'Okay, Sharon.' Izzy's face relaxed into a smile. 'Firstly, I think you should come out from under that table. None of you look very comfortable.'

The girls scrambled out from their cramped hiding place to stand beside Izzy.

'Now, where does your dad work?'

What could she do to smooth this over and save the poor guy's job?

'He's stationed in the loading bay, where the band's limos are kept.' Sharon answered.

Still deliberating the situation, Izzy noticed a pile of signed photographs of the band, stacked in a box on the table. Fishing out four, she handed them over to the girls. 'Here, have one of these, for starters.'

She received a grateful chorus of thanks.

'Now, I need you to come with me. I'll take you back to your Dad, and endeavour to cover this up as a big misunderstanding. But you have to agree with everything I say. Okay?'

Four vigorous head nods. They were onboard.

'Hey, Izzy, have you seen my—' Rick stopped dead in the doorway. 'What's going on here?' he questioned, eyes flicking between Izzy and the teenagers standing before him. 'Is this some kind of Meet and Greet I'm not aware of, Miss Stevenson?'

Four collective jaws bounced off the floor, eyes saucer-like as they gawped at one of their heroes made flesh.

'Em, you could say that.' Izzy answered.

Great! No chance of sneaking them out, with no questions asked.

'But don't worry, I'm returning them straight back to where they belong.' She added hastily.

'Okay.' He nodded at the girls and, thankfully, one of his ice-cream melting smiles appeared. 'Hi!'

'Hi, Rick,' they chorused.

'Well, we'd better get going,' Izzy began, shepherding her charges past him and out into the corridor, fervently hoping none of them decided to faint at his feet. Given the way her luck was going today, that would be the last straw.

'Erm, Rick, you haven't seen them in here, okay?' She hoped he'd take the hint.

'Okay, whatever you say, Izzy. But what do I get for keeping schtum?'He pressed a long slim finger to his lips, winking conspiratorially at the girls.

The girl closest to Izzy giggled and gave a definite sway.

'Just my eternal gratitude,' Izzy replied, hastily looping her arm about the girl's shoulders to ensure she remained upright—just in case. 'I'll fill you in on all the details later, promise.'

10.13 PM

Izzy collapsed into the limo's plush suede backseat, thoroughly exhausted and thanking her lucky stars today was almost over. Only the ninety-minute flight to their next destination —Seattle—to complete, and then they'd be safely tucked up in their beds just after midnight. There was never a dull moment in this job. But some of them she could cheerfully do without.

'We should arrive at the airport in five to seven minutes,' Phil, their driver, advised Izzy and Rick, through the Lincoln's intercom.

As always the car's privacy screen was firmly in place. Marc insisted on it.

'And traffic's light, so we should make it no problem.'

With a sigh of relief, Izzy unzipped her hold-all, and began searching inside for her notepad.

'So, after some incredibly fast talking, my pretty lady managed to save Mr Landsberg's job,' Rick commented, echoing their conversation earlier, as he rubbed the beads of sweat from his forehead with a towel.

The band had come straight off stage and piled into the limos without changing tonight; the take-off slot for their onward flight to Seattle confirmed for ten forty-five pm.

'Yes. I rambled on about a mix-up with the timings of the "Meet and Greet,"' Izzy answered, 'and Mr Landsburg got off with a verbal warning. Let's just say, he was extremely grateful.'

She glanced inside her bag. Where was her notepad? Had she forgotten to pack it?

'And thanks for not saying anything to anyone, especially to Davey,' she added, rummaging deeper. 'If he'd got wind of what really happened, he'd have gone ballistic. You know how paranoid he is about dressing room security.'

On the British tour, a fan had barged into their dressing room in Birmingham, pulled out a penknife and asked Davey to autograph her arm in blood. Davey had been apoplectic with rage at the perceived threat; Scottie and Lee lucky to keep their jobs.

'I'm just glad Sab… Miss Warren decided not to publicise it either.' Although, knowing Sabrina, she might still decide to drop that little bombshell, especially if she wanted to set off fireworks between Davey and Marc.

Izzy continued to poke around within the confines of the massive bag at her side. Could she have dropped the notepad while running for the car?

'No problem, and by keeping my mouth shut, I've now earned your eternal gratitude, remember? That should be good for a few favours from my pretty lady.'

With a cheeky wink and nudge, Rick leaned forward to peruse the contents of the limo's mini fridge. 'I'm desperate for a beer. Can I tempt you to anything, Izzy?'

'Yes, I'll take a *Pepsi*, please…'

Her blood pressure was beginning to inch upwards. There was no sign of her notepad. It must have fallen out. If she lost it, she'd be up shit creek without the proverbial paddle. The band's entire life was contained within its pages.

There was no other option. She'd have to divest the bag of its remaining contents. Go through everything with a fine-tooth comb. And if it wasn't there, then she'd really need to start panicking.

Rick snapped off the *Pepsi* can's ring pull, his eyes widening at the never-ending mound of stuff Izzy had begun to dump onto the seat between them.

'Jeez, Izzy, you must have everything in there but the bloody kitchen-sink.'

'Believe me; I've probably got one of those lurking in here too. Thanks.'

Izzy took the proffered can, and chugged down a large mouthful, before placing it in the cup holder at her elbow. 'I'll have you know, the contents of this bag ensures Eclectic Deviation's life runs like clockwork.'

Although if she'd lost her notebook that might not be the case…

Rick picked up the tiny stopwatch on top of the pile. 'Quite literally it would seem.' He eyed it with amusement, before necking more of his beer.

Izzy's bag was now empty, but still no joy. Marc was going to hit the roof when he heard about this. There was confidential stuff contained within those pages. Confidential stuff the newspapers would just love to get their hands on.

Then Izzy's eyes alighted on what appeared to be a piece of thin blue cardboard sticking out from a torn section of lining near the bottom of the bag.

Could it be? Taking a closer look, sure enough, rammed down between the lining and canvas outer layer, was her missing notebook.

Her backside had been saved.

Fishing it out, she gave the notepad a welcome kiss of joy, before quickly repacking the bag. Crisis number three of the day had been averted.

'Hey, better not forgot these.' Rick picked up a bundle of paperwork which had slid onto the floor by his foot, Izzy's passport resting on top.

His face softened into a grin as he picked it up. 'Okay, pretty lady. Let's see what the old passport photo looks like? Can't be as bad as mine?' he quipped. 'I look like a bloody convict. All that's missing is the serial number below my name.'

Izzy froze, her stomach dropping like a stone.

Shit! Shit! Shit! Out of nowhere, she was suddenly staring a worse catastrophe in the face; worse than any of the others thrown at her today, and multiplied by a thousand.

No one in Jack's office had asked to see her passport. They'd accepted her as Izzy Stevenson, with no questions asked. And, given her job had included organising all the band's commercial flights—as well as her own—no one had discovered she was using an assumed name, around here. Rick was now about to rumble her true identity, if she didn't do something pronto.

'Please don't!'

She made a dive across the seat, trying to grab the passport out from his hand. But Rick's reflexes were quicker, stretching his arm upwards and back behind his head, ensuring the passport remained well out of her reach. He chuckled loudly at her flailing attempts to reclaim it.

'Jeez, Izzy, it must be really bad.' He observed, continuing to sip from the beer bottle in his other hand.

Izzy clocked the devilish glint that had entered his eyes.

Damn, he's enjoying this!

Her blood pressure spiked. If he happened to clock her real name and address, as well as that bloody photo, it was game over, her carefully constructed cover blown in an instant.

'I said give it back to me, Rick.'

What the hell was she going to do?

'How much is it worth for me not to look?' His tone was still jocular, but his smile appeared to have wavered a little.

'Please, just give it back to me, Rick, okay? I'm being serious.' Her voice became shriller as she made another desperate—and unsuccessful—lunge. Her body was now pressed up against his, both of them chest to chest, their eyes locked in mortal combat.

'No one sees that picture except Passport Control.' She hissed, her breasts heaving under the tight confines of her jumper.

He had to hand it over. If not, she was *dead* in the water....

'Come on, Izzy. Let me have just one tiny little peak. I won't tell anyone if it's really bad?' He winked again, but Izzy was in no mood for his flirty games.

'I said no! Now give it back!'

Shit! Her eyes were starting to well up. The last thing she wanted to do was burst into tears next. She tried to sniff them away, but too late; a single rogue tear had escaped, rolling down her cheek.

'Jeez, Izzy, don't cry. I was only teasing.'

But her show of emotion had paid an unexpected dividend, the unopened passport was now being held out towards her; Rick's expression apologetic. 'I'm sorry.'

Izzy snatched it back and hurriedly stuffed it into her bag, out of sight. An uneasy silence ensued, before she let out a sigh, breaking the tension that had permeated the confined space.

'No, Rick, I'm the one who should be saying sorry. I shouldn't have gone completely overboard just now....'

She bit her lip, wracking her brains for a suitable excuse for her behaviour. Maybe it was time for a little honesty?

'If you must know, I've got a hang-up about people seeing my photograph.'

It sounded lame saying it out loud, but it was true. She really didn't like seeing herself in photographs, especially ones—like her passport photograph—that held traces of the girl she'd been, all those years ago.

'You must be fed up dealing with neurotic women today?' She attempted a self-deprecating smile.

'Don't be daft. You're probably one of the least neurotic women I've ever met.' Rick's face had relaxed into what looked to be a relieved smile. 'But I don't get it. Why do you hate people seeing your photograph?'

'I don't know. I just do. A throw back to when I was younger, I guess,' Izzy replied. 'I suppose everyone has insecurities about themselves and how they looked growing up.'

And she'd had pretty major ones.

'Too true,' he gave a laugh, 'I'm still gutted Jonny has six inches on me; late growth spurt, apparently. But seriously, you should know you've nothing to worry about in the looks department.'

His voice became husky, those dark eyes sweeping over her. 'You really are one pretty lady, Miss Stevenson.'

But only if the guy's into the sweet and wholesome type, her brain reminded her.

'Why on earth would you think otherwise?' Rick reached over to loop a stray curl of chestnut hair behind her ear. His fingers brushed against her earlobe, making her breath catch, her skin reacting to the gentleness of his touch.

'Any guy would consider himself bloody lucky to have you as his girlfriend, Izzy.'

Except him. As she looked up, her eyes locked again with the unfathomable brown depths of his. 'If you say so.' she answered.

'I do. Believe me, you're a bit of a pin-up amongst the guys on our road-crew.' He winked. 'I've noticed tongues hanging out when you appear up on stage.'

Izzy blushed. 'Don't be so silly.'

'It's true and, for what it's worth, I'm sorry for being an arsehole and pissing you off.' He went on. 'I know you've had a bitch of a day. Are we still friends?'

He stuck out his hand for her to shake.

Izzy couldn't help but take it. 'You know we are.'

'Good.' He paused. 'Because, Izzy, I wanted—'

'Hey, guys, that's us at the airfield!' Phil's chirpy voice cut in through the intercom.

14

RENO, NEVADA

Izzy was munching her way through a second slice of wholemeal toast, perusing the Entertainment Section of the morning newspaper, an index finger absently twisting a tendril of hair. The band still hadn't appeared down for their breakfast meeting. By her reckoning they were currently seven minutes late.

'Hey! It's our sexy Miss Stevenson!'

At the sound of Terry's unwelcome greeting, Izzy's good mood evaporated in an instant and she automatically replaced the toast on her plate; her appetite gone.

What the hell did he want?

Allowing herself a disapproving sideways glance, she could only watch in growing dismay as he collapsed into the chair next to her, resting the ever-present briefcase on the floor between them.

Great! It's a social call.

Leaning over, he picked up the coffee pot from the centre of the table and filled an empty cup.

'Well, did we get a good review last night?' He inclined his head towards the newspaper article. 'Any mention of our little stage invasion?'

He splashed milk into his cup, before reaching for the sugar bowl.

Halfway through last night's gig, a posse of girls had evaded Arena Security and dashed up onto the stage making a beeline for Jonny, but Terry and his team had been ready, apprehending them before they'd got within six feet of their quarry.

'Yes, your heroics did gain a brief mention,' Izzy commented, counting four sugars lumps being dropped into Terry's cup. Not even a bloody mountain of the stuff could make that man any sweeter.

'Nice to see the hired help are getting some acknowledgement for a change.' Terry gave his coffee a stir. 'Want that last piece of toast?' He nodded towards the toast wrack in front of him.

'No. Please help yourself.'

'Well, send us over the butter.'

The butter was duly passed, and he proceeded to spread a heart-attack's worth onto his toast.

'I know you'll be waiting for the lads,' Terry continued, 'so before I go, can I tempt you to anything for later? I've got the old case with me.' Leaning down, he gave the briefcase a reassuring pat.

Izzy rolled her eyes.

He's patting it, as if it's a bloody dog....

'And remember, I can get my hands on anything—and I mean absolutely anything—a classy lady like you might require. And I'm not just talking drugs. I know all about a lady's needs....' He delivered another salacious leer down at her chest.

Izzy bristled. Since when had her mouth been located down there? Didn't he realise women were more than just a pair of breasts on legs? And worse, she'd a feeling she was about to be subjected to another of his sales pitches. Well, he could forget it. It was never going to happen!

'And as with all my first-time customers, I'm sure we could negotiate a generous little discount. Or maybe payment in kind would be better? I've a feeling that could suit us both down to the ground.

Don't you agree?' His eyebrows shot up into the depths of his greasy brown mullet.

In his dreams!

'As always, Terry, thank you for the offer, but I'm quite sure I don't need anything; now or in the future,' Izzy emphasised with a tight smile, returning to her newspaper.

'Izzy, no offence, but has anyone ever told you, you need to relax more?' He licked the remnants of the butter from his knife.

Too late, offence had been taken. The man was rude, as well as having the table manners of a pig.

'You always seem—how shall I say—a little uptight. And you know the old saying about all work and no play…'

How dare he suggest she was uptight?

'Isn't it about time you let the old hair down a bit?' He bit into the toast, chewing noisily, his repugnant chomping making Izzy's stomach turn.

'Please don't worry, Terry, I know exactly how and when to enjoy myself.' Izzy gave him another tight smile; a harder edge to her tone. He was asking for the contents of her orange juice to be poured all over that bullet-shaped dome of his.

'Then, I'm intrigued. How does our Miss Stevenson do that, I wonder?' He mused. 'Something tells me she needs to spend time with the right kind of guy. Am I right? Maybe explore some of her baser instincts, a little?'

His face was now pressed close to hers. He reeked of stale cigarettes, last night's beer, and cheap aftershave. 'And I'd be more than happy to be of service, Izzy. Just say the word.'

With that comment, his left hand shot out, clamping itself to her right jean-clad thigh under the table. Izzy jumped backwards, almost spilling her orange juice over *herself* and the newspaper, in the process.

Instinctively, she tried to pull her leg from his grasp, but Terry refused to take the hint, his great mitt remaining firmly in-situ. She went rigid, heart thumping painfully against her sternum. Terry had never been as close as this before.

'In fact, we could head upstairs, now.' Terry's voice rasped. 'It doesn't look as though those lazy bastards are about to show themselves. And there's definitely something I could do—this minute—that would make you feel very relaxed indeed. It would set a girl like you up for the day.'

With that comment delivered, he moved his lips to her ear and, in nauseating detail, outlined how he intended to make her relax.

Izzy's blood ran cold. Her eyes widening in horror, as the filthy words dripped like poison from his lips. Did the man have some kind of S&M fetish? She couldn't believe *anyone* would even want to do the disgusting things he'd just alluded to or—worse—that he thought *she,* of all people, might actually enjoy it!

His hand continued squeezing her thigh, his body pressed up against her side, all five foot six, and ninety five kilos invading her personal space. She tried hard not to flinch, remain outwardly detached, but inside she was freaking out. She could see the cockroach was positively getting off on this. His breathing had become laboured, those green eyes glittering with unconcealed lust as they openly stared down the front of her blouse. He reminded her of the wolf in *Red Riding Hood.* Only she had a feeling that Terry was way more dangerous than any fairytale character.

'Come on, what do you say, Izzy?' He clicked his tongue. 'Something tells me that under that oh-so-cool exterior, you could be one kinky little girl at heart—if you got the chance.' With that, he dropped a kiss on her cheek.

Izzy resisted the overwhelming urge to wipe its slimy wetness away with a tissue.

The expression 'How about dropping dead?' crossed her mind.

'Look, Terry, I'm flattered that you seem to …like me like that… but I'm really not …' she stumbled to a halt.

You idiot! What on earth was she saying? Had she actually uttered the word 'flattered'? That made her sound as though she might be *interested*. Not in a million years. Not even if he was the proverbial 'last man' standing. Sometimes she was too polite for her own good.

She wracked her brains for something else to say; wishing someone—anyone—would appear and rescue her.

'I'm really… much too busy at the moment,' was the best—and possibly feeblest— excuse, her panic-stricken brain could compute.

Totally pathetic, Izzy! She was conscious Terry's hand had begun inching higher, creeping up her leg. If he reached her crotch, passing out looked like a distinct possibility.

'I've a hundred and one things to finalise before we head off to Los Angeles.'

He'd succeeded in making her babble now. And, given that ever-widening smirk, the git knew it. So much for her bragging to Rick she could handle the 'Terrys' of this world.

Great job I'm making of it—not!

Glancing about herself, Izzy pondered trying to attract the attention of a passing waiter. Ask for more coffee. But typically, they'd all disappeared like snow off a hedge.

It was then that her salvation appeared in the most unlikely of forms. Scottie was weaving his way between the tables, heading in their direction, an anxious expression on his face.

'Hey, boss!' He waved at them. 'We've got an issue with one the Lincolns. Some silly cow has only stripped down to her knickers and handcuffed herself to the front bumper.'

He cast a weary glance at Izzy. 'Sorry, Izzy, am I interrupting something important here?'

'No. It's all good, Scottie.' Somehow, she'd made her voice sound half-way normal. And, she noted with relief, both Terry's hands were now resting flat on the tabletop where they belonged.

'Well, isn't that a coincidence, Izzy?' Terry pushed himself up onto his feet. 'We were just discussing the joys of restraint, too.'

Without waiting for her reply, he turned back to Scottie.

'Fuck that must be the third one in the last two months. Look, ask if the hotel's maintenance department has any tools we can borrow. Bolt cutters, hacksaws, whatever you lay your hands on. You know the drill. I'll be out in a second to supervise.'

'Yes Boss.' Tipping Terry a salute, Scottie headed off back towards reception.

'Well, looks like we'll have to take a rain check for now, Miss Stevenson.' Terry downed a final slurp of his coffee and licked his lips. 'Given we've both got more pressing matters to deal with, but don't worry, we'll be getting together at some point. Explore this further. You've succeeded in whetting this man's appetite.' Stuffing the last remnants of his toast into his mouth, he departed.

Izzy's head dropped into her hands, her heart about to explode out of her chest, knowing she'd had a narrow escape. But Terry's campaign appeared to be stepping up a gear as far as she was concerned. Well, if he thought she'd be happy to indulge him in his sick little fantasises, he had another thing coming.

9.45 AM

What were those two talking about?

Curiosity getting the better of her, Izzy ducked back behind the nearest column, hoping neither Rick nor Terry had noticed her presence in Reception; especially after her run in with the latter less than an hour ago.

From her hiding place, she could see they were involved in some kind of heated exchange. Rick's brow was creased, that beautiful mouth turned down at the corners, while Terry's hand rested on Rick's shoulder, patting it occasionally, all the time nodding vigorously.

Izzy inclined her head a little further, trying to catch a snippet of their conversation over the piped background music, only to be thwarted by Terry picking up his briefcase and leading Rick over to a sofa at the far side of the hotel lobby.

Damn!

Both men sat down. Terry was still leaning into Rick, their conversation becoming—if anything—more intense than before, and Terry had opened the briefcase now, resting it on his lap.

Taking a discreet look around, Izzy edged a little closer, using a bank of potted plants to screen her movements. Now, with an unrestricted view of proceedings, she observed Terry take out a small brown vial of tablets and pass it over to Rick, who hurriedly slipped it into the pocket of his leather jacket.

Izzy's stomach dropped into her shoes. Those had to be the *Teraxapen* tablets. So, Rick had finally succumbed to temptation and given into Terry's constant cajoling. He must be getting desperate.

She felt a tug at her heart. There was nothing else for it. She had to act. Betty had asked that she maintain a watching brief, but she couldn't just sit back and let him take those filthy tablets; become some kind of addict as Betty feared—or maybe worse. She had to do something—help him—before it was too late.

A bundle of notes exchanged hands, Terry stuffing the cash inside the case, and snapping shut the lid. Then, their business transaction at an end, both men stood up.

Izzy darted back behind the safety of the column, all the time pretending to consult her schedule. Some serious snooping was called for. At least, now, she had a pass key to all their rooms in case of emergencies. She'd find some excuse to use it over the next few days, take a nosy through Rick's belongings; find out if her suspicions were correct. Then she'd speak to Betty.

15

LOS ANGELES, CALIFORNIA

The latest after-show party—expertly organised by Izzy—was in full swing within Jonny's suite; its tone deteriorating nicely as far as Eclectic Deviation was concerned.

'Well, Terry's surpassed himself. The place is littered with A-Listers.' Kathy lit her cigarette before delicately blowing out the match, and using it to point out the vast array of people jostling for space within the lounge area. "It reads like the Who's Who of Hollywood Royalty in here."'

Terry was responsible for who landed a golden ticket from the VIP guest list and got access to the band's after-show parties. It went without saying that only the prettiest girls and biggest celebrities made the cut.

'Yes,' Izzy agreed, nodding towards two men, chatting close by over cigars and beers. 'I can't believe that's really Michael Douglas and Jack Nicolson over there. I have to keep pinching myself just to make sure I'm not hallucinating.' She gave a little shiver. 'And don't you think Jack Nicolson looks just as creepy in real life as he was in *The Shining*?'

Yes, about as creepy as Terry Costello himself.

'You need your eyes tested, Miss Stevenson.' Kathy was scandalised at the very suggestion, 'Jack Nicolson oozes sex appeal from every pore.' She exhaled four perfect smoke rings up in the air. 'I wouldn't say no to a night with either of those two!' She sighed, dramatically. 'But hey, I should be so lucky!'

Izzy knew the feeling; her treacherous eyes sliding from the two actors to where Rick sat across the room, cosying up to tonight's date. So much for his declaration that he'd had enough of one-night stands. The pair of them appeared to be getting on like a house on fire; tonight's female could have been a clone of Francesca—tall, slim, big breasted with dark hair and huge almond eyes. Yep, there was no question Rick had a type he was attracted to.

With a sinking heart, she gave her full attention back to her friend. Kathy was still waxing lyrical over Jack Nicolson.

'Just don't tell Scottie I just said that. Okay?'

'Don't worry, I'll keep it zipped.' Izzy pressed a finger to her lips, having no clue what Kathy had just divulged, and took a small sip of her drink, trying not to grimace at the taste. As staff they were only allowed the cheap plonk and this stuff tasted like vinegar. Why wasn't a handy pot plant around when it was needed?

Her eye caught Terry pushing his way through the crowd, heading towards Jonny and Davey. She'd decided not to tell Kathy about the "Terry" situation. Scottie and Terry were big mates, and she'd the feeling Kathy would probably think Izzy was making a mountain out of a molehill. Tell her to treat what he'd said as a joke and move on.

Some joke! He was now standing beside Davey. Both men's attention caught by a young girl who'd stripped down to her underwear and was dancing provocatively in the centre of the room, clasping a Champagne bottle to her chest.

A grinning Terry whispered something in Davey's ear, both snickering loudly before Terry casually strolled over to where the girl stood swaying to the pulsating beat, whipped off his jacket, and gallantly draped it about her shoulders.

In return for his perceived act of chivalry, Terry was repaid with the fluttering of false eyelashes and the offer of a drink from the bottle. Happy to play along, he allowed her to trickle the alcohol into his mouth, before giving an over-exaggerated lick of the lips and supplying Davey with a thumbs-up sign.

Chivalry my foot! Izzy had caught the look of undisguised lust pass across Terry's face. There had been nothing remotely gallant in that loathsome creep's actions. He'd just been singling out tonight's bed partner. Would he putting some of his sick little suggestions to her?

'And, bless him! Terry's come up trumps again. Always makes sure they've got such a wide selection of "ladies" to choose from too.' Kathy's comment brought Izzy straight back to the present. 'He's in charge of a very posh cattle market, and these are tonight's prize-winning heifers being paraded around the ring. You know how it works around here.'

Izzy nodded, she was only too aware of how things worked when it came to the band and their women. She checked the time on her watch. It was well after midnight. She'd made her token appearance. Done the organisation and showed she wasn't a party pooper. It was time to leave. Witnessing this part of the band's "anything-goes" lifestyle, she could happily do without.

'I know, I know, but it always feels so demeaning, somehow.' Izzy swallowed down the last dregs of her wine and popped the glass up on a nearby table. Yep, the only place that stuff was fit for was sprinkled on chips.

'Izzy, come on. You know as well as I do, none of the women here are wide-eyed little innocents. Sleeping with a member of the band is the name of the game at these parties. Gives a girl kudos to say she's been fucked by a rock star. It elevates her status within the sisterhood. And, if she's lucky enough to actually bag the Rock Star at the end of it, she's set for life. Look how it worked out for Sabrina!'

Kathy's lip curled, and a flash of hurt crossed her face. 'And, if they don't score with the band, there's always Terry, Scottie and the rest, happy to step into the breach. That still earns them brownie points in the pecking order.'

Izzy laid a comforting hand on her friend's arm, both silent for a few seconds thinking, before Kathy spoke once more, nodding across the room.

'Hey, and by the looks of it, Rick's decided it's time he was tucked up in bed with his little "*heifer*" of choice. Bet you're hoping this one leaves quietly in the morning?'

Sure enough, Rick was on his feet, addressing a few final words to Steve and Marc, his arm draped casually around the girl's shoulders.

As if sensing he was being watched, Rick glanced back over his shoulder, those chocolate brown eyes connecting with Izzy's. Her heart skipped a beat, feeling that familiar surge of electricity jolt through her body whenever their eyes met. She gave him a casual wave, and mouthed, 'Goodnight.'

It elicited the tiniest of winks and a half smile in reply, before Rick turned away, steering his latest conquest towards the open door of Jonny's suite.

16

LOS ANGELES, CALIFORNIA

Izzy took another sip of orange juice, luxuriating in the feel of the warm breeze kissing her bare shoulders as it filtered in through the French Doors of the VIP dining room. Yep, this was the life. Another sun shiny day outside, with the mercury predicted to push sixty-nine degrees by lunchtime.

How the other half live!

Resplendent in a denim miniskirt and shocking pink Bardot-style T-shirt, perfect for the spring-like temperatures, she pitied her poor parents at this moment. Unlike *ET*, she'd found a five-minute window—before breakfast—to call home, only to discover Scotland was shivering in temperatures well below zero, with five inches of snow predicted by midnight.

Her mum had been over-the-moon to hear from her, wanting to know all the latest gossip about her life on the road, while her dad had predictably kept the conversation to his two favourite hobby horses; work and the Tory Government. He'd been in a foul mood; his grumpy tone signalling to Izzy that he was missing his little girl badly. And she missed them too—so much!

A sudden movement outside the French windows caught her attention, her eyes drawn instantly towards the hotel pool. Someone had dived into it, and was now swimming its length with strong, even strokes, pushing themselves to the limit. Shifting in her seat, and squinting closer to get a better look, she quickly realised it was Rick.

Her face broke into a smile, her mood perking up instantly. She knew he loved swimming—he'd been undefeated, under-sixteen Berkshire County champion in his youth—but this was the first time she'd ever seen him in action.

Topping up her orange juice from the jug on the table, Izzy settled back to enjoy an uninterrupted ogle. He'd never know he was receiving her undivided attention at this very minute. Just a pity she couldn't offer to hold his towel!

Unfortunately, the anticipated ogle didn't last for long. After a further ten minutes, Rick pulled himself from the water, shrugging his muscular frame into a white robe and slinging a towel around his neck, using its edge to mop up the water dripping down his chest.

Izzy bit her lip; unable to stop a frustrated sigh escaping, ruing the misfortune not to have been born as that scrap of incredibly lucky cotton being dragged across his perfect abs. Kathy could keep Jack Nicolson, Harrison Ford and all the other Hollywood A-Listers she raved about. None of them would ever come close to making Izzy feel the way Rick did.

For the millionth time, she tried to ignore the guilt she felt about, a) the way she was eyeing him up; b) the reason she was here in the first place; and c) lying to Kathy that she didn't fancy those itty-bitty black swimming trunks right off him.

He was coming inside now, and by the looks of it heading straight over to her table. Hastily, she pretended to be engrossed in today's to-do list, knowing it was time to exercise some overdue self-control to her short-circuiting erogenous zones. Unfortunately, one look at Mr Hambro, resplendent in his barely there swimming gear, and any self-control just seemed to fly out the nearest window. She needed to get a grip and fast.

Those brown eyes twinkled at her as he sat down and helped himself to some orange juice. God, he'd better not have spied her practically removing those trunks with her eyes.

'And how's my pretty lady this morning?' he asked, grinning.

'She's fine. Did you have a good swim?'

She inclined her head towards the pool, hoping she sounded as cool, calm and collected as any professional PA would, confronted by their boss wearing next to nothing. Desperate, with tongue hanging out, wasn't a good look on a girl, unless she wanted to channel her inner Labrador.

Picking up his glass, Rick told the hovering waitress that he'd like coffee and toast for breakfast and, with a nod, the girl departed.

'Yeah, it was okay.' He was back to giving Izzy his full attention from those mesmerising eyes. 'Usually can't beat it to blow away the cobwebs, but not this morning. For some reason, I'm still knackered. Shouldn't really complain, though, should I? Given it was all self-inflicted?'

Izzy caught the meaning behind his words, and heat went to her cheeks.

'I'll try and grab some shut-eye on the flight later.' He went on, before taking a long draught of the juice, Izzy's eyes widening at the movement of his throat muscles. Even the way he drank was too sexy for words.

'You'd better,' she moistened her lips, 'because the next thirty-six hours are going to be punishing. Have you read today's schedule yet?'

His robe lay open and, from nowhere, a sudden urge to reach over and lick the bead of water that had formed on his left nipple flashed across her mind. She suppressed it, very firmly.

Stop it Izzy!

'Yeah, don't remind me. Cast an eye over it before I came down. Then wish I hadn't bothered.'

He gave the returning waitress an appreciative grin as she popped both his coffee and a round of fresh toast in front of him and the girl positively swooned in reply. Honestly, where women were concerned, he was just like Jonny, permanently batting them off with a big stick.

Rick poured out fresh coffee for both of them.

'So, you're always up early, Miss Stevenson.' He pushed a steaming cup towards her. 'Would I be able to talk you into joining me in the pool one morning? We could race each other to the deep end and back.'

Caught off-guard by his left-field suggestion, Izzy almost spilt her coffee over the table.

'Nope, I'm afraid that's one thing that's never going to happen, Mr Hambro.'

Giving a grimace, she managed to replace her cup safely back in its saucer without her hand shaking.

'And why not?' He cocked his head to the side, giving her an enquiring look. 'Don't think you can beat me? Is that it? I'd play fair. Give you a decent head start and everything.'

As he brushed wet hair back from his brow, she was treated to another blast of that teasing smile.

'Believe me, it wouldn't matter how much of a head start you decided to give me, you'd still win,' she told him. 'I can't swim. The closest I get to indulge my inner mermaid is the bath or shower. Oh, and I've been known to take the occasional paddle in the sea, but that's as far as you'll tempt me.' Her smile was rueful. 'When I was nine, I nearly drowned in the shallow end of our local swimming pool. I had to be rescued by the lifeguard. It was my first—and last—lesson.'

This admission was accompanied by a shiver as she remembered that particular day. Momentarily, she wondered if she'd been too honest, let slip something she shouldn't, but then dismissed it. She doubted he'd have known such a minor detail in Izzy Anderson's life.

'It left me so traumatised, I refused to go back. I recall screaming blue murder at the suggestion. Sharron Davies definitely has no worries about me stealing her thunder!'

'So you never learned to swim?' He sounded genuinely taken aback by her admission.

'Nope, never have.'

'From a safety point of view, everyone should learn to swim,' Rick observed, 'and you're also missing out on a great form of exercise. Have you never thought about going back for lessons?' He scraped some butter onto a slice of toast.

'At my age, I don't think so.' Izzy gave a dismissive shake of the head. 'For a start, I'd feel a total idiot. Everyone would laugh at me, and that would just be the five-year-olds.'

'Don't be daft. You're never too old to learn. And if you feel self-conscious, how about trying one-to-one lessons? Most pools do it nowadays.' He took a bite of his toast.

'I don't know… maybe.' She shrugged. 'To be honest, I've never given it much thought.'

Until maybe ten minutes ago.

'Would you allow me to teach you?'

Izzy did another double-take, her mouth dropping open. 'Are you being serious?'

'Izzy, I wouldn't offer if I wasn't deadly serious,' he answered. 'Michelle and Jonny can both vouch for my teaching skills. I know what I'm doing and I'd take it at your pace.'

Yes, for some reason, this offer appeared to be one-hundred percent genuine, and not one of his usual wind-ups.

'But when would we find the time?' she pointed out. 'Our days are crazy as it is without trying to factor in time for swimming lessons. And I don't even own a swimsuit.'

'Yeah, fun though it would be, skinny-dipping is banned in hotel pools. Read it in the small print.' He grinned. 'Look, Izzy, don't worry, we'd find time. And seriously, there would be no funny business, if that's what you're worried about.'

Yeah, she knew that was a given already—unfortunately!

His brows lifted and he gave them a wiggle. 'Anyway, what have you got to lose? I'd never put you in any danger. For a start, Marc would kill me if I inadvertently drowned our totally lovely—not to say totally indispensible—PA.'

That comment had her laughing out loud.

'And if the worst did happen.' He reached over and placed his hand on hers, giving it a reassuring squeeze, his lips still twitching. 'I'm fully trained in mouth-to-mouth resuscitation. Mum's even got the certificate to prove it somewhere. I could get her to fax through my references, if you want. As I recall, my technique was marked as Highly Recommended.'

Izzy's mouth went dry at the thought.

'References won't be necessary,' was her slightly breathless reply, as she pulled her hand away, goosebumps ricocheting up her arm.

'So do you want to give it a go?'

Izzy almost spilt her coffee for a second time, which made Rick roar with laughter at her shocked expression.

'Relax! I'm only talking about the swimming, pretty lady, not the mouth-to-mouth. See if we can get your nerve back at the very least?' He cradled his coffee cup in both hands, studying her intently over the cup's rim. 'And if you really hate it then we'll stop. But, it could be a lot of fun.'

Izzy hesitated. Rick giving her swimming lessons would be the perfect opportunity for her to find out more about him and how dependent he'd become on those sleeping tablets. But to do it, she'd need to overcome her monumental fear of the wet-stuff first. Did she have the guts to try?

'And it'll give me something to do rather than sit cooped up in my room, hiding from the fans. So much for the glamorous lifestyle of a rock star, being kept under virtual house arrest twenty-two hours of the day for my own safety. No wonder I'm thinking of...' He trailed off and reached for another slice of toast.

Izzy's ears pricked up. That was an odd thing for him to say. What did he mean? She knew the relentless attention of the fans could be wearing but he sounded almost resentful.

Then his expression seemed to clear once more. 'Go on, you know you want to, pretty lady.'

A picture of them together formed in Izzy's mind. Rick holding her close as he showed her what to do in the pool, those long fingers skimming over her body, positioning her, just the way he wanted her. Her hands clutching onto his shoulders for support......

Cut the Mills & Boon, Izzy. She'd self-combust if she conjured up any more of those deliciously provocative fantasies.

Closing her note pad, she stood up. For now, it was time to put some distance between them, and get back to the real world. Making a decision about swimming lessons would have to wait a little longer.

'Look, let me think about it, and I'll come back to you.' she hedged. 'For now, I'd better see if any of those sleeping beauties upstairs have decided to shake a leg.' She checked her watch. 'And you've precisely fifty-nine minutes left to finish breakfast, wash, dress and be ready to check out. I need you in reception by ten-thirty at the latest.'

17

AUSTIN, TEXAS

After a whirlwind forty-eight hours, taking in back-to-back concerts in Arizona and Oklahoma, they'd flown into Austin Texas; land of cowboys and ten-gallon hats. A consignment of which had just been handed over by Lindsay, with a request that the band wear them at the opening of tonight's show. They were guaranteed to drive the fans wild, apparently.

'Hello, Izzy speaking.'

She dumped the pile of hats onto the desk, and flopped down into her chair, her eyes falling immediately onto a new list by the telephone.

Great! Marc had been exercising his red pen again.

'Izzy, how long does it take you to answer the bloody telephone?' Francesca's dulcet tones filtered down the line. 'I've been kept on hold for fucking hours.'

That was an exaggeration if ever Izzy had heard one.

Great! Francesca had just managed to wipe the shine well and truly off her day. Not that it had been going particularly great anyway. She'd just spent the best part of fifteen minutes performing first aid on Jonny's left ankle, after he'd tripped over a cable on stage. In Izzy's humble opinion, it was nothing more than a slight sprain, but to hear Jonny's constant whinging and swearing as she'd applied a cold compress and then a bandage, it sounded as though she'd been performing open-heart surgery without anaesthesia.

'Are you still bloody there, Izzy?' Francesca snapped in her ear, bringing Izzy back to the here and now. 'I need to speak to Rick. And before you ask, yes it's urgent. Get him.'

Just another one who bandied about the 'urgent' word with impunity and expected Izzy to jump. And not even a polite 'Hello, how are you, Izzy?' or even a measly 'please' or 'thank you' tagged on for good measure. Although, if Francesca had started throwing out pleasantries like confetti that would've been a first.

'Yes, of course I'm still here,' Izzy answered. 'Good evening, Miss Reiss.'

London was six hours ahead of them.

'I'm really sorry.' Much as it stuck in her throat, it paid to get the apology in first. 'But Rick's on sound check. At an optimistic guess, it will be another thirty minutes before he's finished. Things are running a bit behind schedule late. Jonny's had a slight accident. Would you be able to leave a message instead?'

She should have known better.

'No, I can't leave a fucking message. I've just said it's urgent! I need to speak to him now!'

Izzy could even hear the exclamation mark.

'Don't you ever bloody listen?'

Francesca had come out all guns blazing this afternoon.

'And spare me any other bog-standard excuses you usually trot out. I'm not some Fleet Street hack wanting an unscheduled interview. As his future wife, I think I've earned the right to a minute of Rick's precious time. So, do your fucking job. Long distance phone calls aren't cheap, you know?'

'As I've said, I'm really sorry,' Izzy repeated her apology for good measure, 'but you know the situation, as well as I do. Sound check is sacrosanct. I'm not allowed to interrupt—'

'And I'm telling you, I haven't got all day to wait around. Get me Rick, *now!*'

'I beg your pardon, but there's no need to raise your voice—.'

The hackles at the back of Izzy's neck were rising. The woman had a bloody nerve.

'Izzy, I'm heading out to a party in five minutes,' Francesca continued to talk over her. 'Do I have to start complaining to Jack that his hoity toity PA doesn't know the meaning of the word 'urgent', and won't let me talk to my fiancé? Or are you going to get off that fat arse, and bring Rick to the telephone? Your choice; what's it to be?'

And she would complain.

Fat arse indeed! Realising she was getting nowhere, except potentially into a whole heap of trouble she didn't need, Izzy knew she'd no other option but to fetch Rick to the telephone.

'Of course, Miss Reiss,' She forced out through gritted teeth, 'if you'll hold for a second, I'll see what I can do.'

She stabbed down the mute button, and grabbed a pen. Pulling off its cap with her teeth, she began scribbling out a note for Rick, her mind made up. As of now, Izzy Anderson was learning to swim!

11.35 PM

No reply to her second knock.

Great! That indicated Rick was still downstairs in the hotel bar, and '*Operation: Teraxapen*' could finally commence.

Using her pass key card, Izzy let herself inside his room, flicked on the light and kicked the door closed behind her, her arms laden with overstuffed bags of dry cleaning; her cover for tonight's snooping exercise.

Dumping them down on the bed, she hurriedly removed the newly pressed garments from their plastic shrouds and hung them up in the wardrobe. Then, bundling up the empty plastic into a ball, she deposited it into the waste bin with a neat little slam-dunk.

With the official reason for her visit dealt with, it was time for the real work to begin, but where to start? There was nothing obvious on display. She'd have to resort to rummaging through the drawers. Not an exercise she was relishing, but needs must.

Trying to suppress the feelings of guilt at this gross invasion of his privacy, she began searching the nightstand first, one ear open to Rick's potential return. Only the top drawer had anything inside: an un-opened box of condoms; an empty chewing gum packet; and a copy of the *Gideon Bible*, but no tablets. Quickly replacing the drawer's contents, she headed over to the large chest of drawers under the window.

Again, the search proved fruitless. Just some spare underwear and a few 'iffy' magazines. No doubt supplied by that 'iffy' cousin of his. Goggling at the unsavoury images on the covers, Izzy resisted the urge to lob them straight into the bin too.

As she turned on her heel, her eyes fell on his suitcase, sitting on the luggage rack at the bottom of the king-size bed, but a quick search found it empty, too. She let the lid fall back into place, folding her arms, seeking inspiration. They had to be somewhere in here, but where?

The bathroom door lay open.

Could they be in there?

Switching on the overhead light, she made a three-sixty-degree sweep of the room.

'Bingo!'

A small glass bottle, jammed with small white tablets, was perched on the shelf below the mirror, jostling for space with his shaving gear and toothbrush. Lifting it into her hand, Izzy scrutinized the label carefully.

'Teraxapen: 15 mg. 30 Tablets. Dosage: one tablet to be taken before retiring'

Retrieving her notepad from the back pocket of her jeans, she jotted down the details for Betty. She had to hand it to Terry. He'd certainly made the prescription look legit. The impeccably printed label listed Richard John Hambro as the patient, together with a doctor's name and Medical Practice located in London's Harley Street, no less. No doubt Terry had a whole contingent of dodgy mates who churned out these labels for a small fee; no questions asked.

She glanced at her watch. Did she have time to count how many tablets he'd already taken? Probably not; Rick could be back any minute. Best leave that to another time. She carefully replaced the bottle in its original position. From what she could see, it still appeared to be almost full. Fingers crossed, he hadn't resorted to swallowing many of them.

It was at that moment she heard the sound of a key card inserted into the lock, and Rick's voice calling out to someone in the hallway.

'Yeah, see you in the morning, Gilbert.'

Shit! Just as well, she hadn't started any counting.

Snapping off the bathroom light, Izzy made a dive for the waste bin, retrieving the dry-cleaning shrouds. She'd begun to scrunch them back into a tighter ball as Rick walked through the door.

'Hey, pretty lady.' He blinked a few times at her. 'To what do I owe the pleasure?'

'Just dropping off your dry cleaning as a favour to Kathy,' she explained, indicating the plastic in her hands, before artfully lobbing it back into the bin.

Going over to the wardrobe, she threw the doors open. 'Everything hung up, and ready for your inspection,' she advised with a flourish of her arm, 'but they couldn't get out the red wine stain on this shirt.'

She pulled forward the offending sleeve for inspection. 'Kathy managed to track down a new one from a local store, similar colour and fabric. She should have it by tomorrow. She asked if you still want to keep this one, or do you want me to bin it?'

'Just bin it.' He shrugged off his leather jacket and tossed it onto the bed, stifling a yawn. 'Thanks, pretty lady. I don't know what I'd do without you.'

Izzy licked her lips. It was now time to launch into the little speech she'd rehearsed. 'Rick, before I go, could I have a quick word?'

'Izzy, you can have as many words as you like. Just can't promise I'll be scintillating company. I'm totally knackered tonight.'

He'd slumped into the chair, boots now toed off and eyes closed, his fingers massaging his temples. The frenetic pace of the last few days had clearly taken its toll and Izzy's soft heart went out to him.

'You look done in. Is there anything I can do to help?' she asked.

'Unless you've invented a miraculous cure for insomnia that doesn't involve swallowing shit-awful pills, the answer's no.' He gave a loud sigh. 'Now, you mentioned wanting to talk to me?'

'Eh, yes. That's right. Look I've been mulling over your offer of swimming lessons and my answer's yes. 'She replied. 'I'd like to take up your kind offer, but only if it's still okay with you?'

For a moment, the lines of strain on his face seemed to partly recede, and she was treated to one of those knee-trembling smiles. 'Of course it is.'

'But,' Izzy hesitated, 'I really don't want anybody to know about our arrangement. I guess I'm embarrassed that I've reached the grand old age of twenty-three, and still can't swim. Nor am I prepared for the endless ribbing I'll get from "*Morecambe & Wise*" down the corridor if they find out. Could we keep this just between ourselves, please?'

'Sure.' He stifled another yawn with the back of his hand. 'Davey and Jonny won't hear a word from me. Although, if you ever go on to win Olympic Gold, it goes on record that I was your first—and best— coach. Got it?' He flicked a wink in her direction.

'Deal, but don't hold your breath!' Izzy stuck out her hand, loving the sensation of his warm palm as he pressed firmly against her own. 'Believe me, Rick, if you get me to swim a stroke, I'll be happy to shout it from the rooftops.'

18

HOUSTON, TEXAS

Izzy sneezed. She tugged a tissue from the box and pressed it to her dripping nose.

Damn! That was the third time in the last ten minutes, and, if she wasn't mistaken, there was a burning sensation spreading like wildfire across the back of her throat. A bloody cold; just what the doctor hadn't ordered!

But then, was it really any surprise? Everyone had the snuffles at the moment. One of the band's female backing singers had lost her voice last night—mid show in Dallas—and Davey had been coughing over everything that moved, complaining he felt like shit. Now, apparently, it was Izzy's turn to succumb to the lurgy.

She let out another loud sneeze. Her first swimming lesson with Rick was pencilled in for tomorrow night. Would she even feel up to it by then?

With that gloomy thought in mind, she stuffed the tissue into her jeans pocket, lifted five boxes of photographs from her desk, and lugged them through to the dressing room. With just under an hour until curtain up, she'd get these autographed for their merchandise people.

'Couldn't you just make a little stamp with my signature on it?' Davey took his box, firing off a suitably filthy glower in Izzy's direction 'It would be so much fucking easier.'

'Sorry, Davey, but you need to do it the old-fashioned way.' She handed him a marker pen, stifling another sneeze herself. 'Just think yourself lucky that you don't have to sign as many as Jonny.'

She was rewarded with another stinging glower. Her bard had gone home. Davey hated being reminded he was the least popular "pin-up" in the outfit.

'That's decidedly below the belt, Izzy,' Jonny commented, appending his flowing signature to the glossy still; his trademark "Little boy lost" pose captured for posterity in black and white. 'Being popular has its drawbacks, Davey.' He flexed his right wrist towards his band mate, pretending to flinch with pain. 'Chronic writer's cramp can be a real bastard.'

19

HOUSTON, TEXAS

'Well, thank God that's over,' Jonny groaned. 'I wanted to deck that arrogant prick by the end of the bloody interview!'

Jonny, Rick and Izzy were being escorted from the rear entrance of the TV studios by Lee, dodging the sea of fans camped out front.

With no concert that evening, the band had been due to guest on a local TV show, but with three members of the band now indisposed—Steve and Marc joining Davey on Izzy's sick list—only Jonny and Rick had done the interview, the others remaining back at the hotel for an enforced early night.

'Well, I'll see you in the morning.' Jonny broke away from them, making a beeline towards the second Lincoln, parked up alongside the car they'd arrived in earlier. Scottie was holding its rear door open ready for Jonny to jump inside.

'And where do you think you're going?' Izzy tried to ignore the icy shivers currently playing tag up and down her spine.

Her cold had continued to develop throughout the day and standing backstage in that overheated TV studio—trying desperately to keep her eyes open as Jonny and Rick had been interrogated by Houston's answer to Terry Wogan—she'd begun to feel decidedly nauseous.

'Just off for a little R&R, Izzy. Surely you wouldn't begrudge your favourite guitarist some down-time.' Jonny sent her an exaggerated eye flutter before jumping inside the vehicle. Scottie closed the door, but its window remained open.

Izzy rolled her eyes. What was the point in arguing? He always did what *he* wanted anyway.

'Well, before you go,' she reminded him—although whether he'd remember, after a heavy night on the town, was debatable—'you need to be up, dressed and with your game face on by nine am. You have a breakfast interview with the *Houston Chronicle*. And, before you ask, yes, you *must* be there. A hangover isn't an acceptable excuse for a sickie. Not when I've got three laid up already.'

Jonny didn't appear to be listening, too busy checking the contents of his wallet.

'Did you hear what I said?' Izzy prompted, the effort hurting her already throbbing throat.

'Yeah, whatever you say, Izzy.' He pocketed the wallet, apparently satisfied with his cash reserves. 'But tomorrow is soon enough to worry about interviews with the *twats*—sorry, *gentlemen*—of the press. Honestly, don't you ever switch off, Izzy?'

'Nope, I'm not entitled to that luxury around here,' Izzy winced, swallowing was becoming harder and harder, 'because if it was left to you lot, nothing would ever get done around here.'

She knew her reply was both rude and uncalled for, but she was past caring. All she wanted was to get back to the hotel as quickly as possible, lie down for a quick five minutes and see if that would make her feel any more human, before the delights of the swimming pool beckoned.

Clearly, Jonny wasn't impressed by her words either. Izzy rewarded by the sight of his middle finger thrust in her direction through the open window, before the car sped off at high speed.

She slid into the limo beside Rick, Lee slamming the door behind her.

Her legs wouldn't stop shaking, and her eyelids were so heavy, it was taking a supreme effort to keep them open. She needed sleep. In fact, Sleeping Beauty's one hundred years sounded just about bloody perfect at this moment.

9.01 PM

'Come on, sleepyhead, we're back at the hotel. You need to wake up for me, Izzy.'

Someone was saying her name, and a hand was rubbing ever so slowly up and down the length of her spine.

It felt so *damn* good. Yep, if she'd been a cat, she'd have been in full-throttle "purr-mode" at this very minute. Very reluctantly, Izzy opened her eyes a fraction, the intruding streetlights outside, painful; her brain still foggy, not registering where she was.

'Don't want to; too tired.' Her cheek was pressed up against the cosiest pillow she'd even known. Was she in bed?

Yes, she had to be, she decided; a satisfied smile settling on her lips. In bed, and snuggled up to Rick. She could even hear his steady heartbeat thudding in her ear, its hypnotic thrum lulling her back towards glorious unconsciousness. Cuddling closer, she allowed herself a soft moan of contentment.

'Izzy, you really need to open your eyes.' Somewhere above her head, the voice repeated more urgently. 'Or I'm going to have to carry you inside.'

Jeez, this dream just got better and better, the voice even sounded like Rick's.

140

Rick! Her eyelids flickered a few times, and then her brain fully engaged first gear.

Damn, it is Rick! They were in the limo parked up in front of their hotel. And worse, her cheek—and every other body part—now appeared to be pressed up against him.

She jerked backwards, horrified by what she'd done, yet not remembering quite how she'd got there. A wave of dizziness washed over her, making the interior of the car spin for several seconds.

'Oh my goodness, I'm so sorry.' She tried desperately to refocus, but her eyes were still being uncooperative. 'I think I must have dropped off for a few minutes.'

The spinning came to a juddering halt.

'Make that closer to ten.' His lovely lips turned upwards in amusement. 'Not that I minded, believe me. Your head kinda bumped onto my shoulder and then carried on sliding downwards. At one point, I thought I was about to lose you inside my shirt.'

He let out a chuckle and Izzy covered her face with her hands, totally mortified. 'I didn't do that, did I?' She looked through her fingers at him.

'Yep, I'm afraid so! You're definitely a snuggler, Miss Stevenson.' He nodded.

Let the ground open up and swallow me, now!

'And you look even more exhausted than I am, tonight.' A tiny vee had formed at the bridge of his nose, 'Are you sure you're okay, Izzy? You don't look up for our swimming lesson?'

It was time to be honest. Getting to grips with her inner "little mermaid" was the last thing on her mind.

'I'm sorry, but I really don't feel well,' she admitted with a shake of the head. 'Would it be okay if we rearranged for another time?'

Izzy hated messing him around. After all, he was giving up his precious downtime for her, but there was no way she was fit enough to go anywhere near a pool, tonight.

'Yeah, it's not a problem; we'll take a rain-check.'

Thank God! He didn't look too annoyed. Or was he just saying that?

'Hope I didn't dribble on you?' She hastily dragged out a tissue from her jacket pocket, pressing it to her leaking nose.

'Maybe a little, but who cares?' Much to her relief, a grin was firmly back on Rick's face. 'When the culprit's you, Izzy, I can definitely make an exception. Now, come on, it's time you were upstairs in bed.'

He climbed out of the car, holding the door open for her. Relieved to be off the hook, Izzy struggled out behind him, only to begin swaying as another bout of dizziness washed over her. Letting out a cry, she made a desperate grab for the door frame, terrified her legs would give way. An accompanying surge of nausea rose up into her throat.

'Shit, Izzy, what is it?' Rick's protective arms went around her straightaway.

'I don't know.' She shook her head in an effort to eradicate the constant spinning sensation, but this time it wouldn't stop. Her stomach heaved again.

She wasn't sure what frightened her most now, Rick letting her go and landing sprawled in the gutter, or possibly projectile vomiting over him. Neither outcome was particularly appealing.

'Everything just keeps moving. I can't see properly.'

He felt her forehead. 'Fuck, you're burning up.'

Izzy was pulled hard into his side. 'Right, we need to get you inside as quickly as possible. Just let go of the door, and lean against me. I've got you.'

Very gingerly, Izzy released her grip.

'Is there a problem, Rick?' Lee, who'd been chatting with their driver, came forward.

'Izzy's not feeling well.'

Lee let out a bark of laughter. 'That explains the shenanigans on the back seat. Thought it was your lucky night, and Izzy was attempting to go down on you, mate.'

His comment was met with a scowl from Izzy, not in the mood for his brand of tasteless humour.

Catching her look, and clearly getting the message, Lee quickly changed tack. 'Need any help?'

Rick shook his head. 'It's okay. I've got this.'

Practically holding her upright, Rick guided Izzy up the steps and through the front entrance, passing a contingent of gawping fans.

The dizziness still wasn't letting up, Izzy realised, as she was half-dragged across the hotel foyer and steered into a waiting elevator. Dots danced before her eyes, and everything had started to go decidedly black at the periphery.

It was as the doors were closing that her legs decided to say "Thank you and goodnight, Izzy", buckling under her completely, Rick only just managing to catch her before she hit the floor. Izzy let out a strangled groan, her embarrassment complete as she felt herself swung high into his arms.

'Ssshhh, pretty lady,' he soothed, 'just put your arms around my neck.'

'I'm so sorry,' Izzy apologised, burying her face into the warmth of his neck and clinging on for dear life. She'd never fainted in her life— unlike the hordes of girls plucked from the band's audiences every night.

After what felt like an eternity, the lift finally juddered to a halt at her floor, Rick ignoring her protests that she be allowed to walk unaided, carried her to the door of her room.

'Right, where's you key card?'

'It's in my pocket; I think.'

It took a lot of fumbling in the depths of those pockets before she finally managed to locate it.

Rick's smile was wicked as he retrieved it from her. 'Pity, I was beginning to enjoy all the groping you were doing!'

With a bit more careful juggling, he had her bedroom door unlocked and Izzy inside, flicking on the overhead light with his elbow.

The waves of nausea were coming thick and fast now, and Izzy had the distinct feeling she was about to lose the contents of her stomach if she wasn't careful. She needed to get to the bathroom and fast.

'I'm really sorry, Rick, but I think I'm about to throw up.'

9.47 PM

Her dignity had been well and truly left at the bathroom door.

Here she was, bent double over the vanity unit, her head in the sink, watching the undigested meal from several hours ago making a second guest appearance.

All the time, Rick's arm remained tight about her waist, steadying her against him while she retched, a damp facecloth pressed to her burning forehead, his calm voice reassuring her that he'd look after her. Somewhere in Izzy's fuzzy brain, those words stirred faint memories.

'I'm so sorry,' she felt the need to apologise again.

'Izzy, will you quit apologising to me.' She was treated to a wry smile in the mirror. 'How many times have you seen me—or the others—like this? Probably more fucking times than you care to remember, right?'

Their eyes locked. 'Stop worrying, pretty lady, I'm going nowhere. I'll be here as long as you need me.'

In an instant, those vague memories crystallised. Izzy transported back to a hot summer day long ago. The bicycle accident; Rick holding her just like this and reassuring her that he'd stay by her side....

'Would you like a glass of water, Izzy?' he repeated.

Izzy looked up, catching sight of her dishevelled appearance in the mirror.

Talk about a drowned rat; not one of her most attractive moments! But water would be good. Her mouth felt completely parched after all that vomiting.

'Yes, please.'

He ran some water into a glass, and passed it to her, its coolness instantly soothing the jaggedness in her throat.

'It appears some people will do anything to get out of a swimming lesson with me,' he commented with a grin, smoothing her damp hair back from her brow.

'But I'm not—' Izzy set down the empty glass. He couldn't think she was faking this.

His burst of laughter told her she'd been had. 'Relax, pretty lady. I'm only teasing. Come on. Let's get you onto the bed. You need to lie down.'

He manoeuvred her back through to the bedroom, and down onto the edge of the bed.

'How about I phone Kathy? She can help you undress.' He flashed a cheeky wink. 'Not unless you'd like me to offer my services?'

'I don't think it would be very appropriate, do you?' she answered ruefully. Even if that's what she'd been fantasising about—in minute detail—for months.

'Yep, Kathy is probably the safest option,' he agreed, reaching for the telephone receiver. 'Might be difficult to explain otherwise, eh?'

A call to reception had him connected to Kathy's room in seconds; Kathy promising to pop along right away.

Putting down the telephone, Rick laid his palm against Izzy's forehead.

'That fever's getting worse, Izzy. Look why don't we take your coat off for starters? Cool you down a bit.'

Immediately, Izzy's hands went to the buttons, but somehow all dexterity in her fingers had vanished completely now.

'I can't.'She gave her hands a perplexed look.

'Then let me.' Rick gently brushed them aside and took over.

Coat dealt with, he knelt and unzipped her ankle boots next, removing both them and her socks. Their faces were now level. 'Feeling any cooler?' he asked.

'Maybe a little.' she conceded. 'I'm sorry. I know I'm apologising again, but I hate imposing on you like this.'

Rick laid a finger against her lips. 'And I told you, no more apologies. You can impose on me anytime you feel like it.'

With that, he tenderly cupped her cheek. 'You're always there for us, Izzy. And being the ungrateful bastards we are, you get fuck all thanks in return. High time I redressed the balance, don't you think?' He stroked her burning skin with his thumb. 'Anyway, what kind of arsehole would I be if I left a damsel in distress languishing in the gutter?'

An unbidden smile tugged at Izzy's lips. If it had been Davey, that's exactly where she'd still be. They were so close in this moment that she knew she could just lean over and press her lips to his. Find out if those full lips were as tempting as she'd imagined. Reward her white knight with a kiss.

Of its own volition, her body swayed towards him, her eyelids fluttering closed. *Just lean in and kiss him, Izzy,* the voice coaxed in her fuzzy brain.

'Blimey, Izzy, you look like death. What's happened?'

Guilty eyes shot open instantly, Izzy realising with horror she'd been about to act upon her fevered thoughts.

'Cheers, Kathy, you really know how to boost a girl's ego,' she muttered to her friend. 'It's just this bloody cold; decided that Izzy A… Stevenson,' she corrected hurriedly, 'is its next lucky victim.'

Shit, her brain was all over the place. First, wanting to plant a kiss on Rick, and now almost disclosing her real name. Thankfully, neither Rick, nor Kathy appeared to have noticed anything unusual.

'Okay, we need to get you undressed.' Kathy quickly took charge of the situation.

'Izzy, I'm going to call down to reception.' Rick had moved towards the telephone on the faraway nightstand 'Ask if a doctor can come take a look at you.'

His anxious brown eyes swept over her for head to foot. 'We really need to get that fever checked out. Don't you agree, Kathy?'

Kathy felt Izzy's brow, nodding her agreement.

'But, I don't need a doctor,' Izzy protested, feeling a sudden bubble of panic. There was no way she could have a doctor up here. For a start, she might have to come clean about her real identity. And she couldn't do that with either Rick or Kathy ear-wigging on any conversation.

'It's just a bad cold or a touch of flu at most,' she downplayed hastily. 'I'll be on the mend by tomorrow; you'll see. Just let me get some sleep. That's all I need.'

'Okay, I guess you know best.' But Rick's hand still hovered, halfway towards the telephone receiver. 'Someone should definitely stay with you. Keep an eye out. You're not well enough to be left alone.'

'I'll be fine—' Izzy began.

'Look, why don't I come back later?' he offered, 'once you're in bed. I can sleep on the chair over there.'

From the corner of her eye, Izzy caught Kathy's jaw hit the floor.

Great! Kathy would never let her live down that suggestion.

'No, that's really not necessary, Rick. You've done enough, already.'

'Don't worry, Rick. I'll stay with her.' Kathy bobbed a curtsey at Izzy. 'Florence Davies reporting for night duty, ma'am.'

'Nobody needs to stay with me.' Izzy delivered a sharp look at Kathy. 'I'll be perfectly okay on my own.'

'Look, for once, stop with the 'Miss Independent' routine.' Kathy scowled back at her. 'I'm staying. No arguments.'

Grudgingly, Izzy knew she had no option but to shut up and accept the offer, too ill to argue the point any longer. 'Okay, you win, Kathy. The chair is all yours!'

20

HOUSTON, TEXAS

'Jeez, Izzy, I never realised you could be so pig-headed?' Kathy rolled her eyes heavenwards, clearly frustrated by Izzy's continued reluctance to remain in bed. 'And don't *even* think about putting one toe on the floor.'

They'd been having this ridiculous argument for the last five minutes, with Izzy digging her size four heels in, determined to get up and face the day.

'You're really ill. I've been the one cleaning up the sick all night! Today, Miss Stevenson, you are going nowhere!'

As promised, Kathy had stayed overnight; Izzy more than grateful for her presence following three bouts of violent vomiting.

'But, I have to.' Izzy gave her watch a horrified glance, before pushing back the duvet.

Shit! She was *really* late now.

But as soon as the soles of her feet made contact with the carpet, her legs began that familiar trembling and a white-hot pain shot through both ankles.

'Oh God,' she yelped. 'It feels as though someone has strapped me onto one of those medieval wracks and given the wheel a few turns, just for fun!'

'See what I mean.' Her vindicated friend answered, hands on hips. 'I've told you already. I can fill for you in today. If you won't see a doctor, you have to stay tucked up in bed. It's your choice, Miss Stevenson?'

'I doubt Marc will be happy if he knows I'm languishing in bed,' Izzy pointed out. 'You know what he's like if I'm not doing the full "Yes Marc, No Marc. How high would you like me to jump today, Marc?"'

Their breakfast meeting should have started five minutes ago.

'Look, Kathy, I really need to be downstairs for our daily meeting. And they've got an interview with the *Houston Chronicle* at ten. I'm begging, please help me. I'm sure I'll feel better once I'm dressed!' She tried to stand up once more, but failed miserably.

'Izzy, I said that's enough.' Kathy was glaring at her. 'Your breakfast meeting has just been cancelled—by me—and Lindsay's more than capable of dealing with an interview. He is their bloody press officer, after all!'

Kathy held the edge of the duvet up, her grim expression daring Izzy to disobey. 'Today you're incommunicado. Now, get back into bed.'

Izzy let out a sigh, before reluctantly pulling her legs back underneath the covers, and allowing Kathy to tuck her in. She didn't have the strength to argue.

'Izzy, last time we checked with the thermometer your temperature was still sky high.' Kathy's voice had softened. 'And we're heading for Baton Rouge tomorrow. You need to be able to walk onto that plane unaided, not languishing in the arms of our dashing Dr Hambro.'

Izzy shook her head, wishing for the millionth time she'd kept her mouth shut on Rick's quick thinking in the lift. Kathy had been ribbing her non-stop about bloody "white knights" and "damsels in distress".

'Okay, stop nagging me. I'll be a good girl. I promise.'

Izzy snuggled backwards into the enveloping coolness of the pillows. She hated to admit it, but Kathy was probably right. There was no way she could do anything constructive today.

'But if you should need me—'

'I know where you are,' Kathy finished off. 'Don't worry; I'll be popping in throughout the day to make sure you're behaving yourself. And if I find you sitting at that desk trying to work, there will be trouble. Got it?'

'Don't think I could, even if I wanted to.' It was time to be realistic. Her brain had the consistency of cotton wool. 'Just sitting on the edge of the bed has wiped me out, completely.'

10.53 PM

'Just as well you'd kept the knickers on, or Rick would have got a full-frontal worthy of a *Playboy* centrefold,' Kathy sniggered.

Dressed in freshly-laundered pyjamas, Izzy couldn't suppress a howl of shame at the picture Kathy had just painted, pressing her hands to her eyes.

'Fabulous! Not content with practically throwing up all over him, yesterday. Today I flash my bits at him.'

'Believe me, Rick didn't look bothered seeing your *bits*. Not if his grin was anything to go by. You know what men are like when it comes to an unexpected glimpse of the female form.' Kathy chuckled. 'But, don't worry, I told him you weren't up to playing Doctors and Nurses just yet.'

Izzy had spent a strange day drifting in and out of consciousness, gripped by crazy dreams, which revolved around Rick and Terry. At one stage, the two men had even been fighting some kind of dual over her, Rick brandishing his drumstick, while Terry's suitcase had acted as some kind of trusty shield.

As promised, Kathy had popped back and forth regularly, and on one occasion had brought an unexpected visitor with her, Rick stepping out of Izzy's fevered dreams to stand at her bedside. But she'd been so out of it, she'd just groaned and rolled away from him, burying her hot face into the pillow.

'You know, with a bit more encouragement, you might be right in there,' Kathy teased, helping Izzy slide into bed. 'Between offering to stay and mop your fevered brow yesterday, then him turning up this afternoon to check on you, he's showing way more than professional interest, if you ask me?'

'I wasn't asking you,' Izzy grumped. 'And he was just being nice! End of story! You know it, and I know it.'

'Perhaps….' But Kathy still had that infuriating smirk on her face.

21

MID FLIGHT, EN ROUTE TO BATON ROUGE, LOUISIANA

'So, how's my pretty lady this morning?'

Rick dropped into Kathy's recently vacated seat, taking a bleary-eyed Izzy completely unawares.

'If you want the honest truth,' she admitted, sitting up straighter and tugging a hand through her decidedly mussed up hair, 'I've had better days.'

Massive understatement; she knew she still looked—and felt—like shit. But somehow, with a lot of help from Kathy, she'd managed to pull on some clothes, and drag herself onto the flight.

'Well, if it's any consolation, you don't look as rough as you did two nights ago.' His eyes travelled over her. 'When I had to do the "white-knight in shining armour" bit and sweep you off your feet—quite literally.'

Izzy flashed him an apologetic smile. 'And thank you again for doing that. I've never fainted in my life before. But don't worry; these old legs—while still a bit shaky—appear to be working okay, today.' She gave them a reassuring rub, hoping desperately she wouldn't have to eat her words when the time came to disembark.

'So, in other words, you're issuing your white knight with his P45.'

Izzy couldn't help smiling at his disconsolate expression. 'Afraid so Rick.'

'Well.' Rick let out a dramatic sigh. 'I kind of enjoyed it. Maybe I should hire myself out. A new career might be on the cards—White-Knights-are-Us— ready to swoop in at a moment's notice whenever a pretty lady needs me.' He arched an eyebrow. 'Think it'd catch on?'

A vision of him dressed in leather and chainmail, and looking seriously sexy up on his white charger flashed across Izzy's mind.

'You'd make a killing,' she agreed with a smile, 'but seriously, I really can't thank you enough for all your help, especially as Kathy's been telling me about the stick the Chuckle Brothers have been giving you since it happened.'

She inclined her head towards the closed door at the end of the aisle, leading to the band's private cabin.

'You think I care about Jonny and Davey taking the piss?' he dismissed, his eyes locking with hers. 'As I said before, you needed me, Izzy. I wouldn't have done anything differently.' He looked at her for a long moment, before continuing. 'Just as well I had the old armour all polished up and ready to pull on.'

He leaned in close to her; his voice lowering, 'And I haven't forgotten about our swimming lessons. We'll pencil in another date. But only once you're feeling up to it. Okay?'

'Okay.' She nodded. 'But I can't help feeling you'll be wasting your time.'

'Well, I don't. I *will* teach you to swim, Izzy.'
The burning intensity of his look sent a tingle of pure unadulterated lust shooting down Izzy's spine, only for Kathy's reappearance to put an end to their conversation.

'What's going on here? I hope you're not canoodling with your patient, Dr Hambro? That's against the *Hippocratic* whatsit, don't you know?'

'I'm just making a quick house call, Nurse Davies; it's all perfectly innocent.' Rick was now on his feet, allowing Kathy to retake her seat.

Izzy blushed, knowing her *own* thoughts were very definitely against the tenets of the Hippocratic *Oath.*

'So, what's your prognosis? See any improvement in our patient?' Kathy directed a sharp—and meaningful—poke to Izzy's ribs.

'Yep, I can see a definite improvement.'

'But she's not got quite as much flesh on display, today?'

Izzy resisted the urge to slap Kathy. This was rapidly deteriorating into the script of a bad *Carry On* film. Barbara Windsor and Kenneth Williams were bound to pop up any second now.

'Very true, Kathy, *that* was an unexpected surprise.' His eyes crinkled up with amusement, before he gave Izzy the tiniest of winks. 'But moving swiftly on, I'd say our Izzy's back on the road to recovery. Just needs a little bit more TLC. Think you can handle that Nurse Davies?'

'Don't worry; I'm on it,' Kathy answered, 'but if this is a house call, shouldn't you be getting the old stethoscope out? I'm still concerned about her cough. Think she'd benefit from a very thorough chest examination, if you know what I mean?'

Izzy's face suffused with colour.

Kathy was so dead!

'Good thinking! Let me dig it out my suitcase and I'll pop back.' He glanced back at Izzy. 'Is that okay with you, Miss Stevenson?'

'Of course, it is,' Kathy jumped in first before Izzy had a chance to reply. 'I'll have her tucked up in bed once we get to the hotel. Make sure she has on that cute little night shirt too — unbuttoned for ease of access.'

Shaking his head with laughter, Rick headed off.

Once he was well out of earshot, Izzy let rip. 'When I'm better, Kathy, I'm going to kill you for that…'

22

BATON ROUGE, LOUISIANA

'You condescending bitch.'

Izzy slammed down the telephone receiver into its cradle, managing to snag a nail in the process. 'Damn and blast!'

She reached for her nail file and proceeded to buff the offending digit to within an inch of its life, all the time slowly counting backwards from one hundred.

It didn't work. She still felt utterly furious after her latest altercation with Francesca. If only she could pick up the telephone and ram it down her patronising throat. Maybe then she might feel a smidgeon better than she did now.

'What's up?' a voice said from the doorway. 'Sounds as though *someone else* has pissed you off, big time?'

Izzy almost jumped out her skin. 'Kathy, you scared the living daylights out of me. Don't creep up on people like that. For a second, I thought you were Rick.'

Izzy tried a tentative smile to test the waters, knowing she'd need to build a few bridges here. She and Kathy had had another massive row this morning, Kathy warning it was still too soon for Izzy to even think of returning to work.

But Izzy—being Izzy—had stubbornly refused to listen and more heated words had been exchanged; all of which Izzy had regretted as soon as they'd flown unchecked from her lips.

'So, still glad you're back in the driving seat?' Kathy's tone was decidedly dry. 'Or are you realising I was right and you should have stayed in bed a little longer.'

It was definitely time to begin the construction work. Izzy hated being at loggerheads with Kathy. A heartfelt apology was long overdue.

'No, you were right,' Izzy conceded, suddenly feeling overwhelmed by the events of the last few days. A few treacherous tears trickled down her cheeks.

Kathy moved to sit on the edge of Izzy's desk. After selecting a tissue from the box, she held it out, urging Izzy to take it.

'And for what it's worth, I'm so sorry. I didn't mean to be so grouchy.' Izzy went on, taking the tissue and, wiping each eye. 'You didn't deserve my impersonation of you know who?'

Immediately, Kathy's face relaxed into a genuine smile. 'And I should probably be apologising too.'

'Why? You've been great. It's me who's behaving like an ungrateful little cow.'

At that, Kathy gave Izzy's arm a supportive squeeze. 'According to Scottie, I can be a nag sometimes,' she answered. 'But you don't appreciate how ill you've been. That was a really nasty bout of 'flu. You need to look after yourself, Izzy. Now come here, and give us a proper hug.'

They hugged, Izzy glad they were friends again.

'Honestly, Kathy, I can't thank you enough,' Izzy pulled back, sniffing away more tears, 'both for looking after me, and stepping into the breach with the band.'

'Don't be daft, that's what mates are for.' Kathy ruffled Izzy's hair affectionately. 'I know you'd do the same for me.'

'Of course, I would,' Izzy's expression became rueful, 'although, you might regret saying that once you've seen my attempts at ironing, or sewing on buttons.'

That made them both laugh.

'Look, I know you've felt guilty about lying in bed,' Kathy went on, 'but, has the world ended because you couldn't trail after Marc for a few days, waving that magic wand and granting his every whim?'

'No' Izzy conceded.

Kathy nodded towards the telephone. 'Now, more to the point, what did you-know-who want this time?'

'The usual,' Izzy expelled a breath, 'and when I said she couldn't speak to him, she decided to indulge in a full character assassination instead.'

'She's nothing if not predictable.'

'Yep, took great delight in telling me how useless I am as a human being, and the sooner my contract was up the better. Francesca is an out-and-out bitch.'

But it was only as the word 'bitch' left her mouth that Izzy clocked Kathy's frantic hand signals and realised the significance of what she'd just said. Sabrina was sitting next door in the dressing room—no doubt with both ears flapping—and had probably overheard her less than flattering comments about Rick's fiancée.

'Shit!' Izzy's voice dropped to a barely audible whisper. 'I forgot we had company. Anyway, I finally persuaded her to leave a message. Her exact words were—and I'm paraphrasing here—their "wedding is about to go down the effing tubes, and Rick better get his effing finger out and do something quick."'

'Don't know how he puts up with her.' Kathy shook her head. 'You'd think the Hambros were Rock's equivalent to the House of Windsor to hear her go on about this bloody wedding. I'm sure Di never gave Charlie this much grief.'

'No, I'm sure she didn't.'

Kathy leaned closer to Izzy's ear. 'Well, newsflash, from what I overheard yesterday, arrangements have gone up another notch in the pretentiousness stakes!'

'What does she want now?'

'Only to release a basket of twenty-four doves at their reception,' Kathy disclosed. 'Supposedly it signifies peace and harmony within a relationship. Utter crap! The poor little sods will have to work frigging overtime to bring peace and harmony to any relationship which includes her!'

Izzy's answering laughter quickly developed into a coughing fit.

'By the way'—Kathy delivered a helpful thump to Izzy's back—'did I ever tell you she punched me when she found out I'd slept with Rick?'

'I'm not surprised,' Izzy gasped, managing to catch her breath. 'She's certainly got a violent tongue in her head.' In fact, she'd need a dictionary to look up a few of the choice words Francesca had called her earlier.

'Came round to my flat yelling her head off and then—wham—smacks me on the mouth. Muhammad Ali would have been proud of that left hook. Word is that Jim and Betty aren't over the moon about their future daughter-in-law. Can't imagine why, can you?'

Izzy grabbed another tissue and blew her nose. That was certainly true.

There was a sudden commotion in the dressing room next door, which only meant one thing, today's sound check had was at an end and the band had returned. And no surprise, from the raised voices, Marc and Davey were at each other's throats again.

'Well, here's your chance to pass on the latest summons from She-who-must-be-obeyed.' Kathy slid off the desk, smoothing down her denim mini. 'You know, I'm surprised she wanted to go to Portugal to get married. With her delusions of grandeur, it should have been St Paul's Cathedral or Westminster Abbey, at the very least.'

Kathy's dry wit precipitated another bout of coughing from Izzy.

Picking up a glass of water, Kathy pressed it into Izzy's hand. 'Here, drink this, quick!'

Obediently, Izzy did as she was bid.

'Now, don't throw *me* any more of *your* verbal punches,' Kathy continued, folding her arms, 'but don't you think you should go back to the hotel and rest up. You still sound bloody awful.'

Izzy nodded. 'Yeah, I think I will. You're only voicing what I've been contemplating myself.'

'Good girl.' Kathy grinned. 'Now, how about I send through our dishy Dr Hambro? I could hint you're more than ready for that chest examination he promised?'

'Kathy, don't you dare—.'

But before Izzy could get the rest of the sentence out, her cough came back with a vengeance.

Kathy departed, her peals of laughter ringing in Izzy's ears.

A few seconds later, Rick stuck his head around the door.

'Hey, Kathy said you were in need of a quick run over with the old stethoscope.' Eyebrows were wiggled in her direction. 'So I got here as fast as I could. What's up, pretty lady?'

Izzy rewarded him with a shake of the head. 'Please try to ignore the very witty Miss Davies. I do; all the time.'

Yes, they might be friends again, but Kathy was in for it later.

'Your fiancée is just off the telephone.' It was time to get down to business. 'Another snag has developed with the wedding. She needs you to call her back, urgently.'

Rick's face fell, his good humour evaporating. 'What the fuck is wrong now?' He groaned. 'Don't tell me there's a world shortage of confetti? Or have those bloody doves decided to follow the miner's example and go on strike?'

'No idea,' Izzy answered. 'But from the way she spoke, it did sound a lot more serious than your doves deciding to stage a mass walkout.'

23

ST LOUIS, MISSOURI

'Hi, Betty; sorry it's been so long!' Izzy settled back into her armchair, her shoes kicked off, and legs tucked up underneath, her personal diary lying open on her lap.

This was a long overdue conversation. Well over a week had elapsed since her snoop around Rick's room, and given her intervening illness, she still hadn't had an opportunity to bring Betty up to date on her discovery.

'How are things back in the UK?' Izzy flicked over to the entry where she'd jotted down all the information relating to the tablets.

'We're fine, love, just fed up with the weather. It's been raining solidly for the last fortnight. In fact, any more of it and we'll all be walking around with webbed feet.'

'It's not been any better here,' Izzy commiserated, her eyes drawn to the large raindrops battering against her hotel room window. 'And the weathermen are talking snow—blankets of it—by the end of this week'

'Snow, beautiful to look at, but a pain in the backside to go to work in,' Betty agreed. 'But enough moaning about the weather, more importantly, how's my Izzy? Are you feeling any better, love?'

'Not quite one-hundred-percent yet, but getting there,' Izzy admitted. 'Still can't go anywhere without a box of tissues clamped to me.' She glanced down at the latest half-empty box lying on the floor. 'And a snot-covered hankie isn't an attractive look for a girl.'

Betty laughed. 'No, I suppose not, but I'm glad to hear you're improving. Your mum called me last night. Said Andrew is threatening to fly over.'

'That sounds just like Dad.'

And he would come over, if given half a chance. Hopefully her Mum could restrain him. She'd spoken to her parents briefly, the previous day, letting them know she'd been ill, but had reassured them she was now on the mend. Obviously, Dad—being his over-protective self—remained unconvinced.

'But, back to business,' Izzy went on, 'now that I'm on my feet again, I thought I'd better call. Check and make sure you'd received all the paperwork for New York.'

Betty was happy to confirm she had.

'Great. I was beginning to worry it might have been lost in the Bermuda Triangle' Izzy ticked off the reminder in her diary. 'I'm sure it's over a fortnight since I posted it out.'

'That's *Air Mail* for you,' Betty laughed, 'totally unreliable. I've filled everything out as requested. As has Francesca; you'll be pleased to know.'

Great that meant she didn't have to lock horns with She-Bitch-from-Hell for the foreseeable future.

'You know,' Betty mused, 'Jim still can't believe we'll be flying supersonic.'

The band's parents were all scheduled to travel into New York on *Concorde*.

'Yes, you'll be flying—officially—faster than the speed of sound.'

'Jim's been telling everyone he hopes that means he doesn't have to listen to the sound of my voice for the duration of the flight.' Betty joked.

'Unfortunately, I don't think it works that way, Betty!'

'No, me neither,' Betty chortled. 'But back to you. Mary tells me it was our Richard who was on hand when you became ill.'

Betty always referred to her son as Richard.

'Yes, he became—quite literally—my knight in shining armour.'

Her mum had clearly passed on all the gory details.

'He's a good lad. We made sure he was brought up properly. Unfortunately I don't know what happened to our Marcus and Jonathan,' was Betty's telling observation on her two nephews.

The mention of Rick's name brought Izzy nicely to the next part of today's conversation.

'About Rick, Betty,' She hesitated, knowing Betty wasn't going to like what she was about to disclose.

'What is it, love? Tell me.'

Yep, Izzy could hear the anxiety creep into Betty's tone.

'It's about the sleeping tablets. There's no easy way to tell you, but Rick's started taking the *Teraxapen.*'

Izzy hastily outlined the transaction she'd witnessed in the hotel lobby, as well as her subsequent snooping exercise in Rick's bathroom. 'According to the label, he's been prescribed by some doctor in Harley Street. The strength is listed as 15 milligrams per tablet, to be taken as directed. The last time I saw it, the bottle looked practically full, so he can't have taken many, but I still haven't had an opportunity to go back and count them.'

Betty's breathing hitched but she remained silent.

'And we both know Rick's not been near Harley Street,' Izzy continued. 'Those tablets came straight out of Terry's suitcase. I saw it with my own eyes.'

'Richard Hambro, what the hell are you playing at?' Betty burst out 'You know, Izzy, when all this band nonsense started; he swore to me he'd always be careful. Never take opiates. That it was a mug's game.

And now, what's he doing? Only popping bloody sleeping pills on the say-so of that reptile Terry Costello; Jim will go spare!'

There was a loud exhale. 'And it would have to be *Teraxapen*. The longer he takes them, the harder it will be to quit, they're extremely addictive. And don't get me started on all the side effects. I spoke Doctor Kendal, and he says they can be lethal if mixed with alcohol!'

There was revulsion in Betty's voice. 'You're only supposed to take them under close medical supervision and only for a very limited time.'

'I'm so sorry, Betty.' Izzy felt powerless in the face of the older woman's distress. 'Please tell me there's something I can do to help. What side effects should I be looking out for?'

Maybe she could find a reason to accidently—on purpose—flush the bloody tablets down the toilet?

Betty began reeling off a list of horrifying side-effects that made Izzy goggle.

'I know my son,' Betty concluded, 'and if he's resorted to taking strong sleeping tablets, there is something seriously troubling him. I've never known his insomnia to be this bad. And now he's taking one of the worst drugs possible. Some doctors are even calling for it to be banned…'

She let out another weary sigh. 'But you know what men are like, Izzy, won't admit to any "weaknesses". And knowing our Richard, he'll keep bottling it all up. Pretend everything in the garden is rosy. If only our Michelle was out there with him.'

'Why?' Izzy asked.

'Because she'd find out what's bothering him in ten seconds flat. She knows her brother inside out, that one; can wind him around her little finger.'

There was more silence at Betty's end before she spoke again, her voice urgent. 'Izzy, I know this is more than I asked originally, but

I'm desperate. Could you try having a word with him? Maybe find out what's going on with him?'

'Me....yes, I can try, but.....' Izzy swallowed. 'I doubt he'd feel happy talking to me about anything personal...' She trailed off, twisting a strand of hair around her finger.

Then it hit her. The potential way-in was staring her in the face all the time. Hadn't she thought of it herself as the perfect way to probe deeper?

'Look, Betty, there might be a way...' She outlined Rick's offer to teach her to swim. 'My first lesson is tonight, after the show.'

In fact, the more she'd thought about their impending lesson, the more she alternated between stomach-churning dread and toe-curling excitement. Unfortunately, the stomach-churning dread had the upper hand at this precise moment.

'But, Izzy, that's perfect.' The relief in Betty's voice was palpable. 'If it's just the two of you, you're bound to have an opportunity to talk about other things besides swimming.'

'Yes, but he could still tell me to mind my own business. Then you'd be back to square one....'

And Izzy's lessons would come to an abrupt end, too. 'I'm not so sure Izzy. I watched the two of you together backstage at the Wembley concert. Richard looks extremely relaxed in your company. He likes to tease you; always trying to make you laugh. And that's how he is with Michelle. Believe me it takes a lot for him to lower his barriers and let people close. His sister is one of very few. As you've probably noticed, most people are kept at arm's length. How Francesca managed to sneak through the barricades, I'll never know.' Betty let out a groan. 'Got a blind spot as far as that one's concerned, probably her plastic chest.... but I digress. He'd never have offered to give you swimming lessons if he didn't feel comfortable around you.

He had to be bribed with new bike before he'd even teach Jonathan a stroke, and that was his cousin! I think this could work….'

Izzy wasn't quite so confident; but she was ready to give it a go. Betty trusted her.

'Of course, if we enjoyed a good relationship with her ladyship, we wouldn't need you out there in the first place,' Betty continued, 'but whenever I've voiced my concerns, she says it's all in my head. That I'm an interfering old cow who can't loosen the apron strings.' Her voice cracked. 'But I'm begging, Izzy, please give it a try. We're desperate.'

'Okay.' Izzy reassured the older woman. 'As soon as the opportunity presents itself, I'll do my best and have a word.'

11.30 PM

The hotel swimming pool was deserted except for Izzy and Rick; Izzy hovering by the pool's steps feeling decidedly awkward in her newly purchased red swimsuit.

She caught sight of her reflection in the mirrored wall opposite, and allowed herself a long overdue eye roll. As she'd suspected, the suit was far too revealing. It had been the only one left in her size at the hotel's boutique, and with no time to shop around, she'd bought it. But this little number was definitely designed for soaking up the rays on a tropical beach, not pretending she was Sharron Davies.

In fact, she took in a sideways view now; both her breasts appeared to be plotting their imminent escape from its plunging vee neckline. She tugged at the fabric ineffectually, praying neither one decided to make an impromptu appearance over the next hour. She'd be mortified.

Not that Rick—already in the water—had made any comment on *her* outfit when she'd slipped off her bathrobe earlier. His eyes merely giving her a cursory onceover, before informing her he'd reserved the entire pool for them in an effort to make her feel more relaxed. And relaxed didn't cover the way she felt at this moment, warily eyeing the expanse of blue-green water before her. She hadn't put a toe in yet. The pungent aroma of eau-de-chlorine hanging heavily in the air, really wasn't selling it to her either.

Her eyes now fell on Rick; looking drop-dead gorgeous as usual in those tiny trunks.

Keep eyes above shoulder level at all times, she reminded herself. They could not be allowed to stray below the waterline tonight.

'I know you're feeling anxious, but don't be. Your white knight's here to keep you safe, remember!' He said, grinning at her.

'I guess so,' Izzy answered with a grimace, making no attempt to venture any closer to the ladder steps.

'Hey, that's not much of a vote of confidence.'

She was treated to an exaggerated pout.

'I mean "yes, of course"' she answered.

Come on, Izzy, you can do this!

If she stood here dithering any longer, she'd be in danger of getting cold feet—literally and metaphorically. There was still time to back out, say she'd just remembered an urgent letter that needed to be typed. Then Betty's anxious voice echoed in her head. No, she couldn't let one of her mum's oldest friends down. She'd come this far. There was no going back. She was learning to swim—and getting Rick to open up to her—in the process.

Squaring her shoulders, and telling herself it was only water— even if it was scaring her witless at this precise moment—she moved determinedly towards the ladder. Izzy Anderson wasn't one of life's quitters.

Gripping tightly onto the metal rails, she lowered herself one rung at a time into the shallow end.

'That's it. I've got you, Izzy.'

The heat of those hands permeated through the fabric of her costume, coming to rest on her waist as he steadied her. She gave a little shiver, her stomach muscles clenching.

Hopefully, he'd read her physical reaction as fear, and not instant arousal. The heat of his touch felt incredible and, on cue, her nipples jumped to attention, practically saluting at him.

Cursing inwardly at her traitorous body, Izzy hastily crossed her arms over her chest hoping he hadn't noticed.

'Well, I'm in. What do I need to do, now?'

'I want you to take a moment,' Rick told her. 'Get used to standing in the water. How does it feel? Not too terrifying?'

'Em, it's okay.'

His hands on her body were more than okay; standing thigh deep in warm water, with the potential for drowning all around her, wasn't quite so appealing.

'Try to relax. Remember, we can stop any time you want. Take some time out.'

He held a hand out to her. 'But for now, we're going for a walk. Let you get confident with the buoyancy.'

After a second's hesitation, she nodded, and placed her hand firmly in his. 'Okay. Let's do this.'

Much to her surprise over the next five minutes, that elusive feeling of confidence did begin to show its face, her nerves slowly receding with every new step taken.

'You're doing really well,' he told her with an encouraging smile, 'but now I need you be confident walking around on your own.'

Dropping her hand, he waded over to the opposite side of the pool, and pulled himself up to sit on the marble surround.

'Walk towards me and stop just there.' He pointed to a spot right in front of him.

Taking a deep breath— it was only walking and what could possibly go wrong—Izzy began to navigate the short distance towards the spot he'd indicated, one careful step at a time.

She'd almost made it to Rick when her right foot slipped out from under her, and then she was down, pitching head first into the water and emitting a loud scream, her arms flailing in all directions.

Instantly, an awful sense of déjà vu washed over Izzy as her face hit the water with a resounding thwack. This was what had happened all those years ago. Water squirted up her nose and inside her mouth, panic setting in as she quickly found herself unable to breathe.

Somewhere about her, she heard the words 'Fuck, Izzy!'

With a splash, Rick was back in the water, beside her in two strides, and scooping her up into his arms.

'You're okay. It was just a slip.' He reassured her. 'Now, breathe for me, pretty lady. That's it, slowly in and out, try not to panic' he instructed, smoothing her hair back from her face, and still holding her close. 'There. No harm done.'

Somehow Izzy wasn't quite so sure; her chest continuing to heave as she dragged more air into her lungs.

'Better, now?' he asked, when her breath finally caught and steadied

Izzy nodded, gazing back at those concerned brown eyes. 'Yes, I'm fine, thanks.'

Temptation stirred inside her. Being wrapped in his strong arms, with her nose pressed up against the warmth of his chest, all she could think about was pulling that gorgeous mouth down to hers, feel the reassuring touch of his lips. Remind herself that she—Izzy—had just survived a second close encounter of the aquatic kind.

Instead, she made a conscious effort to pull herself together and step back; hoping he hadn't noticed the goosebumps which had erupted on her skin where he'd touched her arms.

'Good! So, how would you feel about venturing a little deeper?' he coaxed.

'You mean *the deep end*!' she squeaked.

He has to be joking.

'No, not the deep end,' he was quick to reassure her. 'Just until the water is up to your waist, and I won't be leaving you this time. I'll be holding my pretty lady's hand, all the way.'

But Izzy shook her head firmly. That belly-flop moment had completely shattered what modicum of confidence she'd just built up.

'Em, not yet, Rick…'

'Okay, maybe later,' he didn't push any further in the face of her refusal. 'How about I teach you how to float, instead?'

'You mean take my feet off the bottom?'

His second suggestion sounded worse than the first.

'Yep, that's generally what floating entails,' his smile was teasing, 'but it's easy.' His arm was already pressed to her spine, the dark hairs tickling the exposed skin.

'All you have to do is lean backwards over this arm, just until your head rests on the water. At the same time, I need you to slowly lift your feet off the bottom. Let me and the buoyancy of the water do the rest. You won't go under. I promise.'

Somehow, the calm reassurance shining in those impossibly gorgeous eyes was making her trust him, implicitly.

'Okay. What have I got to lose?' she heard herself say.

Very gingerly, doing as he'd instructed, Izzy began to lean backwards, relying on Rick to provide the necessary support, until finally her head was resting on the pool's surface, her feet completely off the bottom.

'There, you're officially floating, Miss Stevenson!'

'I am.' Her wonder-filled eyes met his. 'But don't you dare take your arm away.'

'I won't. I'm not letting you go, Izzy. Now, point your toes and kick your feet; splash as hard as you can.'

Izzy began to kick, tentatively at first and then with more determination, soaking Rick in the process, unable to stop her giggles at the absurdity of it all.

'Okay, I think that's enough. This time I'm flipping you onto your stomach,' he said, slowly pitching her forwards until her chin rested on the water line.

As well as kicking her legs, he now made her incorporate arm rotations, explaining a bit about the catch and pull technique she'd need to develop as a swimmer.

'You, pretty lady, are extremely quick on the uptake,' Rick told her. 'But we still need to get your face under the water. Only, this time, let's do it in a controlled way.'

Izzy felt a pang of trepidation. Her impromptu ducking ten minutes ago had been more than enough. But, not wanting to look a complete wimp, she accepted his challenge.

'Well, first, I need you to relax more.' He winked at her. 'You're still much too tense.'

He made Izzy stand facing him, capturing her hands securely in his, and shaking her arms up and down.

'That's better. We're both going to crouch down until our faces are under the water,' he explained. 'Before we go under, take a deep breath. We go on three. Okay, ready.'

'Ready, as I'll ever be.'

'Remember, just keep looking straight into my eyes and you'll be fine. I'll be holding onto you. Nothing bad will happen. One, two, three, deep breath, and down for three.'

And down they both plunged, Izzy clasping onto his hands.

Within seconds, they'd resurfaced again, Izzy rewarding him with a beaming smile.

'Rick, I did it.'

Letting out a whoop of pure joy, she launched herself at him, wrapping her arms around his neck tightly, and hugging him close.

'I actually did it, Rick, without trying to drown myself,' she repeated, beginning to laugh with pure joy.

'Yes, you did'

He was staring back at her, smiling; his head bent down towards hers and Izzy's heart give a crazy lurch. That overwhelming urge to kiss him reasserted itself.

Just one kiss, Izzy.

For an age, they remained as if frozen, neither of them saying a word, their eyes locked into position before—much to Izzy's disappointment—Rick removed her arms from around his neck and placed them firmly by her sides. That strangely charged moment evaporating completely.

'And as I'm so impressed,' his voice sounded strangely gruff, 'I think we should do it again. Check it wasn't a fluke. Don't you?'

It wasn't.

They remained in the pool for another twenty minutes, Rick keen for her to repeat everything she'd learnt so far.

'Well, thanks to you, I've definitely gained more self-belief now,' Izzy reflected, tugging herself back up the ladder and onto dry land, their session drawing to an end.

'Yeah, your confidence is really building. We'll definitely make a swimmer of you yet, Miss Stevenson,' he agreed, winking at her as he picked up a towel from a nearby lounger, and wrapped it about her shoulders. 'But I think that's enough for tonight. Let's hit the shower.' His faced reddened slightly. 'Well, not together—obviously,' he amended.

'No.' Izzy agreed, looking away, and rubbing the water from her limbs.

An intimate image of them pressed together in a tiny shower cubicle had taken up residence in her brain and refused to budge. She didn't want tonight to end. It had been wonderful just being here alone with him. Not that they'd had an opportunity to talk to him about anything other than swimming. But then, this was just the start, she reminded herself, with a secret smile. They'd been so easy in each other's company. She'd do better next time. Betty was relying on her.

24

ST LOUIS, MISSOURI

'Hey, pretty lady!' Rick slid into the chair next to Izzy's, his plate piled high with scrambled eggs and pancakes just collected from the breakfast buffet.

Izzy looked up from scribbling in her note pad, her jaw dropping at the mound of food he intended to tackle. 'Someone's hungry this morning!'

As ever, Izzy was a cereal and toast girl.

'Yeah, giving my PA swimming lessons is proving to be hungry work,' he whispered against her ear, before picking up his knife and fork. 'Sleep okay? No nightmares after last night?'

Quite the reverse, but she wasn't about to share any of her x-rated dreams with their leading man. 'Nope, all good,' Izzy replied, hoping her cheeks didn't give her away.

'So, you're happy to continue?' He prompted.

'Yes. I've got a feeling I'm going to enjoy learning to swim.' She replied, before taking a sip of orange juice.

'Glad to hear it. Because, here's the deal, I'm enjoying teaching you.'

Butterflies started fluttering in her stomach.

'I can't believe how patient you are.' Izzy helped herself to another slice of toast, before reaching for a tiny jar of marmalade.' I don't know if I could be quite as patient, if the roles were reversed?'

Unscrewing the lid, she loaded some marmalade onto her knife.

'Izzy, you're super easy to be patient with. It's clear you want to learn.' A loaded fork of scrambled egg was halfway to Rick's mouth. 'Now our Jonny was another story. I was all for drowning the little bastard at the end of our first lesson, but Mum and Dad had promised me a new bike. I just kept repeating '*Chopper Bike, Chopper Bike*' like a bloody mantra when he was being particularly obnoxious, which was most of the time. He wouldn't do a fucking thing he was told.'

'No change there.' Izzy laughed, remembering his *Chopper* bicycle.

'Yeah, you said,' Rick chuckled. 'But you did really well, last night. I could feel you shaking in my arms at the start. I realise how scary you found it, just being there again after all these years. Now, we need to have a second lesson, make sure you don't lose any of that new-found confidence.'

Thank God! He hadn't realised all that trembling had been for another reason entirely.

Marc and Jonny appeared, and were heading their way, their breakfasts collected. Marc was complaining loudly about another run-in with Davey.

'I'm telling you, Jonny. I've just about had it with his fucking moods. If he starts on me again…'

'Look Izzy, before Marc monopolises all your time…' Rick stole a glance at his rapidly approaching cousins. 'Could you do something for me, today?'

'Of course, you know you only have to ask. What's up?'

'I need you to chase up some paperwork for me.' Rick's face had become grave. 'And, unfortunately, it's urgent. I should have spoken to you about it sooner, but with everything going on it was never the right moment.' He sighed. 'In fact, if I don't deal with it now, Francesca says she'll have my bollocks for earrings.'

'That sounds painful!' Izzy pulled a face.

'Remember, when she rang a few days ago, saying there was a big problem with the wedding?'

How could she forget!

'Well, she wasn't wrong,' Rick admitted, 'there's a problem with the validity of the paperwork we've lodged in Portugal. And unfortunately, it has to be sorted out in the next three days, or we can kiss goodbye to our preferred date for the wedding. I'm hoping with your magic wand, you can fix it. Or I'll be fucking toast as far as my fiancée's concerned.'

'I see. So we're talking very urgent indeed. Tell me what you need me to do?'

Marc and Jonny were now seated. While she'd received an unexpectedly chirpy 'Good morning' from Jonny, the look on Marc's face was enough to sour the milk in her coffee.

It's going to be one of those days!

'If I'm honest,' Rick continued, 'it sounds as though Francesca has made an arse of filling out our application form but won't admit it to me.'

Izzy reached for her notebook and opened at a new page.

Focus, Izzy! She had to stop thinking about them splashing around in the pool last night. She needed to be on the ball here.

Rick quickly sketched out the situation. Due to his tax exile status, the Portuguese authorities were requesting a breakdown—with dates—of his living arrangements over the last 12 months. Without it, their application would be void. 'And if that happens,' he finished, 'we'll have to put the wedding off for at least another six months due to the band's schedule.'

'Sounds like 'bollocks for earrings' time, cuz,' Jonny pronounced sagely, before disappearing behind his *Daily Mirror.*

Izzy gently tapped her pen against her teeth, considering how best to tackle this quickly.

'Surely, they just need to know you're a British Citizen and see a copy of your passport. You're a musician, not some criminal mastermind on the run from Interpol.'

That comment provoked laughter from Rick and Jonny, but Marc's lips remained firmly clamped together, not registering any amusement whatsoever. Instead, he helped himself to a copy of today's itinerary from the pile at Izzy's side, and whipped out his red pen. Within seconds, a bold slash had been drawn through the first item on the agenda.

Catching the movement, Izzy's eyes narrowed.

'Shit, that's your "Secret Agent" cover blown, Ricky boy!' Jonny commented from behind the newspaper. 'MI6 won't be happy.'

'Seriously, Rick'—Izzy was trying her best to ignore Marc and the continual slashing of the pen—'leave it with me. I'll get started on it, this morning.' She gave Rick a reassuring smile.

'Eh, not so fast, Izzy,' Marc interjected, his head snapping upwards, 'you'll have to deal with Rick's matrimonial woes, later. It's band business, first. I need you to deal with these changes.'

He shoved the itinerary he'd been working on back across the table. There was red pen everywhere.

'I'm really not happy…' he began.

25

SAINT PAUL, MINNESOTA

Rick opened his suite door, hopping on one leg, while simultaneously rubbing his big toe.

'*For fuck's sake!* What is it now, Marc?' he snapped, his head lifting at the last moment to look Izzy in the eye. 'Sorry Izzy! Didn't realise it was you.'

'What have you done to yourself?' Izzy's voice was full of concern as she glanced down at his foot.

'I thought Marc was back to annoy the fucking life out of me, again,' he explained with a grimace, 'then stubbed my bloody toe on the way to answering the door.'

'Do you need me to take a look at it?' she asked.

He waved away her concern as he let her inside. 'No, I think I'll live.'

'Well, you'll be pleased to know all the paperwork's sorted at last.' Izzy held out a large manila folder, with a beaming smile. 'It's all systems go for twelve noon on June Twenty-second.'

'Thanks.'

He took the envelope, but failed to smile back.

Izzy's good mood faded a little; not the reaction she'd expected.

'Everything is in there,' she went on. 'And they no longer think you're on Europe's Most Wanted List.'

'Great.'

His monosyllabic answers were beginning to disconcert her. Surely, he should be happier that his problems were solved as far as the wedding was concerned.

The last four days had passed in a bit of a blur; the band whizzing through three more states—North & South Dakota and Nebraska— before touching down in Minnesota, with Izzy devoting most of her time—when Marc allowed—liaising with the band's legal team in London, the British Consulate and Lisbon's Civil Registry.

Given the time and locational differences involved, her task had become—at times—little short of nightmarish, with Izzy spending ages either 'on-hold' or waiting impatiently for someone who'd promised to "call her right back" but hadn't. On top of that she'd her regular day-to-day duties to factor in.

But thankfully, her contacts had come up trumps, and by seven pm American time—midnight in the UK and Portugal—Rock music's wedding of the year was back on.

It was unbelievable the amount of chaos Francesca had managed to create by ticking the wrong box on Rick's residency status. But Izzy was more than happy for him to drop that particular bombshell into the lap of his beloved fiancée.

'The covering fax is your final confirmation. You just need to take that along on the day of the wedding. Oh, and say "I do" of course!'

'Fine.'

There it was; a third one-word answer.

'Rick is there anything else bothering you?' she asked carefully.

He really didn't look or sound himself. In fact, thinking back, he hadn't been himself over the last few days. Spaced out; not really firing on all cylinders and spending most of his time hiding behind a pair of aviator sunglasses. Could the tablet's horrific side effects finally be showing themselves?

'No, I'm just knackered as usual,' he answered, 'and Francesca has landed me with more shit to deal with—as if this wasn't enough.' He waved the file at her. 'Believe me; you don't want to know what's happening between her and Mum now.'

Izzy's ears pricked up. Here was her chance, the perfect opening to a conversation with him. But was the wedding really at the root of all this?

'Well, why don't you try me? You know what they say about a problem shared?' She gave an encouraging smile. 'And I can see its annoying the hell out of you. I'm a good listener and offloading helps, especially as I'm not directly involved.'

A slightly disingenuous statement there, but she ignored her prickling conscience. She had to make him talk to her.

'Nah, I wouldn't know where to start, Izzy.'

She felt a stab of disappointment. Just as she'd suspected; he didn't feel comfortable taking her into his confidence.

'Of course you could.' She decided to give a final push. 'Look on me as a convenient shoulder to cry on or sound off at. Take your pick! I'm not doing anything now, and you look as though you need to get it off your chest.'

Rick let out a breath and gave her a tired smile.

'You really want to know?' He asked, raising his eyebrows.

'Consider my listening ear payback for my swimming lessons.'

'Well, in that case, do you fancy a drink downstairs?' He asked at length, his hand pulling at the back of his neck. 'If I don't get out this bloody room, I'll suffocate. We can take a look at this paperwork while we're down there.'

Success! She'd got him to go downstairs with her.

Within five minutes, they were sitting in a secluded corner of the dimly lit hotel bar, each sipping an ice cool glass of *Chablis*, the paperwork still lying unread on the table.

'So, you mentioned your mum and Francesca. I take it they're not seeing "eye to eye" over the big day?' Propping her elbows on the table, she rested her chin in her palms, giving him her full attention.

His arm came to rest along the back of the booth behind her head.

'Yep, you could say that.' Expelling a slow breathe, he began relating the conversation he'd had with Francesca earlier that afternoon regarding the seating plan for the wedding breakfast. Needless to say, there had been more fireworks between Francesca and Betty.

'The way things are heading,' he concluded, 'I doubt the *UN Peace Keeping Force* could break the deadlock. They've never got on, but with the wedding looming ever closer, every day brings something new. If it's not the seating arrangements, it's the bloody menu. If there is something to argue over, believe me, those two will find it.'

'Well, planning weddings can be very stressful,' Izzy answered, inwardly thanking her lucky stars that she and Alex hadn't got that far. 'I remember my cousin Annie's vividly. Two of my aunts nearly came to blows over the shade of pink for the bridesmaids' dresses. They're talking now,' her eyes sparkled with undisguised humour, 'but the wedding was four years ago.'

More success! She'd succeeded in making those lips twitch, and the tension was definitely leaving his hunched shoulders.

'I'm sure Francesca wants it to be perfect for you both,' Izzy continued, 'that's probably why she's stressed-out all the time. All brides are the same. It goes with the territory. After all, it's supposed to be the happiest day of your lives.'

God, she was cheerleading for She-bitch-from-Hell.

'And so does your mum,' she hurried on. 'With you out the country, she probably feels she has an obligation to step in, lend a hand with the decision-making.'

Rick drank down more of his wine before he answered, 'Oh, Mum's doing that alright. But it's degenerated into a game. All they want to do is score points off each other. Everything Francesca decides, mum disagrees with and vice versa. Then, they have a huge slanging match, and next thing I know, they're both on the blower hounding *me*, saying I need to be more involved. But how can I? Being on tour is hard enough, without me having to referee their fucking spats, long distance.'

He shook his head. 'And the latest is I'm eating *Lobster Thermidor* for the wedding breakfast. All the best weddings have it apparently. And while she knows I loathe lobster, Francesca's exact words this afternoon were "tough shit; you're eating it, you bastard".'

He pinned Izzy with a look. 'Sorry, that sounds unbelievably petty, but you did say you were a good listener.'

'Not a problem. Swear as much as you want. I'm tough. I can take it.'

She had to be around here.

'Believe me, if I fucking start, I'll never fucking stop.' He gave a rueful grin, swirling the remnants of the wine in his glass. 'So, if it was you, what kind of wedding would you want? And if I was the poor groom, would you force feed me *Lobster Thermidor* at our wedding breakfast?'

'Me?'

For a second, Izzy was completely thrown by his question, especially the tagged-on comment about being the groom. If only he knew.

'Well…' She considered his question for a little longer before answering. 'For a start, I'd want my wedding in the UK. And it would have to be small, just surrounded by the people that meant something to us as a couple, maybe sixty at the very most. I hate big weddings. You never get a chance to talk to anybody,' she smiled, 'or finish a drink.'

'At the last count, there's three hundred coming to ours,' Rick supplied, 'and would you believe we've got two lists, the 'B' List is filled with bloody celebrities. Last time I looked, Elton John and his new wife have made it to the top.' He rubbed a hand over his face. 'I've met the bloke precisely three times, Izzy. In Francesca's book that means we're now bosom fucking buddies and it necessitates an invitation to our sodding wedding!'

'Well, I can honestly say Elton won't be getting an invite to mine.' Izzy let go a bubble of laughter.

'Trust me, and no offence to Elton, but I don't want him turning up at my big day, either,' Rick muttered.

'Personally, I'd want the whole day built around the commitment we're making to each other,' Izzy continued, getting into her stride now. 'Simple and straightforward, with nothing glitzy or showbizzy, and I'd definitely want my husband to be happy with the food. Not spending half the wedding night with his head down the toilet with food poisoning.'

'Exactly my point; a wedding night is too important to fuck up.'

The wistful look in his eyes made Izzy quiver, her fertile imagination envisaging what a wedding night with Rick might entail. Maybe the two of them rolling around on a four-poster bed, their naked limbs entangled in white silk sheets…

Then she realised that with her 'too-honest' answer she might have inadvertently criticised Francesca.

'Not that I'm saying what Francesca hasn't planned isn't pretty spectacular,' she back-pedalled hastily. 'I'm sure it will be great. Just not for me, that's all.'

'Don't worry, Izzy, what you've described sounds just about perfect. But thanks to my fiancée, I've got a three-ringed bloody circus, and I'm the fucking clown with the cheque book, paying for it!'

'Don't be silly,' It was time for some reassurance. 'When it comes around, you'll love it, you know you will. An occasion neither of you will forget.'

'Yeah, Francesca's making sure of *that*.'

'But before I get too carried away planning weddings,' Izzy considered, 'I'll have to find the right guy first. After all, bridegrooms are a pre-requisite for the big day, not just an optional extra.'

And even if she knew she was looking at him, there was no way Rick Hambro would ever be the groom perched on her wedding cake.

'And you haven't found him yet? I don't believe it. Not someone as lovely as you, Izzy?'Rick shook his head. 'You're seriously telling me, you've no one waiting for you back home?'

'Nope, I'm young, free and single as *Radio One's* Gary Davis would say. I ended it with my fiancé last year.'

'You were engaged?'

'Yes, to… James,' she substituted Alex's middle name. 'We met at university. He was my first really serious boyfriend.'

She thought back to their first meeting. 'He was a very studious guy, who reminded all the girls of *Clark Kent*.'

'Don't tell me, the cape and red underpants were a dead giveaway?'

More giggles overtook Izzy at the very idea of Alex decked out as *Superman*—fat chance! But she liked how Rick's dry sense of humour was reasserting itself.

'No, the look he had before his transformation. All dark rumpled hair, with those tortoiseshell glasses that kept slipping down his nose. And he always wore tweed jackets, with leather patches on the elbows.'

'Nice.' Rick rolled his eyes.

She could tell he was less than impressed by her description. 'Let's just say, at the time, I thought that look was ever so sexy.' She answered. 'Anyway, we got talking one day in the library, and by the end of our conversation, he'd asked me out and that was us for the next three years.'

Izzy paused. This conversation wasn't going as she'd hoped. They should be talking about him. 'Sorry, I'm the one who should be listening to you, not monopolising the conversation. You don't want to hear about my disastrous relationship.'

'Believe me, Izzy, it's a welcome distraction to the soap opera that my life's become. You said you got engaged. What happened? Why did you end it?'

'Because, as much as I thought I loved him, there was a nagging doubt that something was missing.'

Her blue eyes met brown.

'What do you mean?' He'd moved closer, and Izzy could feel the warmth emanating from his body; the smell of his subtly sexy aftershave enveloping her, awakening goosebumps across her skin.

'There wasn't any passion in our relationship. Well, not on his side anyway.' She looked down. 'James was the first man I slept with, but…'She bit her lip, not knowing how to phrase it.

'He didn't make the earth move.' Rick had reached over to pick up the wine bottle and was now topping up their glasses.

'No.' Izzy took a quick sip from her re-filled glass for courage. 'Turns out, we weren't very compatible in the bedroom. It lasted two minutes at most, and then he'd roll over and go to sleep.'

'Didn't you say anything to him?'

'No 'Izzy's shoulders sagged, colour suffusing her cheeks. 'I was too embarrassed. I would have had to admit to…. you know… pretending….' She expelled a breath. 'None of my girlfriends back home know the depressing truth about my less than perfect sex life,' she admitted. 'James much preferred a good debate to making love.'

Rick almost spilt wine over his jeans at that comment. 'What the fuck? Sorry Izzy, I know he was your fiancé, but from what you've said, the guy sounds a bit of a dick to me. No wonder you had to fake enjoyment. He's got someone as great as you, and all he wants to do is talk.' He shook his head. 'Not that I'm saying conversation isn't important in a relationship. Of course it is. I need to be able to have a decent conversation with a woman, but for me there has to be good sex; a connection between us a physical level, too. What was his problem?'

'It was just the way he was.' Izzy felt duty bound to defend Alex. 'I suppose everyone's different in what they find attractive in another person.'

After all, Rick's preferences didn't run to the 'Izzy Andersons' of this world.

'And knowing James, saying he loved me for my brain was the ultimate compliment. Only, I realised pretty quickly that wasn't enough for me. I needed the physical connection too. And when we did make love, it was always lights off, missionary position, and no talking. He said it put him off the job, so to speak.'

Rick shook his head. 'Fuck, Izzy, you had a lucky escape!'

'Looking back,' Izzy spread her hands, 'we acted more like friends than lovers after the first year and a half, and we certainly never ripped each other's clothes off.'

'And have you ever wanted to rip the clothes off someone, Miss Stevenson?' Rick waggled his eyebrows. He was teasing her again.

Izzy shook her head. She certainly wasn't about to tell the man sitting opposite she regularly dreamed about ripping his clothes off, as well as doing a whole lot more besides.

'But James thought everything was great between us,' she went on, addressing her next words to the glass in her hand. 'When I suggested doing something a bit more adventurous, he'd always look hurt. Close the conversation down. And he was such a sweet guy, I didn't want to hurt him, it would have been like kicking a puppy. So, in the end, I just kept quiet and kept pretending.'

'And what did you suggest as being more adventurous?' Rick asked. 'You have me intrigued, pretty lady. Are we talking being tied up and whipped by any chance?' His grin widened, and he bestowed her with a large wink. 'I tried it once; Jonny's idea to visit a sex dungeon in Berlin. Interesting experience…'

'Nope, James would have had a heart attack if I'd presented him with a whip.' The blush in her cheeks got worse. 'I just suggested me on top. He said nice girls didn't do that sort of thing.'

Rick let out a shout of laughter. 'I was right. The guy is a dick!'

'Who knows? As I said, he never wanted to talk about sex. Ec…. Politics,' she hastily substituted; Rick was bound to have heard Isabelle Anderson had graduated with a first class degree in Economics. 'It was his first love. He ate, slept and breathed it. And at the time, I thought I was in love with him. But looking back, I wasn't. I was just flattered by the attention.'

Yes, what she'd felt for Alex hadn't been close to love. Not now she'd been swept away by all the crazy, passionate, feelings she had for the man sitting before her. Feelings she knew he'd never reciprocate.

'So, what's your definition of being in love, Izzy?'

Izzy was aware he was studying her intently, his eyes fixed on her face. She paused for a brief moment, trying to articulate the feelings she held inside. Put into words the way she felt about him, but without giving the game away.

'Well, all the physical stuff. You know, like your hearts about to explode in your chest whenever your eyes meet, and those butterflies going crazy in your tummy.'

Just like now.

'All you can think about is spending every available minute with them, wanting to know everything about them; what they think, what they feel. They're the last thing on your mind as you fall asleep at night, and the first thing you think of when you wake up. And you dream about them in-between.' She smiled. 'Or maybe I've been reading too many trashy novels.'

If anything, Rick's eyes had become even more intense, as if he was trying to see inside her.

'I guess it's knowing that he's the *one*,' she pressed her palm flat against her thumping heart, 'the person you want to spend the rest of your life with.'

'And you didn't feel that way about James?' His voice had dropped.

'Not really. Maybe a bit at first, but it fizzled out pretty quickly. Being together became a habit,' she admitted. 'But Mum and Dad thought he was a real catch. Right up there with Prince Andrew in the husband stakes. By the time he proposed, he'd graduated, secured a good job with a fantastic salary, his future all mapped out. What more could a girl ask for? I heard myself saying yes, even though I was having these stomach-churning doubts. My parents were over the moon, but I couldn't confide in Mum how I really felt. Couldn't say I needed a fulfilling sex life too. That would have meant admitting I'd slept with him.'

'You mean your mum didn't know you were sleeping together?' Rick's jaw visibly dropped. 'Hadn't she guessed? What bloody era is she living in? This is the 1980s, not the 1880s.'

'In our house, sex before marriage is a big no-no. Respectable girls wait until their wedding night, don't you know.'

'That's nothing but out-dated crap, Izzy.' Rick retorted.

'Sometimes it felt James was more suited to being their child than I was.' Izzy gave a shrug. 'With my parents, it's easier to keep your head below the parapet. Say nothing. Not rock the boat if you want a quiet life.'

'So, that's what you did.'

'Yes, but the thought of actually being married to James was beginning to scare me. We hadn't started planning the wedding, but I'd a feeling we'd have ended up hating each other inside six months if it had gone ahead.'

'So, you decided to finish it?'

'Yes, I told him that I didn't love him anymore. And, as I said the words, it was one of those real light-bulb moments.' She fiddled with the stem of her glass, remembering the guilt she'd felt calling a halt to their relationship. 'He was devastated, begged me to reconsider. But I wouldn't change my mind. I gave him the ring back. Predictably, my parents were furious. How could I turn my back on perfection?'

'And how do you feel, now?' Rick cocked his head to the side, leaning closer. 'You're not regretting it, are you?'

'Absolutely not,' she told him, honestly. 'Kicking my engagement into touch was the best decision I've ever made. But I'm sorry I hurt him; led him on for so long. But my parents are still hoping for a full reconciliation.'

'Has he tried to contact you?'

'A few times, but I've stuck to my guns, maintained it was for the best. Said that I hoped he'd find someone else.' She bit into her bottom lip. 'Does that make me sound a bad person?'

'Shit, Izzy, don't be daft. You're one of the kindest, most thoughtful people I've ever met. You put everyone first except yourself. I see it day in and day out with the band.' He grinned. 'You knew getting married to James would end in tears, and put a stop to it. You did him a favour. And he'll see it too, eventually. Believe me, the right decision is the hardest one you ever have to make.'

He gave sigh, before downing the last of his wine and setting the glass on the table. 'And the right guy for my pretty lady is out there. Maybe even be closer than you think?'

Izzy gave a sad smile. 'Well, they say you've got to kiss a lot of frogs before you meet your *Prince Charming*. And when the time is right, I guess I'll have a lot of fun putting that into practice.'

She looked up to find Rick watching her again, and for a long moment she allowed herself to be lost in the depths of those dark eyes, mesmerised by tiny gold flecks at their centre. She wanted it to be him so badly, and he'd no idea how she felt.

'Well, I suppose I better familiarise myself with the paperwork.' Rick turned away, reaching over to pick up the envelope. 'No doubt, I'll get the third degree the next time I speak to Francesca,' he went on, taking out the covering fax and giving the typewritten pages beneath a quick scan.

'Yep, it's officially full steam ahead,' he concluded at length, returning the sheaf of papers to the envelope. 'Thanks, Izzy, I know you've jumped through hoops to get this done in double-quick time. At least Francesca can't accuse me of sitting back and doing fuck all. But then, knowing her, it'll be something else I need to do by tomorrow!'

At that moment, Jonny stuck his head round the side of the booth. 'There you are, you bastard!'

Two extremely pretty girls—one blonde, the other brunette—were hovering by Jonny's side; inane grins on their pretty faces, and eyes fastened on Rick.

Izzy, however, could feel Jonny's eyes resting fully upon her.

'Don't tell me I'm interrupting something?' His expression was eloquence itself, as he hitched a thumb towards the door. He wanted her to beat it, in double quick time.

Taking the hint, Izzy got to her feet. 'I should go…'

'Yeah, great idea Izzy…' Jonny replied, now sliding his long limbs into the booth, and taking up the seat Izzy had just vacated,' I'm sure you've probably got some typing to be getting on with….'

His two companions followed suit.

'I've been thumping on your bedroom door for the last five minutes, Ricky?' Jonny accused.

'Izzy and I have been having a quiet—and extremely pleasant—drink. Haven't we?'

Rick flashed a heart-stopping smile in Izzy's direction, before turning his attention to the brunette, cosying up at his side. Izzy noticed the smile he'd deployed towards her no longer reached his eyes; the exhaustion was back.

'You *said* you were going, Izzy…' Jonny gave another meaningful inclination of his blond head.

'Yes, of course.' Izzy turned away.

'Izzy, wait…' Rick caught her hand in his and, as always, an intense pulse of electricity shot through Izzy's body.

His thumb brushed lightly against the centre of her palm, as he nodded towards the envelope on the table. 'Thanks again for everything.'

'Don't be daft. It's what I'm here for. Remember?' Her smile encompassed everyone. 'Enjoy the rest of your evening!'

Great! She'd just spent the entire time talking about herself. And more to the point, she still got the feeling that Betty, Francesca and the forthcoming wedding didn't come close to what was really niggling Rick. A sixth sense was telling her there was more to this than a neurotic bride-to-be and her endless war-of-words with his mother.

26

INDIANAPOLIS, INDIANA

'So it was purely a change of scene; the reason why you applied to come and work with this band of reprobates?' Rick joked, bumping her shoulder.

'Yes, you could say that.' Izzy answered, staring out across the pool to the darkened windows beyond; Rick's ever-more probing questions were getting too close to home. 'It allowed me to get away from the pressure of Mum and Dad were exerting after the split with James. But my dad wasn't keen. Thought I wasn't street-wise enough to handle a bunch of hardened rockers.'

It was three nights and another two states later—Wisconsin and Indiana—and they were sitting on the edge of yet another hotel pool, taking a well-earned breather, their feet paddling idly in the water. Izzy had just reached the milestone of swimming eight complete strokes, before losing her rhythm, necessitating an emergency rescue by Rick.

'Let's just say there were lots of arguments and stony silences.' Izzy wiped some droplets of water trickling from her brow.

Somehow she had to turn this conversation back to him. At the moment it was *her* under cross-examination.

Think, Izzy. Quick!

'Yeah, your dad does sound a tad over-protective,' he agreed.

'A tad?' Izzy rolled her eyes. 'More like over-protective with bells and whistles! Trust me it's incredibly suffocating being wrapped in cotton wool twenty-four-seven. Dad's convinced that six months under the influence of Eclectic Deviation, and there will be no hope for me. I'll come back some kind of chain-smoking, champagne-swilling nymphomaniac.'

'Hey, don't dismiss it completely. You might enjoy it,' Rick teased, giving her a large wink. 'Stick with me, Izzy, I could show you a thing or two. But only if you let me!'

Izzy let out a laugh; she didn't doubt it.

'Seriously,' Rick sobered, 'I'd probably feel the same if *I* was in his shoes and it was my daughter.'

Izzy swallowed. An image of Rick cradling a little baby girl in his arms crept unbidden into her head. Instinctively, she knew he'd make a wonderful dad.

'Dad refuses to believe that I'm perfectly capable of making my own decisions. I'm twenty -three and all grown up. I don't need his protection from anybody! I can look after myself.'

'And don't I know it, Miss Stevenson. You can be one scarily independent lady,' he answered; reaching over, he wiped away more water droplets which had collected on her brow.

The tender gesture made her thighs clench with desire. As ever, being this close to him was a constant battle for self-control.

'Even if you do have the odd hang-up about water; people looking at your photograph; and flying,' he bumped against her once more.

'I didn't say I was perfect. A girl's allowed to have some quirks,' she reminded him airily. 'It makes her much more interesting, don't you know.'

'Quirks; you left pit marks as I recall.' He pretended to examine his unblemished knuckles. 'So, what does this overprotective dad do for a living? He's not a policeman by any chance?'

'You must be joking!' Izzy shook her head. 'He works in an office; middle management. Don't ask me what he does all day. Every time he starts droning on about work, I mentally check out.'

He was an accountant for *Shell UK*; Rick would know that.

'Mum's a housewife.'

'And you've no brothers or sisters?'

'Nope; so the pressure's all on me.' She sighed. 'Anyway, once I get home, Dad expects me to apply for a "proper job". No more PA-ing for louche-living rock stars.'

It was time to nudge him on the shoulder.

'And what's his definition of a proper job, Miss Stevenson?'

'Somewhere I can use my expensive education. Steady job, steady wage, and definitely no bad influences of the Eclectic Deviation kind.'

It was then it struck her. The perfect route to divert their conversation, make him talk about himself.

'But enough about me, the mundane life of Izzy Stevenson is much too boring compared to yours. More to the point, what would you have been doing if you hadn't joined the band?'

As if she didn't know!

'Easy. Apprentice electrical engineer at SSE in Reading. You have Employee Number 98246 completely at your service.' He doffed an imaginary cap at her. 'Believe it or not, a month before we were signed by *Virgin*, my dad delivered the 'proper job' ultimatum too. I'd been finished college for about a year, just bumming around, playing drums with Jonny and Marc at local gigs and working shifts in a dive of a bar. As far as Dad was concerned, drumming was fine as a hobby, not a career.'

He exhaled loudly. 'Anyway, this apprenticeship came up at SSE Energy—my Dad's a Senior Manager—and yours truly was frog-marched along to the interview. Unfortunately, despite my best efforts, I impressed them—got the bloody job, didn't I! Well, either that or Dad was pulling strings behind the scenes. You must employ my son—or else!' He sliced a finger across his throat. 'But then the call came through. *Virgin* wanted to sign us, and the big time beckoned. So, Employee Number 98246 never officially took up his position.'

'What did *your* dad say to that?' Izzy pulled her knees up to her chin, encircling them with her arms, eyes trained on his lips as he talked. She liked hearing him talk about his life; made her feel close to him.

'Not a lot,' he continued. 'Told him I was signing the record deal and if he didn't like it, tough shit. But we make a pact that if the band flopped within a year, I'd be a good little boy and go back to electrical engineering.'

'But you didn't,' Izzy pointed out with a grin, 'and now your parents are extremely proud of you and what you've achieved.'

'I guess so.' He ran a hand through his dripping hair, but something in those three little words made Izzy hold her breath.

What did he mean by "I guess so"? Those words definitely sounded pregnant with some kind of hidden meaning.

Rick swallowed. 'Don't get me wrong, Izzy, I love music. But this glamorous life you think I'm leading…' he paused for a few seconds before continuing, 'is becoming one gigantic pain in the arse. You know the expression "if you can't stand the heat". Maybe it's time for me to do just that, get the hell out while the going's good and I've still got some sanity left.'

He gave an ironic smile. 'I could ask Dad for my old job back. I still—just about—remember how to wire a plug.'

'And it's a very handy skill to have.' Izzy agreed, but she could tell there was more behind his flippant remark; a worried frown had settled onto his brow.

Then she remembered, he'd said something similar a few weeks ago. It was incredible, but it sounded as though he might be questioning his whole future with the band. Could she be inching a little closer to the real reason for his sleepless nights?

'Well, from what I can see, Eclectic Deviation is at the very pinnacle of its success. You've got the world at your feet: four bestselling albums, a whole string of number-one hits, not forgetting your poster on every teenage girl's wall from here to Timbuktu. Everything Eclectic Deviation touches turns to gold.'

She knew she was going to be a touch disingenuous here. 'And you never give the impression that you're not enjoying your jet-set lifestyle.'

'Maybe I've learnt to be a good actor over the years.' That frown had deepened. 'Recording music and playing live is still the best ego boost in the world. To hear all that screaming, knowing they love what you're doing is amazing. It still gives me fucking goosebumps every time I step out on stage—just like the first time. But it's all the bullshit that goes with it. I'm living in a constant bubble, shut up in five-star hotels and guarded by a bunch of heavies for my own fucking safety. My life isn't my own anymore, Izzy. I can't do anything I want without running it past at least six different people. And, usually, they all say *NO!*'

He pulled a face. 'And don't get me started on all the lying, insincerity and backstabbing that go on. This business is cutthroat. You've read about the fickleness of fame, well, I live it every single day. One minute everyone is kissing your arse, and the next they're burying a knife between your shoulder blades. You can't trust anybody. I used to be a pretty good judge of character, but not anymore. I've been let down too many times.'

A horrible stab of conscience hit her, at his words. She'd have to let him down too but, hopefully, he'd never get to know about her duplicity.

'I'm probably one of the people who always tell you "no".' she reflected, shifting uncomfortably at his side. 'Pointing out where you need to be and what you have to do. In fact, I'm surprised you want to spend your off-duty in my company.'

'No, Izzy, that's where you're wrong, having you around has been great. Especially the way you field all the day-to-day crap. In lots of ways, you've made my life a little easier,' a brief smile appeared, 'although the colour-coded schedule is starting to piss me off, big time. I half expect seeing you in the gents standing over me with that bloody stopwatch when I'm taking a pee!'

A cheeky little picture formed in her mind.

'Now, that's an interesting idea. Maybe we should try it.' She tapped an index finger to her temple, grinning. 'See how long it actually takes, and then I can refine my calculations.'

'Don't you even think about it or I'll have you in the deep end in ten seconds flat.'

With that, he made a grab for her, Izzy letting out a squeal of surprise, play-fighting against his half-hearted attempts to push her back into the water. But all the time she was secretly revelling in the strength of those strong arms wrapped around her, the brush of his chest hair—so wonderfully prickly—against the smooth skin on her back. Would it feel just as good brushing the tips of her naked breasts? She'd love to find out.

'Getting back to the point, Mr Hambro,' she finally managed to pull free of his arms, wagging a restraining finger at him, 'if you're really not happy, finding it too intrusive, you can always say no to the media stuff. I'm sure Marc's more than happy to be the soul mouthpiece of Eclectic Deviation.'

'He is already, which hacks Davey off no end,' Rick said dryly, 'but in answer to your question, until now, I've just tried to grin and bear it.'

He'd begun that habit of gripping the back of his neck. 'At the end of the day, dealing with the media and the fans is part of the job. If I want to be in this band, I need to pull my weight. But some days, it feels like I'm a bloody hamster on a wheel, just running to keep up.' Those broad shoulders sagged. 'I'm so bloody exhausted, Izzy. Everyone wants a piece of me—all the fucking time—when all I want to do crawl into a corner and sleep the clock round.' He let out a mirthless laugh. 'And I can't even to do that, because my fucking insomnia won't let me.'

He looked off into the distance for a few seconds. 'I first started using sleeping tablets at the end of last year. I'd spoken to a Doctor. They weren't very strong; just something mild to get me over at night.' He let out a long breath. 'And initially they were great. But pretty soon, their effect wore off, and I was back to square one.'

Those must have been the tablets Betty had found in his wash bag. Izzy held her breath. He was finally opening up to her.

'I always swore to Mum I'd never get mixed up in hard drugs. That it's a mug's game. Who'd want to be wired to the moon twenty-four-seven? But I've learnt my high ideals are easier said than done. In this business you have to be "on", all the time. Grab sleep when—and if—it comes along.' He pushed his hair back from his brow. 'The rest you probably know. Things got so bad I finally gave in. Spoke to Terry about getting me something stronger and he sourced the *Teraxapen*. Not that I've taken many; maybe half a dozen at most. You don't want to know the fucking awful side effects.'

He dropped his head into his hands, and let out a low groan of frustration. 'The bloody cure's worse than the disease, Izzy.'

Izzy laid her hand against arm, gently stroking the skin with her fingertips. She'd experienced the spaced-out Rick on several occasions now; one of the horrible side-effects Betty had disclosed. But he was probably talking about all the stomach churning others; the nausea; sweats; diarrhoea, and loss of appetite.

She had to come up with some alternative to him taking these filthy tablets, find some way to help. But for now it was time to take the bull by the horns, find out if her mounting suspicions were correct.

'Rick, are you trying to say you're seriously re-considering your future with Eclectic Deviation?'

Something in her gut was telling her this was the crux of his problem. And if she was right, it was massive. Given Eclectic Deviation's massive worldwide popularity, him leaving would be up there with the *Beatles* splitting. But would he admit it to her?

For the longest time, he didn't answer, his face impassive, and Izzy worried that she might have over-stepped the mark, probed too hard, too soon.

'The jury's still out, Izzy, I just don't know?' He placed his hand over hers, twisting their fingers together, and giving them a gentle squeeze, before resting their clasped hands against his thigh. 'Sometimes I think it's what I need to do. Other times I'm not so sure. But my sleep problems are connected. Whenever I'm struggling to come to a decision, sleep's always the first to go.'

He rolled his neck from side to side.

'And lately, I've started getting this bloody pain across my neck and shoulders that won't shift, no matter what I do. It stops me sleeping, too. Some days, when it all gets too much, I think about jacking it in. Walking out the door and not coming back. Then I tell myself things have to get better; that the pain and insomnia is just a blip. I've worked my arse off since I was nineteen to get where I am today. I can't give up now.'

Izzy rested her head on his shoulder, gazing at their interlinked fingers. She knew it had taken a lot for him to make that admission to her.

'Have you shared any of this with Francesca?'

For a second, she felt his body tense, and then he seemed to relax once more. 'No. Not yet. There's never been a good time.'

'Maybe if you did—' she began.

But the mention of his fiancée appeared to throw some kind of switch; Rick unfurling his fingers from hers, withdrawing both mentally and physically.

Izzy watched as he slid back down into the water with a soft splash.

'Jeez, it's nearly one-o'clock in the morning.' He pointed towards the clock above the Fire Exit. 'You've probably had enough of me spilling my guts, pretty lady. Let's have a final five minutes in the pool, and then we'll call it quits. You are way too easy to talk to. If I'm not careful, you'll know my deepest, darkest secret. And we can't have that.'

He winked at her as he reached out and placed his hands against her hips, before very gently tugging her down into the pool beside him.

'Seriously, Izzy, you won't mention what I've just said, will you?' His eyes burned into hers, and Izzy saw genuine fear there. 'You're the only person I've told about what I'm thinking, and it has to stay that way.'

'No, I won't say a word.'

God, she hated herself for uttering that hollow assurance, knowing she was duty bound to pass on his disclosure to Betty. 'Talking is good, Rick. Everyone needs someone when the going gets tough. I'm honoured you felt you could trust me with this.'

He nodded, brushing a tendril of hair from her brow, and cupping her cheek. His thumb slid over her lip, and Izzy felt herself leaning into his touch.

'It's crazy, but you remind me so much of Michelle,' he said. 'I can talk to her so easily too.'

They exchanged another long look, before Rick broke away. 'But enough talking, it's time to get back to work...'

27

CHICAGO, ILLINOIS

'Run that past me again, Izzy, what time is Caroline's flight due to land?' Steve looked up momentarily from reading the *Daily Mirror* over Jonny's shoulder, their breakfast meeting almost at an end for another day.

Typical Steve! Not listening as per bloody usual.

'Caroline and Jilly's flight is scheduled to land at O'Hare, just after noon,' she repeated, fixing their front man with a stony glare, but it was a waste of both time and energy. He'd gone back reading over Jonny's shoulder.

Thank God, it was only Caroline and Jilly arriving today; Francesca safely off on her modelling assignment in Marbella.

'Oh, almost forgot, Izzy,' Jonny emerged from behind the newspaper, fixing Izzy with his best ingratiating smile. 'Need you to do something for me, urgently.'

Unable to stop herself, Izzy rolled her eyes meaningfully at Rick and he winked back.

It was magic wand time.

'Yes, Jonathan, what can I do for you?' Izzy swivelled in her chair, and gave the lead guitarist her full attention, her chin resting on her palm.

What miracle did he expect her to perform, now?

'Want you to pop out and buy a little pressie for Jilly,' Jonny continued.

'What kind of present do you have in mind?'

No doubt it would be something tacky and very expensive.

'Need you to get something that looks like this.' He'd retrieved a crumpled piece of paper from his hip pocket and deposited it on the table before her. It appeared to have been torn from one of his dodgy stashes of magazines. A playboy reading *Playboy;* the man was a walking cliché. And she'd been right about the tacky; the picture was of a scantily clad female resplendent in a minuscule red bra, panties and suspender belt.

'I take it you only want me to buy the underwear?'

Knowing Jonny, it was always better to check.

'Well, I don't expect you to go out and 'buy' her, do I?' Jonny snorted with laughter, before sobering to give Izzy a thoughtful look. 'But that's an interesting idea, Miss Stevenson. Select a potential girlfriend from the pages of a magazine. I've never done that before. You've given me something to consider for future reference.'

And the really sad thing was—Izzy realised—the idiot actually meant it.

A chorus of sniggers went round the table.

'But for now, maybe concentrate on the underwear.' Jonny went on.

Izzy hastily shoved the picture into the back of her notebook out of sight. 'So, what size do I need to buy?'

She had a feeling Jonny wouldn't have thought about the basics here. The next few minutes would be a game of twenty questions 'ping-ponging' between them, until she found out all the necessary requirements.

Sure enough, Jonny's brow creased in consternation. 'What do you mean… size? You know what Jilly looks like.'

Obviously those five words were meant to convey everything as far as Miss Fletcher's vital statistics were concerned.

'Yes, I know I regularly work the oracle on your behalf, Jonny, but Jilly's bra size is still a bit beyond me,' she deadpanned.

'Bra size… em maybe about a thirty-four something….' That comment was accompanied by a helpless shrug.

'Jonny, I know you're speciality is getting them off in ten seconds flat, but I really need the actual size here. And do I buy a Size Eight or a Size Ten for the knickers and suspender belt?'

Jonny glanced at his band mates, his expression puzzled. 'I don't think she should be any more than a Size Ten? What do you think guys?'

'She'd be furious if you said she was anything more than a size ten!' Davey chuckled.

By now, the whole table was crying with laughter, even Marc had stopped slashing at the schedule with his red pen, everyone enjoying the joke at Jonny's expense.

'I can see this part of your education has been woefully lacking,' Izzy observed. 'Never mind, leave it to me. Izzy'll fix it.'

As usual! It was time for a bit of inspired thinking.

4.37 PM

'Thanks a lot, Izzy!' Davey stormed into her office, slamming the door hard behind him. 'You just buggered off and left me.'

He slapped down the receipt for the taxi fare onto her desk. The glower was back in those beady hazel eyes. 'Do you know I had to pay for a fucking cab? Twenty dollars that cost me, and the driver was an arsehole. Talked the whole fucking way here about how bloody *Metallica* is the best fucking rock band on the planet. When he asked for a tip, I was ready to deck him. That's 10 minutes of my fucking life I'll never get back, thanks to you.'

Izzy studiously ignored both the over-dramatic gestures, as well as the expletives. A reaction was just what Davey wanted. He was playing the blame game again.

And as for him having to hail a taxicab to get to the arena, she hoped that had given him a timely reminder on how ordinary mortals still lived. Although, where had the money come from to pay for it? Most of the time, the band acted like royalty, none of them carrying cash; except if they were in a betting mood or required to "powder" their noses. Everything else went on the *AMEX*, or Bank of Izzy picked up the tab.

'If you'd just waited another couple of minutes longer, Izzy, I'd have been back at the hotel. I was only playing fucking pool downtown.'

So, he'd been out playing pool had he? It was nice of him to let her know.

'Instead, I get back to be met with the last fucking limo pulling out into the traffic. What was do you expect me to do, fucking fly here?'

So far, that made seven instances of him using his favourite word.

'I'm sorry, but we didn't have the luxury of waiting for you any longer.' Izzy deliberately kept her voice neutral, picking up the receipt and making a note of the amount owed.

'Complete bollocks, you didn't wait because it was me.'

If looks could kill, Izzy didn't fancy her chances.

'Don't be so ridiculous, Davey. You know time is precious whenever we've a fan meet and greet to factor in before a show.'

She shot off an icy glare in his direction. He wasn't the only one who could annihilate with a look.

'Huh, don't feed me that old chestnut. If it had been any of the others, you'd have fucking waited, and you know it!'

'And your point is?' Arms folded, she sat back in her chair, waiting. She could guess what was coming next.

'You treat me differently. Always have done! If it'd been Rick, our resident Knight in the Shiny Stuff, or Marc—Boy Bloody Wonder sitting through there like butter wouldn't melt— the limos wouldn't have fucking moved. It's one rule for them and another for me.'

That permanent chip on his shoulder was showing.

'I certainly do not.' But Izzy could feel her cheeks begin to warm, knowing there was a grain of truth to his accusations. 'It wouldn't have mattered who was late, we're all supposed to keep to the schedule.'

'And, unlike Marc, you know I'm never late for sound check. I was on my fucking way, Izzy.'

He leaned in close, his expression venomous. 'I'll be speaking to Jack about this.'

Honestly, he was like a dog with a bone, refusing to let the argument rest, and as for his threat to speak to Jack? A hollow one; Jack was a stickler for punctuality too.

'You didn't leave word with anybody as to where you'd gone this afternoon,' she refused to be intimidated. 'Nor am I telepathic. If I'd known you wanted to play pool, I'd have organised a limo to take you there and then onto the arena. You only had to lift the phone. But, as per usual, you decided to cut me out the equation. I'm your PA. I need to be kept in the loop.'

'PA? You've got that bit right; stands for *Pain* in the fucking *Arse!*' A threatening finger was now levelled at her. 'And, anyway, who pays the wages around here? I don't have to answer to some stuck-up little bitch every minute of the fucking day.'

He headed for the door, before glancing back momentarily. 'Just watch your step, Izzy. Your card's just been fucking marked, big time! Got that?'

Thirteen; a new record!

'And that's the amended version of tomorrow's schedule.'

Izzy handed Rick the neatly typewritten sheet reflecting last-minute changes. Its contents weren't for the faint-hearted. Eight hours of media commitments and another two-hour show at the end of it.

'For fuck's sake, Izzy, what's the Record Company trying to do to us?' Lines creased Rick's brow. 'When do we get the chance to breathe? Or even take a piss? Or have you been consulting that stop-watch again and decided it's too time-consuming?'

"I know. It's a bit full on,' Izzy conceded with an apologetic smile at his understandable grouchiness.

That had been the rest of the band's consensus when she'd dropped off their copies earlier. After reading his, Davey had scrunched the copy into a ball and thrown it back at her before he'd retreated inside his suite and indulged in a bit of childish door slamming. She'd made sure a second copy had been posted underneath— just in case.

Rick turned the sheet over, his face falling even further as he took in the additional typewritten instructions on the reverse. 'Well, I suppose I'd better try and get some sleep.'

He stuffed the schedule into his robe pocket, his eyes drifting reluctantly towards the bottle of *Teraxapen* sitting on his nightstand

Izzy knew the insomnia had been particularly bad over the last few days, and that Rick—out of desperation—had swallowed another tablet. Consequently, he'd been almost comatose today, barely going through the motions behind those dark glasses. He'd also been disappearing off to the toilet more than usual. Maybe it was time to float the idea she'd come up with to tackle his sleep problem. See if he'd go for it.

'Have you ever thought of massage as an alternative?' she ventured.

'Are you suggesting I indulge in something naughty just to get some relief, Miss Stevenson?' He treated her to a half-hearted smile. 'You know what happened last time the band tried that.'

'It's well documented that massage has positive benefits for both insomnia, and pain relief.' She gave him a hard look, knowing only too well the incident to which he was referring.

Last summer, the band had been caught up in a raid on a—supposedly—reputable Massage Parlour in London's Soho by the Met's *Vice Squad*. Needless to say, the story had been announced to the world in an exposé, courtesy of the *News of the World*; the band lucky to get off without a caution.

'All I'm suggesting is a regular massage of your neck, shoulders and back,' Izzy went on, primly. 'Nothing remotely seedy involved. In fact, if you're agreeable, I'd like to hire a physio and have them travel with us. I really think it could help make you relax more. What do you say?' She raised her eyebrows expectantly.

'No, I think I'll pass, if you don't mind.'

'Why?' Not the reaction she'd hoped for. What was wrong with her idea?

'With my luck, I'd get some butch female built like the side of a house, offering me optional extras in a thick Russian Accent.'

'Don't be so ridiculous.' Izzy rolled her eyes in exasperation. 'Physiotherapists are professional people, Rick. They deal with injured sports stars all the time. And they certainly don't offer quickies on the side; no matter what you might have read to the contrary.'

'Nah, not happening, Izzy. Could you imagine the stick I'd get from the others?'

True….

Would he go for her rapidly forming Plan B instead? And more to the point, did she actually have the bottle to carry it out? Exercising supreme self-control during the swimming lessons was hard enough, but putting Plan B into action might be taking it to a whole new level.

'Then how would you feel about… me… giving you a massage?'

There, she'd said it. Her heart banged uncomfortably against her chest as she awaited his response.

'You, Izzy?' Rick's look was decidedly sceptical.

'I did evening classes in Sports Massage about a year ago,' she hurried on, flushing. 'One of my friends wanted to learn, and I was dragged along as moral support. She thought it would be a good way to chat up men. Big mistake! It was a female only class.' She chuckled, remembering her friend's disappointment. 'We both ended up dropping out, but not before I'd learnt the basics.'

'Miss Stevenson, you never cease to amaze me…'

'Well, as you told me with the swimming lessons, what have you got to lose by giving it a try? You're in pain, and together with the lack of sleep, its driving you to distraction. Anything has to be better than downing those filthy tablets,' she reminded him.

'True.' He rubbed his chin.

She wiggled her fingers at him. 'And I can guarantee these fingers come with no adverse side effects, whatsoever.'

His lips twitched. 'You really think so? I'm a guy, remember. I can think of a pretty major one, when a woman starts running her hands over my body.'

'I won't be massaging down there!' she retorted, trying hard to ignore the innuendo behind his words.

'You won't have to. As the American's say, it doesn't take much for the old "wood" to appear.' He grinned.

'Okay fine. Then take the tablets. It was just an idea' She turned away, suddenly annoyed at his continual leg-pulling.

'Hey.' His hand snagged her arm and he twisted her round to face him. 'Don't be like that. I'm sorry. You're right. It's a good idea. As you say, what have I got to lose?' His face relaxed into a smile. 'Okay, pretty lady, I'm in. And I'll try and behave myself down there too.'

Izzy became business-like, trying to put that image out of her mind. 'Well, there's no time like the present, why don't we get started? Slip off your dressing gown and lie down on your front, on the bed.'

'You mean we're giving it a go, right now?'

'Yes. Why not?'

'Well for a start, I'm not wearing any underwear.' He chuckled. 'Is this just some elaborate way to see me with my kit off? Swimming trunks not enough, eh?' He winked at her, his hand going to the belt in his robe.

'Don't be silly.'

The jingle *Liar, liar pants on fire* echoed in her brain.

Still grinning, Rick turned his back and let the towelling robe drop at his feet. Izzy got a brief, but tantalising, glimpse of his bare—and very firm—backside, before he leapt beneath the sheets and lay down on his front, pulling the duvet up to rest at hip level.

'Okay, I'm decent! Ready when you are!'

Izzy came to stand beside the bed. 'Now, I need you to relax, and close your eyes.'

Very gently, she tilted his head to lie sideways on the pillow, all the time trying to ignore the nerves fluttering in her tummy.

Those chocolate brown eyes were wide open, honed into her every move.

'Your hands are a bit cold?' he observed. 'Shouldn't they be warmed up a little before we start?'

Unable to curb a loud tut of irritation, Izzy rubbed both hands together, blowing hot air between her palms.

Jeez, he's not making this easy.

'Better?' she asked, replacing them on his back and trying not to savour—too much—the familiar feeling of his heated skin and hard muscle resting beneath her palms.

She had to be totally dispassionate here.

Imagine its Davey!

Yeah,' he smirked, 'they'll do.'

'Okay, you have to concentrate on your breathing. Very slowly, in for three and out again for three.' She instructed.

'Am I allowed to yell if it hurts?' That comment was accompanied by one of his customary winks.

'Rick, I'm not going to hurt you, so there will be no need for yelling,' she rebuked. 'Now, just close your eyes and do as you're told.'

'Shit, I don't recall me being this bossy during our swimming lessons.' His chuckling only got louder.

'That's different. The whole point of this exercise is to make your body relax, and you can't relax if you won't stop talking. Now, are you going to take this seriously or not?'

'Point taken, I'll shut up.' He closed his eyes but he was still grinning.

'And stop grinning at me!'

With considerable effort, he straightened his face.

Taking a deep breath, Izzy began to very slowly, but firmly, run her hands up over his shoulders. She really should have some kind of oil to make the hand motions easier—for both of them. If he wanted her to do it again, she'd buy some *Baby oil* and brace herself for the leg-pulling, which was bound to follow.

Growing more confident, she began to make circular movements up over his shoulder blades towards the base of his neck, then swept down again towards his upper arms, feeling the harness of his biceps under her fingertips. Between all his swimming and constant drumming, he really was in fantastic shape.

Slowly and steadily, she now repeated each movement, manipulating the knots beneath his skin. No wonder he was in pain. There was way too much tension in his upper body. She began to knead his skin more firmly; calling to mind all the different techniques she'd learnt to work the kinks from the body's soft tissue, methodically moving around each muscle group in turn.

'Just breathe slowly in and out,' she reminded him, finally feeling some of the stiffness beginning to ebb away under her ministrations. 'Now, how does that feel?'

Stupid question, she knew how it was making her feel. She'd the strongest urge to lean over and place a line of soft kisses between those powerful shoulder blades.

Rick let out a low groan. 'I have to admit,' he said, his eyes remaining closed, 'this feels bloody fantastic.'

'Don't sound so surprised.' Izzy allowed herself a little smirk of satisfaction.

'Ahhhh.' He let out a long breath as she manipulated the skin at his nape. 'And what you did just there felt fucking amazing.'

'You mean this? Izzy repeated the twisting movement to relax his neck muscles.

He moaned again. 'Yeah, in fact, I could let you do that to me all night?'

The undisguised pleasure in his voice ensured her stomach butterflies went berserk.

For another five minutes, she repeated her hand motions, and as she worked, she began to hear a definite change to the timbre of Rick's breathing. Stilling for a second, she leaned in closer, listening carefully. No, her ears weren't deceiving her. His breathing had definitely evened out; a slow and steady in and out.

He'd fallen asleep on her.

'Izzy, I think your work here is done,' she murmured, before finally succumbing to temptation and placing a kiss to her fingertips and pressing it between his shoulders.

'Goodnight, my love.' She whispered.

28

CHICAGO, ILLINOIS

'I don't know what the hell you did to me, pretty lady, but they should prescribe you on the NHS.' Rick slid into the chair next to Izzy at the breakfast table.

'I take it you slept well?' Izzy held her breath, awaiting his answer. Had he made it all through the night?

'Understatement of the century; I went out like a light. One minute you were there, doing whatever it was you were doing,' he flashed a cheeky grin, 'and then I don't remember another thing until seven this morning. I was out cold for nearly seven hours. Those hands of yours definitely cast some kind of spell.'

'Glad to hear it.' She resisted the urge to do a fist pump. 'But more to the point, what about the pain in your neck, do you feel any improvement, there?'

'I'm not going to lie, I'm still tired,' he conceded, 'but yeah, the pain seems to have gone for now. And I definitely didn't wake up feeling like shit.'

A glow of satisfaction ignited deep within her.

'So, we can safely say "Massage one—*Teraxapen* nil" ' Izzy licked her finger and drew an imaginary line in the air. 'Have I convinced you to hire a physio yet?'

'Well, last night was definitely promising,' he agreed, 'but it might have been beginner's luck. I think we need to give it a few more tries— just the two of us—before I'd even consider hiring anyone.'

'In that case, are you up for engaging in a little experiment with me?' she asked.

He wanted her to do it again. She allowed herself another mental fist pump.

'I knew it. You're trying to lure me into something kinky…' He nudged her shoulder.

'Get your mind out of the gutter, Mr Hambro!' Izzy batted him away playfully.

Now, it was time to see if he could give up the tablets entirely.

'I want you to hand over the *Teraxapen* for safekeeping,' she proposed, 'and in return I'll give you regular massages for the next week. If the massages continue to work, we look at hiring a proper physio for the remainder of the tour.'

He looked a little thrown by her idea, his teeth sinking into his lower lip. 'I don't know, Izzy. What if they don't? I'd still feel better having something to fall back on. As I told you, I've not taken many of them, but still…'

'They make you feel awful, Rick.' Her smile was both sympathetic and determined. 'Is it really worth it?'

'Yeah, I guess but…'

'Please, let's try. I think it might work.' Izzy's eyes met his and she gave a little nod of encouragement.

'Okay. You win, pretty lady. Pop up to my room after breakfast.'

At that moment, the dining room doors were thrust open, admitting Marc and Steve.

'But this is between us, Izzy.' Rick nodded towards his fast-approaching bandmates.

'They know nothing about the massages. Okay?'

'My lips are sealed.'

29

CLEVELAND, OHIO

'Want Booze and ice in the usual place, Izzy?' Lindsay was leaning against the stacked trolley of alcohol he'd just lugged into Davey's suite, breathing heavily with the exertion.

Izzy hastily scrawled her signature on the catering receipt before looking up, her face breaking into a smile. 'Yes please, Lindsay. Just pop them in the bath. People can help themselves, as usual.'

She handed the receipt back to the hotel's catering assistant hovering at her elbow, and then cast a satisfied glance round Davey's suite.

Food and drink now in place—check!

Not bad, given she'd had a mere four hours' notice that Davey wanted to throw an impromptu party after tonight's show. She checked the time on her watch. They'd be back any minute.

On cue and despite the torrential rain bucketing from the heavens outside, high-pitched shrieking could be heard from a small group of dedicated fans, congregated under umbrellas on the pavement below.

Izzy nipped over to the window and, pulling back the heavy drape, peeped outside. Sure enough, six floors below, the band's convoy of three limos had pulled up, the yellow beam of their headlights illuminating the front entrance to the hotel.

Perfect timing as always!

And no surprise, tonight's host was the first member of the band to make it upstairs and through the door of his suite, Davey bouncing around like a rock-star version of *Zebedee* from *'The Magic Roundabout'*. And by the looks of it, he'd already powdered his nose with a few lines of cocaine, just to get into the party mood.

Grabbing an open bottle of champagne, Izzy watched as the guitarist made a beeline for a group of young women standing beside the buffet table, a cheeky smile plastered all over his face. The chat-up lines were about to be rolled out.

'Good evening, ladies, Davey Eastman, completely at your service,' He clicked his tongue, performing an overblown theatrical bow before them. Its impact somewhat ruined when he managed to spill some of the alcohol onto the Persian carpet.

'Get this fucking mess cleaned up, Izzy,' he hissed at her out the side of his mouth, before swinging seamlessly back to his enthralled audience. 'May I say you all look absolutely stunning, ladies? Good enough for a man to eat, if you get my meaning.'

Giggling ensued.

Izzy resisted the urge not to vomit as she hastily dealt with the spillage with some napkins. Didn't he know those sexually charged chat-up lines didn't work on modern women?

Or maybe they did.

The rapt expression on each girl's face showed they hadn't read the script. Davey had his audience eating from the palm of his hand.

'Now'— he indicated the bottle—'which one of you lucky ladies would like the chance to be topped up first?'

Izzy suppressed a groan as four glasses were thrust towards Davey. The king of the 'double entendre' had struck again.

As she disposed of the sodden napkins in a nearby bin, her eye caught Rick's. He was standing in the open doorway, glancing about the room with a barely disguised scowl.

Her breath caught in her throat. He looked awful. Today's punishing schedule had clearly taken its toll. Gone was the relaxed guy she'd chatted to over breakfast. From his grim expression, he didn't look to be in the socialising mood, his eyes red rimmed with tiredness, and he was trying—unsuccessfully—to stifle a yawn with one hand, while his other gripped the back of his neck.

'Rick, would you like—' Izzy tried to make a move towards him, but she was too late; Davey had barged her out the way, and shoved a glass of champagne into his band mate's free hand.

'You have to meet these birds, Rick. They're fucking gorgeous, man!'

Before he could raise any protest, Rick was dragged off by the elbow to meet Davey's harem, Izzy receiving a helpless shrug as he went. The bass guitarist was clearly determined that Rick enter into the party spirit—whether he felt like it or not.

But—Izzy comforted herself—at least Rick had handed over the *Teraxapen* tablets to her safe-keeping. And they were safe alright; safely flushed down the toilet and out of his reach —permanently. With any luck, they'd be swirling their way through Cleveland's sewage system— at this very moment—anaesthetising the local wildlife.

'I'll give you a penny for your thoughts, Miss Stevenson?' Kathy had appeared; carrying two open bottles of *Pepsi* and handing one over to Izzy.

'Just wondering if Mr Eastman will find anything to complain about, tonight? You know what he's like,' Izzy observed, taking in the rapidly filling hotel room as more A-list guests arrived. But, she noted, still no Marc and Sabrina; both conspicuous by their absence.

'Where's Marc?' She asked.

'You'd already left for the hotel when Madam announced she has one of her "heads".' An expressive eye roll accompanied Kathy's comment.

Izzy understood instantly. 'So, Marc's not allowed out to play with the big boys.'

'You said it. No doubt she's feeling neglected again, hence the spontaneous "'migraine'". Kathy shook her head in disbelief. 'How much more attention does that woman need?'

'Your guess is as good as mine!'

'Marc needs to wise up and fast. Sabrina's got him dangling on a string.' Kathy downed some of her drink, and then grimaced at the bottle. 'Honestly, Izzy, I don't know how you can drink this stuff straight. It definitely needs vodka in it. No bloody kick, otherwise!'

With that, Kathy whipped out a small silver hip flask from her back pocket and poured a liberal measure of the spirit into her *Pepsi*, before offering the flask to Izzy.

'That's better. Can I tempt you?'

Izzy placed a hand over the lip of her bottle, and shook her head. Kathy knew she wasn't a vodka girl. 'No thanks. I intend to sit tight for another ten minutes. Make sure Davey doesn't have any last-minute gripes, and then I'm out of here. I feel a long, hot soak beckoning.'

30

CLEVELAND, OHIO

Izzy awoke with a start to the shrill ringing of the telephone in her left ear.

She took a one-eyed glance at the alarm clock. Who the hell was calling her at this time of night? She'd only been asleep an hour—if that.

Rolling onto her back, and letting out a loud groan towards the ceiling at the unfairness of it all, she rubbed the sleep from her eyes.

The phone continued to ring out. Knowing her luck, it'd be Marc. He'd done it before. Full of hare-brained schemes he wanted her to implement urgently! The middle Hambro—a real night owl—was totally oblivious to the fact normal people actually needed sleep at this hour. Well, if it *was* him, he'd receive the sharp edge of her tongue.

Yawning, she reached out and drew the receiver to her ear. On principle, she refused to lift her head an inch from the comfy indentation she'd made in her pillow.

'Hello, Izzy Stevenson, speaking.'

'Hi Izzy, its Rick.'

Izzy was bolt upright in seconds. 'Rick, is everything okay?'

She ran a flustered hand through her mussed-up hair, trying to flatten her unruly curls, before remembering he couldn't actually see her.

'Not really.' His voice sounded flat. 'Look, Izzy, I'm sorry to disturb you, but I can't sleep and the pain is off the fucking scale.' He paused. 'I found a couple of tablets in my washbag. I was going to take one, but...' There was a long drawn-out breath before he continued. 'I know it's late, but would you come up? Give your magic fingers another go? I'm going off my fucking head here.'

He sounded desperate. But more to the point, why did he still have some of those tablets in his possession?

'Of course, just give me a couple of minutes.' Izzy was already kicking back the covers and swinging her feet onto the floor.

Then she remembered his potential sleeping arrangements.

'Wait, don't you have company tonight?'

She reached for her discarded jeans. There was no way she was setting foot upstairs to perform a massage if his latest floozie was snuggled up beside him. That would be too weird for words.

'Eh….no, I didn't invite anyone back. I wasn't in the mood.'

Strange; not like Rick at all.

'Okay, give me a few minutes to pull on some clothes.'

'You really don't have to, Izzy.'

Well, at least that comment was more like it.

'I'll pretend I didn't hear that. Be with you shortly.'

2.46 AM

A fully dressed Izzy let herself into Rick's room.

He was lying propped up in bed, his head resting against the headboard, eyes closed. Both hands were grasping the back of his neck.

'Hi.' She closed the door, and came to sit by his side.

'I've got someone beating me over the back of the head with a bat,' he said, opening pain-filled eyes to look at her. 'I was so bloody tempted to take that tablet. Make it all go away.'

Izzy detected a flash of anger and despair in their brown depths.

'But you didn't. You phoned me instead,' she reached out and rested a comforting hand over his, giving it a reassuring squeeze, 'which is what we agreed, remember?'

'Yeah, but it was a close-run thing, Izzy. I felt like such an arsehole disturbing you.'

Izzy knew it was time for some tough love before she got started. 'Don't be daft. But first, I need you to hand over the last of those tablets. And I mean all of them, Rick.' She held out her hand.

With an embarrassed flush to his cheeks, he opened the bedside drawer and, after a quick rummage inside, dropped the two remaining tablets into her outstretched palm.

'And you don't have any more?'Izzy channelled her best school teacher look. If he was serious about the experiment, there could be no more lapses.

'Nope, those are the last.' His jaw tensed.

She pocketed them. They'd be heading straight down the toilet, too.

Without her asking, Rick shuffled down the bed, and flipped onto his front.

Izzy drew out a small bottle from her jean pocket. She'd purchased it earlier in the day.

'I've managed to get my hands on some lavender oil,' she explained. 'The vapours will make you relax; feel sleepy. It'll also make the actual massage easier for both of us. Are you happy for me to use it? Some people can't stand the smell.'

'Izzy, you can knock me out with a fucking brick if you think it'll do the trick.'

'I'll take that as a "yes" then.'

Unable to hold back a smile, she poured a little oil onto her palms, rubbed them together and placed them on the skin at his nape.

'Now concentrate on your breathing, and the feel of my hands. Take it slowly. In for three and out for three….'

Izzy set to work, but unlike the previous night, the knots of tension in his muscles were stubbornly refusing to play ball.

'Rick, please stop fighting against me.' Her tone had become exasperated after several minutes wrestling with uncooperative rotator cuffs.

'I'm not,' was his snapped reply.

'Yes you are.' Izzy ignored his burst of temper. 'Just breathe. Go with the touch of my hands….'

A stubborn grunt was all she got in response to that instruction, but very gradually over the next five minutes, the muscles began to loosen, Izzy continuing with slow circular movements, always working towards the heart as she'd been taught.

Gliding her hands upwards to the tops of his arms, she manipulated around his left biceps and Rick let out a low moan.

'Does that feel good?' she asked.

She got no coherent words of reply, except what sounded like another satisfied moan. Confident things were finally moving in the right direction, she repeated the movement, before turning her attention to his other biceps. He still wasn't asleep, but his eyelids had closed over and she could tell by his breathing that he was gradually edging closer to that sweet spot.

'You're almost there, Rick,' she whispered against his ear. 'Just let go for me…'

It took just under another five minutes before a deep sigh finally escaped with a whoosh from those softly parted lips, all the tension leaving his body.

He was asleep—at last.

She lifted her hands away to rest in her lap and smiled in satisfaction.

Or was he? She gave a little jump as Rick's left hand snaked out unexpectedly from beneath the quilt, his fingers catching hold of hers.

'Stay.' His eyes remained closed, his voice strangely childlike.

'Rick, I can't.' she whispered back, uncertain he could even hear her.

'Need… you … stay….can't …sleep ….without you…..'

Well, that's what the disjointed mumbling sounded like.

Izzy frowned. He had to be dreaming—surely? Then the awful realisation struck her. He *was* dreaming and he thought *she* was Francesca.

She tried a gentle tug, endeavouring to free her right hand from his grip, but he just clung on tighter. A further —stronger—tug proved equally ineffectual. Nope, he didn't look to be surrendering her—Francesca's—hand any time soon, and certainly not without a fight. What on earth did she do now?

She glanced down at those long fingers inter-twined with her own. Would it really hurt to-do as he'd asked? Maybe lie down and stay with him for a few minutes. Pretend she *was* Francesca, and if it got him back into a deep sleep…

'Okay. But just for a few minutes.'

Toeing off her shoes, she climbed onto the bed, all the time trying not to analyse her behaviour too closely. This was seriously pushing her professional boundaries into unknown territory. And what if he woke up? What would she say then?

She lay down on top of the covers, trying to make herself comfortable on the narrow strip of mattress he'd left vacant.

Rick gave an unexpected movement, and Izzy froze. His dark head had started to nudge against her shoulder. Was he about to wake up and get the biggest shock of his life?

But, after a few more nudges, he appeared to find a suitably comfy spot and settled against her, the warmth of his breath fanning her throat. Her hand was still wrapped up in his, but now he had it pressed flat against the wall of his chest; the steady thump of his heartbeat reverberating against her fingertips.

Izzy stifled a yawn, and turned on her side to face him. He looked so contented.

Not quite what she'd expected when she'd answered his cry for help. Her eyelids were beginning to grow unbearably heavy, closing over of their own volition as the lavender oil's scent wove its soporific spell. She'd just lie here for a few minutes longer, make sure he was really out for the count, and then sneak back downstairs. He'd never know…

5.55 AM

The sounds of a slamming door and loud curses roused Izzy back to consciousness, only to find she couldn't actually move. A deliciously warm male body was curled into her back. Rick's head was now resting against her own on the pillow, a heavy arm pinned across her stomach, holding her captive against him.

It took a few seconds for her to realise she definitely wasn't dreaming again. This was wonderfully, beautifully real. She was in bed, being held within Rick's protective embrace. Her face creased into a smile as she breathed in his familiar male scent. She didn't want to move from this spot. It felt too good.

But, *damn*, she'd have to! He couldn't wake up and find her here. The first fingers of grey light were beginning to creep in through a crack in the damask curtains, and a quick check to her watch told her she'd been here for nearly three hours.

It was time to galvanise herself into action, before Rick—or anybody else for that matter—discovered she'd enjoyed an impromptu sleepover. Otherwise, it would become all-sorts of embarrassing. How the heck could she explain herself? Could she really say she'd just taken the opportunity to close her eyes for a few seconds, and three hours later she just happened to be still here?

A likely story!

Another quick glance told her Rick was still dead to the world, breathing deeply.

Slowly and carefully, her stiff muscles protesting, Izzy began inching both legs towards the edge of the bed, all the time keeping a watchful eye on Rick. After what felt like an eternity, she was able to gradually twist her body and place both feet firmly on the floor. Now, for the hard part, she had to extract herself from underneath that arm. Taking a deep breath, and performing a manoeuvre worthy of any limbo dancer worth their salt she finally made it upright to stand beside the bed.

Rick murmured something and appeared to stir—Izzy's heart skipped a beat—before he rolled onto his stomach, and burrowed his face into the hollow she'd just vacated.

Thanking her lucky stars she still hadn't been sprung, Izzy retrieved her shoes from under the bed and pulled them on. He'd never know she'd been in his bed.

With one eye still pinned to the sleeping figure, Izzy tiptoed to the door, and opened it carefully. Briefly, checking the coast was clear—all quiet on the western front—she stepped into the corridor and hurried off in the direction of the lift, letting out a huge sigh of relief, the suite door closing behind her with a soft click.

31

DETROIT, MICHIGAN

'If I didn't know better, I'd say you've been avoiding me?' Terry smirked, giving Izzy the once-over as she scrambled out from the rear of the Lincoln.

They'd just arrived within the parking lot at tonight's venue, Detroit's Cobo Arena.

Spot on, sunshine!

Izzy had done just about everything to avoid being alone with him over the last few weeks, praying he'd forgotten their last repugnant conversation, but apparently no such luck. The sleaze-bag had just been biding his time.

She pointedly ignored his question, all the time smoothing down her denim mini-dress, making sure she wasn't showing off too much leg. She'd no intention of making that creep's day with an eyeful of her thighs, even if they were encased in thick black woolly tights to keep out the cold.

He slammed the door shut, falling into step by her side; the band and their entourage all heading for the sanctuary of tonight's dressing room.

So far, it hadn't been the best of days. On the journey here, Izzy had endured another dressing down from Marc. Furious that she hadn't managed to secure tickets for some avant garde play showing in Ottawa—an up-and-coming destination on their tour—and now, given the way Terry was eyeing her, it looked like another indecent proposal was heading her way.

'Well, Izzy.' Terry leaned close to her ear, his voice low enough to ensure only she was privy to his next words. 'It's been a few weeks, now. Isn't it about time I start paying you some of that very personal attention we discussed?'

'I beg your pardon?' Izzy stopped in her tracks. He had to be joking, right?

'Tut tut, don't tell me you didn't take our recent discussion, seriously, Miss Stevenson.' His grin was positively menacing. 'Oh, I was deadly serious, darling. And don't try to deny it. I could see you were just as turned on by the idea, as I am.'

Turned on!

Izzy's insides shrivelled in revulsion. He'd been the one getting off pouring those filthy fantasies into her ear. She'd just felt sick to her stomach. And if he thought it was ever going to happen, he was on a hiding to nothing.

'Or have you decided to leave me dangling; now that you've hooked yourself a bigger fish?'

Izzy didn't like the speculative look she was getting. Bigger fish-what on earth was he hinting at now?

'I don't know what you're talking about, Terry.'

'Don't you?' Terry feigned disbelief. 'Saw you disappearing into Rick's room late last night and then—lo and behold—you don't make another appearance until gone six this morning. Good night was it?' He tapped his nose with his index finger.

Izzy swallowed. Terry must have been lurking out of sight watching all the comings and goings on the band's floor. That was his remit after all. The band's very own resident *'Big Brother'*. And the voice that had awoken her this morning, none other than the man himself; barking orders to some of his sub-ordinates.

Damn! Damn! Damn!

'Rick wasn't feeling well,' she answered in a tight voice. 'I popped up to check on him….twice.' She added as an afterthought. 'It was all perfectly innocent.'

Which it was, if she left out the 'falling asleep and staying the night' part!

But from Terry's sceptical expression, he didn't believe a word of her explanation.

'Pull the other one, Izzy! You were in there the whole fucking night. You know it and I know it. I sent his bird home in a taxi when he blew her out. And as for him not feeling well; bollocks! He just had a cosy little assignation lined up with you, instead. I saw the grin on your face when you left his room. You looked one—very satisfied— young lady.'

With that, he caught her elbow and shoved her roughly through the open door of her office, kicking it closed behind them.

'It's time to stop bullshitting me! I know exactly what's been going on over the last few weeks,' he rasped, his face inches from hers. 'Witnessed some of those cosy little meetings in hotel swimming pools, haven't I? Teaching you to swim is he? Or is that just a convenient cover story for something else?'

Izzy's heart plummeted. He knew about the swimming lessons…

'Don't look so shocked, Izzy!' His smile was mocking. 'Remember, I make it my business to know exactly what goes on around here—and with whom! Their personal safety is my concern twenty-four-seven.'

His eyes raked over her, before coming to rest on her breasts. 'By the way, a great pair of tits tucked away in there. You could give Jonny's bird a run for her money. I'm not surprised Ricky can't keep his hands to himself!'

His grip bit harder into her elbow.

'You're hurting my arm, Terry.'

She tried to twist free, but he appeared to be in no mood to let go. All she got in return was a wolfish grin.

'Am I? Well, here's the deal, Izzy. Just because you're being screwed by the band's drummer, it doesn't mean I'm going to stand aside and wait patiently—forever!'

'I don't know what you think you saw, Terry, but there's nothing going on.' Panic bubbled up inside her.

'Liar! Behind the Miss Goody Two Shoes façade, you're just another little gold digger on the make.' He gave a harsh laugh. 'I meet your kind day in and day out. But don't worry. I'll keep your dirty little secret safe—for now. After all discretion is part of the job. But if I've got to exert a little pressure, remind you that I'm next in line to enjoy Miss Stevenson's favours, these old lips might start flapping.' He delivered another sharp squeeze to her arm. 'Got that, Izzy?'

The words 'loud and clear' went through her brain.

'Didn't catch what you said?' he prompted. 'Or do you need—'

Whatever else Terry had been about to say was cut short by a furious Jonny exploding through the office door.

Terry released Izzy so suddenly she overbalanced, stumbling backwards, her hip making contact with the sharp edge of the desktop.

'Owwwwh!'

'Izzy, why are you never around when I fucking need you?' Jonny snapped, totally ignoring both her cry of pain, and Terry's looming presence by her side.

'Think over what I said, Izzy?' Giving them both a salute, Terry disappeared outside into the corridor.

Izzy rubbed her hip, trying to get her erratic pulse rate under control.

Great! She'd just landed in the eye of a colossal shit-show.

'Izzy, when you're quite finished flirting with our Head of Security,' Jonny bit out, scowling at her from under his fringe.

'I wasn't flirting.' Izzy snapped back, collapsing into her chair. Couldn't the idiot see she'd just been scared out of her wits? Then she remembered. Jonathan Hambro saw absolutely nothing, unless it involved him.

'What do you want, Jonny?'

Opening her note book, she grabbed a pen, willing her hand to stop trembling. 'And make it quick, Marc's already given me another list to deal with.'

'Okay, keep the wig on, this won't take long.'

Jonny was obviously in a filthy mood.

Well, that makes two of us!

'I need you to get onto our hotel, ASAP.'

Somehow, she got the sudden feeling trouble had returned to paradise? No doubt, "Little boy lost" was about to be laid on in spades, any minute now.

'I need the TV replaced in our room.'

She got the look. His alter ego had entered the building.

'What's happened?' As if she couldn't guess.

'I might have accidentally put a bottle of vodka through the screen.'

So, her female intuition had been right. Sparks had started flying between Jonny and Jilly, and they'd only been together a matter of days! And as for *accidently* putting a bottle of vodka through a TV screen? No "*might*" about it, not where Jonny and Jilly were concerned. They'd just had another frank exchange of views, and the TV had miraculously "jumped" in the way when the ammunition had started flying.

Izzy made a quick note —'*TV damaged when a vodka bottle inadvertently slipped from Jonny's hand*'.

'Anything else I need to tell them?'

Was it too much to ask that the TV was the only casualty?

'The mirror's got a bit of a crack too, Jilly lobbed a bottle of tequila at me, I ducked, and…' He gave a shrug, as if no further words were necessary. 'Fatima Whitbread would have been proud of that shot at the Olympics.'

'And you're sure that's everything?'

On principle, she refused to see the funny side of the "Fatima Whitbread" comment, but at least the rest of the lounge remained intact.

'How much more do you bloody want, Izzy?' Jonny demanded. 'Just because you and lover-boy Costello have had words, there is no need to get sarky with me.'

He couldn't be serious; lover-boy Costello!

'And don't be starting anything with Terry.' He was stalking back towards the door. 'Jack doesn't like any fraternising between employees. Remember the shit-storm Angie stirred up between Scottie and Kathy.'

'I can assure you I am not "fraternising" with anybody; least of all Terry Costello!' she yelled back; her raised voice earning her a one-fingered salute from Jonny's departing figure.

Still fizzing with anger, she picked up the telephone receiver, and punched zero for an outside line. How could that arsehole even suggest such a thing?

6.14 PM

'Right, it's time to spill the beans. I've just overheard an extremely juicy titbit of gossip about the lovely Miss Stevenson.'

'What kind of gossip about me?' Izzy's eyes widened in shock, as she allowed Kathy inside the office. Had Terry decided to shoot his mouth off, after all? Let slip about her swimming lessons, or worse, that he'd seen her leaving Rick's suite early this morning?

'And what's with all the added security? Kathy inclined her head towards the door as she flopped down into a chair. 'Your office door is never kept locked.'

'Sorry, I must have snibbed it by mistake.' Izzy retreated to her seat, and pretended to fiddle with some papers. But there had been no mistake. She'd locked the door deliberately after Jonny's departure, terrified Mr Costello might pay a return visit.

Kathy tossed tonight's dinner, courtesy of the local '*Kentucky Fried Chicken*' outlet, into Izzy's lap.

'Jeez, that's better. My feet are bloody freezing.' Her boots had been toed off and Kathy was now flexing her sock-clad feet against the two bars of Izzy's electric heater. 'Anyway, you and I are supposed to be best mates? Why am I the last to know? I need details, Miss Stevenson.'

'Details?' Izzy asked.

'About what's going on with you and Terry, of course?' Kathy opened the polystyrene container sitting in her lap, and drew out a large chicken drumstick, eyeing it like a lion that hadn't seen a decent wildebeest in weeks. 'I'm so ready for this.'

Izzy's skin crawled at the mention of Terry's name. 'Nothing's going on.' She kept her tone neutral.

'Sure about that?' Kathy chomped into the chicken with relish. 'Shit, this tastes good,' she said, licking the grease from her fingers. 'I overhead Jonny and Terry chatting earlier, Jonny mentioned something about walking in on a lover's tiff—his words not mine—so what gives?'

A full-scale cross-examination was mere seconds away, Izzy knew it. The light bulb in Kathy's eyes had been switched on and was shining directly in her face.

She took a tiny nibble of the burger in her hand before setting it down on her lap.

'Jonny walked in on us having a slight disagreement. That's all. It certainly wasn't some kind of lover's tiff; far from it.'

'Then why did Terry drop a couple of none-too-subtle indications that there might be something more going on. Answer me that?'

'He did what?' Izzy's jaw slackened in disbelief.

'Unless I heard it all wrong, he was definitely hinting that you two might be indulging in a bit of horizontal jogging, in the not-too-distant future,' Kathy wiggled her eyebrows, 'if, he played his cards right. Terry's words not mine.'

The tiny morsel of chicken Izzy had been chewing momentarily lodged in her throat. She reached for her can of *Pepsi*, gulping down a large mouthful of the fizzy liquid, trying hard not to choke.

How dare he insinuate such a thing? But then, given the loathsome individual he was, should she really be surprised?

'He was just winding Jonny up.' Izzy gave a dismissive shake of the head.

'So you're not...'

Izzy was treated to more wiggling eyebrows from Kathy.

'I've just said so, haven't I? And before your imagination starts running wild, I certainly don't fancy him.'

'Well, I did wonder, given how much you have the hots for Rick.'

'Nor, do I have the hots for Rick, either.' Izzy ground out.

'And as I've told you, I don't believe a word.' Kathy gave a maddening smile. 'But we're straying from the point. So, for the record, it's not true; you and Terry?'

'How many more times do I have to say it?' Izzy threw up her hands in frustration. 'There is no me and Terry. Not now. Not ever!'

Kathy let out a relieved sigh and, without looking, expertly tossed the now-stripped chicken leg in the waste bin. 'Thank God!'

'Excuse me; you were practically buying a hat for our "wedding" two minutes ago.'

'Eh yeah …I'm sorry about that.' Kathy gave an apologetic smile. 'To be honest, Izzy, I was totally floored when I heard what they were saying. You know Terry's less than spotless reputation around the ladies.'

'Of course, I've got eyes and ears, remember.'

'And the thought that you—of all people—might suddenly be interested in him…' Kathy paused, before continuing in hushed tones, her eyes trained on the closed door as though it might burst open any second. 'I got this from Scottie, so don't repeat a word. According to him, Terry's into some seriously weird stuff in the bedroom. Not just your average bit of rough sex. We're talking the whole BDSM scene. You know whips, chains and manacles. And while a bit of variety can be okay, there are limits…'

It was Kathy's turn to blush beetroot red. 'Terry gets a real kick out of inflicting pain and lots of it. He's not someone to be mixed up with.'

'You don't say.' Izzy's tone was decidedly dry, 'and you seriously thought—even for a second—that I might be into that sort of thing too.'

'Well no…' Kathy reached for her boots and began pulling them on, not looking Izzy in the eye. 'You've never given that impression, but you're not exactly one of life's open books either. I've got to prise everything out of you.'

'Jeez, just because I don't shout my private life from the roof tops doesn't mean I'm a closet whip-welding dominatrix.'

For several seconds there was an uncomfortable silence between them, before Izzy let out a sigh. Maybe, it was time for her to let down the drawbridge. Open up a little. Tell Kathy about the real situation with Terry, get her take on it, but only if she could be trusted not to blab to all and sundry.

'So, given what you've just said, what's your honest opinion of Terry?' she asked.

'The truth or what I tell Scottie?'

Izzy just looked at her, eyebrows raised.

'Terry Costello scares the crap out of me,' Kathy answered. 'I don't know for certain, but there was a rumour that he was behind Angie's departure, but it was always denied. But then, as I've told you, Angie and I were never bosom buddies, after I caught her and Scottie in our bed.'

Terry playing a part in Angie's departure didn't surprise Izzy in the slightest. She moistened her lips. 'Then, if I tell you something, can I trust you not to repeat it, and definitely not to Scottie?'

'Izzy, you should know by now, there are loads of things I don't tell Scottie.'

Kathy leaned forward, head to the side looking expectant, but Izzy was still debating how much to divulge. It went without saying the swimming lessons and massages were definitely off-limits—Kathy would light up like the Blackpool Illuminations if she got wind of either—but she desperately needed some advice.

'Somehow I've got myself into a really awkward situation with Terry, and I've no idea how to get out of it,' Izzy admitted. 'That's what Jonny walked in on.'

With that, she filled Kathy in on all her conversations with Terry to date, before rolling up her sleeve and showing off the angry bruise that had developed around her elbow where he'd grabbed it. Kathy's eyebrows shot upwards, as Izzy outlined all the things Terry had said to her.

'So, was that why the door was locked? In case he popped back with some of his toys for a trial run?' Kathy shook her head. 'Shit, Izzy, why did you keep this to yourself? You should have told me, sooner!'

'Naively, I thought he might have forgotten,' Izzy admitted. 'Convinced myself it was all a bad joke. But then this afternoon, I finally realised he was deadly serious, and the joke's entirely on me.'

'You have to tell Jack.'

'Kathy, I wasn't going to tell you until two minutes ago. I was convinced you were big mates with the man.'

'I only pretend because of Scottie,' Kathy confessed, 'figure it's safer that way.'

'And what good would it do telling Jack?' Izzy's shoulders slumped. 'He's miles away in London, and anyway, Terry's his right-hand man. Jack must know what Mr Costello's like, given he's been with them since the year dot. And if I said anything, it would be my word against his. Terry's in a position of real power. I'd just be seen as some kind of troublemaker.'

Especially if, as a consequence of her making a complaint, Jack decided to investigate her fictitious background and found out the truth.

Taking a deep breath, Izzy got to her feet, binning the remnants of her burger. 'Look, there's nothing else for it, I just need to keep avoiding Terry as much as possible until the end of the tour. That's what I've been trying to do so far. What do you think?'

Kathy didn't reply for a long moment, looking up to the ceiling and tapping her finger on her chin.

'Look, what about saying something to Rick?' She suggested at length.

'Rick? No, I really can't…'

Why on earth had Kathy suggested Rick of all people?

'Hear me out.' Kathy waved her silent. 'He's the one decent guy around here. Remember how great he was when you were ill? Strike that, he's lovely to his "pretty lady" *all* the time. A girl can get jealous you know.' Kathy rolled her eyes comically. 'But I'm sure, if he knew Terry was harassing you, he'd step in. Have a quiet word.'

Izzy thought over what Kathy had said for a brief moment. Telling Rick had briefly crossed her mind too. After all, Kathy was merely voicing Rick's own offer, from weeks ago. Should she call in that favour? They had a lesson was pencilled in for later. That would give her an opportunity to raise the subject.

Or should she? Something held her back. Did Rick really need—or want—her running to him with out-of-school tales about Terry Costello? Rick had enough on his plate at the moment: what with the wedding; managing his insomnia; and reaching a final decision on his future with the band.

Plus, just like speaking to Jack, there was still the chance that her real identity might— somehow—tumble out in the wash. And, no matter how small the risk, that wasn't one she couldn't afford to take.

No, on balance, telling Rick was a non-starter.

Izzy shook her head, her mind made up. 'I can't. I've imposed enough on his good nature.'

'Well, I guess you know best.' Kathy patted her shoulder. 'But, don't worry, as of now, Kathy Davies has got your back.'

11.36 PM

'Okay, Izzy, that was great!'

She was rewarded with another of Rick's pulse-rocketing smiles.

'We'll try one more length, and then call it a night. Are you up for it?'

Izzy nodded, but failed to share his obvious enthusiasm. Given she'd just swum a whole length of the pool—unassisted—she should be swinging from the rafters in unparalleled joy, but truth be told, she felt anything but joyful. Her mind was still too full of the conversations with Terry and Kathy, their words repeating on one endless loop in her brain.

Looking up, she caught Rick scrutinising her closely. He'd been doing that a lot tonight. No doubt, wondering what had got into her. She knew she'd been unusually quiet. Strike that, she'd been downright standoffish; failing to engage in any of their usual teasing banter. Worse, she'd taken to physically distancing herself if he got too close, worried that Terry might be lurking in the shadows, taking in their every move and dreaming up even more repulsive things he'd like to subject her to—if he got half a chance!

'Izzy, is everything okay?' He laid a gentle hand on her arm and, instantly, Izzy went rigid, before jerking away from his touch.

'Look, if you're still pissed about me calling so late last night—' His brows knitted together; those deep brown eyes searching her face.

'Of course I'm not upset about that. Don't be so ridiculous!' Izzy cut him off, then immediately regretted the sharpness in her tone. 'Look, Rick, I've told you, I'm on call whenever you need me,' her voice softened, 'no matter the time of night. I've just got a bit of a headache; that's all. I've not been able to shake it off all day.'

It goes by the name of Terry Costello.

'Then, do you want to stop?'

'Please, if you don't mind.'

Without awaiting his reply, she waded towards the nearest ladder, and quickly hauled herself out of the water, leaving Rick to follow.

Reaching for the towel laying on the nearby lounger, he wrapped it around her shoulders.

'Don't worry; we can take up where we left off, next time,' He began to rub her arms dry. 'You're doing really well!' She received a bone-melting smile.

Very deliberately, Izzy took a step backwards out of his reach.

'Thanks. But if you don't mind, I can dry myself, Rick.' Her voice held a trace of impatience.

Was Terry getting off on the little floorshow they were providing?

Glancing up she caught the momentary look of puzzlement—or could it be hurt—that flickered across Rick's face, and instantly she felt contrite. What she'd said had been rude and unnecessary. The last thing she wanted to do was upset this wonderful, sexy man who was always so kind and patient with her. She'd no right to take her bad mood out on him.

'I'm sorry. It's just the headache talking. Please ignore me. Do you need me to pop along later?' she tagged on a half-hearted smile.

'Nope, funnily enough, tonight's swim seems to have done the trick.' He rolled his neck. 'But it looks like I should be returning the favour. I'm sure massage must be great for headaches too. Want me to give it a go?'

Izzy shook her head. 'That's a very kind offer, but not necessary. Look, I'll be off. See you in the morning.'

Wrapping the towel tighter about her shoulders, she made to walk away, but Rick snagged her arm, tugging her gently back to face him.

'Izzy, are you sure I haven't done anything to upset you?'

She tried to avoid that searching gaze, those eyes that seemed to take in everything, leaving her feeling suddenly exposed and vulnerable.

'Shit, if I've … maybe touched you,' he gestured towards her lower body with his hand 'then I apologise. It was completely by accident.' He began. 'Seriously Izzy, I don't want you thinking I'm some kind of pervert. I'd never do anything—'

'Don't be silly, I know you wouldn't,' she jumped in hastily, 'you're always the perfect gentleman.'

More's the pity!

Again, for the briefest of moments, the thought of telling him crossed her mind, the words hovering on the tip of her tongue. Then she backtracked, her nerve deserting her. Rick's problems were in a whole different league. Way more important than her issues with Terry. And what could Rick do, anyway? Probably nothing, except make a bad situation potentially catastrophic if the real Izzy Anderson was accidently unveiled in the process.

'I'd like to think that we've become good friends, Izzy.' He moistened his lips. 'That with the lessons and everything else, we've moved way beyond you being just my employee.'

'Of course we have.'

His acknowledgement of their friendship warmed her insides. It felt so good to hear he now looked on her in that way. Then her conscience chose to kick in. Friends didn't spy on each other.

'But I can tell something's eating up my pretty lady. And it looks way more than just a headache.' He gave her a tentative smile, reaching out to cup her cheek. 'And I was told that a problem shared…'

She'd been hoisted by her own petard.

'It's nothing you need worry about, Rick. I promise.' Izzy answered, fighting the overwhelming urge to lean into the protection of that hand.

'I've heard Marc mouthing off over Sabrina's birthday. Acting like a total dick as per usual. If he's giving you a hard time…'His thumb had started to stroke her skin and, as always, prickles of awareness shot down Izzy's spine. 'I can have a word with him. Believe me; the way he's been throwing his weight around lately, it would give me the greatest of pleasure.' His eyes twinkled with amusement. 'I'd even punch him, but only if you really wanted me to.'

'Punching your cousin is definitely off limits, Rick,' she insisted, finding the strength pull away from the tenderness of his touch.

'And what about Terry,' Rick continued to scrutinize her, 'has he stopped making a nuisance of himself?'

Terry! Where had that totally left-field question come from? Had Jonny said something about finding her and Terry alone together?

'Eh, yes, everything's good in that department.' Somehow, the lie tripped glibly off her tongue. 'You could say we finally understand each other.'

32

PITTSBURGH, PENNSYLVANIA

'Don't tell me you're still locked out?' Izzy had arrived outside Jonny's suite to be met with more yelling between him and Jilly, Jonny trying—unsuccessfully—to gain access to his clothes.

After a second sell out night in Detroit, they'd arrived in Pittsburgh, but only just. A massive snowstorm had blown up prior to their departure from Michigan, making it too dangerous to fly, and leaving no option but to cover the intervening two hundred and ninety miles by road.

During that car journey, hostilities had broken out again between Jonny and Jilly, culminating in a foul-mouthed argument between the two in the lobby of their Pittsburgh Hotel; Jilly finally delivering a nifty right hook to Jonny's face, before storming off upstairs and barricading herself inside their suite.

After a further two-hour slanging match, conducted through their suite door—with Jonny stuck outside in the corridor—the guitarist had been left with no option but to spend an uncomfortable night on Davey's sofa.

Having witnessed most of the drama, Izzy estimated it would take more than a new pair of sexy undies to win Jilly around this time.

'Thanks for stating the fucking obvious, Izzy.' Jonny delivered another vicious thump to the door with his fist. 'Jilly, open the fucking door now or I'll kick it in. Do you hear me?'

'Piss off!' was the immediate response from his fiancée.

'Jonny, please stop!' Izzy laid a restraining hand on his arm. 'We can't afford to replace a door next. I've only just settled the invoice for the TV and the mirror.'

'Not funny, Izzy; I couldn't give a shit how much this costs me' he snarled, his foot now making contact with the wood. 'Jilly, I'm warning you. I want my clothes, now.'

'If you take one step inside this room, Jonathan Hambro, I'll throw the contents of your suitcase out the window into the snow. Do you hear me?'

Izzy groaned inwardly. She could just picture the scene; Jonny's clothing floating serenely down onto the sidewalk, and being leapt on by a pack of rabid teens. Worse, it would be down to her to try to retrieve them, and Eclectic Deviation fans didn't give up their spoils easily. She'd learnt that the hard way, receiving a split lip when trying to repatriate a pair of Steve's sunglasses.

'Why don't you let me talk to her?' Izzy suggested.

After another couple of harsh bangs, more in frustration than anything else, Jonny finally admitted defeat.

'Feel free,' he delivered with a sarcastic little bow, allowing Izzy to take his place.

She gave the door a gentle knock. 'Hi Jilly, it's Izzy. Is there anything I can do to help?'

She felt, rather than saw, Jonny's eye roll.

'If that's your opening gambit, I doubt I'll get my fucking clothes this side of Christmas! Just tell her to open the bloody door!'

'And you can tell my fiancé, he can go to Hell!' the banshee shrieked back.

Izzy turned back to Jonny. 'Look, you're not helping the situation. Why don't you go back to Davey's room? Let things cool down a bit for now?'

'I'm not coming out until that bastard apologises, Izzy.' Jilly was in no mood to compromise.

The furious look on Jonny's face told Izzy that an apology wouldn't be forthcoming from that direction any time soon.

'If my memory serves me correctly, I apologised—several times—darling!' he thundered, 'and that's all you're getting out of me.'

'You call those snivelling attempts to justify your disgusting behaviour, an apology?' Jilly gave a derisive laugh. 'I want a proper one!'

'Then you'll be waiting for a cold day in Hell!'

Izzy saw red. Jonny was currently missing an interview due to this nonsense. The official line being he was "indisposed". At this moment, she could cheerfully *dispose* of the pair of them. 'Not another word, Jonny. Go!' She pointed towards Davey's suite.

Most surprisingly, after a couple more choice expletives, Jonny did as he'd been told; the door to Davey's suite slammed shut behind him.

'Jilly, he's gone now,' she relayed.

'Good.'

But there was still no move to let Izzy inside.

'Jilly, please let me in. I really want to help.'

After another brief pause, she finally heard movement inside Jonny's suite. It sounded like a heavy piece of furniture being scraped across the floor, then the key rasped in the lock and the door swung open.

Jilly stood before her, channelling a very convincing impersonation of *Alice Cooper's* more attractive baby sister. Tears, mascara and blue eye shadow streaked over her lovely face.

'Why is he being such a bastard, Izzy?'

The screaming 'fish-wife' of two minutes ago had vanished, leaving a truly pathetic creature in her wake.

Stepping inside, Izzy picked up a box of tissues from the coffee table, and handed it over. On cue, Jilly burst into uncontrollable sobs, leaving Izzy with no option but to comfort her as best she could.

'I just don't understand it,' Jilly hiccupped at length. 'I caught him with some maid in our bloody bathroom, of all places. He was at it, right under my bloody nose!' She gave a large snort of disgust. 'He didn't even have the decency to take her to a different floor. Then he'd the cheek to tell me it was all a misunderstanding. Said he'd just been asking for clean towels, and *she* jumped him.'

So that was the story. Jonny was reverting to type as usual.

'I don't know why he feels the need to shag every female in sight? It's not as if I keep him short of sex.'

Izzy wasn't sure she was qualified to answer that question, settling for a diplomatic, 'Mmmm' instead.

Jilly wiped her eyes, calmer now after five solid minutes of tears and snot.

'Is it always going to be like this? Me forced to look the other way like Caron and Francesca? Humiliated, every time there's another story splashed across the tabloids?'

She blew her nose loudly, before giving her long curtain of blonde hair a dramatic toss. Shades of the real Jilly were re-asserting themselves. 'Well, I've had enough. I deserve better.'

Hallelujah, the real Jilly had re-entered the building. Her "Road to Damascus" moment had arrived— at last—far as Jonny Hambro was concerned.

'Leopards never change their spots.' Jilly's crystal blue eyes fell onto her suitcase by the bed. 'I want to go home. Can you arrange a flight for me, Izzy? This afternoon, if possible?'

'I'll see what I can do. Obviously, it depends on the forecasted blizzard, but I'll do my very best to get you on the first flight out.'

Jilly gave her a grateful smile, something Izzy had never received before.

'Thanks Izzy.' Jilly fiddled with her engagement ring for a few seconds. 'Can I ask you something?'

'Of course, fire away?'

'Was it you who came up with the idea behind the roses? You know the red ones meaning "I love you" and the single yellow rose signifying "I miss you"?'

'Eh, not exactly, I can't take full credit.' Izzy's cheeks flushed, knowing her admission might land Jonny in it even further. 'It's an old Japanese Flower Custom apparently, and I thought it would be nice—'

'No. Don't say any more.' Jilly held up her hand. 'I might have known it wouldn't be his idea. And I suppose I have to thank you for the grovelling card, too.'

Very reluctantly, Izzy nodded her assent.

The final nails had just been hammered into Jonny's metaphorical coffin. Unfortunately, it was at that moment, he chose to re-enter the room.

Jilly's eyes alighted on an ash tray on the table. Without a word, she scooped it up, and took aim.

'You lying, cheating bastard!' she screamed, launching her missile directly at Jonny's head.

He ducked just in time, and the lump of glass made a resounding thump against the far wall, shattering into a million pieces.

Much to Izzy's relief, another mirror had been missed by a good six inches.

'That's it.' Jilly wrenched off the engagement ring. 'As of now, we're officially over, Jonathan Hambro.'

'Good evening, it's your friendly pizza delivery service,' Izzy announced, as the door swung open to Marc's suite, her arms laden with the large pizza boxes she'd just uplifted from Reception; a gift from the Band's tour Sponsor, *Rock TV*.

The band had retired to Marc's room for a council of war, Jack making his presence felt on speaker phone. But for some reason—and not that she was complaining in the slightest—Izzy hadn't been asked to attend and take notes. No doubt it would be some pretentious idea Marc had dreamed up and was trying to sell to the others. Then, she'd be wheeled in at the eleventh hour, told to get the old magic wand out, and actually make his next "big idea" come to fruition.

'Cut the comedy routine, Izzy. I'm not in the fucking mood.' Davey scowled at her. 'You can leave the bloody pizzas and get out.'

Then without waiting to be asked, Davey grabbed the top-most box from the pile and retreated to the sofa.

Izzy could sense a definite chill in the air. There had clearly been words already. Choosing to ignore Davey's petulant behaviour, she placed the pizzas on the table where Steve, Jonny and Marc were congregated.

'The card says with the compliments of *RockTV*, in recognition of an extremely successful tour, to date,' she explained, before directing a comment to the speaker phone. 'Hi, Jack. Sorry, but no pizza for you, today.'

'Not a problem, Izzy.' He let out a loud chuckle. 'As long as they keep sponsoring us, I'll be happy.'

Izzy looked around room, suddenly realising Rick wasn't there.

'Where's Rick?' she asked Marc.

'Said he was knackered, and headed off to bed.' Marc's lip curled. 'Despite me emphasising the importance of tonight's meeting. Honestly, he's always sloping off to bed these days. He's turned into Rip Van *bloody* Winkle.'

'And always on his own, too,' Jonny commented, retrieving his pizza box. 'He seems to have gone off the old rumpy-pumpy, big time.' He exchanged a wink with Steve. 'Don't think he's been laid since Minnesota. That must be at least twelve whole days without sex. I'd be climbing the walls if it was me!'

'Yeah, for some reason he's suddenly decided to take a vow of fucking celibacy,' Steve replied, and the two men sniggered.' Any longer with this sex drought and his dick will shrivel up and die.'

'Rick's given me his proxy vote,' Marc continued to address Izzy, 'so I don't suppose it matters.'

But Izzy caught the gloating look he now shot Davey. So that's what the argument had been about. The proxy vote hadn't been given to Davey— Rick's future brother-in-law-to-be—and Mr Eastman's nose was seriously out of joint.

'If Rick's pizza is up for grabs,' Davey studiously ignored Marc, 'I'll take it. I could eat a fucking horse tonight.'

So, as well as being in a foul mood, Davey had a touch of the 'munchies', too. A sure sign he'd been over-indulging in the old weed again. It always affected his temper and his appetite. Well, there was no way Izzy was letting him get his thieving hands on Rick's pizza.

Whipping up the remaining box, Izzy turned on her heel and headed back towards the door. 'Don't worry, Davey; I'll drop it off to Rick on my way downstairs. He might not be asleep, yet.'

'Well, if he doesn't want it, bring it back!' Davey yelled after her. 'It's got my fucking name on it.'

'Cheers, Izzy, this is just what the doctor ordered!' Jonny sent her a quick thumbs, mid-munch.

For a man whose engagement had ended less than six hours earlier, he didn't look too devastated by the turn of events. No doubt he'd be expecting Jilly to crawl back on her hands and knees—given the number of times she'd flounced off in the past. But Izzy had a feeling this time was different. Jilly—like the indomitable Mrs Thatcher before her—was in no mood for turning.

Jonny inclined his head towards Marc, who was still scribbling frantically in his notepad.

'Something tells me it's going to be one of "those meetings".'

Picking up his meaning, Izzy gave him the briefest of nods. Jonny was right. Marc had that 'terrier' look about him. The look that said he wasn't about to be thwarted by anyone, no matter what barriers Davey decided to throw up along the way.

'And Izzy, before you disappear, any joy with those tickets?' Marc asked.

Typical! He was back on her case; she'd been asked twice today already.

Izzy let out an irritated sigh. 'As I told you earlier, Marc, the answer is still no. As soon as I have them, you'll be the first to know.'

11.10 PM

'For you,' Izzy held out the pizza box to Rick, 'with the compliments of *RockTV*.'

Her breath caught in her throat. Never mind the pizza, the man standing before her in the open doorway, looked good enough to eat. Just out the shower, his dark hair damp and rumpled, with a white shirt open to the waist over faded *Levi 501s*, positively oozing her kind of sexy with a capital 'S'.

'Marc said you were heading for bed.'

Rick took the box out her hands, eyes lighting up immediately as he flipped the lid back to reveal the steaming food.

'That's what I said to get him off my case,' he admitted with a grin. 'But to be honest, I couldn't face another two hours of him droning on about some new god-forsaken idea, Davey objecting, and then the pair of them going at it hammer and tongs for the rest of the night. I gave him my vote and told him he could do whatever the hell he wanted with it.'

With that, he sniffed at the pizza appreciatively, reminding Izzy of the *Bisto Kids* advert on TV.

'Chicken and pepperoni; this is my absolute favourite, pretty lady.'

'Why do you think I kept this one especially for you?' she flashed a cheeky smile. 'After all, it's my job to know all the band's preferences, remember?'

'Well, you don't know *all* my preferences but, as ever, we'll not go there.' His dark eyes danced with barely concealed amusement. 'Jeez, it must be hours since I've eaten...'

He picked off a large piece of barbeque chicken and popped it in his mouth, before letting out a deep groan of undisguised appreciation. 'That tastes so bloody good.'

'Well enjoy! I need to get back downstairs.' She turned away. 'I'll see you in the morning.'

Rick snagged her arm. 'Not so fast. Aren't you going to stay and share this with me, first?' He indicated the box.

'Much as I'd love to accept the kind invitation, I can't. ' Izzy replied with a sad smile, 'I'm still on the trail of those wretched theatre tickets, remember? I was supposed to call the Box Office in Ottawa at eleven, speak to the manager. I'm ten minutes late, already.'

'You mean you'd rather do that than share my pizza!' he groaned. 'Shit, I must be losing my touch. I don't usually get a knock-back when asking a pretty lady to have dinner with me' He gave her a tiny wink.

'Especially, as you're the only person I'd give my last slice of chicken and pepperoni to!'

That comment made Izzy laugh out loud. He made it sound like the *"Rollo"* Advert. 'Thanks, but if I don't get those tickets, Marc will have *my* head on a platter for *him* to eat.' She made a slicing action across her throat.

'Come on, Izzy,' he cajoled, 'you can make the call from here. I won't tell if you don't. Then we can relax. Enjoy the pizza.' He cocked his head, resorting to a "puppy-dog-eyes" look, his eyelashes fluttering. 'Go on, you know you want to.'

'Okay. You win,' she conceded. Her taste buds were watering in more ways than one. 'I'm rather partial to chicken and pepperoni pizza, myself.'

'Great. Make yourself at home and I'll get some drinks organised.'

She was about to step inside, when a flicker of movement out the corner of her eye made Izzy hesitate, her eyes glancing sideways down the corridor. But there was no one there.

'Something wrong?' Rick asked.

She gave him a dismissive shake of the head before following him inside. But she couldn't dispel that horrible feeling that Terry was watching them again.

33

PITTSBURGH, PENNSYLVANIA

'Come on, Izzy! Are you serious? Not Donny fucking Osmond!' Rick snorted, slapping his thigh in amused disbelief.

'If you tell anybody about my teenage crushes, I'll deny everything.' Izzy shook a remonstrative finger at him, slightly giddy with the amount of wine she'd consumed tonight. She'd gone over her usual two glass quota. This had to be her third or was she onto her fourth now?

Once Izzy had finally made her call—still no joy with the tickets— they'd spent the rest of the time munching on the delicious pizza and downing the extremely good Sauvignon Blanc, Rick had produced from his mini bar.

Izzy glanced down at her watch. 'Jeez, it's quarter to two. I really should get going.'

As always, her time in his company was disappearing, all too quickly.

'Yeah, time flies when you're having fun, ' he grinned, 'but seriously, I never had you down for a "Donny" fan. Brian Ferry, yeah. *Roxy Music* is a class band, but the *Osmonds*—' He pretended to be sick. 'All I can say is thank God your musical tastes have improved with age and you're working with us, now.'

'Donny was a good-looking boy. Still is come to that.' Izzy was unable to stop her lips twitching 'And when he sang *"Puppy Love"* my teenage heart just melted' She pressed a hand to her chest and let out an exaggerated sigh. 'Now, where did I put my boots…?'

Leaning over the arm of the sofa, she began to hunt for the footwear she'd kicked off earlier. 'I've still to double check tomorrow's schedule before I turn in….'

'You are much too dedicated.' He answered. 'Look, the schedule can wait a little longer, surely? We haven't finished the second bottle yet? Who knows what I might get you to admit to with another glass of wine?'

He reached down to pick up the almost finished bottle, but Izzy shook her head, placing a hand over her glass.

'No thanks, I think I've had enough for tonight.' Any more wine and she might admit to something she shouldn't; like her feelings for him…

'Spoil sport.'

There was easy silence between them as Rick poured himself another, but his humour of a few moments earlier had receded slightly. Izzy could see a vee settling between those dark brows.

'How's the neck, tonight?' she asked.

'Its fine' he dismissed, 'but if you've got time, I've been chewing over something I'd like your take on. If that's okay…' He sunk his teeth into his lip.

'Of course it is. Fire away.' She put the ongoing search for her missing boots on hold.

She had feeling she knew what was coming. 'Have you come to a decision about the band?'

'Yeah, I think so.' Rick took a swallow of the wine then fixed her with those melted chocolate eyes.

Staring back into them, Izzy sensed immediately what he was about to say. 'You've decided to leave, haven't you?'

'Yeah, at the end of the tour,' he gave a brief nod, 'it's for the best, Izzy. I know I won't feel any better until I take back some control in my life.' His expression was thoughtful. 'Do you think I'm making a mistake?'

'Rick, it's not what I—or anyone else thinks—that's important here,' she replied. 'It's what you think that matters. What you feel here.' Reaching over, she pressed her hand against his heart to emphasise her point. It jerked under her touch. 'But leaving is so final. Are you sure a permanent break is what you really need?' she asked. 'Wouldn't some kind of a sabbatical make more sense? That would give you some breathing space—say six months—to step away and really consider all your options?'

He rubbed his chin. Her words had clearly struck a chord.

'The sabbatical would certainly be a compromise. I hadn't thought about anything like that. It would give me time to clear all the crap up here.' He tapped his forehead. 'Because all I know is, if I stay put feeling like this, I'll go fucking crazy. Some days, I think I'm half way there already.'

'Then maybe the sabbatical would be the perfect solution.' She smiled. 'Work out what you really want, Rick. Don't just jump ship and then find you've made a colossal mistake.'

'Why are you always right?' he asked, before downing another large mouthful.

'Believe me, I'm not always right.' Her conscience prickled again. 'But I take it you've had some initial thoughts at what you might want to do? I don't see you going back to wiring plugs.'

'Nope, those days are long gone. But I've got a germ of an idea, and if I do leave the band, it wouldn't involve moving away from music.'

'Go on.' Izzy moved closer, resting her chin in her hands.

'I've always wanted to get into the production side of the business. Plough some of my ill-gotten gains into a recording studio. Give other young bands the break we had. You know, produce records that sort of thing. I'm very fond of twiddling little knobs.' He gave her a cheeky wink. 'But you're right, I need time; time to get my head sorted first. Take those 6 months you suggest...'

'And now you've said this out loud, how does it make you feel?' she asked.

'Honestly? Fucking relieved.' He drained the last of his drink, and placed the glass on the floor. 'But I still don't know how I'm going to break it to the lads. This was our dream from the moment we got the band off the ground. But I've had it with life in the goldfish bowl. I need to break free. '

Those dark eyes of his were still pinned on her. A shiver went down Izzy's spine. It felt like he was trying to read her mind.

'I get it,' she said, softly. 'I couldn't live the way you do, with your every move under scrutiny. Being your PA is bad enough, with all the over-the-top attention I get. But I had a funny feeling this could be on the cards, but I didn't want to pry. It's none of my business.'

Great! Yet another Pinocchio moment had just come and gone.

'Izzy, I've made this your business. You know how much I trust you.'

The use of the word *trust* made her stomach sink through the floor.

Rick reached over and took her hands in his, twisting those warm fingers through hers, squeezing tightly.

'It's so easy when we talk. I can say what I feel. Know I won't get any hassles or arguments.'

Was that a subtle dig at his high-maintenance fiancée?

'I'm glad that using me—as a sounding board—helps.' She smiled. 'It's time you made peace with yourself, Rick.'

'Yeah, I guess so.'

'And if you explain how you're feeling to Marc, Jonny and the others, they'll understand,' Izzy went on. 'You five are closer than brothers. In the long run, they'll want what's best for you, I'm certain of it.'

'I hope so.' Rick looked down at their interlinked fingers. His thumb had begun to absently stroke backwards and forwards over her knuckles, sending sparks of electricity to every nerve ending in Izzy's body.

'And, at the end of your sabbatical you might decide to come back,' Izzy reminded him, forcing herself to concentrate on their conversation, not those stroking fingers. 'There might be a way to combine the band, the studio and a private life away from the spotlight.'

'Who knows? Anyway, Marc's always threatening to replace me with a drum machine. He's going to get his wish now.' Rick grimaced.

'And once you speak to Francesca, let her know what you're contemplating. She'll understand too. It will work out. You'll see.'

Although, Izzy got the feeling Francesca might not be very receptive to life out of the spotlight. Worse, she'd go positively stratospheric if she found out Izzy had been in on Rick's secret first.

'Yeah, I know, but it's not something you can blurt out over the telephone. Is it? It's too important. I need to have a face-to-face conversation with her.' He inhaled a large breath. 'I'll tell her when she comes out to New York. One thing for sure, this is going to fuck up her five-year plan.'

'What's that?'

'She has this plan; what we're going to achieve as a couple.' He rolled his eyes dramatically at Izzy. 'Let's just say, it's worse than your bloody schedule, times about one hundred.'

They were both quiet for a few moments, Rick's eyes looking off into the distance, his thumb continuing its hypnotic caress across her knuckles.

'One thing's for sure, I'll need to be out of London to do my thinking,' he spoke up at length, 'too bloody claustrophobic. Between the press and the kids camped permanently on my doorstep, I won't get a minute's peace. I've got this mate whose dad's a builder. Last time we met up, he spoke about them working on a development of luxury villas outside Southampton; all with stunning views overlooking the Solent. Maybe I'll rent one—if my tax exile status lets me.'

'That sounds a great idea,' she agreed. 'Hampshire is beautiful, and my…someone I used to know lived there,' she corrected quickly.

Rick had met her Hampshire-based uncle on that holiday fifteen years ago.

'Izzy, you'll keep all this to yourself, won't you?'Suddenly his grip tightened; his expression urgent. 'This can't leak out. Not even accidently. Not to anybody. Understand?'

'You know I won't say a word.'

She felt physically sick as the lie passed her lips; hating the subterfuge and knowing she was duty bound to tell Betty.

It was all she could do not to shudder as he lifted both hands and kissed the backs of her fingers. The touch of those firm lips against her skin making the blood throb in her veins.

'Being able to talk like this,' he went on, 'it's like having Michelle around, except you aren't quite so blunt with me.'

'It's all part of the Izzy magic,' she answered.

Great! She reminded him of his sister, again.

'You're the type of girl a guy could fall for—very easily.'

Somehow, during their conversation, the distance between them on the sofa had narrowed; both facing each other. She watched as his eyes lowered, and for a second she was certain his gaze rested on her lips. Her pulse surged. Why had he looked at her mouth? Was he…?

No, totally impossible. Don't be Daft, Izzy!

And yet, she could feel her breath becoming shallower, unable to tear herself away from those mesmerising eyes opposite, and the way they held hers captive.

Why could neither of them look away? Her eyelids began to flicker lower, her body swaying forwards. If only he would kiss her…

There was a colossal bang on the door, followed by an irate bellow from Davey. 'Open the fucking door, Rick!'

Several more loud thumps ensued, harder than the first. 'Or do I have to smash it to bloody smithereens to get some attention around here?'

Rick's head snapped sideways, looking towards the door, frowning hard.

With Rick distracted, Izzy pulled her hands free and jumped to her feet. It took less than a second to locate her discarded boots from under the sofa and tug them on.

'I need to go' she said unnecessarily.

'Shit.' Rick had flopped backwards onto the cushions, eyes glaring upwards at the ceiling. 'What the hell does he want?'

'Do you hear me?' Davey's decibels had increased further.

'There's a good chance the dead can fucking hear you, Davey!' Rick yelled back.

Izzy had made it to the door. 'Don't worry; I'll let in "Raging Bull" on my way out.'

'Look, Izzy. Wait a minute, please—'

But the door was already open, Davey bulldozing his way inside.

'That's it! I've had it with Marc. Either he backs down this time, or I'm walking.' he blustered. 'And, as God is my witness, I'll rip his fucking head off before I do it!'

He kicked out a chair in his temper sending it flying. 'Why the hell did you give him your proxy vote! Shit, I'll be your brother-in-law in just under three months. That vote's supposed to be mine, mate!' Davey sucked in a breath. 'Do you have any idea what that idiot wants to do now? Who he wants to install—permanently—on the bloody payroll…'

He trailed off, turning to glower at Izzy. 'What the fuck is she doing in here?' He jerked his thumb in her direction.

'It's alright, Davey.' Izzy knew she'd outstayed her welcome. 'I'm just leaving.'

2.48 AM

Lying in bed, Izzy couldn't stop thinking about what had happened in those intense few moments in Rick's suite.

Had they really been on the verge of kissing?

Nope, definitely not, Izzy! Don't be so stupid!

It was just her over-active imagination playing games; putting two and two together and coming up with an answer that made absolutely no sense, whatsoever. Why would he even contemplate kissing someone like her? He didn't think of her in that way. Hadn't he said, she reminded him of Michelle? His little sister! All thoughts of them kissing were in her mind. It was just her desperate need to see feelings on his part that weren't there.

He doesn't go for the sweet and wholesome type. Her knickers were perfectly safe from any interference by Richard Hambro. And that bit about her being the type of girl a guy could fall for easily? Huh, just empty words. He'd been talking about guys in general, not himself.

Izzy struggled into a sitting position, flicked on the bedside lamp and buried her head in her hands, letting out a frustrated groan.

Nope, she'd never be anything more than a surrogate sister to Rick. A substitute sounding board, just as Betty had wanted. And okay, he might tease and get flirty with her, but it was only ever done in a jokey way. He'd be shocked if he thought she actually took any of it seriously. She had to stop over-thinking those few minutes in his room or she'd drive herself crazy. When it mattered—in the pool or while she was massaging him—he'd never crossed that invisible line of propriety. And that was because he'd didn't want to cross it—full stop!

34

CHARLESTON, WEST VIRGINIA

Another little cross was appended to the date on the calendar, before Izzy hurriedly reached over to quell the insistent ringing of her telephone.

The days were flying by now, New York drawing ever closer and the band's three night date with destiny at Madison Square Garden. Next stop was Toronto—with Ottawa hard on its heels—and she'd still had no joy with those theatre tickets. Marc was going to kill her.

'Hello, is that you, Izzy?'

'Hi…. Betty.' Izzy cast a quick glance over her shoulder, checking no one was around. Then she noticed the office door lying slightly ajar.

Damn! She couldn't take the chance of someone—especially Rick—inadvertently barging in from the dressing room beyond, and overhearing their conversation.

'Just give me a sec; I need to close the door.'

Within seconds, she'd dealt with the door and Izzy could relax. 'So, how are you, Betty? It's just under a month until New York. Are you and Jim getting excited?'

'Yes, I suppose we are.' For some reason Betty sounded strangely deflated, not her usual chatty self. 'Look, love, could I have a quick word with Richard. Is he about?'

'I'm sorry. They're currently tied up with some media commitments out in the auditorium,' Izzy explained. 'But they need to finish up any minute for the sound check. Could I get him to call you back in an hour? I'm afraid it's the best I can do.'

'Typical. He's never around when I need him!' was Betty's irritated reply.

Something was definitely up in the "Betty" camp.

'Sorry, Izzy, that was uncalled for. Let's just say, I'm rapidly losing patience with my daughter-in-law-to-be.'

And without further prompting, Betty launched into an account of her latest altercation with Francesca, repeating word for word the vulgar names she'd just been called earlier in the afternoon.

'Honestly, it's got to the stage we feel like boycotting the wedding. But we can't, he's our only son.' She exhaled a loud huff. 'The latest is that we can't stay at the castle. Suddenly, there aren't enough rooms apparently, and because Francesca has the larger family—and needs every last one of them dancing attendance on the day—she thinks the Hambros should book into some hole-in-the-wall affair five miles down the bloody road.'

The Lisbon *Intercontinental* wasn't what Izzy would call "some hole-in-the-wall" hotel, but she could see Betty's point.

'But isn't Michelle one of Francesca's bridesmaids?' Izzy queried.

At the last count, there were five bridesmaids, four ushers, three flower girls and a couple of page boys. A partridge in the pear tree would have been the cue for a song. Francesca didn't subscribe to the 'less is more' concept.

'Yes. But for all Francesca cares, my daughter can get dressed by herself, then jump on a bloody donkey and make her own way to the registry office.'

'But that's part of the fun, getting ready with the other bridesmaids. Having your hair and make-up done together. Getting the first glimpse of the bride in her dress and drinking gallons of champagne; it's tradition.' Izzy could feel herself growing annoyed on Michelle's behalf.

'Exactly, but according to Francesca, with the cast of thousands already on board, our Michelle is suddenly surplus to requirements. Lord knows why she even asked her to be a bridesmaid in the first place.' Betty clicked her tongue in exasperation. 'And given the fact I just heard we nearly didn't have a wedding—by the way, thank you for stepping in and fixing things, love—I'm at the end of my tether.'

'Well, I suppose we all make mistakes,' Izzy felt bound to point out, even if Francesca's had been a pretty monumental one. 'I don't suppose it's very easy organising a wedding when your fiancé is half way round the world.'

'No,' Betty conceded, 'but I'd be happier if she'd just get the basics right first, instead of worrying about all the fancy extras. Every week it's something new. She fails to see it's about commitment, love and putting the other person first. And I've seen precious little evidence of Francesca putting Richard first since they got together! It's what *she* wants every time, and Richard just meekly goes along with it. He's not paying attention to what she's doing.'

All of which was true, but then Rick had much bigger things on his mind than worrying about doves, bridesmaids and wedding favours.

'This is a terrible thing to say,' Betty continued, 'but I think she's more in love with his money, than the man himself. And ever since he met her, our Richard's changed. He's become hard and cynical; just like her! We hardly ever see him and when we do, she's always in tow. Making sure he only says what she wants us to hear.'

Betty was on a roll this afternoon. 'She's not what Jim and I imagined for him. In fact, Francesca—and that whole ghastly family of hers—leaves a lot to be desired.'

Silently Izzy agreed, but outwardly she said, 'Maybe once the dust settles, things will get better.'

'I doubt it. When Richard was home at Christmas, he said the band is booked solid until next September, what with recording another album and then more touring. I don't know how he's going to cope without some proper rest. And now with him relying on *Teraxapen* to sleep…..'

Izzy knew she had so much more to tell Betty, but time had caught up with her again.

'When they're married, we'll probably see even less of him, not to mention any children they might have.' There was a catch in Betty's voice. 'Although, according to Francesca, children won't be on the cards for at least another five years; Jim and I will be past it by then.' Her voice wavered again. 'And I know Richard's desperate for his own family.'

In her mind Izzy could picture two beautiful dark-eyed children—a boy and a girl—running at Rick's heels before being swung up into his arms; all of them laughing.

'But will Francesca make a great mother?' Betty ploughed on. 'I doubt it; given how that sister of hers—Caron—is dragging up Rosie. Jim has warned me not to interfere any further. As you know, it was almost divorce before he finally agreed to you getting involved. But how can I stand back? Richard might be twenty-eight next month, but I'm his mother. I worry. It's what mums do. It's in the small print.'

Rick's birthday was another entry on Izzy's "Still to Be Organised" list.

There was a knock and the door opened, Lindsay poking his head inside. Izzy could almost discern the steam coming seeping out from his ears.

'Marc wants you, *now*!' he barked without preamble.

Izzy rolled her eyes. What earth-shattering disaster had occurred now? If it was those tickets again, she'd swing for him…

'Look, I'm sorry, but I'm going to have cut short our phone call.'

She gave Lindsay a quick thumbs-up sign, and he withdrew, muttering oaths under his breath.

'I've just been summoned to see your nephew. But before I go…' Izzy took a deep breath. After the day from Hell Betty had just described, Rick's mother deserved a bit of good news.

'Rick's stopped taking the *Teraxapen*.'

There was a pause from Betty, then, 'He has? Are you sure, Izzy?'

'Yes, because I flushed every last one of them down the toilet,' Izzy informed her triumphantly. 'Not that I've shared that with Rick yet. I've got him trying something else, something that appears to be working much better. Touch wood.' She rubbed her temple to back up her words.

'And what's that, love?'

Momentarily, Izzy wondered about Betty's reaction when she came clean about the "something else".

'Massage.'

'*Massage*!' The other woman's consternation was clear; definitely not what Betty had been expecting to hear.

'Don't worry, it's nothing dodgy like their exploits last year,' Izzy was quick to reassure her.

'You mean you've hired some kind of physiotherapist?'

'Well, not exactly. Rick wasn't very keen on that idea.' Izzy paused. 'So, for the moment, he's agreed to me doing it, with a view to maybe hiring a professional in future.'

However, their initial week's experiment had expanded, somewhat. For some reason, Rick was still dragging his heels on the "hiring" front.

'You are?' For a second Betty sounded a little taken aback, but then appeared to recover. 'Oh yes, I recall Mary mentioned something about you doing a course…'

'Yes, it was a pretty basic one, and I didn't finish it, but I know roughly what I'm doing. And, while I don't want to tempt fate, I think the massage is working. He's sleeping again, Betty...'

There was another knock at the door; louder this time.

It was Lindsay again, and given the venomous look he fired off in her direction, he was less than enamoured to find Izzy still on the telephone.

'Marc is doing my fucking head in, Izzy!' he spat out, making no concession to who might be on the other end of the line. 'Can you get your arse out here and deal with him, *NOW*? He won't listen to a bloody word I say.'

'Okay, I'm just coming.' Izzy sent him a placating smile.

It didn't work; the door was slammed so hard, its vibration made her coffee cup jump in its saucer.

'Look, Betty, I really need to go….' Izzy got to her feet.

It was time to wind up their conversation, now that World War Three had kicked off next door.

'Things sound a bit tense over there,' Betty commented.

'Yes just a bit. Look, we'll talk again soon, but please stop worrying. Everything's good with Rick. I'll get him to call you, later.'

35

CHARLESTON, WEST VIRGINIA

WEDNESDAY 13 MARCH 1985 - 8.36AM

Davey, in dark sunglasses, was bearing down on her.

Great! First member of the band down to breakfast and, given the presence of the sunshades, he was clearly nursing the "mother and father" of all hangovers.

'Want some coffee?' Izzy asked, picking up the coffee pot, but not bothering to lower her voice. If it hurt him—tough!

Davey merely grunted what she took to be an affirmative, slumping into the chair opposite and shoving an empty cup across the table to her.

'Good party?' she asked, pouring out the coffee.

But she should have known better.

No reply was forthcoming. Instead, Davey merely took back his cup, chugged down a large mouthful of the liquid, before holding out his right hand. She knew his 'hangover' routine off by heart. He needed painkillers. A jackhammer was going off inside his skull and medication was required before he could even begin to function like any normal human being. There would be no attempt at conversation until the headache situation had been rectified. Delving into her handbag, she extracted two *paracetamol* tabs and dropped them into his outstretched palm.

These were washed down with another mouthful of coffee before Davey finally uttered his first words. 'God, I feel like fucking shit, man.'

Lovely choice of words, Davey!

He wasn't getting any sympathy from her.

A waitress appeared to take his breakfast order, but Davey waved away all suggestions of food, opting instead for another pot of strong black coffee.

From past experience, Izzy knew it took at least two to three cups to get him back to the land of the living.

'I've got two things I need you to do, Izzy.' He'd fished out his lighter and a packet of Marlboro Lights from his jacket pocket. Extracting a cigarette, and popping it between his lips, he lit up before continuing.

'First, tell that dickhead of a singer from our so-called support act to stop eyeballing me.' He exhaled a large cloud of white smoke in her direction.

Izzy wrinkled her nose, eyeing him with distaste. He'd been on the coke last night. Paranoia was a classic side-effect, and there were still telltale traces of white powder sticking to the end of his inflamed nostrils.

'I beg your pardon, Davey.'

Really, who the hell did he think he was?

'You heard me. He's been pissing me off for days. Bastard did it again in the lift on the way down here. Would you believe *he* tried to start up a fucking conversation? Do I look like I want to talk to someone like *him* at 8.30 in the fucking morning? When I'm about, he makes no eye contact, whatsoever. Got it?'

'Of course, I'll speak to their management right away.' She dutifully made a note in her pad. That promised to be an interesting discussion.

'And if he does it again, tell the bastard I'll fucking flatten him.'

This job required more diplomacy than working for the United Nations.

'And number two, I need you to organise back-stage passes for the final Madison Square Garden gig. Got some mates coming over; want to know how we—real musicians—do it.'

The man is modesty personified. Izzy gave the piece of paper he'd just handed over a quick scan. It contained a list of names and addresses scribbled in blue biro. The writing was even more atrocious than Marc's.

'No problem, Davey. I'll get onto that today.'

She tucked his note into the front of her notebook and then looked up. The sunglasses had been pushed onto the top of his head and Davey was now staring at her from bloodshot hazel eyes. He clearly had something else on his mind, but what?

She shifted nervously under his scrutiny. And why did she get the feeling she wasn't going to like it when she *did* find out?

'Well, Izzy…' He exhaled another cloud of cigarette smoke towards the ceiling. 'You'll never guess what I heard last night.'

For some reason, Izzy liked neither his choice of words, nor the overly smug demeanour. Whatever he was building up to was speeding towards her like an out-of-control juggernaut.

He leaned forward. 'So, here's your starter for ten. How long has Rick been screwing you?'

Izzy's mouth fell open, not sure she'd heard him quite right.

'Come on, Izzy, simple question.' One hundred percent fake smile. 'Terry and I had this really interesting conversation last night. You know how guys like to shoot the breeze over a few lines of coke.'

Terry! She might have known. He'd decided to loosen his tongue, and it would have to be Davey he'd dropped hints to. The git knew how much Davey despised her. Ever so subtly, Terry was beginning to turn the screw on her.

'Spun me this fantastic tale about how you and Rick regularly meet up in hotel swimming pools in the *wee* small hours.' His eyebrows arched incredulously. 'Not to mention, you being clocked doing the "walk of shame" from his hotel room on more than one occasion.'

Davey took another brief drag on his cigarette. 'It certainly blows Rick's current vow of fucking celibacy out the water, doesn't it? So, I'll ask again, how long, Izzy?'

He reached over for the ashtray at the centre of the table, and casually flicked ash into it, his eyes never leaving her face.

'I really don't know what you're talking about.'

Izzy was doing her best to remain calm, but her brain was in overdrive. By the sound of it, Terry had added some pretty major— not to say blatantly untrue—embellishments to whet Mr Eastman's appetite for gossip.

'Come on, Izzy, Terry's seen you all over each other. And don't forget I caught you in Rick's room the other night. No wonder you were so keen to give him his *"pizza"* or was that a euphemism for something else, entirely?' He cackled at his own tasteless joke. 'Bet me showing up spoilt your fun. Or did you pop back later to provide *'dessert'*, once the coast was clear?'

'Davey, I don't know what Terry's implied, but there's absolutely nothing going on between me and Rick.'

'Bollocks!'He dismissed her with a wave of his hand. 'We all know Ricky's been a bit off lately, especially when it comes to entertaining the ladies. We were beginning to worry he'd gone off shagging completely, but it all makes sense now. He's getting it on tap from the hired help.' Davey pushed a stray lock of lank brown hair behind his ear. 'So, when did it all start? That night you did your "woe is Izzy" act and puked at his feet? Or was it going on before then? After all, he's always waxing lyrical about his "pretty lady".'

'You're barking up the wrong tree entirely.'

'Bullshit!'

She was treated to a disbelieving eye roll.

'Remember, Terry's paid to be our eyes and ears, Izzy. He knows everything—and I mean everything—that goes on! Admit it; Rick's been fucking you for weeks now?'

'He certainly has not!' Izzy snapped back, and then wished she hadn't. Losing her cool had only made Davey's gloating smirk widen even further; let him know he'd succeeded in getting under her skin. Probably make him think she *did* have something to hide.

'Although, I must admit it did come as a surprise. Miss Goody Two Shoes happy to provide extras in the bedroom? Wonder what odds I'd have got if I'd dropped into *William Hill* with that one? Maybe we should review your contract, make sure you're suitably remunerated for all the extra effort you're putting in "out with regular business hours"?'

There was a deliberate pause to allow the dig to sink in.

The Vicious, pony-tailed little yob!

'But you do realise,' Davey lowered his voice, making a show of glancing around theatrically, feigning discretion. 'Rick's only using you. It's not as if he'd ever be seriously interested, Izzy. Hate to burst your bubble, but if it came down to a choice, Francesca will win, hands down.'

Don't rise to his bait again, she reminded herself, but he was starting to really push her buttons now.

'What, no smart comeback? That makes a fucking first!'

Davey picked up his coffee cup, and took another long chug. Izzy hoped it choked him.

'You must have realised by now that the girls we sleep with on the road mean less than nothing. So don't get any ideas you'll be any different!' he informed her. 'And don't think I'll be sticking to the adage "what happens on tour, stays on tour" either. Naturally, I won't be saying anything to Rick—or the others. Who we choose to shag is our business,' Davey's eyes flicked over her disparagingly, 'even if Rick's taste is verging on the questionable. But my sister-in-law has a right to know you've made a move on her fiancée. So, don't worry, I'll make sure the wife passes on the good news, as soon as possible.'

Izzy's breath caught in her throat, her cheeks blanching at his coup de grace.

Shit! Shit! Shit! The little git *was* threatening her! And no doubt once Caron had filled her in, Francesca would be on the phone breathing all kinds of fire and brimstone.

'Now, as a matter of interest,' Davey went on, 'getting back to your schedule. Just how many precious minutes do you allocate Rick for all those little extras he's getting?'

11.09 AM

Izzy stared out of the window, absently twisting a curl of hair around her finger, feeling just as miserable as the grey West Virginia day outside, her thoughts becoming louder and louder, crowding in on all sides.

Her discussion with Davey had had been the last straw. Those two—Eastman and Costello—were truly a match made in Hell, and worse, she didn't doubt Davey would make good his threat and tell Caron. And when that happened, Francesca would be out for blood; Izzy's type 'O' to be exact.

There was a knock on her bedroom door.

'Who is it?'

She hesitated; her hand resting on the door chain, reluctant to open up, just in case thinking about the "gruesome twosome" might conjure up their malevolent presence.

'It's the Bellhop, ma'am. I have a fax for you; marked *URGENT.*'

Giving a relieved sigh, Izzy slipped the chain, and took delivery of the bulky A4 envelope, being held out to her. She scrutinized the fax's cover sheet stapled to the front. It was from Jack.

With that, her telephone rang out. After slipping the bellhop a ten-dollar bill for his trouble and receiving a respectful salute in reply, she dashed over to answer it. Jack's booming voice came down the line, eager to find out if his latest communication had landed safely in Izzy's lap.

'Yes, Jack, Just this minute. Give me a sec and I'll open it.' Slitting the envelope with her nail, she drew out the extensive paperwork. It was a contract in her name and an extremely generous one too. Izzy re-read the salary figure twice, just to make certain she wasn't hallucinating.

'Jack, I'm looking at it now.'

Sinking down onto her bed, she skimmed the rest of the document. From what she could see, the band wanted to employ her permanently as their PA. Just another complication she really didn't need.

'Well, Izzy, I don't think I need to go into too much detail,' Jack's voice continued to rumble in her ear, 'when I say how impressed we are with you,' he took in a long draw from his ever-present cigar, 'especially after a slightly bumpy start over riders and other things.'

That comment was accompanied by a hearty chuckle. 'But your loyalty, efficiency and work ethic have been second to none. I just wish all my people were as half as diligent. As such, after a brief discussion with the lads in Pittsburgh…'

Recognition dawned. That was what the mysterious meeting had been about. No wonder Davey had been spitting feathers when he'd descended on Rick's room. This job offer had Marc's 'name' written all over it—in big red letters.

'We'd like you to stay on,' Jack continued. 'You'll see from Condition Two, your salary would increase significantly, and we're happy to pay rent on any accommodation required until you get settled in London, up to a period of six months. If it takes longer, we can renegotiate.'

Izzy's eyes dropped to the clause he'd just referred to.

'Then, there are the usual conditions relative to pensions, insurances, holidays etc.,' he rhymed off, 'as well as the usual non-disclosure clause.'

In other words, say anything about the band to the media, and they'd sue the backside of her. Momentarily, she wondered if it covered discreet conversations with frantic 'mothers'? Hopefully, she'd never get to find out.

'It's really very generous, Jack…' Izzy paused.

How was she going to dig herself out of this latest mess?

'But, as you know, this job was supposed to be merely a stop-gap until I found something more suitable to my qualifications.'

'I think you'll find the salary being offered is better than any university graduates are receiving nowadays.' Jack's confident counter punch came straight back at her.

But staying here wasn't a viable option. There was no way she could perpetrate her cover story indefinitely. She wasn't a good enough liar. Correction, she didn't want to be a good enough liar!

'And I don't think I need to emphasise how much Marc wants this to happen,' Jack was piling on the emotional blackmail. 'He's been harping on about having a permanent PA for years. He's constantly singing your praises, Izzy. Emphasising what a god-send you've been after the whole "Angie" debacle.' The life was sucked from his cigar once more. 'Says you understand the job inside out, and I have to agree. Although, how you've dealt with his constant whinging is beyond me. You must have the patience of Mother Theresa!' Jack gave another hearty chuckle.

Yes, Marc was always going on about how he couldn't do without her. How she did everything the way he wanted. And, in Marc's world, that was the clincher. People doing everything *he* wanted—*when* he wanted!

She let out a slow breath. Marc would be unbearable if he knew she'd already said a definite "no". He could bear grudges on an epic scale. The best idea would be to play for time, and then turn down the offer at the last possible moment.

'Well, you've certainly given me a lot to think about,' Izzy admitted, chewing her lip, 'and to be honest, I'm a bit thrown. Would you allow me some time—maybe a couple of weeks—to think things over, consider your very generous offer?'

"Please say yes, Jack!" circled on repeat in her brain.

'I don't see why not,' Jack replied. 'Just let me know when you're ready, Izzy'

36

MONTREAL, QUEBEC

'Good show?' Izzy handed Rick a towel, as he leapt off the final step down from the stage.

His band mates—surrounded by the usual backstage hangers-on and rubberneckers their concerts attracted—were already easing their way along the corridor, heading towards the sanctity of their dressing room.

'From a technical point of view, not the best,' he considered, draping the towel about his neck, and taking a corner to soak up the beads of sweat dripping from his brow. 'The heat up there was incredible. Felt like I was having a two-hour sauna. But, on the plus side, what a crowd! Did you hear the noise they were making?'

'Hear them?' Izzy couldn't help but smile at his elated expression. 'At one point it was so noisy down here; I thought they'd managed to storm backstage.'

Rick ran a hand through his hair. 'Just a pity our sound system wasn't quite up to scratch. I suppose you heard Marc throwing a strop.'

'Yep, I got it with both barrels when he came off,' Izzy confirmed. 'Poor Donnie has already been summoned to the dressing room. No doubt, he'll be getting the full carpeting, any second now!'

Looking down, she caught sight of a little cuddly dog clutched in Rick's left hand.

'Who's your new friend?' she asked. 'And more to the point, Mr Hambro, does he have clearance to be backstage?'

They'd begun to make their own slow progress towards the dressing room, Rick falling into step at her side, acknowledging the words of congratulations from the onlookers with a tired smile.

'Yeah, he'll probably need one of those 'Access all Areas' passes,' he replied, taking Izzy's hand, and dropping the toy into it. 'Present for my pretty lady. Someone lobbed him straight at me as I was taking my bow. Nearly took my eye out, but he looked so cute, I thought you might like him.'

'Why thank you, kind sir! He's gorgeous!' Izzy cuddled the little scrap of fur under her chin. She still had the rose he'd given her weeks ago, pressed between the pages of a book, and hidden at the bottom of her suitcase. 'Think I'll keep him on my desk. Might be useful protection against the bunch of crazy rock stars I work for.'

'I hope I'm not included in that description.' Rick laid a sweaty head on her shoulder and batted his eyelashes comically.

'Okay, I'll tell him to play nicely whenever you're around,' Izzy wrinkled her nose in mock disgust, 'but only once you've seen the inside of a shower.' She batted him away playfully, trying to dismiss all thoughts of Rick in the shower with her welding a very large sponge…

They'd finally reached Izzy's office.

'I want the sound system issue addressed, Donny. I don't care if you and the guys have to do an all-nighter to fix it. Do I make myself clear?' Marc was already in full flow in the dressing room next door.

And by the purely one-sided conversation, it was clear the sound engineer wasn't being allowed to get a word in edgeways.

Out the corner of her eye, Izzy noticed Rick's hand had strayed to the back of his neck. The pain was back.

'Want me to pop up, later?' she asked, leaning in close to avoid any potential eavesdroppers.

'Yeah, that would have been great but, unfortunately, we're heading out. Jonny's just been handed free tickets for some Gentleman's Club, downtown.'

'You mean strip joint.' Izzy wasn't fooled for a minute.

'Got it in one,' Rick gave a one-shoulder shrug, only to wince at the effort, 'and I'm really not in the mood…..'

'Then don't go.' She'd pushed open her office door, hovering on its threshold, resting her head against the jamb. 'Nobody says you have to put in an appearance.'

'Nice thought, but you know what Jonny and Davey are like when they start badgering…'

'Then call me the minute you get back. And don't worry about the time. I'll be waiting….'

37

TORONTO, ONTARIO

'Izzy, it's out of the question that we're being asked to do all this additional stuff,' Marc complained. 'There aren't enough hours in the day for the shit he's got here.'

Izzy and Marc were sat side by side in the final limo, pouring over a draft of the schedule for the band's upcoming five-day stint in New York, Lindsay having sneaked in several more engagements much to Marc's displeasure

The Eclectic Deviation Bandwagon had jetted into Toronto at one pm local time, to be met by hordes of screaming fans at the Airport. After penning hundreds of autographs, they'd been whisked straight to the studio of Canada's weekly chart show to lip sync their latest Number One single, and then back into the limos and off to record a live thirty-minute interview at a local radio station. Interview over, they'd made a short detour back to the hotel for a twenty-minute freshen up and change of clothes, before heading out to the grand opening of Toronto's newest nightclub, '*Night Games*', special guests of its owner—and Steve's elder brother—Charlie.

'I understand that'—as usual, it was Izzy's job to pacify him—'but with your first three albums shooting up the *US Billboard Charts*, the record company still feel more media exposure would be good. The four shows that Lindsay has listed are all syndicated across the country.

According to *Virgin's* marketing department, an appearance on these shows has the ability to boost sales by at least seventy per cent—including the album you're plugging at the moment.'

'I do so hate that word 'plugging'. It reeks of commercialism.' Marc flashed her one of his haughty looks, before taking a long drag of his cigarette. 'Remember we're artists, first and foremost, Izzy. And while I'm all for selling more records, we're on a tight schedule as it is, without all these extras.' He rapped the paper with his hand, all the time providing her with another petulant scowl from his considerable repertoire.

'Does Lindsay have any idea of the pressure we're under?' He went on. 'We need time to re-charge our batteries. We're not fucking robots. You can't just wind us up, point us in front of the cameras, and press play.'

Yep, Marc's feathers were well and truly ruffled.

'Each appearance will be fifteen minutes, tops,' Izzy pointed out, knowing that would make little difference to Marc's grumpy mood.

'That's not the point. It's the hanging around, all the travelling beforehand, as well as running the gauntlet with fans whenever we break cover. Sometimes, I wonder if I'll get back to the limo with parts of me missing.'

Marc gave a shudder as he looked across at his cousin, who was perusing his own copy of the schedule. 'You agree with me. Don't you, Rick?'

'Yeah,' Rick lifted his head and fixed Izzy with a searching look, 'is there really nothing you can do? I'm knackered just reading this crap.'

'I know.' Izzy's lips tilted upwards with a sympathetic smile. 'Look, let me go back to Lindsay. Maybe I can negotiate dropping the number of personal appearances or even broach the possibility of doing some kind of hotel-link up instead. Would that help?'

'Slightly better, I suppose,' Marc conceded.

Rick nodded his assent too.

'But you do realise Mr Negative will flip his lid, regardless of whatever changes you make?' Marc exhaled another large cloud of smoke at the mention of Davey. 'And now, please tell me you've had more success with those tickets? Sabrina's birthday is on Sunday.'

As if Izzy could forget. Marc was making such a song and dance about it. Sabrina's forthcoming birthday—and all its elaborate preparations—were beginning to induce nightmares.

But at least tonight Sabrina wasn't around to voice her equal displeasure. She was back at the hotel, nursing one of her "heads" and reportedly in a huge sulk that Marc hadn't remained behind with her; Caroline had been the one to draw the short straw.

'Yes, Marc.' Izzy nodded, reminding herself she'd need to keep tabs on Steve; ensure he didn't get into any compromising situations when he was out from under his girlfriend's eagle eye.

'And….?' Marc prompted, giving a sharp inclination of the head.

It was time to give him some good news. 'Before I left the hotel, the play's director finally got back to me. His two daughters are *huge* fans. So much so, he's made available two tickets. You and Sabrina are to be his personal guests. You've also made it onto the Guest List for drinks with the cast in the Green Room afterwards.'

'Great. And what do I have to do in return?' Marc gave a comical eye roll. 'After all, you dropped a hint about his daughters being "*huge*" fans,' he made quotation marks in the air, 'so I'm sensing a trade-off here?'

But there was a whiff of a smile playing on his thin lips. Izzy knew she'd succeeded in pulling the rabbit from the hat.

'I've promised four VIP seats and the opportunity to meet you all before the Ottawa Show.'

'Typical,' Rick muttered turning away to look out of the window, lifting a weary hand to acknowledge the crowd of fans congregated in front of the nightclub's entrance.

Their limo braked sharply, drawing to a halt beside a rolled-out red carpet. Flashbulbs had starting to pop, courtesy of the ever-present paparazzi.

'Well, if it has to be done, it has to be done, Rick.' Marc's tone was resigned as he sat forward, making ready to exit their car, but he'd definitely cheered up.

Izzy smiled; she'd made it back onto Marc's Christmas card list.

8.22 PM

Before entering the nightclub, the band posed for the obligatory photographs, all looking suitably mean and moody, and then Steve cut the ribbon, declaring in solemn tones, the venue officially open.

On cue, their escorts for the evening—five extremely beautiful hostesses—shimmied forward on sky-scraper heels, and linked arms with the band, all of the women resplendent in barely-there silver playsuits. Jonny looked as though he'd died and gone straight to heaven as he allowed himself to be ushered inside by two Amazonian blondes—one glued to each arm.

Izzy made to follow them but a Sylvester Stallone look-alike—dressed in sharp black suit and shades—materialised out of nowhere, barring her way.

'Sorry, ma'am, but you can't come in.' He glowered down at her, arms folded, his expression daring Izzy to disobey his barked instruction.

'But I'm with them.' Izzy answered, momentarily nonplussed by his brusque manner. 'I'm Izzy, Eclectic Deviation's PA.'

'Sorry, ma'am, don't care who you are. You can't come in tonight.' The oaf was refusing to budge an inch.

'Look, you don't understand, I really do work for them,' she stressed.

This was new. She'd never been refused entry before. Where the band went, she went. Even if it meant the gents toilets, her back turned, taking more orders from Marc as he relieved himself.

'Here, this is my ID.' She dug out her Access-all-Areas pass, flashing it at 'Sylvester'.

He lifted the shades, gave it a cursory once-over, and then let the sunglasses fall back into place, shaking his head. 'Nope; you still can't come in.'

'Is this some kind of practical joke?' Izzy's voice held a definite hint of frustration. 'I'm working, and I really don't have time to argue about this. I'm needed inside.'

She'd had her fill of this gorilla's intransigent attitude.

'Don't care. Not happening. Now, move aside.'

She was being dismissed. Just like that.

'What's the problem? You still haven't told me why can't I come in?' Two could play at that game. Izzy folded her arms and glared back, equally determined to stand her ground.

The bouncer let out a weary sigh. He looked like he wanted to fly-swat her into the middle of next week.

'You're wearing denim.' Eyes were drawn downwards over Izzy's skin-tight stonewash jeans, and she was treated to a lip curl.

Great! Wearing denim clearly equated with a nasty case of bubonic plague around here. And Steve hadn't mentioned any dress code—not that the band would have complied with it, anyway.

'Strict rule, ma'am. No denim allowed, especially stonewash; *No* exceptions!' Another menacing glower was tagged onto emphasise his final point. 'So, I suggest you move along. We need to let the paying guests in.' He'd stepped towards the rope cordon; his hand out ready to lift it.

Tonight's paying guests—without a hint of stonewash in sight—began surging forward; Izzy picking up several voices murmuring their displeasure at being kept waiting. The natives were getting restless.

'But—'

If he thought she was backing down, he'd another thing coming. This conversation wasn't over yet. He'd met his match with Izzy Anderson.

'Ma'am, the rules are clear.' Another bouncer had appeared at Stallone's shoulder, every bit as big, wide and insistent. 'My friend's told you nicely. So, unless you have a dress in that itsy-bitsy evening purse and you change on the sidewalk, you *can't* come inside. Got it?'

Something in his insolent manner reminded her of Terry. Was this attitude part of standard training at Bouncer School?

'Or, will I be forced to call the cops.' He added.

Izzy drew herself up to her full five-foot-two inches in heels. This was getting silly now.

'Wait a minute; I don't think Eclectic Deviation would be very happy that you're threatening to have their PA arrested. Nor would your boss, given he's Steve's brother.'

'I'm well aware of who my boss is. But I'm telling you, ma'am—'

'Izzy?' Rick's voice cut into their conversation.

They all turned to see him standing in the open doorway, arms folded and brow furrowed, and clearly awaiting some kind of explanation as to why Izzy still hadn't made it inside.

'He's wearing denim.' Izzy pointed at Rick in triumph, and Rick's eyes dropped to his faded black Levi's.

'Special guest of the boss,' Stallone answered. 'Special guests are exempt from the dress code.'

'But you've just said there aren't any exceptions,' Izzy countered, her lips pursing. 'Anyway, I work for him, what's the big difference?'

Was this guy being deliberately obtuse or what?

'Izzy's our PA,' Rick stepped forward and flashed Izzy a smile.

'Sorry, sir, but she's breaking the dress code. And as she's only your employee, we can't make an exception.'

All this power had obviously gone to Stallone's head.

'But, if my memory serves me correctly,' Rick replied, 'you've just let in our minders, and I don't recall any of them wearing three piece suits.'

'Security,' Stallone's mate jumped in, as if that explained yet another unfathomable exception to their draconian rules.

Rick gave a little tut of impatience. 'This is fucking ridiculous. What if I said that as well as being our PA, Izzy happens to be my girlfriend? Does that make any difference to your so-called "rules"?'

Izzy tried hard not to let her jaw drop.

Rick gave her the briefest of winks, clearly urging her to play along with his little bit of improvisation.

'Or do I have a word with Charlie myself? Complain about members of *his* staff...' His boot-clad foot had begun to tap in irritation.

Stallone exchanged an uncertain look with his colleague.

'Eh, in that case…she'd probably fall into the category of special guest,' he answered at length.

'Finally, we have the right answer.' Rick grabbed Izzy's right hand, pulling her up against his side. 'And as my girlfriend,' he continued, Izzy's hip receiving a comforting squeeze, 'I think she deserves an apology for your rudeness. Don't you?'

There was a moment's hesitation from the two minders, and Rick raised his eyebrows. 'We're waiting?'

Izzy had never seen Rick resort to pulling rank; doing the full 'Do you know who I am?' routine but, if this worked, she was more than happy to play along. Plus, seeing him like this was such a turn-on!

'Sorry, ma'am,' Bouncer Number Two muttered, sounding as though uttering an apology was giving him as much discomfort as a tooth extraction without novocaine.

'Yeah, you should have said,' Stallone spoke up too, barring his teeth in an unapologetic grimace.

'That's okay.' Izzy could afford to be magnanimous. Her white knight had come up trumps again.

8.39 PM

'What the hell kept you, Izzy?' Marc demanded; grey eyes accusatory as they rested on the approaching Izzy and Rick. 'I turned around and you weren't there.'

He had the ability to make it sound as though her absence equated with the crime of the century, somewhere on par with *Brink's Mat* and *the Great Train Robbery*.

'I had a slight problem getting inside.' Izzy plonked herself down on the nearest neon pink pouffe, off-loaded her bag onto the table and began unzipping her suede biker-jacket.

In truth, she still felt a little stunned at being passed off as Rick's girlfriend—and the bouncers actually falling for it. Not that she was objecting. His ingenious deception had more than served its purpose.

'Apparently, she didn't comply with the club's strict dress-code.' Rick leaned over and picked up the open champagne bottle from the ice bucket at the centre of the table. After pouring out two flutes of the pink bubbly liquid, he handed one over to Izzy.

'I think you deserve this,' he said with a grin, 'Cheers! And don't worry. As always you look pretty damn good.'

Izzy took a grateful sip of her champagne, flushing with pleasure at his unexpected compliment. She'd now dispensed with her pink scarf and jacket to reveal a pale pink camisole top underneath and, although she said so herself, she did look good tonight. But Thank God it was so dark, and Rick wouldn't be able to see her skin blush as pink as her boots.

Izzy turned her attention back to Marc. 'There's a No Denim Rule apparently, but somebody forgot to brief me,' she explained, casting a nod in Steve's direction. 'Rick had to resort to some quick thinking to get me inside.'

Marc gave her jeans a cursory glance, before his eyes went to the glass of champagne in her hand and frowning. 'Well, it's not as if you're here to enjoy yourself, Izzy? I hope you stressed you're just an employee of the band?'

She knew the subtext. *Quit guzzling the free booze. You've got work to do.*

Marc always liked to remind the little people of their place. And being a lowly PA equated with his definition of little people.

'Of course I did.' She tried not to let her irritation shine through as she replaced her glass on the table. 'What do you need me to do first?'

Marc consulted his *Rolex*, letting out a bored yawn. 'First, find a bloody telephone in this rabbit warren and call Sabrina. Ask how she's feeling. Reassure her I'll be back by midnight at the latest. Hopefully she'll be speaking to me by then…'

11.54 PM

'Izzy! Are you listening to me?'

She snapped to attention at the sound of Marc's voice, a guilty flush heating her cheeks.

'Sorry Marc.'

With considerable effort, she dragged her attention away from Rick on the dance floor, swaying to the music with his hostess; or rather a hostess who'd morphed into the human equivalent of an octopus, her tentacles going *everywhere.*

It had been like that for the last ten minutes. Izzy had timed them. Every time Rick had looked to be making a break for freedom, the female had only latched on tighter. Her fingers had clearly been replaced with suckers.

'What can I do for you?' She painted on a suitably contrite smile, knowing she'd have to pick up the thread—of whatever Marc had been pontificating about—and fast.

The middle Hambro cousin was surrounded by a select group of Toronto's 'glitterati', his hostess having shipped out long ago. He'd succeeded in boring the pants off her too.

'Well, when you've quite finished daydreaming, Izzy,' Marc muttered, before nodding towards the "Andy Warhol" wannabe sitting opposite him. 'Vince, here, has just invited Sabrina and me to a preview of his inaugural Show, tomorrow night. I need you to be a darling and pop out in the morning, pick up a catalogue for me.'

'Yes of course.' Izzy smiled across at Vince Osborne, expecting him to disclose the necessary address of the Gallery, but frustratingly she received no reply. In fact, on first impressions, the guy appeared dead behind his Windsor glasses.

It took several more moments of painful silence, the two of them trying to out-stare each other out, before the address was finally disclosed by a lackey seated off to Vince's right. Like Marc, the artist had obviously brought along his own assistant to converse with the little people.

Izzy stifled a yawn as she scribbled down the gallery's address. It was shaping up to be a long night. It was time for a trip to the ladies.

'I see my damsel in distress requires to be rescued—again. That's twice in one night, pretty lady.'

Izzy gave a startled jump at the sound of Rick's husky tones in her ear; his breath warm against her cheek. She hadn't noticed him approach their table. Even better, he looked to be alone; his *octopus* nowhere in sight.

'You looked bored to tears,' Rick hunkered down by her side, his voice remaining low. 'I thought it was about time your white knight stepped up to the plate. Rescue you from my pretentious prick of a cousin.' He flashed a quick wink. 'How about a dance with your surrogate boyfriend? You still owe me from Christmas, remember?'

Izzy's stomach muscles clenched with instant excitement. Did she ever?

'Won't your "hostess with the mostess" object?' she asked, lightly.

'Nope, she's disappeared off to rustle up some drinks. Thank God!' Rick gave a shudder. 'Her bloody hands were everywhere, Izzy— and I mean everywhere! At one stage she was trying to grope inside my jeans. It felt like dancing with a fucking octopus.'

Izzy couldn't help it. She burst out laughing.

'What's so funny?' He asked; his expression puzzled.

'Nothing.' Izzy hastily pulled her face straight.

Great minds....

'Yep, she was about as subtle as a bloody Sherman Tank.' Rick rolled his eyes. 'Don't know what she'd been told about keeping the band happy, but spending the night with yours truly isn't part of the deal.'

So, tonight's date wasn't getting to first base either.

'You do realise you'll be in for more stick from Davey and Jonny if you don't take her back to the hotel,' Izzy heard herself saying.

'Trust me, Izzy. I'm passed caring what those two think about my sex life—or lack of it. Its no-one's fucking business but mine who I choose to sleep with. ' His dark eyes met hers. 'Anyway, I told you. I've had it with one-night stands. There's only one woman I want in my bed, and if I can't have her, I'm not settling for second best.'

As he uttered those words, the intensity of his look invoked a shiver down Izzy's spine. She could tell he was missing Francesca.

'And if the lads think I've taken a fucking vow of celibacy, or whatever; let them!' Rick's face broke into a cheeky smile. 'To get out of her clutches, I concocted this wild story about being caught up in a steamy affair with you. She seemed to buy it.'

'You said what to her!' Izzy spluttered. 'You're not afraid she'll blab that piece of information to the newspapers?' The potential consequences of his throwaway remarks loomed large in her mind. 'It could generate lots of unwanted publicity. Lindsay won't be happy if he's got to field rumours about you and me next.'

Not to mention a plethora of other people if they ever got wind of any so-called "affair".

'Don't worry. It won't come to that. Anyway, the important people here—you and I— know it's not true.'

At his words, a totally irrational wave of disappointment crashed over her.

'Now, as tonight's put paid to our swimming lesson, let's go dancing ….' Rick reached for her hand and tugged her to her feet.

They'd barely gone three steps, when Marc's voice stopped them in their tracks. 'Izzy, where the hell do you think you're going, now?'

Marc was already on the move, shrugging into his oversized silk jacket. 'You know I need to get back to Sabrina,' he reminded her, removing his curtain of hair from the collar and fluffing it out around his shoulders. 'And I also want to do a final run through about the arrangements for her birthday. Make sure you've got everything covered. We'll do it in the car on our way back to the hotel.' With a final tweak to his fringe, the consummate rock star was clearly ready to face the flashbulbs waiting outside.

Izzy bit back a pithy retort. Typical Marc, he was expecting her to drop everything—in this case, Rick—and just trot after him like some little dog.

'Marc, can't you give Izzy a fucking break?' Rick interjected at her side. 'You've had her running around like a blue-arsed fly for weeks— between securing those tickets and arranging the sodding party—what more do you want…blood?'

'Sabrina's 21st birthday is important, Rick. Especially as her parents can't make it.' Marc snapped back.

According to *The Sun* newspaper, Sabrina's parents were reportedly unhappy their daughter had "quit" her blossoming modelling career to become a rock star's trophy girlfriend. They'd refused to fly out for the party. Not that Sabrina appeared to be unduly upset at their non-appearance.

From the corner of her eye, Izzy spied Rick's hostess rapidly advancing on them, the drummer firmly in her sights.

'Watch out, human octopus is approaching at two o'clock,' she hissed, but too late, a possessive hand had already stolen around Rick's waist, red tipped nails coming to rest on his belt buckle.

'Hey, lover, you're not leaving already, are you?' the girl purred, pressing a kiss to his cheek, her brown eyes narrowing as they alighted on Izzy.

The message was clear; she was up for another crack at Rick, torrid affair with Izzy or not.

'I'm afraid so.' Rick pointedly extracted her hand, before helping Izzy on with her jacket.

The girl pouted prettily. 'Oh, come on, Ricky. Stay a bit longer? I've got the champagne on ice waiting for us, upstairs,' her voice was decidedly wheedling, 'and we were having so much fun….'

She flashed him a seductive smile, her fingertips coming to rest against his chin. 'If you're really going, I could grab my purse and come along with you…'

'As I told you earlier, Maria, the answer's no.' There was a definite edge to his voice.

'Don't need to leave on my account, Rick.' Marc intervened, checking his watch. 'Izzy, we need to leave go now…'

'Yes I do, Marc,' Rick growled at his cousin. 'I'm suddenly all ears about what you two have cooked up for Sabrina's birthday.'

38

TORONTO, ONTARIO

Pocketing the pass key, Izzy let herself inside Rick's suite, kicking the door closed behind her as she juggled several large suit shrouds and assorted shoe boxes, all containing the clothing and accessories he'd need for the next day's photo shoot.

This was usually Kathy's job, but Scottie had whisked his girlfriend out on an unexpected date to discuss their relationship. Izzy—knowing that Kathy's romance needed all the help it could get— had been happy to step into the breach.

After dumping them all onto the bed, she began unzipping the first shroud, drawing out the tuxedo jacket, tight black leather trousers, white shirt and black silk bow tie, checking against Kathy's list that all the items had been sent and were the required sizes.

Everything looked to be in order.

For a moment, she smoothed her hands lovingly over the light wool lapels of the tuxedo, wishing it was covering the man himself. She had a real thing about men in evening dress— or more accurately— men in dishevelled evening dress. She'd a feeling Rick could pull off "dishevelled" with bells on.

A smile settled on her lips as she gave reign to fantasy. He'd be lying back on a bed, that bow tie undone, together with maybe a few shirt buttons, revealing an expanse of that snugly chest. His brown eyes dilated with desire as he glanced up at her, before reaching up to tug the bow tie free from his collar. Every move done frustratingly slowly, his eyes never leaving hers…

The bathroom door opened and Rick strolled out, drying his hair, the rest of him completely naked.

In an instant, Izzy's eyes had settled on places they shouldn't before she swiftly remembered herself and turned away, pressing a hand to her face, just in case she was tempted to take another ogle.

'Oops, I'm sorry!'

'Shit, Izzy, where did you spring from?' Not that he sounded overly fazed by her unexpected appearance, or the fact she'd caught him in the nude.

'I… I did knock… twice. I thought you'd already left.' She stammered.

The previous night, on the ride back to the hotel, Marc had invited Rick along to Vince's show.

Izzy took a breath; her heart was pounding so hard, it felt close to exploding. Having only ever seen him in his swimming trunks or Y-fronts—or that snatched glance of his bare backside weeks ago— she'd naturally wondered what he'd look like totally naked. And, boy, she wasn't disappointed. He was exquisite; big—much bigger than Alex—but totally exquisite.

'It's okay, you can turn round. Towel's in place. I'm decent.'

Izzy swung back, hoping her expression was suitably dispassionate. But she knew her cheeks would probably still be a dead giveaway.

The answering grin he gave her, told her she'd been right.

'These are the things the boutique sent over for tomorrow's shoot.' She advised, moving to the wardrobe and hanging up the first set of clothing. 'Sizes have been checked and they should be fine. If you have any problems, just let either me or Kathy know tomorrow.

Everything has a red label. If you quote us reference number, we'll source something else from the master list.'

She now reached for the next shroud and began to unzip it. It contained more casual attire, comprising a short hip-length zebra print PVC jacket, faded blue jeans and red leopard print T-shirt.

Rick's brow wrinkled as he took in the second selection of items being laid out onto the bed.

'Let me guess. Marc was responsible for choosing these.' He pulled a face. 'I suppose I should be grateful it's not a crotch-less leotard or leather G-string!'

'He's put them on the reserve list!' Her expression was dead pan.

Rick picked up the jacket, giving it a brief inspection, before tossing it back on the bed with a loud groan.

'Good to know Marc's taste hasn't improved any!' He turned his attention to the leopard print T-shirt. 'I can hear him now. "You've got to get with the concept, Rick",' he mimicked Marc's affected drawl with ease. 'Although quite what the concept is, I'm not sure.'

'If it's any help, Jonny's jacket resembles a green and white fluorescent chess board.'

'Is it bad?'

'I'm pleading the *Fifth Amendment*.'

Some of the things Marc had picked for the band to wear over the years had been little short of grotesque. But in a crazy way it had got them noticed—Eclectic Deviation dubbed the 'Beau Brummell's of Rock Music'. Their very individual fashion sense, together with their crossover pop/rock sound, had set them apart from the run-of-the-mill 'jeans, leathers and big hair' heavy metal groups.

'Just wait and be amazed!' She tapped the side of her nose as she closed the wardrobe door.

'Well, I guess I'd better get moving. So, what are your plans tonight, pretty lady?'

Izzy smiled. 'I've been dreaming about a bubble bath, bed, and a good book all day.'

She'd started re-reading *Pride and Prejudice*. But Jane's *Mr Darcy* wasn't a patch on the man standing before her in all his semi-naked glory. And she was sure the prim Miss Austen—if she'd been here to cop an eyeful—would have agreed wholeheartedly.

'Want to come along to the gallery with me? Marc said I could bring along a plus one?'

'I don't think I'm quite what Marc envisaged as your plus one, do you?' Izzy replied, with an ironic smile. 'Anyway, it's a private function, not official band business. Marc rubbing shoulders with the great and the good of the art world. I doubt my gate-crashing would be welcomed.'

'Precisely, it'll be Marc hanging out with a bunch of pretentious arseholes. All up themselves; just like him. That's why I need you there, Izzy. Someone who's down-to-earth, good fun to be around…' He clasped his hands before him. 'Would you be willing to do Richard Hambro the biggest favour, and come along as my guest?'

She was treated to an exaggerated Darcey-esque bow, making her melt inside, especially when the towel was nearly dislodged in the process.

'Shit! Nearly gave you another eyeful…' Rick grinned, securing the towel once more. 'Apparently, it's all surrealist abstract.' He went on. 'Totally up Marc's street. He'll be making all the right noises about concept and imagery. And I'll be standing there thinking someone's just had a serious accident with a tin of emulsion.'

Izzy couldn't help but laugh at the pitiful picture he'd just painted with his words.

'You can't say no to me, Izzy. Plus, I might need your protection from any more predatory females, ready to pounce and sink their claws into an un-chaperoned rock star.'

'So that's it. You only want me to protect your body?'

With a shake of the head, she pretended to give his request thoughtful consideration for precisely two beats. 'Well, in that case, I suppose I'd better. After all, I'd hate for you to fall victim to another human octopus.'

She checked her watch, before pointing at her jeans. 'Do I have time to get changed out of these? I don't want to get us flung out on our ear because I'm not meeting the dress code. If you give me five minutes, I'll meet you down in the lobby?'

11.38 PM

'And now, we have the incredibly famous 'blue blob' by our esteemed Mr Osborne,' Rick pointed out the canvas with his half-full champagne glass, 'which looks as though it's taken him all of two seconds to paint?'

At the white canvas's centre was a perfect circle of ultramarine paint and nothing else. Izzy tried to keep her face straight, but it was becoming increasingly difficult as the minutes ticked by. Rick had been providing her with a running commentary since their arrival, supplying his—less than complimentary—thoughts on the paintings they'd already viewed. She hastily took a sip of her own champagne, doing her best to suppress another giggle erupting. Several times, she'd been unable to stop herself giving way to fits of laughter at his bitingly accurate observations, only to receive censorious looks from other guests who'd clearly overheard, but failed to appreciate Rick's sense of the ridiculous.

'Rick, will you behave? Its proper name is the "*Secret of Tranquillity*",' Izzy corrected him, peering at the small card pinned to the wall next to the canvas, 'and it can be yours for a very reasonable fifteen thousand dollars.'

Then she noticed the little red dot on the top left-hand corner, indicating its sale. 'Sorry, too late. Someone's already bought it.'

Rick let out an exaggerated sigh. 'Shit, just what I was looking for, too.'

They exchanged another amused glance.

'You mean some idiot has actually bought this monstrosity?' He leaned closer to the painting, frowning. 'I'm definitely in the wrong game. It looks like it's been done by a five-year-old. Maybe I should take up painting during my sabbatical. I think I could just about replicate that.'

'Shh, someone might hear you,' Izzy said, giving a little tug to the hem of her red mini shirtdress and glancing about herself.

At least she didn't look too out of place tonight. Her outfit fitted in with the other women milling around. Even better, no one had tried to forcibly eject her from the premises for allegedly not meeting any so-called dress code.

The Wightman Gallery, located in a former Clothing Factory overlooking the harbour, was mobbed with the great and the good of the Canadian art world, all crowding round the various pieces on display.

And Rick had been right. They were all utterly pretentious; trying to outdo each other with their supposed intellectual knowledge of modern art. To Izzy, there was the odd painting which caught her interest, but most of it—in her humble opinion—was rubbish; very expensive and not very well painted rubbish.

Marc came into view, being steered around the nearby exhibits by the gallery's owner; while Sabrina trailed in their wake, a bored expression marring her elfin features. She was clearly not enjoying this unexpected birthday surprise from her boyfriend.

Worse, by the looks of it, they were heading in their direction. Thankfully, Marc had made no comment at Izzy's unexpected appearance, but Sabrina had bestowed one of her customary snotty looks, before reverting to her default position, ignoring Izzy completely.

'And here we have the one you've already purchased, Marc.'

The gallery owner, Neville Wightman—Izzy was certain he was wearing a badly fitting toupee that drooped over one eye—indicated the canvas Izzy and Rick were looking at.

'"*The Secret of Tranquillity*" by my young protégé Vince Osborne. I believe you had the pleasure of meeting him met last night. Don't you just love how the colour draws your eye to the very depth of the canvas, its clarity firing your soul?'

The one little piggy eye, not obscured by artificial hair, gazed at the painting in undisguised ecstasy. To Izzy, he'd clearly never seen anything so beautifully awful in his life.

'Its simplicity just cries out to you. I always say the purity of Vince's work is thought provoking, don't you agree, Marc?'

On cue, Marc nodded sagely, while Rick took the opportunity to roll his eyes at Izzy. She could tell that he was—like her—suppressing the urge to burst into even more hysterical laughter.

'And my darling boy will be along later,' Neville continued. 'He's been temporarily held up; boyfriend trouble,' he confided, tapping his nose, before mopping his sweaty forehead with a spotted handkerchief.

The toupee moved, making Izzy's lips twitch.

Rick bent his head to whisper in Izzy's ear, 'Let me introduce you to the idiot who's bought this monstrosity, Izzy. Step forward Marcus Robert Hambro.'

Unable to hold it back any longer, Izzy let out a snort, which she quickly turned into an exaggerated cough, placing a hand over her mouth.

'Excuse me,' she apologised, as she received combined glowers from Neville, Marc and Sabrina. 'I think my drink went down the wrong way.'

'You actually bought this?' Rick asked his cousin, when Neville had moved away to mingle with other guests.

'Of course I've bought it.'

Marc fancied himself as an art buff and clearly didn't want Neville—or anyone else—thinking otherwise.

'Osborne originals don't come cheap. In fact, Rick…' Marc's face was now wreathed in smiles, 'this little beauty here happens to be your wedding present. Francesca told me you were desperate to own more contemporary art.'

'Francesca said what?' It was Rick's turn to almost choke on his champagne.

'Effusive thanks would be good, cuz. I've just spent fifteen thousand dollars on you,' was Marc's withering putdown.

'And I expect it to be displayed prominently,' he went on. 'With the high ceilings and all that natural light flooding into your flat, the walls are crying out for decent artwork.' He stroked his chin thoughtfully, gazing at the painting. 'In fact, it would be perfect in the master bedroom, positioned opposite the bed. From what I've read, that would guarantee great Feng Shui in your relationship.'

Leaving Rick to contemplate that remark, Marc turned to Izzy. 'Just as well you're here, Izzy. Be a darling and sort out the shipping arrangements, will you? Speak to Tabitha, Neville's assistant.' He gestured towards a red-haired girl hovering at Neville's elbow, looking just as fed up as Sabrina. 'And then I need you to come with me. There are quite a number of paintings I'm currently swithering over. Rick won't mind….'

'Actually Rick does—' Rick began.

'Off you go, Izzy.' Marc shooed her away with a dismissive wave of the hand.

Setting down her half-drunk glass on a passing waiter's empty silver tray, Izzy turned to Rick, pulling a face. 'Sorry, but I appear to be working again. Any preference as to where you'd like me to ship your latest acquisition?'

She could feel Marc's disapproving stare upon her.

Rick leaned in close. 'How about rustling up a one-way ticket to Outer Mongolia? I'd be ever so grateful!'

12.10 PM

Rick was backed up into a corner, two attractive females vying for his undivided attention. At first glance, they reminded Izzy of a couple of praying mantises, licking their lips as they contemplated tonight's dinner dish. She could make out Rick's anxious brown eyes darting around the room. Was he looking for her? One thing was certain; he looked seriously uncomfortable at the prospect of being this pair's main course of choice. It was time for Izzy to embark on a rescue mission.

She'd just spent the last half hour traipsing after Marc as he'd deliberated over more paintings to add to his already massive art portfolio. So far, every painting he'd purchased— eight at the last count—had been more ghastly than the last. But Marc being Marc, indulging in rock-star excess, was flashing the cash as though it had gone out of fashion.

"These will be the antiques of tomorrow" he'd advised Izzy, confidently. She'd merely nodded; deciding if was safer to keep her mouth shut. But she'd serious doubts. They were more like the contents of the bargain bin at a local jumble sale.

'Hey Rick, I'm back. You look as though you've missed me.'

Izzy was rewarded with a relieved smile, as she looped an arm about Rick's waist, and plastered herself his side. She made sure to zap an over bright— and totally insincere—smile in the direction of his two companions. Predictably, both women appeared somewhat taken aback by her unexpected—and not to say—extremely unwelcome appearance.

Inwardly, Izzy rubbed her hands together. It was time for her to really rain on their parade; play the 'girlfriend' role to the hilt. But could she make it look convincing? Easy, she just had to imagine he was really hers for the next few minutes. He'd never guess she was playing it for real.

'Hey, pretty lady, you made it, and not before time!' The lines of tension had disappeared from around his mouth. 'Ladies, let me introduce my beautiful girlfriend, Izzy.'

She received an extremely welcome kiss to her cheek.

'Izzy, this is Rachel Steyn and her friend Claire Eden.'

'It's so nice to meet you.' Izzy extended her hand to the tallest of the duo—the one he'd called Rachel—and the one she'd observed doing most of the over-blown flirting. 'Are you both artists by any chance?'

'No, I'm just a collector… of extremely beautiful men,' Rachel drawled back, ignoring Izzy's extended hand, her jade green eyes devouring Rick.

Izzy's hand dropped like a stone. So that was how Rachel wanted to play it.

'Then it appears we've got a lot in common, Rachel.' Izzy placed her palm possessively on Rick's chest, feeling the reassuring thump of his heart under her pink-nailed fingertips. 'I'm a bit of a collector too. And where I come from, possession is nine tenths of the law. Isn't that right, darling?'

She fluttered her eyelashes at him dramatically, and was pleased to note how his eyes flashed with barely concealed amusement in reply. He was clearly enjoying her little performance as a femme fatale.

'As *I* was saying, Rick,' Rachel flicked a long strand of dyed black hair over her shoulder. 'The club promises you an experience you'll never forget; particularly, if you like to live life on the edge. Isn't that right, Claire? We could get a private room, just the three of us. Have some fun together; maybe indulge in a bit of role play….'

Rachel threw her partner in crime a sideways glance; Claire instantly picking up the not-so-subtle cue and running with it, nodding at Rick eagerly.

'I'm sure Lizzie won't mind us dragging you away.' she simpered.

'It's Izzy and yes she would.' Izzy narrowed her eye menacingly, pleased to note Claire automatically took a step backwards.

Keep walking, sister!

'Thanks for the kind invitation, ladies, but I'll have to pass,' Rick answered, moulding Izzy even closer to his body. 'It sounds more up my cousin Jonny's street. Pity he's not here tonight. He'd jump at the chance. Wouldn't he Izzy?'

'Definitely' Izzy replied, swallowing. His hand had begun to trace little circles against her lower back, through the silk of her dress. And, as always, at the touch of those fingers, he was making it hard for Izzy to concentrate, especially as she needed to remember to breathe at the same time.

'Izzy and I have somewhere else we need to be. Don't we, sweetheart?' He prompted.

She looked up and his eyes locked onto hers, his expression suddenly intense. The way he'd said the endearment 'sweetheart', making her heart bounce against her sternum.

Then before Izzy knew what was happening, Rick's head had swooped down and he was bestowing a slow lingering kiss on her parted lips.

Izzy froze, her eyes snapping shut. Too astonished to do anything else but respond as the kiss seemed to go on and on. The world, the art gallery, the ghastly presence of Rachel and Claire melted away to nothing, leaving all Izzy's senses zeroed in on the wonderful pressure of his mouth, moving sensuously against her own, his tongue flicking her lower lip, seeking access.

But then, just as suddenly as it had begun, Rick pulled away and reluctantly Izzy's eyelids fluttered open. She expelled a slow breath, still gazing up at him and not sure what to say. They'd kissed and—jeez— the needle had shot completely off the *Richter* scale. Those sparks he'd brought to life were now surging through her, completely out of control. If he could make her react like that with just the touch of his lips, what else was he capable of?

She licked her lips slowly, savouring his taste.

'Don't we, sweetheart?' he gave her a little nod.

He was clearly expecting her to say something, not just stand there gawping at him like some kind of idiot. After all, they *were* supposed to be feigning a passionate relationship.

Say something, Izzy!

'Eh, yes…' With difficulty, she somehow managed to get her thoughts into some kind of coherent order. 'It's way past Rick's bedtime,' she continued, falling into her stride, 'and he needs to be tucked up for the night. Don't you, darling?'

'Yes. And I can't wait to find out what you're planning once we get there!' He winked at her. 'But I'm sure it won't involve much sleeping. Am I right?'

'You know me so well, Rick,' Izzy purred back. 'This body is in need of your full and undivided attention for the next few hours. Think you can handle it?'

Was that a flicker of surprise she saw in his eyes?

Shit, maybe she'd over-egged it with last remark? But clearly not as far as Rick was concerned, he'd already swung back to the two gaping women standing opposite.

'Sorry, ladies, but it would appear Izzy has an urgent orgasm that I have to attend to.'

Izzy goggled. She'd practically had one with that kiss.

'Well, I guess there's no answer to that,' Clare was the first to speak. 'It's been great to meet you, Rick. Hasn't it, Rach?'

'Yeah, maybe we'll catch up, next time you're Stateside?'But Rachel's final parry was decidedly lacklustre.

'I think that's extremely unlikely.' Izzy drawled, and with one final barring of teeth, she hooked a finger through Rick's belt loop and tugged him away.

'Wow, you certainly told them,' he observed, once they were out of earshot.

'You didn't do too badly, yourself, Mr Hambro.' she countered. Her central nervous system still hadn't stopped short-circuiting. 'I could see decisive action was needed. Rachel was ready to eat you alive back there. And if there had been any leftovers, Claire would have been first in the queue, brandishing her knife and fork.'

'But my pretty lady proved more than capable of taking them out.' Rick chuckled. 'Rachel had been stalking me from the moment you left. Then she joined up with Claire, adopting a full-scale pincer movement. They wanted to drag me off to some kind of sex club.' He shook his head. 'Thanks for playing along. I hope neither the kiss, nor the orgasm joke, embarrassed you.'

His eyes were pinned on her, and Izzy looked away quickly, fearful she might somehow betray her true feelings in that moment.

'Don't be silly, Rick. Our play-acting had to be convincing.'

Yes, play-acting; on Rick's part anyway.

With the depressing thought that it *had* been a game of pretend for him, she allowed herself to be dragged over to another obscure looking canvas

'So, when will I be in receipt of that hideous painting?' he asked.

'Should be with you by mid-May at the earliest,' Izzy answered, trying to give the impression that kissing rock stars was merely a formality on a PA's never-ending to-do list.

'Yippee.' Rick grimaced. 'I always thought Marc had more money than sense. After tonight, I'm convinced.'

'At the last count, he's bought eight canvases, and the band is down eighty-five thousand dollars. He's got me to put it all on the *AMEX.*'

'He's what?' Rick's jaw hit the floor, gawping at her. 'So, technically, he's spending *our* money on this rubbish.'

'Yep, and he's just acquired another Osborne.'

'Don't tell me that bloody painting comes as a pair?' Rick's eyes had widened in horror.

Izzy toyed with teasing him a bit more, but he looked so genuinely concerned at the prospect, she decided to put him out of his misery.

'No. This one is a red hexagon called "*The Secret of Identity*". According to our esteemed Mr Osborne—who's now arrived with boyfriend in tow—it's based on a molecule of Human DNA. Marc wants it for himself. He feels it's life-affirming.'

Rick stopped a passing waitress, helping himself to two glasses of champagne. 'Well, no secret to our Marc's identity. He's got MUG tattooed across his forehead.'

'Thanks.' Izzy accepted the glass he was holding out to her. 'Now, any thoughts about where you'll hang *your* painting?'

'Nope, but I refuse to wake up to a face full of that, every morning!'

'Oh, I don't know…' She shot him a wide-eyed look, unable to resist playing devil's advocate. 'You might get to like it!'

'You mean you'd be happy have a big fucking blob of blue paint on your bedroom wall, Izzy? Perfect, I'll gift it to you.'

'No, that won't be necessary,' Izzy backtracked hastily, giggling. 'Anyway, according to Marc it's a wedding present, and Francesca says you're both desperate to own more contemporary art.'

'Funny. Don't recall ever having that conversation with my fiancée,' he observed before swallowing down another large mouthful of his champagne. 'What time is it, Izzy?'

Izzy checked her watch. 'It's just left twenty to one. Do you want to leave? Phil's waiting for us outside. He's ready to go whenever you say the word.'

'Yeah, I don't know about you, but I've seen enough tonight. Come on, let's drink up. Leave Marc to it. Pray he hasn't bankrupted the rest of us by tomorrow morning.'

39

TORONTO, ONTARIO

'So how much money do you think he's spent now?' Izzy speculated as they wandered back along the corridor towards her hotel room door. Rick had insisted on seeing her inside.

'Don't even want to think about it, Izzy. Knowing Marc and the way he flashes the cash, we'll probably need to play an additional three gigs just to recoup tonight's losses.'

They stopped outside her door, and Izzy took out her key, placing it in the lock and giving it a swift turn. The door clicked open, revealing the darkened bedroom beyond.

'Thanks for asking me to come along. I had fun.' She smiled up at him.

'Me too, but then we always have fun together, don't we?' he grinned. 'You're one feisty lady when you get going, Miss Stevenson.'

'You better believe it.' She gave a little swivel on the heel of her boot, reluctant to take that final step inside and bring their night to a close. 'And who knew the art world could be so entertaining? Whenever you need me to step in and play your 'decoy' girlfriend, just give me a shout. I'll scare them off for you.'

'Yep, Sally Field better keep her *Oscar* locked up!' He let out a laugh, before sobering. 'Seriously, I don't think I've never met anyone like you, Izzy.' His eyes met hers.

A flush crept over her skin at the compliment *Yes you have, Rick. You just don't remember, and I'm not in a position to remind you.*

Her heart began beating erratically; those eyes were so damn intense, as they looked back at her.

'I'm really nothing special, believe me, Rick.' Out of nowhere, she felt that familiar little jab to her conscience.

'Yes, you are, Izzy. You're very special indeed.' Reaching out, he brushed his fingertips softly against her cheek. 'I hope I didn't offend you when I kissed you earlier?'

Izzy shook her head. How could she be, when it had been the best moment of her life to date?

'It had the desired effect...'

Those melted chocolate eyes were hypnotising her, making her insides quake with longing. And was it her imagination or had that strange tension sprung up between them again?

She watched as Rick moistened his lips, wanting so badly to feel the heart-stopping pressure of those lips once more.

'How would you feel about me kissing you again; as a 'thank you' for saving my arse, tonight?'

'I… if you want to,' she heard herself saying, still stunned by his unexpected request.

Jeez, this man really is a mind-reader.

His arm slid around her waist, pulling her up against him as his other hand cupped her cheek. And all the time, his eyes stared deeply into hers.

'Thank you, for being my life-saver, in more ways than you'll ever know, Izzy,' he murmured as his mouth lowered and touched hers.

His lips were firm and warm as they moved with determination against hers, imploring her to kiss him back. He tasted of the vintage champagne they'd enjoyed earlier, intoxicating Izzy, making her head spin, a million fireworks exploding in the pit of her stomach.

Without questioning her actions, she instinctively reached up and wrapped her arms about his neck, pulling him closer, letting him know this kiss definitely wasn't someone-sided affair, her fingers twisting into the hair at his nape.

Unlike his subtle teasing earlier at the gallery, his tongue entered her mouth now, finding hers, duelling with it, and she gave a little moan back in her throat. This was what she'd dreamed about for so long—being thoroughly kissed by Richard Hambro—but she needed more, wanted all of him, here and now, this very minute.

As if reading her thoughts, he began to walk her backwards, until Izzy felt the wall pressed hard against the small of her back. A hand stroked down her sides, before reaching round to cup her bottom through the fabric of her dress, drawing her into the intense heat of his thighs.

She had to be dreaming, nothing could feel this good, this right—surely? And even better, he appeared to be just as caught up in the moment, as turned on by their eager searching kisses as she was; the physical evidence of it, pulsing through the barrier of his jeans against her stomach. His mouth brushed down over her chin, pressing a line of soft kisses along her jaw, before settling on a deliciously sensitive spot at the juncture of her ear and throat.

Izzy had never felt anything so intensely arousing in her life, unable to quell a soft moan of pleasure, her head falling to the side allowing him better access, holding him tighter.

'*Don't stop, please!*' screamed the voice in her head.

The lift doors pinged open, and Davey stumbled out into the corridor, colliding with an adjacent rubber plant.

'Who put the fucking *Triffid* in here?'

Izzy felt Rick's body stiffen; his hands falling away from her as he stepped backwards. Her eyes fluttered open in confusion, feeling bereft at the loss of his heated touch.

Davey's eyes were on them as he disentangled himself from the plant's clutches; that infuriating smirk growing wider and wider.

'And who do we have here? Why it's our Ricky and the lovely Miss Stevenson.'

Damn! He'd seen them kissing! Izzy could feel incriminating heat flooding her cheeks and hastily looked away. It would have to be Davey who'd sprung them.

'Don't mind me,' Davey parodied a little mock salute in their direction, 'just off to see Terry; in need of a little pick-me-up!'

And without another word, he was gone; barrelling down the corridor before finally disappearing through the fire doors at the far end.

Rick expelled a long breath. 'I'm sorry, Izzy. I think I got a bit carried away there…'

Those dark eyes had become guarded. For a second, he reached out a hand, as though wanting to touch her again, before thinking better of it.

Izzy blinked, her stomach plummeting to her toes as the meaning behind his words sank in. He was apologising to her. And men only apologised for one reason, when they'd realised that kissing a girl had been a monumental mistake.

She watched as Rick's eyes strayed towards the closed elevator doors. Yes, she got the message, loud and clear. He wanted to make a quick exit; get away from her as quickly as possible. Swallowing down her own disappointment, Izzy knew she'd have to be the one to let him off the hook; pretend it was all a mistake on her part too.

'Me too; probably all that vintage champagne we've been drinking tonight…' She forced an over-bright smile to her still tingling lips. 'Look, why don't we just forget about it? The kiss… I mean…'

She gave a dismissive wave of the hand and took a conscious step inside her room, putting further distance between them. 'I'll see you in the morning.'

God, why couldn't the ground just open up and swallow her? 'There are several things we need to go through prior to the photo shoot.' She heard herself babble on 'Lindsay will be attending...'

8.58 AM

Typical! Not one of them had bothered to show face.

Izzy had been sitting alone at the breakfast table for the best part of half an hour, drumming her fingertips on her notepad, growing more and more enraged as the minutes had ticked by.

She tried to stifle another yawn, feeling totally drained by her sleepless night. Not surprisingly, she'd been unable to drop off, continuously reliving those moments in Rick's arms and its aftermath over and over again.

And what complete knee tremblers his kisses had been. The nerve endings in every part of her body short-circuited every time she recalled the expert way his mouth had plundered hers. No one had ever kissed her like that before; least of all, Alex.

When she'd actually got any kisses from Alex, his lips had remained frustratingly jammed together— his excuse being he didn't like the taste of lipstick—and he'd certainly never attempted to use his tongue. That would have been a complete 'no-no' for the strait-laced Alex Fairbairn.

However, given Rick's closed-off reaction in the minutes afterwards, he'd clearly reached the same conclusion that kissing Izzy equated to a complete 'no-no', too. She winced, remembering the anguished look that had flickered across his face before he'd finally left her. Talk about a dead giveaway. Kissing Izzy was clearly something he didn't wish to repeat—on pain of death.

But had those few minutes ruined their friendship? Was last night's lip lock going to make things hopelessly awkward between them from now on?

Izzy ran a weary hand down her face. He was bound to realise—by the way she'd practically sucked the face of him—that she harboured strong feelings for him. She'd put her heart and soul into those few minutes in his arms. Would he be embarrassed that she might have feelings for him?

She hoped not. There was only a matter of weeks until the end of her existing contract. Not being able to spend any more time— alone—with him would be torture. Surely, they could they just ignore last night? Treat it as a stupid one-off aberration? They'd both been a little tipsy; granted Rick more than her. Could they just call it a silly drunken fumble and move on? After all, alcohol could be blamed for anything. She couldn't lose him as her friend; not yet. She'd her whole life ahead of her, without him.

Izzy glanced down at her watch again and reluctantly got to her feet. Lindsay had stopped by five minutes ago, livid at the band's no-show and somehow she'd got the blame. The photo-session was due to start in under an hour, and what the hell was *she* going to do about it?

"Short of dragging them out of bed by their back-combed locks', Izzy had flared back; there was precious little she could do.

She headed for the bank of lifts in Reception. No use waiting down here any longer. They weren't coming. It was time for her to go and bang on a few doors.

A bleary-eyed—and completely starkers—Jonny answered his door on Izzy's third fist thump.

'Oh, it's you.' He yawned, tugging a leisurely hand through his decidedly messy mane, and taking an age to reach inside for his robe.

No doubt he was hoping she was totally bowled over at the sight of his wedding tackle, and going weak-kneed with desire. Fat chance! He wasn't a patch on his eldest cousin in that department!

'What do you want, Izzy? It feels like the middle of the fucking night.'

Hung-over didn't begin to cover Jonny's appearance at this precise moment. Completely wrecked looked to be a more apt description. Izzy didn't bother asking what he'd been up to. She was pretty sure the old cliché—sex, drugs and rock'n'roll—had it more than covered.

'Well, who did you think it would be at nine-fifteen am?' she snapped back. 'I need you up, dressed in Outfit One and downstairs to 'hair and make-up' within the next fifteen minutes. The photographer's here, together with his army of stylists. We're running horribly behind and Lindsay's on the warpath.'

'Don't sound too happy yourself.' Jonny opined, and Izzy bit back a pithy retort.

'I'm not in the mood for smart-ass remarks. None of you bothered to show up to our breakfast meeting. How are Lindsay and I supposed to do our jobs if you lot don't meet your end of the bargain?'

The sound of rustling sheets filtered out from inside the room. So last night's 'date' was beginning to surface, was she? Well, she'd better ship out pronto, Jonny's day job called.

'What do you mean Outfit 1?' Jonny squinted at her.

'The clothes you have to wear for the Photo Shoot.' Sometimes, Jonny could be unbelievably dense. 'It's hanging on the outside of your wardrobe, marked with a red label. I dropped it off, last night.'

Jonny gave a noisy yawn. 'Right, didn't notice. Bit tied up with other things when I got back.'

His saucy grin wasn't reciprocated. 'Spare me the details, Jonathan. I don't want to know.'

Davey didn't answer, despite several knocks that would have woken the dead. She decided to come back later. He was probably sleeping off whatever little commodity he'd purchased from Terry's bag of tricks. But more to the point, had the little git brought Terry up to date on seeing her and Rick in a compromising position?

Knowing Davey, the answer was probably a big fat "*yes*".

Sabrina let her in without a word, not even acknowledging Izzy's entirely forced, 'Happy Birthday', while Marc—still in last night's clothes—was slumped in an armchair, head in one hand, *Bloody Mary* clamped in the other, and a metal waste bin rammed between his knees, lamenting loudly that he was dying.

Not wishing to see what he'd just vomited up, Izzy made suitably sympathetic noises from the far side of the room, all the time hoping the band's bank account wasn't in equally dire straits.

However, Marc's imminent demise was clearly a gross exaggeration as, with his next breath, he promised to be dressed and downstairs by the required time. Izzy would believe it when she saw it.

Steve was in one of his *I-really-can't-be-bothered-talking-to-someone-as-unimportant-as-you* moods. After abruptly assuring Izzy that he'd be down when *he* felt like it "and *not before*" the door had been slammed in her face.

Then she remembered. Caroline was flying home later today. No doubt, Steve was trying to get in as much "quality-time" as possible with the Honourable Miss Lansing before she disappeared back to good old Blighty. Izzy decided she'd be generous and allow the couple another ten minutes—but no more.

She headed back towards Davey's room.

'Davey,' she yelled, hammering the door. 'Are you up yet?'

There was still no answer from Room Five Hundred and ninety two.

'Davey, I said are you up?'

For the first time, there were definite signs of life within; the tramp of heavy footsteps making their way towards the door. He'd surfaced.

'You need to be dressed and downstairs for the photo-shoot. Have you got that?'

'Fuck off, Izzy!' was the grumpy reply. 'And what am I supposed to wear, anyway?'

'Outfit One. It's in your wardrobe, marked with a red label.'

The footsteps retreated again.

Use your bloody eyes, she wanted to add but stopped herself, just in time.

'Jeez, Izzy, what time is it?'

The door opposite had opened, and Izzy was confronted by a yawning Rick, hastily tying a knot in the sash of his bathrobe.

'It's twenty past nine.' she snapped at him, and then wished she hadn't sounded quite so snippy. Not when he looked so dammed adorable standing there, bed-head hair all over the place, and that too-short robe barely decent. Unbidden, images of their frantic kisses filtered across her mind.

'I'm guessing if you've resorted to banging on doors, I'm not the only one who's late?' He gave her a lopsided smile as he rubbed his eyes.

'Yes. And you've missed the breakfast meeting too. But don't worry, so did everyone else.' Adorable or not, he wasn't getting around her so easily.

'Shit; I'm sorry.'

'Lindsay is going ballistic downstairs….' Izzy added, unable to look him in the eye.

There was an awkward silence before Rick spoke up. 'Look, Izzy, about last night...' He paused and Izzy shot a quick glance at him. A pulse flexed in his jaw.

'It was my fault, entirely. I stepped over a line between us...I'd had too much to drink.' He bit his lip. 'Not that I didn't enjoy our kiss,' he added. 'I did. You're a great kisser, but...'

He stumbled to a halt, and the phrase "just not what he wanted from someone like her" echoed within Izzy's brain.

'Rick, I get it.' Izzy fidgeted with the button on her sleeve, shifting from one foot to the other. 'I really do.' It was time to undertake more damage limitation. 'As I said last night, let's just forget it ever happened...'

She really couldn't face listening to any more—regardless of whether he thought she was a good kisser or otherwise. She'd a feeling he'd only tagged that bit on to soften the blow.

'I got carried away with all the play acting,' she went on, 'there's no harm done. I can assure you.'

Both hands were gripping the back of his neck, his eyes staring at her, intently. 'Then are we okay, Izzy? I'd hate for last night to make things awkward between us.'

Like it is at this precise minute, Rick?

'Don't be silly. Of course we're okay.' Izzy feigned a lightness of tone, forcing herself to give him a bright smile. 'It would take more than a couple of silly drunken kisses to spoil us being mates. Let's just move on, shall we? I can, if you can?'

Izzy surveyed Marc's lounge, allowing herself a well-deserved pat on the back. Although she said so herself; the room looked just about perfect for Sabrina's party, with streamers and balloons everywhere. The DJ had finished setting up his turntables in the corner, and according to her watch, the band—plus the birthday princess herself—should be arriving back from their posh dinner in Toronto's renowned *Chinatown*, any second now.

The room itself was already heaving with Sabrina's specially invited guests, a plethora of well-known faces from the world of modelling. It could have been backstage at *London Fashion Week* given the body count of supermodels, all dressed to the nines and guzzling the free champagne and canapés on offer.

Smile on, Izzy shifted seamlessly into professional mode, refusing to be intimidated by all the glamorous party goers. With practiced ease, she directed them towards the circulating waiters and waitresses, their trays over-flowing with champagne and a selection of cocktails, the latter complete with miniature umbrellas.

In pride of place, by the window, stood a three-foot-high shocking pink birthday cake, surrounded by an archway of more pink and white heart-shaped balloons, 'Sabrina' and 'Twenty-one', printed in elaborate gold lettering on each balloon. Sabrina's birthday had cost the band a bloody fortune, Marc ensuring his beloved's Twenty-first was the "Coming of Age" to end all "Coming of Ages".

On cue, high-pitched screaming came from outside, and within minutes, Sabrina had made her entrance, waltzing through the door and—in Izzy's opinion—faking a bit too much over-the-top enthusiasm at the transformation to their hotel room. From the DJ's speakers, Stevie Wonder started belting out *'Isn't she lovely?'*

Izzy wrinkled her nose and allowed herself an exaggerated eye-roll. Not quite the song she would have picked for the occasion. Elton John's *'The Bitch is back'* sprung to mind…

Her gaze fell on Marc, standing by Sabrina's side, those hypercritical grey eyes conducting a mine-sweep of the entire room. He was making sure Izzy hadn't skimped on his final three-page set of instructions. If it wasn't up to the Boss's satisfaction, she'd soon hear about it.

Not that Izzy would be allowed to stay and enjoy tonight's handiwork. This party was strictly 'by invitation only' and Izzy's had been lost in the post. She was just expected to organise the whole shebang and then piss-off back to her room without even a smoked salmon canapé touching her lips. Marc's eyes met hers and he delivered a short sharp nod of approval. He was happy.

'Hey, Izzy, I'm over here!' Kathy was waving frantically at her from the other side of the packed room.

At the sight of a genuinely friendly face, Izzy eased her way through the crowd towards her. Kathy was perched on the sofa, a heaped plate of food balanced on her knees, stuffing her face with what looked to be a salmon mousse canapé.

'So, who did you bribe to get in, Miss Davies?' Izzy collapsed down beside her friend, ready to enjoy a quick breather. 'Tonight's party isn't open to riff-raff like us, remember? All gate crashers will be formally ejected. You've been warned. And you're not supposed to be eating the food, either.' She pointed at the remaining three canapés.

'Just said I needed a brief word with Scottie,' Kathy confided, 'Anyway, if it came down to it, I'd like to see Madam try and throw either of us out.'

She flung a disparaging glower at the birthday girl's rear view.

'Well, I'm only allowed to stay until I finish swishing the old magic wand,' Izzy reached over and swiped one of the canapés.

What the hell, it's a birthday party!

'Then it's "There's the door, Izzy, please use it. And don't even think about sneaking out a cocktail!"'

'You have to. I've had two already; the *Mai-Tai* are out of this world.' Kathy grinned, swallowing down the last remnants of her canapé and licking her fingers noisily.

'Knowing my luck, Marc would catch me. He's probably got them counted, as we speak,' Izzy replied, making fast work of her own piece of contraband.

That made them both laugh.

'Anyway, I just wanted to let you know, I've got it on underneath.' Kathy provided Izzy with a little shoulder shimmy, looking pleased with herself.

They'd popped out that afternoon to indulge in a rare couple of hours' retail therapy; Kathy falling in love and purchasing an extremely expensive silver lace and leather playsuit.

'So, that's why you're here.' Realisation dawned for Izzy. 'Letting Scottie know it's his lucky night, and he'd better get back to your room double quick if he knows what's good for him. I thought he was looking a bit hot under the collar.'

Kathy's purchase hadn't been to Izzy's taste, but she hadn't wanted to burst Kathy's bubble, knowing Kathy was desperate to regain Scottie's diminishing interest. According to Kathy, their date, the previous night, hadn't gone well. Hence the need for their lingerie shopping trip, today.

'Yes, and let me tell you, he sounded extremely keen when I whispered a sexy little suggestion about how he could help me get out of it.' Kathy gave a throaty giggle.

'More information than I really need to know, Miss Davies.' Izzy held up a hand.

'But to be honest,' Kathy continued with a grimace, 'getting him to do that won't come a minute too soon. It's ever so tight, Izzy. I'm beginning to realise what a *Bernard Matthews'* turkey feels like just before Christmas.'

'At the price you paid for it, there is no way it should be uncomfortable.'

'You're telling me. But I've a confession to make. At the last minute, I swapped it for a smaller size. I hoped it might make my figure more voluptuous.' Kathy's laugh became decidedly awkward, as she smoothed her hands down her body. 'But with hindsight, that probably wasn't one of my better ideas. The old boobies were supposed to stand to attention; look all perky, just like yours.'

Both Kathy's boobs still resembled poached eggs. 'All it's doing is cutting off the circulation in my legs!'

'You idiot!' Izzy couldn't suppress a chuckle.

'Honestly, Izzy, there must be an easier way to make him commit to me?'

'Why don't you just tell him how you feel?'

'I don't want to look too keen.'

'I hate to state the obvious, but you are keen.'

Not that Izzy could see the attraction. Scottie Taylor was just another Terry Costello in training.

'I know, but we've been casual for so long. I don't want to scare him off by suddenly getting all heavy, suggesting we move in together.'

'Maybe if you talked to him a bit more, you might find he wants something permanent, too.' Izzy mentally crossed her fingers, but she didn't like Kathy's chances.

'But what if he just likes things as they are, or worse, wants to cool off entirely? I told you how badly last night went. If I go jumping in with both feet, he might dump me. Say I'm pressuring him. And I'd rather have part of him, than nothing at all.'

For once, Izzy could appreciate Kathy's position. She'd rather Rick continue to see her as an honorary kid sister, than have last night's kisses destroy their close friendship.

Izzy decided to change the subject, hating the despondent look which had settled on her friend's face. In her opinion, Kathy was too good for Scottie, and she should be aiming far higher.

'Well, Madam is certainly enjoying her moment in the spotlight.' Izzy nodded towards Sabrina, air kissing late-arrivee, Jerry Hall; Mick Jagger by her side, and exchanging a few words with Steve and Marc.

The last she'd heard Jerry couldn't stand to be in the same room as Sabrina, not even bothering to RSVP. And now, here she was, large as life—with Mick in tow—and eating for two again, if the tabloid rumours were to be believed. Thank God she'd made a last-minute decision to increase the catering.

'Yeah,' Kathy agreed, 'and what the hell is Sabrina wearing? She looks like Andy Bloody Pandy in that outfit.'

'It's is a *Zandra Rhodes* original,' Izzy supplied. 'She's one of Princess Diana's favourite designers. And if it's good enough for the Princess of Wales…'

'It's good enough for Sabrina Warren. Yep, message received and understood,' Kathy finished. 'By the way, did you clock the bracelet on her wrist? I'd need *Securicor* chained to my other arm if I ventured out with that.'

'There wasn't much change out of Four thousand dollars for that little beauty.' Izzy answered.

'Jeez, *Austrian Crystal* is so expensive these days. But, seriously, that one will bleed Marc dry. Like the first commandment in the Gold Digger's Manual, Sabrina's mission in life is to marry money, and he's so bloody besotted, he doesn't see she's halfway there.'

'Yes, she does seem to consider his bank account a bottomless pit. But then, after Marc's shopping spree last night, he's clearly of the same opinion.'

Izzy had just taken possession of the final tally for last night's crazy trolley dash around the Wightman Gallery. The amount made eye-popping reading.

'Miss Davies, I'm here to remind you that tonight's party is by invitation only, and that includes the food!' Terry cut into their conversation.

Izzy' groaned inwardly.

What does he want?

Over the last few weeks, Kathy had effortlessly slipped into the role of faithful wing-woman watching Izzy's back in case Terry made another move in her direction. Not that he had; too many other security and band issues claiming his time.

But here he was large as life.

'And according to Miss Warren, you don't receive one.' Terry's eyes narrowed.

'Sorry.' Kathy jumped to her feet, brushing the incriminating crumbs from her jeans onto the carpet. 'I just need a final word with Scottie. Then I'm out of here. Give me two minutes, Terry.'

'Well, make it quick. Any longer, and I'm instructed to remove you by force—if necessary!' He nodded towards Sabrina.

Kathy turned back to Izzy. 'Fancy a drink downstairs?' Her head now resembled that of a nodding dog. 'I could do with more advice about what we were discussing a few minutes ago.'

'No problem.' Izzy answered, still eyeing Terry warily.

With that, Kathy scooted away.

Great! Now what's coming?

'So, as the cliché runs, we're alone at last, Miss Stevenson.' Terry's smile was altogether too smug for her liking. He held out his half-drunk beer bottle towards her. 'Can I tempt you to a drink?'

'No, thanks,' Izzy declined politely, 'and Sabrina needn't worry about me, either.' She added. 'Just a couple of final checks and I'll be on my way, too.'

She tried to stand up but—too late—Terry had plonked himself down into the space vacated by Kathy, effectively pinning Izzy into the sofa's arm rest, rendering a quick getaway impossible.

'Oh, I think you'll be allowed to stay a bit longer. Told Sabrina, I needed a quick word with the delectable Miss Stevenson.' His serpent-like eyes did their customary sweep of her body, before settling on their favourite spot; down her cleavage.

Izzy resisted the urge to do up the blouse's buttons. The git had her trapped, with his tongue practically rammed down the front of her top.

'So, how're things going between you and Rick?' Terry enquired.

Izzy bristled. He was making it look to the casual observer as though they were having an entirely innocuous conversation. And was it her imagination or had his leg started to rub, ever so subtly, against her thigh?

'Hear Davey finally caught you two in a bit of a clinch?' he went on.

So, Blabber-Mouth Eastman has spoken. No surprise there.

'Not that Rick looks to be missing you, now?' Terry remarked, directing the neck of his bottle towards Rick.

Rick was locked in conversation with one of Sabrina's model friends; her arm about his shoulders, laughing provocatively at the punch line to some comment he'd just delivered.

'If she gets any closer, she'll be in the bloody shirt with him. Worried she might be the one, Izzy?' He taunted.

'What do you mean?' Izzy's voice was husky, her eyes still on Rick, jealousy twisting in her gut.

'The girl who might take your place in Rick's bed,' he gave a humourless chuckle. 'Jeez, you've got Jonny and Steve seriously worried about the dip in Rick's libido. But we know better, don't we?' Terry took another draught of beer, eyeing her. 'Is that a glimmer of the green-eyed monster rearing its head, by any chance?'

His hand had come to rest on Izzy's denim clad knee, his fingertips applying a light pressure with his fingertips.

Izzy shifted uncomfortably at his touch.

'And if Rick's interest is waning…' He left the rest unsaid, but Izzy got the message.

'Terry—' she began, only to feel the most agonising pain rip through her right kneecap. A horrified gasp escaped her lips. 'Please don't do that.'

'I find women who continue to say no, a real challenge.' He continued. 'You don't know how much our little cat-and-mouse game is turning me on!'

'You're hurting my knee.'

'Come on, that's just a playful squeeze. If I really wanted to hurt you, I'd do this…'

The vice-like pressure intensified, and Izzy felt tears prick the inside of her eyelids. The loathsome git was taking perverse delight in making her suffer.

'I won't put up with being ignored for much longer, Izzy,' he went on. 'Others have found out to their cost what happens when they do that. And my patience is wearing thin. Do you hear me?'

More indescribable pain; Izzy certain her kneecap was about to be pulverised any second now.

'I didn't catch your answer, Izzy.'

'I hear you.'

'Good. I suggest you start giving "us" some serious thought, in the *not* too distant future,' he took another chug of his drink, eyebrows raised. 'If not, I'll be taking matters into my own hands.'

With that threat left hanging in the air, he released her knee and got to his feet, his bottle raised in salute towards Sabrina, clearly indicating Izzy had been dealt with, too.

'It's time for you to leave, Izzy.' Without another glance, he sauntered off towards Lee and Scottie.

Izzy watched him say something as he approached his two henchman and all three men sniggered, their heads swivelling—as one—in her direction. Impotent rage bubbled up inside her.

'Jeez, Izzy, are you okay?' Kathy was back.

Izzy rubbed her throbbing kneecap. 'Do I look okay?' she bit out.

'You have to say something. He's just assaulted you in full view of everyone.'

'Yes he did. And look what happened,' Izzy retorted, 'precisely nothing, Kathy. No one paid a blind bit of notice.'

Not even Rick; too wrapped up with Sabrina's pal to notice.

She stood up and gingerly put some weight onto her leg. She could just about walk.

'Right, I need a quick word with Marc, check there are no more instructions, and then we're going.' Sabrina was still blasting them with icy glares every ten seconds. 'I'm sure that will please her Ladyship, no end….'

40

OTTAWA, QUEBEC

'We've finally made it to Ottawa, Betty. Another gorgeous city! From what little I could see of it on car-journey here.'

So much for Mum's idea of seeing the world; it was mostly airport, hotel and arena these days, with precious little time for sightseeing.

Wedging the telephone receiver between her left ear and shoulder, Izzy hauled her suitcase up onto the bed, unzipping its lid.

'How's Richard?' Betty asked. 'I hope those wonderful hands of yours are still working their magic?'

But Izzy could hear a lingering trace of anxiety in her voice.

'Yes, he's fine,' Izzy was happy to report, removing her nightshirt from the suitcase, and slipping it under her pillow.

A dreamy smile lit up her face at the memory of last night's massage. Rick had been dead to the world in just under ten minutes flat, and more importantly, their friendship completely back on track; any remaining traces of awkwardness between them gone.

'And you're certain he's not got *his* hands on any more *Teraxapen*?' Betty checked.

Izzy placed her travel clock and book on the nightstand.

'Nope,' she reassured Betty, 'in fact, I overheard Terry trying his sales pitch again this morning, and he received a very emphatic "no thanks" for his trouble. Neither of them knew I was around, so Rick was being completely honest.'

'Thank the Lord!' Betty breathed.

Izzy had dug out the little cuddly dog from her case, kissing its nose before placing it on the pillow. She'd christened him Buster.

'But for some reason he's still staying "no" to hiring a full-time physio. I was only supposed to be temporary….'

Not that she was complaining about his intransigence in that department.

'Izzy, if it's a toss-up between a pretty girl, and some chap built like a rugby prop pummelling the life out of him, there's no contest.' There was a throaty chuckle at Betty's end of the line, and Izzy couldn't help but join in.

'But more to the point, are you any closer to finding out what's wrong, Izzy? Why he needed the tablets in the first place? Has he said anything, love?'

Izzy sank down heavily beside her open case. The moment had arrived but she was balking at the thought of spilling the beans. Betraying all the trust he'd shown in her.

She exhaled a breath. Realistically, she'd no choice but to put Betty in the picture. It was why she'd been sent here, after all. It would be unfair to keep Betty in the dark, when she—Izzy—now knew the whole story; the expression rock and a hard place sprung to mind.

'Yes, but no one else knows, Betty.'

With that caveat made, she began her story, all the time trying to assuage her conscience, reminding herself that her first loyalty was to Rick's mother.

'He's decided to leave the band after the end of the current tour, initially for a 6-month sabbatical, but perhaps permanently.' She concluded.

'So that's it,' Betty murmured.

'Now, please remember, he's told me this in confidence.' Izzy bit her lip. 'You can't say anything; to him, or anybody else for that matter. Neither the band nor Francesca has been informed yet. He's going to speak to everyone in New York.'

'Don't worry, love,' Betty reassured her. 'Jim and I will act just as surprised as everyone else when the time comes. You don't know how relieved I am to finally know what's going on. I knew it was big, but I never dreamed he'd actually be leaving the band.' She paused. 'I was hoping it might be the wedding he wanted to place on hold— permanently.'

Nope, that's definitely still going full steam ahead!

There was a moment's silence at the other end of the line, before Betty spoke again, 'It must have taken him a lot of soul searching to reach this decision. The band is his whole life.'

'It has,' Izzy agreed. 'That's been the major stumbling block. All the turmoil he's felt has manifested itself in his insomnia. His body was telling him it was time to step back and take stock, but emotionally, he refused to listen.'

Izzy twisted a strand of hair through her fingers nervously, guilt gnawing at her gut. 'Even though he's finally admitted taking a break is the right thing to do, he's still hurting badly. He thinks he's being selfish, letting everyone down. Music and performing are his first love and it's a huge step for him to walk away.'

'And we'll support him, love,' Betty resolved. 'At the end of the day, I just want him to be happy. I was convinced if things carried on much longer, he'd end up in hospital or—'

'Don't worry. I think Rick reached that conclusion, too.' Izzy cut in hastily.

'I'm so glad he was able to talk to you, love. Something told me you'd be the one to finally get through to him.'

But Betty's words did little to comfort her. Izzy had never felt so desolate in all her life; breaking her promise to Rick leaving a particularly nasty taste in the mouth.

'He said I reminded him of Michelle.'

That comment made Betty laugh. 'I knew it…'

'I'm just sad that we'll never be able to maintain our friendship,' Izzy went on. 'It's been so lovely getting to know him all over again.'

'I know, love.' Betty's voice was soothing. 'Jim and I will always be grateful for your help. There's nothing I'd have liked more than for you, Rick and Michelle to be friends when all this is over. Just like me and your lovely mum…'

But that could never happen. And the senior Hambros' gratitude didn't provide any balm to the pain ripping through Izzy's chest at this particular moment. A large lump of unshed tears had lodged itself in her throat, and she tried to swallow it away as she checked her watch, only to goggle at the time. She'd have to get her skates on. She was expected downstairs in the next two minutes.

'Look, Betty, duty calls. They've got an interview at Three o'clock. I have to go now…'

3.52 PM

The band had spent the last thirty minutes sitting propped on bar stools, swigging beers and being quizzed by a roomful of teenagers; the ratio of girls to boys at least three to one. Izzy was tucked away at the back of the room, watching proceedings with interest.

'Okay, sadly, we've come to our final question,' Lindsay rechecked Izzy's typewritten notes, and there was a collective groan of disappointment from the audience. 'Where's Paulette Jones?'

Paulette stood up, smiling nervously, her fingers plucking at her chunky blonde plait.

'Okay, Paulette, I understand your question is for Rick?'

Paulette nodded. 'Thanks. We know how close you all are, and you always say in interviews that you are family first and a band second. But, is it hard to maintain friendships with people outside the band? Trust them not to run to the press telling lies about you?'

All at once, the air seemed to be sucked from Izzy's lungs. It felt as though Paulette had physically punched her. The question's subject matter a little too close for comfort.

'Yeah, it can be,' Rick agreed, fixing a blushing Paulette with his melted chocolate stare, 'you have to be very careful in this business.'

He looked thoughtful for a few seconds, contemplating the beer bottle in his hand, before expanding on his answer, 'We're all lucky that the people we grew up with are still our mates today.'

Collective nods of agreement came from his bandmates

'And we know they won't leak stories to the press, or let slip things we may have told them in confidence. In the music industry, you will always meet people who you think are trustworthy and go on to let you down—massively. It never stops being a pain in the arse, knowing you've opened up to someone, and then they've stabbed you in the back. You learn to be wary. So, when you do meet someone you can trust, it kind of restores your faith in human nature.'

Rick inclined his head towards Izzy, in the briefest of acknowledgments, and automatically her lips widened in reply. What would he say if he knew she'd just sold him down the river—to his own mother?

'Well, well, well, if it isn't Rick's pretty lady! We speak at last.'

Shit! Izzy's blood froze her veins at the sound of Francesca's decidedly arctic tones.

Zero hour had arrived.

'And she's been a very busy little lady too. Hasn't she?'

Izzy had known it was only a matter of time before Francesca confronted her; had dreaded hearing the sound of her voice, every time she'd lifted the telephone to her ear. There was no option now; she had to brace herself for the onslaught.

Moistening her lips, she set her coffee cup down on the desk, and slid into her chair.

'Miss Reiss,' she replied, hoping she'd kept the nerves from her voice. 'What can I do for you this evening?'

'Well, I need to speak to *my* fiancé but, I think we should have a chat first. Don't you?' Francesca went on. 'Given the enlightening conversation I've just had with Caron.'

This is it, Izzy. Brace yourself.

'Does shagging my fiancé in hotel swimming pools—every bloody chance you get— ring some bells for you?'

Francesca clearly didn't believe in beating about the bush.

'I…' Izzy tried to speak, but somehow no words would form.

'Thought so; your silence speaks volumes. Why don't I put you in the picture about how this is all going to play out from now on?'

Yes, she was about to be warned off—big time.

'Just to make sure there's no misunderstanding,' Francesca emphasised. 'The moment we met, I knew you'd be trouble. And— hey presto—my gut instinct wasn't wrong. Don't think I didn't clock all those lust-filled little glances directed at Rick whenever you thought no one was watching. Well, news flash, bitch, his fiancée clocked every single one of them. I knew it was only a matter of time before you'd manoeuvre yourself into his bed. After all, we both know what Rick's like on tour. Happy to fuck any stuck-up little slut that bats an eyelash at him.'

Izzy winced.

Stuck-up little slut—nice choice of word, Francesca!

'Not that I'm worried about Rick,' Francesca carried on, 'I've learned to accept the band's rules. And as you're probably realising, you're just the latest in a very long line. But here's the deal, Rick and I trust each other—implicitly.'

The cards were being laid on the table. 'After all, it would be unfair of me to expect him to go without sex for months on end when I can't be there. So, he has my blessing, because I know there's a line that Rick will never cross with *anyone*. Provided he always uses a condom and feelings don't come into it, he's free to do whatever he likes and I won't consider it cheating. But get this. I only tolerate this type off arrangement when I'm not around.'

Somehow Izzy managed to find her voice at last. 'But really, you've got things so wrong Francesca—eh, I mean Miss Reiss.'

If only Francesca knew the real truth. That Rick only pined for her in his bed; Sabrina's pal the latest to be spectacularly blown out by Francesca's fiancé—much to Izzy's relief.

'Rick and I aren't. We haven't— '

'Come on, Izzy, we both know it's exactly like that,' Francesca cut her off. 'So let's be grown-up and stop pretending, shall we? I've met your kind before. Think you'll be the lucky one to finally lure him away from me?'

Izzy tried again, 'Rick and I are just friends. You have my—'

'So that was just a chaste little kiss between friends in the corridor the other night, was it?'

Great! She knew about the kiss, too!

'That was a mistake. We both agreed it should never have happened. We'd been drinking—'

'Izzy, stop treating me like a fool. Rick's never been just "friends" with any woman in his life. You're no different.'

'But—'

'Look, if it comes down to your word against my brother-in-law, I know who I believe. You just want your claws into my fiancé.'

'Fran… Miss Reiss, it was a totally meaningless kiss—'

Well, for Rick, anyway.

Francesca continued to talk over her, 'You must think I was born yesterday. But don't delude yourself into thinking you'll be different. Rick's more than happy to fuck you. Take what you're offering on a plate, but that's as far as it goes.'

Izzy winced. Francesca's mouth resembled the underbelly of a sewer when she got started.

'I can see it doesn't matter what I say.' she sighed.

What was the point in arguing? She'd been cast as the villain—end of story.

'Do you want to speak to Rick or was the purpose of today's call to remind me of my place?'

'Of course I need to speak to him. But hear this, bitch. I'll be out there very shortly and when I arrive, your little romance stops. Do you understand? Rick's mine and always will be.'

11.58 PM

Izzy thumped her pillow, letting out a groan of frustration and rolled onto her front, endeavouring to get comfortable in yet another strange bed. But, tonight, it was proving impossible. She was too wound up to even think about sleeping yet.

Not only was the guilt of finally telling Betty truth eating away at her conscience, now, thanks to Davey's big mouth, Francesca was on her case and accusing her of all sorts. And to cap it all, Terry had subtly ramped up his campaign since the night of Sabrina's party, trying to intimidate her at every turn, with either a look or carefully chosen word.

She was getting further and further out of her depth. And Rick might be her dashing white knight, but he wasn't in a position to slay any of these particular dragons— much as she might want him to. No, packing her suitcase, and leaving the band high and dry, was becoming an altogether more attractive proposition.

After all, Rick was off the sleeping tablets and Betty knew the truth about her son's future plans. Being Terry's plaything or deputising as Francesca's punch bag wasn't what she'd signed up for.

But, realistically, she knew escaping wasn't an option. Not yet! She'd committed herself fully to both Betty—and the job—and she didn't break her commitments. Somehow, she had to find a way to last out until they reached New York. Izzy Anderson was made of sterner stuff. She didn't buckle under pressure or bail out when the going got tough. But, jeez, it was getting harder and harder.

41

PHILADELPHIA, PENNSYLVANIA

'Izzy, I need to get out of this sodding hotel, or I'll go crazy. Will you come with me?'

Another seventy-two hours and two more Cities—Quebec and Syracuse—had come and gone. They'd now touched down in Philadelphia.

Rick was propped against the door jamb of her room, arms folded, brow wrinkled and that wonderful smile had gone distinctly AWOL.

'What's up?' She allowed him inside.

'I'm so fucking bored. I feel like a bloody prisoner trapped in this place. And there are only so many times you can get excited winning a hand at Solitaire.' Brown eyes rolled expressively as they met her blue ones. 'Plus I've watched everything the Porn Channel has to offer.' That comment was delivered with a cheeky wink.

Izzy gave him an exasperated shake of the head. 'I'll ignore that last remark. So, where would you like to go?

'How about I take you shopping? I *know* you like shopping.'

'Shopping?' Izzy bit her lip, her eyes drifting to her paper-stacked desk. Lindsay had just off-loaded a heap of schedule revisals for here in Philadelphia, as well as their next port of call, New Jersey. She really didn't have time....

'Go on, you told me you like shopping.' He nudged her shoulder, turning on those "puppy dog eyes" to full beam.

'But I've got loads of typing…'

She was so tempted to say 'yes'. Take the chance to enjoy two of her favourite things—Rick's company and a bit of retail therapy.

'And I'll throw in lunch,' another nudge was delivered, 'entirely on me.'

'We'd need to be back here for quarter to four—at the very latest,' Izzy considered.

'Don't worry, I'll have my pretty lady back in plenty of time, I promise.' He treated her to another flutter of those lustrous eyelashes.

'Okay. You win. Let's go.'

Trying to ignore the typing glaring at her from her desk, Izzy reached for her denim jacket lying on the bed. Lindsay had indicated he needed to be in possession of the new schedules by five pm at the latest. That would potentially give her an hour when she got back. It would be tight, but do-able.

'By the way, I like where you've got your friend,' Rick commented, helping her on with the jacket, and nodding towards the toy dog perched on her pillow.

Izzy followed his gaze as she pulled her curls from the jacket's collar, a smile creasing her lips.

'Has he got a name?' Rick prompted.

'Yes. Let me introduce you to Buster,' Izzy replied, digging out a pair of fingerless woollen gloves from her jacket pocket and tugging them on.

For a moment an odd look passed across Rick's features. 'Where did you on earth did you dig that name up from?'

'I don't know. It just came to me.' Izzy gave a shrug as she swept up her room key from the nightstand and followed him to the door. 'I thought he looked like a "Buster".'

'Well, that's a coincidence.' Rick stepped out into the corridor, his expression still quizzical. 'I'd a dog called Buster when I was a teenager.'

'You did?' Izzy's hand froze in mid-air while reaching for the door handle.

Shit, so he did! Great! A total *'Casablanca'* moment; of *all* the names in the world, why had her brain conjured up that one? Being around Rick had obviously dragged it back from the dark recesses of her sub-conscious. Thinking back, she remembered Buster, so well. He'd been on holiday with them. A very bouncy Collie/Labrador cross and Izzy had adored him on sight, just like his master.

It was time to move the conversation away from dogs—past and present.

'Jeez, almost forgot. I need to call Phil. Get one of the limos brought around to the front entrance for us.'

'Do we have to do that, Izzy?' Rick placed a restraining hand on her arm before Izzy was able to retrace her steps back inside. 'Can't we just sneak out through the kitchens? Hail a cab at the end of the street. I don't fancy trailing round a store with either Scottie or Lee shadowing our every move.'

'But they're there for your safety?' she reminded him. 'Just in case, the presence of Richard Hambro creates an international incident. You haven't forgotten how long it took us to get into this hotel, last night?'

Their cars had been surrounded for at over an hour, until the local police, hotel security and their own minders had managed to clear a path through the two hundred-strong crowd of hormonally charged teenagers.

'Precisely, this is why I want to leave incognito. Remember, what it's like to be half-way normal. If we leave by the front entrance, it's guaranteed to descend into chaos.'

He looked so despondent that against her better judgement, Izzy found herself falling in with his request. 'Alright, I suppose so. But if it all goes pear-shaped, please don't blame me.'

11.53 AM

'We're still being tailed,' Izzy warned Rick, casting a worried glance behind them; her worst fears confirmed. His disguise of dark glasses and baseball cap—pulled down low over his face—clearly hadn't worked.

'Great. You mean I've become the *Pied Piper* of bloody Hamlyn again?' Rick muttered, returning the black leather bomber jacket to the rail. 'They'll be a total pain in the arse to get rid of.'

They'd made it to *Macy's*, congratulating themselves on a job well done, exiting via the kitchens and hailing a passing taxicab. Their car had sailed past the fans milling around the main hotel entrance; the teenagers oblivious to the fact one of their quarry had just pulled off a successful getaway under their noses.

However, for the last fifteen minutes, they'd been trailed by a posse of six girls. Izzy had first noticed them five minutes after entering the store, lurking behind a column, lust-filled eyes trained solely on Rick, and she'd been keeping a discrete watch on them ever since. As soon as they'd popped up again within the designer menswear department, she'd been certain. Teenage girls had no interest in men's clothing, just the particular man she was chaperoning about town, today.

'I did warn you.' Izzy thought for a moment. 'Look, I've got an idea. How about we do a deal with them?'

'What kind of deal?'

'You turn on the charm,' she explained at his sceptical look, 'maybe add a burst of those "puppy dog eyes", and sign some autographs. But all on condition they stop following you and leave the store.'

'And you seriously think they'll go for that, Izzy?' He shook his head. 'Sorry. Not convinced. It'll become a bloody circus.'

He held up another jacket and Izzy gave it a nod of approval. He'd look totally sexy in that. Then she caught sight of the price-tag and sucked in a breath. She'd never be able to afford something like that in a month of proverbial "Sundays".

'Come on, they got me to come shopping with you?' she coaxed. 'It has to be worth a try?'

'Okay.' He gave a reluctant grin. 'So you like my "puppy dog eyes", do you?'

'No. Only said that to persuade you to talk to your fans,' she replied dryly, before letting out a laugh at his crestfallen reaction. 'Got you, sucker!'

Leaving him, Izzy hurried over to where the girls stood.

At her approach, they suddenly appeared terrified, huddling together around a rail of shirts, looking everywhere but at the determined figure of Izzy bearing down upon them. Izzy guessed they probably thought she was an undercover store detective out to arrest them.

'Hi, girls,' she smiled, knowing she had to get them onside for her idea to succeed, 'I'm Izzy, Rick's PA. We noticed you've been following us. Is there something you wanted?'

Six bodies visibly squirmed in front of her.

'We didn't mean any harm.' One of them answered, the others looking at the floor, the walls, the ceiling, anywhere but actually making eye contact with Izzy.

'Don't worry you're not in trouble,' Izzy went on kindly, 'but Rick's entitled to his privacy while he's shopping. And being followed around the store really isn't fair. Is it?'

More squirming, but she received a few reluctant nods. The penny appeared to be dropping.

'Look, he's prepared to do a deal with you.'

It was carrot and stick time. Instantly, the expressions perked up, the girls keen to hear more about the mooted 'deal'.

'I'll take you over to meet Rick,' Izzy explained, 'and you can have a chat with him. He's more than happy to sign a few very discreet autographs, but on condition that you agree to leave afterwards. Now, do we have a deal?'

There were a few furtive glances exchanged between the girls.

'Because, if not'—it was time to get tough—'I'll have no option but to speak to the store manager and have you removed. We really don't want to do that, do we?'

Seeing she was playing hardball, and her threat was serious, the girls met her offer with vigorous head shaking. A deal had been struck.

Ten minutes later, six ecstatic girls left the store, clutching autographs to their heaving teenage bosoms; meeting a member of Eclectic Deviation had made their year.

'And now that the ever-resourceful Miss Stevenson has dealt with that problem, can I tempt her to some lunch? Don't know about you, Izzy, but I'm bloody starving.'

Rick had finally bought and paid for a leather jacket—the one Izzy had pronounced to be her favourite—and was now steering her towards the nearest escalator.

'So, where are we headed?' Izzy stepped on board the moving stairway, looking up at him expectantly. Her stomach had been rumbling for the last half-hour.

His arm had dropped to rest against her hip, and he gave it a light squeeze. 'Well, it just so happens there is an award-winning Italian restaurant on the top floor of this building,' he informed her. 'Apparently, it has superb panoramic views over the city, and the food is amazing. Plus, it's confession time,' he winked at her, 'I booked us a table this morning. I knew I could persuade you to play hooky with me!'

2.18 PM

'Have you got it on yet?' Rick called through the curtain of Izzy's cubicle, before retreating to the chaise longue opposite. Izzy heard him collapse down onto it with a groan.

'I'm ready for the grand reveal.'

'Just give me a minute!' Izzy took a final look at her reflection.

The dress definitely wasn't her usual style. She pulled a sultry pose in the mirror, pouting at the glass, channelling a look she'd seen Sabrina use on Marc a hundred times. The dress was definitely more for the 'Sabrinas' of this world but, nonetheless, it looked absolutely breathtaking.

Rick had been right. With its simple strapless bodice, and sweetheart neckline, it fitted like a glove around her slender frame, giving a tantalising peek at the curviness of her breasts beneath, while its silk skirt flared out in soft godets of fabric to mid-calf. But it had been the colour that had made her pause for a second look when pointed out by Rick—a rich sapphire blue. Visually, when teamed with her eyes, it was nothing short of stunning.

After some pretty persistent coaxing from Rick—not to mention full deployment of his "puppy dog eyes"—she'd finally agreed to try it on. And now here she was, gazing at herself—or rather a girl who looked remarkably like her but altogether much sexier—in the fitting-room mirror.

'Here goes nothing, Izzy,' she murmured, before grabbing the curtain and pulling it back to face Rick.

'Ta daa.' She struck a dramatic film-star pose, leaning against the side of the cubicle. 'What do you think?'

'Wow.' Rick's eyes swept down over her from head to toe. 'Izzy, you look…' He stopped, and his eyes did a reverse sweep, this time much slower; his expression unreadable.

'Okay?' she hazarded when he still hadn't uttered anything more. 'A bit of dog's dinner… a sack of potatoes…hideous…..'

'You look fucking beautiful,' he managed, sounding strangely croaky.

He did like it!

With a pleased giggle, Izzy performed a little pirouette for him.

'It's totally made for you.' He was on his feet now, moving forward towards her.

Heat crept up her neck as he approached. 'It's just a pity I'm all dressed up with nowhere to go,' she told him, giving the bodice a little self-conscious tug.

With all her exaggerated posing it had slipped slightly, and knowing her boobs, they'd be spilling over before long. It was a beautiful dress, but it would need a good strapless bra underneath to keep her figure in check.

She stepped back into the cubicle, making to close the curtain. 'Okay, you've seen me in it. Give me a few minutes, and I'll be right with you.'

'But you are going to buy it.' Rick had stepped in behind her, placing his hands on her shoulders, stilling her movements, his eyes catching hers in the full-length mirror. 'You—pretty lady—look breathtaking. You can't just leave it here on the hanger. This has 'Izzy' written all over it.'

Predictably, goosebumps popped on her upper arms at the sensation of both his hands and his warm breath against her bare skin.

'Well, I suppose it makes a change from seeing me in tight jeans or a denim mini,' she conceded.

'And you rock those too.' He leant his head against hers. 'But this dress is in a different league, Izzy. You'll need more than Buster for protection when you step out wearing that.'

She met that comment with a dismissive shake of the head, pretending to give him a swipe with her hand. 'Stop exaggerating!'

She took another critical look in the mirror.

'I can't buy it. For starters, I've nowhere to wear it to?'

Could she really justify the three-figure price tag for it to just hang in her wardrobe? Then she remembered. 'Wait a minute….our neighbours' daughter is getting married in the summer. I guess it would be perfect for her wedding.'

'Yep, you'd definitely pull the best man in that.'

'Will you please be serious; for once in your life?' Izzy rolled her eyes at him. .

'I *am* being serious. Nobody will be able to take their eyes off you.'

Their eyes collided, and desire twisted in her stomach. Her breath hitched in her throat, and an answering smile spread across Rick's face.

'Sorry I took so long. I was beginning to think I was on a wild-goose chase.' The sales assistant—who'd introduced herself as Madeleine—bustled into the fitting room, carrying a shoe box and giving Izzy a relieved smile. 'But I've finally found the matching shoes. I knew we had them.'

She opened the lid and drew out a pair of silk court shoes in Izzy's requested size. Izzy slipped them on, immediately gaining three inches in height, the sapphire-coloured shoes proving to be the ultimate

finishing touch, plus—Izzy took a couple of steps to walk them in—
they felt surprisingly comfortable, too.

'I have to say, your wife looks amazing in that dress. Don't you
agree, sir?' Madeleine commented, standing back to survey Izzy with
a contented smile.

'She certainly does.' Rick smiled.

If only!

'Oh, I'm not his wife,' Izzy felt obliged to set the record straight.
'I'm just his—'

'Beautiful girlfriend,' Rick threw a teasing wink in Izzy's direction.

He was at it again. Although, maybe just as well. His presence in
a ladies fitting room—with his half-dressed PA—might raise a few
eyebrows, otherwise.

'So, is it going to be a yes?' Madeleine looked hopeful, her honey-
coloured eyes flicking expectantly between Izzy and Rick.

Izzy bit her lip, deliberating. The dress and shoes were perfect. She
really wanted to splurge on them, but she'd need a bit more reassurance
before signing on the dotted line. Her eyes automatically shifted to
Rick.

'What do you really think—? ' she began.

'Just say yes,' he mouthed.

'Em… yes,' she heard herself say out loud.

'That's great.' Madeleine clapped her hands together, beaming at
Izzy. 'You won't regret it. I'll leave you get dressed. Bring everything
to the sales desk when you're ready.'

She moved to the doorway of the fitting room. 'Oh, I almost
forgot; underwear. That type of dress needs a really well-fitting
strapless bra. Give's a girl more confidence bending over. In fact…'

Izzy could see the cogs beginning to turn in the older woman's
head.

'I've a stunning little bustier set that came in yesterday which would be perfect for you. Give that lovely figure a little more support.'

The woman is a mind-reader.

Very reluctantly Izzy shook her head, knowing that—unfortunately—she'd have to shut down the suggestion. New underwear was out of the question.

For a start, it would be altogether too embarrassing. Rick was bound to react like a typical bloke and start ogling whatever Madeleine produced for inspection, then say something totally inappropriate into the bargain. Plus buying the dress and shoes would be putting her precariously near the bread line until she got paid. She couldn't afford to buy anything else.

'No, I'm good for underwear, thanks, Madeleine.'

'Come on, Izzy, at least take a look at what's on offer?'

Izzy caught the flirtatious wink Rick sent the shop assistant.

He's at it already.

'After all, a girl can never have too many sexy undies, don't you agree, Madeleine?'

'You said it, sir.' Madeleine was clearly lapping up his unashamed flirting. 'Now what size should I bring along, ma'am?'

'Really, you don't have to…' Izzy hesitated, but at the woman's raised eyebrows, she took the hint—arguing had just become futile.

'Thirty Four C, Size Ten.'

She'd been ambushed by two experts.

'Why did you have to say that?' Izzy challenged Rick as soon as they were alone. 'There is no way I can afford to buy anything else; least of all designer underwear.'

'Come on, Izzy, humour the woman. She's thinking about all that lovely commission heading her way.' He rubbed his hands together. 'Maybe you could model it for me? Go on, I dare you…'

'Not a chance, sunshine,' Izzy muttered, watching him flop down on the chaise and stretch out his legs, crossing them at the ankles.

'Awwww, come on, Izzy. Not even a little peek?' he cupped the back of his head with both hands, his grin decidedly teasing. 'We blokes never pass up a chance to see a pretty girl in sexy underwear.'

With a final glower in his direction, and trying to ignore his throaty chuckle, Izzy stepped back into the cubicle, shutting him out with an annoyed swish of the curtain.

Two minutes later, she heard Madeleine make her comeback; the sales assistant and Rick 'oohing and aahing' over whatever the older woman had just brought in.

Exiting the cubicle, back in her jeans and sweater, Izzy found Rick giving the underwear an altogether too close inspection. The bustier and panties were in a matching shade of deep sapphire blue, the former made of delicate boned lace with silk trim, while the latter was two barely-there triangles of lace, held together with ribbon ties.

'Look, Izzy.' He was holding up the miniscule panties by the side ribbons. 'These are seriously hot. Don't you think?' He flashed an incorrigible grin.

'Yes, they're from a new line we're carrying, called "*Sensuously Yours*",' Madeleine chimed in. 'Guaranteed to add a bit spice in the bedroom. How about I leave you both to have a think?'

With that she made a discreet withdrawal, but not before Izzy caught the knowing look she and Rick had exchanged. He was such a wind-up.

Deliberately choosing to ignore them, Izzy checked out the price tag on the bustier and did a double-take. It was more expensive than the dress.

'So?' Rick prompted.

'I'm not paying over two hundred dollars for a matching set of underwear,' was Izzy's indignant reply.

'Izzy, I didn't ask you what you thought of the price, I asked if you liked them.'

Izzy rolled her eyes at him. 'Of course I like them. They're beautiful. How could I not?'

She allowed herself to run her fingers over the intricate lacework of the bustier cups. The matching set really was exquisite. She'd love to own it, but only if she had the cash.

'But I also don't want to starve until my next pay cheque. And if I buy this, that's probably what's going to happen. Correction, that's definitely going to happen.'

'Then how about I buy them for you?'

'What?' The unexpected proposition made her splutter out loud. 'Don't be so stupid, Rick.'

'Come on, Izzy, why not? I've never said a proper thank you for all the extra hours you put in sorting out Francesca's cock-up with the wedding. Call this a long overdue thank-you gift?'

'Rick, I don't need gifts for doing my job,' she reminded him. 'It's what I get paid for, remember; sorting out all your problems.'

And certainly not gifts of a sexy little bustier and panties. If two triangles of lace held together with ribbon could be classified as panties?

'But, Izzy,' he protested, nodding towards the dress and shoes that she held clasped to her chest, 'it would finish off the whole look. I'm always buying stuff for Michelle. What's the difference to me treating you for a change?'

Those "puppy dog eyes" had made another appearance. Well, they wouldn't work their magic this time!

'It wouldn't feel right,' Izzy replied.

'Why?'

Isn't it obvious, Rick?

Izzy let out a sigh. 'Well, for a start, Michelle's your sister; I'm just your employee...'

'For fuck's sake, Izzy; you know you're way more than that.' He dismissed her argument with a wave of his hand. 'You're someone I consider pretty bloody important around here. Look, we could put it down as a well-earned bonus if that makes you feel any better.'

'No, it wouldn't.'

That would make it ten times worse, given what Terry, Davey, and now Francesca thought they were up to.

She tried to ignore the way he was holding the underwear in his hands, his fingertips caressing the lace. Her brain had started to conjure up all sorts of sensual images of him doing the same to her while wearing it. Biting down on her lip, she turned away, heat creeping up her throat. It was getting way too hot in here.

'Izzy, you can be so frustratingly obstinate sometimes? It's just a gift from me to you to say "thanks". What's the big deal? I can afford it.' He was clearly getting annoyed at her continued refusals.

'For your information, I neither want—nor expect—any of my friends or family to spend that kind of money on me—and certainly not for a set of underwear. You, Richard Hambro, are not the exception to that rule just because you happen to be a multi-millionaire. Got it?'

Her conscience wouldn't allow it.

Picking up her bag, she slipped it onto her shoulder. 'Now, come on. We need to get a move on. You have a sound check in thirty minutes. And I've still got all that bloody typing to wade through. This discussion is closed.'

She'd found the silver box waiting for her on the desk ten minutes ago; *Macy's* logo emblazoned on its lid.

'*Damn!*' Izzy tried to ignore the way molten heat flooded to the pit of her stomach as she approached it. He hadn't. Had he?

And more to the point, how on earth had he managed to buy it and get it over here in double quick time?

Quickly removing the lid, she found a small square of white card nestled on top of the blue tissue paper. Picking it up, she read Rick's handwritten note.

Please don't be mad at me, xxx

Beside the words, he'd drawn a little cartoon puppy with huge pleading eyes.

Those stomach muscles clenched tighter.

The sneaky so and so!

She knew she should be annoyed—and she was a little—but if she was honest she was more thrilled than anything else. Underneath the tissue paper was the matching bustier and panty set; both items in her correct measurements; Thirty Four C, Size Ten.

If only she could model it for him as he'd jokingly suggested! In her fantasy world, she could see those brown eyes smouldering with desire as he stripped it slowly off her body. Rick on his knees before her, his long fingers hooking into the panties, and sliding them agonisingly slowly off her hips and down her legs. His lips reaching over to press soft kisses against her…

'Stop, don't go there, Izzy!' she muttered, snapping out of her reverie.

But it still didn't feel right to accept the gift. The underwear was too expensive. Worse, if Francesca ever got wind of him splashing out on this type of thing for her…

'Izzy, we've got a bit of a crisis brewing…' Kathy's voice echoed down the hallway.

Izzy hurriedly dropped the card inside the box and stuffed it and its contents inside her filing cabinet out of sight.

Never mind Francesca; if Kathy got found out about this little lot, she'd demand details, lots and lots of embarrassing details. In fact, knowing Kathy's powers of interrogation, she'd have been an asset to the *Spanish Inquisition* back in the day.

No, she'd speak to Rick later. He'd have to take it back.

7.43 PM

Face to face, with the office door closed behind him, shutting out the rest of the world, Izzy was beginning to feel more than a little daunted at the conversation she was about to initiate with Rick.

And, given the huge grin he wore as he leant casually back against the door, he'd obviously guessed why he'd been called into the Headmistress's Office. With those arms folded, his brown eyes fastened onto her, Richard Hambro looked too damned sexy and self-assured for his own good. How was she going to play this?

Worse, the cut-away vest he was wearing, with its strategically placed rips across the chest area, was seriously distracting her, big time. It was time to concentrate on the grubby mark on the wall above his left ear, and not that cute little rip over his heart, with those wisps of dark hair poking through, just asking to be tousled.

'Rick.' She moistened her lips, and then berated herself inwardly for dithering. 'Thank you'—her hand rested on the box—'but as I told you earlier, I can't accept this gift.'

Damn, that smile wasn't disappearing.

'As the card says, Izzy, don't be mad at me.' He gave her one of those infuriatingly cute little winks. 'You'll look amazing.' Then he added, 'And if you should ever feel the need to model it...'

On cue, her cheeks flushed at his empty teasing.

'Stop with the jokes. I'm being serious. I really appreciate the thought,' she continued, not wanting to sound an ungrateful shrew, 'but as I explained earlier, it's way too expensive.'

Not to mention too personal!

'And as I told you, Izzy, you are a fantastic PA,' he grinned, 'but—more importantly—you're someone I've come to care about—one hell of a lot. You know I have. I don't give out swimming lessons to just anybody, remember?' He shook his head. 'You know my feelings about the people we meet in this business. But from day one, somehow I knew I could trust you. You're the kindest, most loyal person I've ever met in my life. So, please accept the present. Not just as a belated 'thank you' for sorting out the whole wedding fiasco, but for just being you; for being there for me with no hidden agenda.' He'd straightened, flashing a wicked smile. 'And it's not as if I can take it back to the store. Is it?'

Izzy gave a helpless shrug. He was right; the shop would be closed by now. But the 'no hidden agenda' phrase was niggling at her conscience.

'But I still think—'she tried to argue once more, only to be silenced by him holding up a hand.

'They're yours, Izzy. You don't know the trouble I went to, to get the lovely Madeleine to sort this for me.'

Out of nowhere, Izzy felt her eyes brim with tears. He was so bloody lovely, and she deserved neither the gift, nor his kind words. With difficulty, she managed to blink the tears away, hoping he hadn't noticed their glisten.

'And it's not as if I can wear it, myself,' Rick observed with a chuckle, his hand on the door handle. 'Sorry, but I don't get off on parading around in women's underwear. Now, Jonny on the other hand, you never know. He'll try anything once…' He waggled his eyebrows.

42

ATLANTIC CITY, NEW JERSEY

Davey was watching her from the doorway, hands stuffed into his too-tight jeans, a lit cigarette dangling from his lips and—Izzy swallowed—the little toad was smiling at her. Correction; make that more like sneering. And when Davey sneered, it was never a good sign. It spelt trouble, and always for her.

'Davey?' She forced herself to be pleasant, but she hadn't forgiven him for dropping her in it with Francesca. All her wits were now switched to high alert; she was probably going to need them over the next five minutes.

'Izzy?'

Yep, his reply was cordial, too cordial; Davey at his most dangerous when pretending to be nice. It meant the knife was about to be plunged right between the shoulder blades.

'What can I do for you?' Izzy asked, watching him saunter into the office, arrogance personified.

And make it quick, she wanted to add. She didn't have time to indulge in any of his verbal fencing matches. She was knee-deep in the organisation of Rick's birthday.

'Just chasing up those Access-all-Areas passes. Have you processed them yet?' He came to perch on the edge of her desk, a foot swinging. 'Spoke to our Gary last night and he says he hasn't received anything.'

He let out a loud tut. 'Don't tell me the super-efficient Miss Stevenson has slipped up for once? Been too busy looking after other things, or—should I say—other people?'

Yep, the first dig of the day had been expertly delivered.

'For your information, they were sent out last Friday, first class *Air Mail*. They should arrive any day, now.' Izzy's voice was clipped as she rechecked the entry in her diary.

Hopefully, her prompt confirmation would make him leave. 'But if you like, I can give him a call myself—'

'Not necessary,' he cut her off quickly, giving Izzy another of those evil little smirks, making her doubt that was the real reason for his visit. 'Should never have doubted you for a second, should I?'

Beady hazel eyes stared at her for a few more unsettling seconds. It was time to get rid of him. 'So, if there's nothing else, Davey…?'

But Davey clearly didn't want to leave just yet. Inclining his head, he leaned over to peruse the list of notes written on her notepad, letting out a low whistle.

'So, finalising the details for Ricky's birthday? And is that your idea for the cake?' He pointed at her extremely rough doodle with his cigarette.

It was a cake in the shape of a drum kit. Or rather Izzy's best attempt at one. Art hadn't been her finest hour at school.

'I thought that might be appropriate,' she answered, immediately on the defensive.

Davey pulled a face, clearly not impressed by either her idea or her artistic talents.

'Yeah, might have known *he'd* be your top priority,' he observed. 'Anyway, I've had a fucking perfect idea for the cake. So, hold fire with whatever *that* monstrosity is meant to be. I need to run it past the lads, first.'

'Fine!' Izzy muttered, scoring a heavy line through her drawing. 'Let me know as soon as possible. We don't have much time left.'

Davey folded his arms, raising a speculative eyebrow. 'Anyway, more to the point, what does Izzy intend to give our Ricky for his birthday?'

Good question! She still had no clue. What did a girl buy a millionaire?

'No doubt, you'll be giving him a bit more of the old slap and tickle eh!'

She didn't appreciate his seaside postcard humour.

'And as I've told you numerous times,' Izzy's eyes were cold, 'there is nothing going on between Rick and me.'

'So that kiss I witnessed was Scotch mist, was it? I'll believe you, thousands wouldn't.' he crowed 'Anyway, isn't it about time you and Rick knocked things on the head? Francesca will be here soon.'

As if Izzy could forget the imminent arrival of She-Bitch-from-Hell courtesy of her supersonic broomstick.

'And Caron and I don't need some jumped-up little tart causing trouble with the wedding just around the corner.' Davey slid off the desk, sucking on his cigarette as if his life depended on it. 'And despite my very vocal objections, Marc—our resident Boy Wonder— made sure you've been offered a fucking permanent post. But I think it's about time you called Jack; turned down the job offer. ...' There was a pause, pregnant with meaning.

She caught the menacing glint reflected in his eyes. Here was the real reason for his visit. He wanted her out.

'Is that a threat, Davey?'

'Let's just say, I could make things pretty fucking uncomfortable around here if you chose to stick around beyond the last concert in New York....'

Yep, he *was* threatening her, but Izzy didn't get an opportunity to respond, the office door was propped open, and a frazzled Lindsay stuck his head inside.

'There you are, Eastman! Meet and bloody Greet, remember! Get your arse in gear!' he barked. 'And wait till you see the bunch we've got tonight. Talk about over-excited. Four faints already. Bloody medical attendants don't know which way to turn.'

Izzy gave grim smile, knowing Davey's imminent appearance wouldn't garner the same response.

'I'll be right with you. Just need a couple more minutes with Izzy?'

'No can do.' Lindsay consulted the clipboard in his hand. 'According to Izzy's schedule, you're on now. In fact; you're already one minute and twenty eight seconds late…'

43

ATLANTIC CITY, NEW JERSEY

Avalon Beach was bathed in glorious early morning sunlight. A soft breeze was blowing in off the Atlantic Ocean, gently whipping up the foaming breakers that washed back and forth over the golden sand. Up above, cotton wool clouds were engaged in an endless game of kiss-chase across the palest of blue skies.

The start of another New Jersey day found Izzy and Rick, their shoes in hand, walking the shore line, Izzy's arm linked through Rick's. The surrounding beach was virtually deserted at this hour, apart from a couple of dog walkers and the usual early morning joggers, meaning Rick didn't need to worry about being pestered by over-zealous autograph hunters or teenage girls.

During their swimming lesson the previous night, he'd asked if she fancied accompanying him on the forty-five minute journey south, and Izzy had jumped at the chance.

While Rick enjoyed a quick dip in the ocean, she'd been content to sit by the water's edge, holding his clothing at the ready, and watching the world go by. There was nothing pressing in the band's diary until they left for the return flight to Philadelphia, in four hours time.

In fact, Izzy mused, smiling up at him now, she and Rick could be any young couple in the first flush of romance enjoying an early morning date on the beach. Except of course, they weren't.

'Isn't this stunning?' she exclaimed, stopping for a moment to shield her eyes from the glare of the sun, and take in the full beauty of her surroundings. 'I wish I could stay out here all day.'

'Yeah, me too,'

At that moment, a large wave crashed onto the sand at their feet.

With a yelp, Izzy just managed to jump clear, before the water soaked through her rolled up jeans, but Rick just laughed at her, content to stay where he was, the foam swirling about his bare ankles.

'I love being beside the ocean,' he commented. 'It's got so many moods. One minute calm and serene; the next, whipping itself into some kind of angry frenzy, out to destroy everything in its path. I think that's why I'm looking forward to taking that house in Southampton. I'll get to sit on my terrace and watch it all day. And you, pretty lady, will be most welcome to visit. We could even fit in a few swimming lessons. What do you say?'

Izzy shook her head sadly; she knew she'd never get to see this new home by the sea. 'I don't think I'm quite good enough for sea swimming, yet. Do you?' she hedged.

'Oh, I don't know. You're progressing really well. We could give it a quick try, now?'

With a cheeky wink, he made a playful lunge towards her, clearly intent on gathering her up in a fireman's lift and dragging her back into the surf with him.

'Don't you even think about it!' she squealed, managing—at the last minute—to dodge out under his outstretched arms, and make a getaway.

Only after some gentle coaxing, was she finally persuaded to return to his side, tucking her hand back through his proffered arm.

'I'm thinking of getting a dog,' he mentioned, as they set off once more, pointing towards a dog walker up ahead, throwing a ball for a gambling retriever, 'and a boat.'

'You're buying a boat?' Izzy's eyebrows shot up in surprise. 'I didn't know you were into sailing.'

'Technically, I'm not. But it's something I've always fancied giving a try,' he told her, with a slightly wistful look, 'never had the time or the cash before.'

He leaned down to tenderly brush a couple of stray curls that had blown onto Izzy's lip.

'There something ever so appealing about just casting off and going wherever the mood takes me. Ever tried sailing, yourself?'

'No. Well, not unless you count the Dover to Calais ferry—twice?'

'No, that's not quite in the same league.' He chuckled. 'And are you a good sailor, pretty lady? Ever been seasick?'

'Never,' she answered proudly, before rubbing the top of her head with a giggle. 'Touch wood.'

'Good. A guy always needs a hardy crew he can rely on.'

With that enigmatic comment, they walked on in silence, finally reaching a rickety wooden pier that jutted several metres out into the ocean; its boards bleached white with the sunlight and salt water.

Rick clambered up first and then tugged Izzy up to stand at his side, her hand held fast in his.

'Have you given any more thought to what you're going to say to Francesca,' Izzy asked tentatively, glancing at their clasped hands, 'about your sabbatical?'

Knowing Francesca and the fact image was everything, Rick's career change—even if it was temporary—would go down like the 'old lead balloon'. His fiancée enjoyed the kudos of being one half of a famous rock-star couple.

'Yeah, a little bit.' His jaw had visibly tightened at the mention of Francesca's name, but he didn't say anymore.

'Once you have a chance to talk face to face, she'll realise it's for the best.' Izzy rested her cheek against his shirt clad biceps, squeezing his fingers.

'I suppose so,' he gave a little shrug, 'but to be honest, I don't really want to dwell on Francesca going ballistic at me. It's too beautiful a day.'

He exhaled a long breath. 'Look, Izzy, there's something I really need to ask you before we head back?'

'What is it?'

Rick was looking down at her now, studying her closely, while biting his lip.

'Jack has asked you to work for the band, and I know you're still mulling it over?'

'Yes.' She still needed to extricate herself out of that tricky situation.

'Made any final decision yet?' he asked.

'I'm still considering my options.' Izzy's eyes shifted away from Rick to gaze at a large yacht which had appeared on the horizon. 'Obviously, it's an amazing opportunity.'

Shit, how did she sidestep this one?

'But if *I'm* being honest,' she went on, choosing her words with care, 'I'd really like something with regular working hours and much less travelling.'

Is this a good enough excuse?

'So, you're going to say "no" to Jack?' He sounded genuinely surprised.

Izzy nodded. 'Yes. Don't get me wrong, touring with the band has been an experience I'll never forget; with the emphasis on "experience".' She rolled her eyes. 'But, I'm just picking the right moment to speak to him. When Marc finds out, I've got a feeling things could turn awkward. The word "no" isn't in his vocabulary. Is it?'

'Only if he's the one saying it,' Rick agreed.

He clearly knew his cousin inside out.

'Yes. You won't say anything, will you?'

Jeez, she had a nerve asking that of him.

'Don't worry, I'll keep it zipped.' He pointed at his lips. 'But that leads me nicely onto what I need to ask you. He treated her to a bone-melting smile. 'Would you maybe consider working for me instead? If I want to pursue my idea of setting up a studio, I'll definitely need a PA.' He gave her a small wink. 'The hours would be more human and there would definitely be less travelling. Obviously, it's not going to happen straightaway, but I'd match Jack's terms when the time came.'

Keep a poker face, Izzy. She'd never felt so elated and so defeated in the same instant.

'You'd really want me to work for you?'

'Told you, a guy needs a crew he can rely on,' he joked.

'But, what about Francesca, shouldn't she have a say?' Izzy blurted the name out before she could stop herself.

There was no way Francesca would agree to her working for Rick. Cancel that. What was she even thinking? Izzy Anderson couldn't work for him—full stop!

'What do you mean?' Rick frowned.

'Well, surely she'd want to be involved with the setting up of your studio idea? Taking on staff…' Izzy replied.

'Knowing Francesca, I doubt it. For a start; she can't type to save her life. Too terrified she'd break a precious fingernail.' He grimaced. 'No, office work isn't her thing. She's blessed in… other ways.' He pinned her with those all-seeing eyes. 'So, what do you say? Interested in becoming my *Girl Friday*?'

'Well, it's a great offer…' Izzy moistened her lips, that rabbit-trapped-in-the-headlights feeling gripping her. How could she let him down gently?

'But…?' The frown on Rick's face had deepened and Izzy hated seeing the disappointment creep into his eyes.

If things were different, she'd bite his hand off. No questions asked….

'There's a potential PA job back home.' she invented. 'I'd be working for a friend of mum's. I kind of promised I'd look into it when I get back. Try and get back in mum and dad's good books.'

Another whopper of a lie had passed her lips.

'Although, what you've offered is way more appealing,' she added hastily, 'but I just need to check things out first—keep the parents off my back. You know how it is with them. I won't keep you waiting very long for a final answer.'

Just the rest of his life!

44

PHILADELPHIA, PENNSYLVANIA

Picking up her pen, Izzy appended her signature to the letter, formally declining Jack's offer of a new contract. She'd also—reluctantly—reached another very necessary decision. It was time for her to exit stage left—as soon as possible.

The official end of her contract with the band was the last day of April, but after the final concert in New York would be good enough. After all, that seemed to be Davey's preferred date for her departure. She'd grant the little git's wish, but Jack couldn't know she was bailing early.

Everything—Rick, Jack, Davey, Francesca, Terry—it was all becoming much too complicated. She'd told so many lies in the last four months, keeping track of them was becoming little short of exhausting. The phrase "oh what a tangled web…" kept running through her mind. It was one of her mother's stock phrases—and it was her Mum who'd landed her in this situation in the first place!

And despite all her brave internal pep-talks—that quitting early was the coward's way out —it was time to go. With Rick safely off those pills and Betty knowing the truth, her mission was effectively over. Yes, she'd see things out to the final night at Madison Square Garden and then she'd head for home.

Her mind made up, she organised herself a flight from New York to London with an onward connection to Glasgow. If she was clever, no one would realise anything was amiss until it was too late and she'd be on her way home.

Taking the completed letter, Izzy hurried down to reception, asking for it to be faxed through to Jack's home number as soon as possible. She'd barely got back upstairs when the telephone by her bed rang out.

It was Jack, stunned by her decision.

'Is there really nothing I can say to change your mind?' There was genuine disappointment in his usually gruff voice. 'Nothing I could add that would make you stay?'

'Jack, you've been more than generous as it is,' Izzy reassured him. 'I've loved every minute of my time with you. I really have. But I think, going forward, I need something with a lot less travelling and shorter working hours.' She hoped he'd swallow the same line she'd used on Rick. 'But I do appreciate the trouble this will cause, once Marc finds out.'

'Yeah, Marc being Marc, he's already talking as if it's some kind of done deal.' Jack sighed. 'Never mind, he'll just have to live with it. If you want to leave at the end of April, I can't stop you.'

'I really am sorry, Jack.' Her conscience gave a twinge, knowing she'd be departing a lot sooner than that.

Jack took a drag of his cigar. 'But you're going to be missed, Izzy! And I never thought I'd say that after your first week with us!'

'Yes. It was a real baptism of fire until I got to grips with all the competing egos around here.'

'Yeah, apart from Rick, who—by some miracle—has managed to remain a thoroughly decent bloke,' Jack chortled, 'I've never met four more self-absorbed narcissists in my life. Sometimes, I think I've created monsters.' He let out a sigh. 'Okay, thanks for confirming your thoughts. And don't worry; you've more than earned another glowing reference.'

'Thanks, Jack.'

Not that it would be forthcoming once Izzy Stevenson did her "Houdini" act.

'Jack, one last thing,' Izzy hesitated, hoping what she was about to ask would go down okay. 'Could we keep my decision under wraps for a little bit longer?' She paused. 'Not say anything to *anybody*, especially the band? It might make the last few weeks difficult for all concerned if Marc knows I've said 'no'. Everyone is stressed enough with New York looming large on the horizon. I don't need him bearing a grudge and becoming…' she hesitated, 'difficult to work with.'

Mentally, she crossed her fingers, hoping Jack would agree.

'Not a problem, Izzy. Totally see where you're coming from.' There was amusement in his tone. 'This is just between the two of us; nobody else. '

45

PHILADELPHIA, PENNSYLVANIA

The lights had dimmed out on stage once more, and intermittent screams rang out in the darkness, the audience realising it was nearing tonight's encore.

Izzy was secreted out of sight behind a large bank of amplifiers, awaiting Steve's signal, and doing her best not to inadvertently do a "Michael Jackson" and set her hair alight with the cake's twenty-eight oversized candles.

She looked down at it now, wrinkling her nose in disgust at Davey's supposedly inspired idea; a pair of women's boobs encased in a lacy white bra—size Thirty-two Es to be exact— a nod to Rick's beloved fiancée.

At least Rick had no inkling about this unscheduled departure to tonight's proceedings; the rest of the band getting ready to launch into an un-rehearsed rendition of *"Happy Birthday"*.

Through the gloom, Izzy could make out Steve exchanging a final few words with Jonny and Davey and, as soon as they'd returned to their respective microphone stands, she received the agreed thumbs-up sign. Her walk-on part had arrived.

The stage lights went up.

Taking a deep breath, she stepped out into the glare of overhead spotlights, fifteen thousand pairs of eyes instantly swivelling in her direction.

A wall of sound erupted around the auditorium; the whole place going wild as an image of the burning cake flashed up on the overhead video screen. Taking Izzy's appearance as his cue, Jonny strummed the opening cords on his guitar, and everyone began singing with gusto.

Izzy picked her way across the stage to stand at Steve's side. She'd made it without tripping—or worse—ending up with a face full of sponge boobs.

Rick was still firmly ensconced behind his drum kit, a drumstick being twirled absently between his fingers, a ghost of a smile on his lips. But he wasn't allowed to remain there much longer.

'You're in trouble for conspiring with these mad bastards, pretty lady,' Rick shouted in her ear, having finally been dragged forward by Davey and Marc. 'You know I asked for no bloody fuss, today.'

'But we couldn't let your birthday pass without either a song or a cake,' she protested at Rick's disbelieving expression, 'and a good PA always does what she's told, remember?'

Although procuring a cake resembling a pair of breasts had been pushing it—massively.

'What a cake!' He grinned, giving the twin mounds of pink and white icing a quick onceover. 'Are they supposed to remind me of someone by any chance?'

Izzy pretended not to hear him.

The singing at an end, Steve delivered a short speech congratulating Rick on reaching the grand old age of twenty eight, making much of the fact that there was only two years of his twenties left until he hit the big 'Three Zero'. Then, Steve's few words at an end, Rick was finally allowed to blow out his candles—and not before time as the icing was beginning to melt in places—Steve joking that they had Philadelphia's Fire Department on standby as a precaution.

Candles extinguished, Rick grabbed a microphone, and thanked everyone for their birthday wishes, as well as the mountain of cards, flowers and presents that had deluged their hotel earlier that day. He finished by reminding Steve it was just under three months until his own twenty eighth birthday and that he should watch out, Rick fully intended on getting his own back.

After giving each member of the band a hug, Rick leaned over and broke off one of the boob's protruding nipples and popped it in his mouth, wiggling his eyebrows comically as he chewed.

'Mmmm.' He licked his lips. 'I think I'm definitely a nipple man. Thanks, Izzy.'

She received a quick brush of his lips to her cheek, which resulted in more screaming from the packed arena. Around eight thousand people clearly wishing they were in her shoes at that moment.

Flushing at such a public show of affection, she looked down, catching sight of the silver and leather thong bracelet nestling on Rick's left wrist. She felt a rush of pleasure. He was still wearing it. He'd seemed genuinely touched when she'd presented it to him at breakfast, slipping it on straightaway—with Izzy receiving another kiss on the cheek—but she'd caught Davey's eye roll towards Jonny. He'd been distinctly underwhelmed by her present; probably thought she'd got it out of a Christmas cracker.

With a final wave towards the audience, Rick scuttled back to the safety of his drum kit, allowing Izzy to make her own escape. The first part of his birthday celebrations complete.

'Why are guys so bloody predictable?' Kathy groaned against Izzy's ear.

Both women exchanged disgusted glances at the sight of the scantily clad female gyrating around Rick's crotch, all her clothes removed now except a gold thong and sky-high scarlet heels, her mammoth chest jiggling everywhere.

The rest of the assembled—mainly male—cat-calling audience were crammed into the bar of their Philadelphia hotel, and thoroughly enjoying the stripper's raunchy display; her presence, another dubious gift to the birthday boy.

'Come on. I've seen *more* than enough of this.' Izzy grabbed Kathy's arm, and propelled her towards an unoccupied booth on the far side of the room.

'Honestly, one glimpse of a pair of breasts and men regress to teenagers, Kathy opined, collapsing onto the banquette, but still keeping a weather eye on the floorshow.

'You can say that, again! Having to parade about with that bloody cake was bad enough.' Izzy harrumphed, her back defiantly to the proceedings. 'Let me know the minute this spectacle's at an end. I've still got to pay her.' She removed an envelope from her jeans pocket and slapped it down onto the table. 'You won't believe how much strippers charge for their services?'

'I can make a guess,' Kathy replied, picking up her drink, swirling it with her straw. They're de-riguer for birthdays on tour. And the good ones are always more expensive, especially if they're into providing a few optional extras; if you know what I mean?'

Izzy was subjected to the old 'nudge-nudge, wink-wink' routine; but she tried not to dwell on the insinuation behind Kathy's words. She didn't want to think about this one providing Rick with any optional extras.

'Although, given Rick's vow of celibacy, that part of the deal might not be required,' Kathy went on, 'but if he's looking for someone to step into his shoes, our Terry looks to be more than up for the job. Look at him!'

The girl had moved away from Rick and was getting intimately acquainted with their Head of Security, his head shoved into her ample chest. A cursory glance at the nauseating spectacle was enough for Izzy.

'Yuck!'

More whooping and words of filthy encouragement followed over the next few minutes. Her performance was clearly moving towards some kind of crescendo.

Chanting began; '*Off! Off! Off!*'

'And that's it, Izzy. We have the highlight of tonight's show, the thong is off, and the negligee is on,' Kathy reported as the room burst into rapturous whistles and applause, 'and Rick's having the privilege of her tongue being rammed down his throat. Is that a prelude to what comes later, we ask ourselves?'

Izzy whipped around, her green-eyed monster stirring deep inside. *No, he couldn't. Please not with her!*

'Wish that was you. Don't you, Miss S?' Kathy observed over the rim of her wine glass, her grin wicked.

Izzy pursed her lips. 'You're beginning to sound like a broken record.'

'Honestly, Izzy, face facts. You fancy the guy. Just admit it to me!' Kathy shot back. 'I won't tell anybody.'

Izzy slumped back into her seat, feeling defeated. Kathy was right. What was the point in denying it any longer?

'Okay, you win,' she conceded, tracing a line of condensation down the side of the Pepsi bottle she was holding. 'I do like him. But girls like me aren't on his radar for meaningful relationships. You said so yourself.'

'True,' Kathy agreed, eyes sparkling mischievously, 'but who said anything about having a meaningful relationship with him? I'm talking about good old-fashioned sex.'

'Rick isn't interested in me like that.' Izzy gave her friend a frustrated shake of the head. 'He's not interested in any woman at the moment; you just said so, remember?'

Except his flaming fiancée - She-bitch-from-hell!

'Scottie says he's refused all offers of hook ups for weeks now.'

'Exactly, why do you think we've got the luscious...,' Izzy double-checked the name on the envelope, before rolling her eyes ceiling-wards, 'Lynette tonight? And I'm quoting Jonathan Hambro here, if anyone can tempt Rick's "dick" out of hibernation' Izzy pulled a face 'she'll be the girl to do it.'

'But it still doesn't get away from the fact—vow of celibacy or not—that Rick's always very flirty with *you*, Izzy. And I'm sure I've caught him checking you out a few times, when he thinks no one's watching.'

'Believe me. I know for a fact. I'm the last one he's checking out.'

Kathy gave a disbelieving laugh, before taking a slurp of her drink.

'It's' true.' Izzy emphasised at Kathy's scepticism. 'Yes, we may get on well together. Have a really good laugh together. But we're mates, nothing else. If you must know, he says I remind him of his sister, Michelle. Surely, that says it all? There's definitely no romantic interest on his part...'

'You remind him of Michelle. Do me a favour, Izzy! That's not what *those* looks were telling *me*.'

'It's the truth. That's what he said.'

The booths and nearby tables were beginning to fill up. It was time for Izzy to steer the conversation away from Rick.

'Anyway, Francesca will be with us in precisely ten days time.'

'Please don't remind me!' Kathy pretended to retch over the side of the banquette. 'And she'll be accompanied by that Rottweiler of a sister, Caron. Our cup will runneth over with all that enforced loveliness heading our way, courtesy of *Concorde*.'

Kathy's accurate observation on the Reiss Sisters reduced them both to hysterics.

'But I still think there's something between you two.' Kathy sobered 'Just can't put my finger on what it is. And it's nothing to do with you channelling his little sister. He's so relaxed around you, Izzy. Relaxed in a way he's not with other people. Even me, and I've slept with the guy!' Kathy tapped her shoulder. 'Go on; why not give him the come-on. Just a little bit? See what happens? You never know. It might surprise you!'

'And end up mortified when he turns me down flat!' Izzy retorted, remembering the aftermath of their kiss and his emphasis on just wanting them to be friends. 'No, Kathy. You're so totally wrong here, it's laughable….'

46

PHILADELPHIA, PENNSYLVANIA

'Hi' Izzy smiled as Rick allowed her inside.

'Thanks for coming up, Izzy.'

He ran a hand through his damp hair. 'I took a bath but it hasn't helped. The pain in my neck just seemed to start out of nowhere.'

Izzy gave him a reassuring smile. 'No problem. I wasn't doing anything special anyway.'

She'd been unable to settle too. Her brain constantly churning over what Kathy had said, analysing every conversation she'd ever had with Rick, and she was still unconvinced—two kisses, a few charged looks and some flirty comments aside—that Rick was interested in anything more than friendship. Yes, he was relaxed around her. They had fun together; could talk about anything under the sun. But it was a bit of stretch to say that meant he was attracted to her.

Izzy glanced discreetly around the room; empty. Had Jonny's little scheme back-fired too?

'If you're looking for Lynette, she's not here.'

Izzy jumped guiltily. It was uncanny how accurately he could always tell what she was thinking.

'She's probably cuddled up with my little cousin as we speak.' Rick flashed a wicked grin.

Typical, she might have guessed Jonny would have taken advantage of the situation. That one would be chasing women in his *Zimmer* frame.

'Not that they didn't make it clear I could join them, should I change my mind.' He winked at her, before undoing the belt of his robe and diving between the sheets.

'But birthday present or not, a threesome wasn't what I wanted,' he continued. 'Last I heard Davey and Terry were drawing lots for the privilege of taking my place.'

'Charming!' Izzy tried—and failed—to hide her distaste at the little scene he'd just conjured up.

'So, do you want to do my neck or shoulders first?' He'd flipped onto his stomach, his head resting on crossed forearms; those eyes never leaving her face for a minute.

'Probably better to start with your neck,' Izzy considered. 'That seems to be the root of your problems.'

The intensity of the look she was receiving now was slightly un-nerving, as though he was trying to see right inside her; read her mind again.

Could he…? No, stop being stupid Izzy!

Taking a deep breath, she placed her hands on the nape of his neck and began the massage.

'So, did you enjoy your birthday?' she asked after a few minutes of intense concentration working those persistent little knots of tension which never seemed to disappear entirely.

'Yeah, cake was great. And I love my bracelet, but I could have done without the whole "stripper thing"'

'Jonny told me strippers were traditional for band birthdays. You know, up there with turkey and sprouts for Christmas dinner.'

'Yeah, and back in the old days, they were a rite of passage,' he gave a rueful grin, 'but somewhere along the line, I seemed to have changed. I guess it's been the questioning of my future with the band that's done it. It's made me look at life differently; look at *me* differently. Realise that there are aspects of my behaviour with women that I'm not proud of.'

A strange, almost sad look passed across his face. 'Maybe I'm finally growing up, deciding what's important? What I really want? And believe me, top of the list, casual sex with strangers has lost its appeal; big time.' He let out a long sigh, and Izzy sensed a distinct shift in his mood.

'Look, Izzy, can we stop, please?' With that he shifted away from her to sit up, raking both hands through his hair.

'Have I done something wrong?' Izzy sat back, biting her lip in puzzlement.

Why had he asked her to stop? His eyes had taken on a serious look, those full lips pursed together. Something was annoying him, but what?

There was a long pause before Rick moistened his lips and began to speak. 'No, of course not, you've done nothing wrong, pretty lady. It's me. I'm the one at fault here.' he said. 'I'm sorry, but I got you up here on false pretences, tonight.'

'What do you mean false pretences?' Izzy's eyes widened.

'I'm fine. I… don't need a massage.'

Was that a trace of embarrassment she could see now? His cheeks had reddened.

'I lied to you, Izzy.'

'You lied to me. But why…'

What was going on?

Reaching out, he took her hand in his, entwining their fingers together, grasping her hand tightly.

'You see…' His eyes flicked towards the ceiling, his teeth sinking into his lower lip, before he looked at her straight in the eye. 'All I really wanted for my birthday was to spend some time alone with you. Maybe take you out to dinner first, and then we could…'

He paused, the pulse in his neck throbbing, before he spoke again. 'The thing is Izzy; I can't fight the way I feel any longer when I'm around you, no matter how much I try...'

'What you feel…?' Izzy's mouth dropped open in astonishment.

Had Kathy been right, after all?

'Izzy, I think about you all the time.'

'You do?'

Her heart began hammering painfully against her breast bone. So hard, she was sure he'd be able to hear it. Was she dreaming all this? Or was she about to wake up any minute?

She blinked several times but couldn't say anything, her throat too constricted at his admission.

'Ever since I met you, you've bewitched me. And this is not just some cheesy line.' He continued. 'Given all the stuff with the band and the wedding, I told myself I didn't need any more complications in my life; especially being attracted to another woman. I tried to push my attraction to the side, ignore it. Keep everything strictly platonic between us. Pretend it wasn't happening.'

He continued to stroke her fingers. 'But every day, I've been fighting a losing battle with myself. I've become addicted to being around you, Izzy.' He gave a short humourless laugh. 'You're the one who's put me off casual sex. All I want is you.'

'You do?'

She was the reason behind his vow of celibacy, and not Francesca? Could she really believe him?

'Yes, all I can think about is being with you. I'm fed up being just friends. What I'm feeling inside is anything but friendly, and definitely not brotherly.' He gave brief chuckle. 'I hate having to watch everything I do and say whenever we're together. Never step over that invisible line. Give into my attraction. And, from watching you, being around you, kissing you, I kind of think—maybe hope—you have feelings for me too. That this connection I'm feeling between us isn't all one-sided?'

Molten desire flooded the pit of her stomach as his final words hit home. He actually felt something for her. Okay, it sounded to be purely sexual attraction too, but he definitely felt something.

'See what you're doing to me by just being here.'

He took the hand he'd been holding and pressed it against his chest. His heart thundered against her palm; its frantic beat mirroring her own.

With a slow smile, and trying not to think if this was the right thing to do or not, Izzy leaned forward and brushed her lips lightly against his.

'Yes, you're right,' she murmured, pulling back before he could return her kiss properly, her hand sliding up to caress the skin at the back of his neck. 'But I kept telling myself that you'd never be interested in someone like me.'

'Believe me, pretty lady; I've never been more interested.'

Reaching over, Rick cupped her face in his hands and suddenly he was back in control, his mouth crushing down on hers. Kissing her like a parched man who'd finally found water after the longest of searches.

Need washed through Izzy, every part of her pulsing and vibrating as his mouth continued its expert exploration of hers. His tongue flicked boldly against hers and after a moment's hesitation, she responded, their tongues dancing now, tasting just as they'd done before; their frantic breaths mingling.

Rick's hand went to her waist, bunching up the thin fabric of her blouse and tugging it from the waistband of her jeans, ready to slide underneath.

Izzy could tell he wanted to move things on, remove the barrier of clothing between them. And she wanted that too—so much—but if his hands continued their wandering, he'd guess her secret. And she wanted— no needed—to be in control of that final revelation.

Reluctantly, she pulled her lips away, placing her own hand over his, stilling his progress.

'No… no… wait. Not yet, Rick.'

Rick lifted his head, his breathing ragged, and passion still dancing in the dark depths of his eyes.

Izzy shivered, why had she never noticed it before?

'I know. I'm going too fast.' He sighed. 'I thought maybe you wanted to take this further… Have I pushed too hard, tonight? If you're not ready, or really don't want to. I understand, really I do…' He looked suddenly awkward.

'No, it's not that. Believe me, I more than want to.' She gave him tentative smile as she stroked her fingertips down his cheek. 'But there's something I need to do first. Can you give me a few minutes, please? I won't be long.'

1.21 AM

Izzy braced herself against the sink, gazing at herself long and hard in the mirror, trying to steady her nerves. It was decision time. Did she take this further?

Suddenly her mother's words came back to haunt her.

'We're not asking you to sleep with him, Izzy.'

Her Mum would be appalled to know she was contemplating just that. She wanted this so much, and yet there were thousands of good—and entirely sensible—reasons why she should stop now and walk away, regardless of everything he'd just told her.

There could be no Happy Ever After for them. At the end of the day, he'd admitted his physical attraction to her—one Izzy was still trying to get her head around—but that was all. There was still Francesca in the background; the forthcoming wedding. He wasn't in the market for any kind of long-term relationship. This was just another one-night-stand for him. Izzy just a need—an itch —that once he'd scratched, he'd get out his system.

But if she slept with him, it would only lead to heartbreak for her.

She shook her head at her reflection and let out an ironic laugh. Who was she kidding? Her heart was already in little pieces loving Rick Hambro and knowing she could never have him. For self-preservation sake, the sensible thing to do would be to backtrack, maintain she only wanted the wonderful friendship they'd built up over the last few months. That taking things further tonight would make it all too real, and messed up for all concerned.

But, in her heart, she didn't want sensible. She wanted—no her body craved—the knowledge of what it would be like with him. He'd set a fire inside her, and if she didn't take the chance on offer now, it would never happen again; not with Francesca swooping in to reclaim her fiancé in ten days' time. Why was it so complicated? What did she do?

Well, one thing was clear; she couldn't stand in this bathroom all night arguing with her reflection.

'Stop over-thinking, Izzy', she gave herself a stern look, 'go with your gut. What's that telling you? What do you really want in this moment? Make a decision. Tomorrow can look after itself.'

It was an east question to answer. Her heart—and her gut— told her she wanted Rick; full stop. She was a grown woman. Surely she was mature enough to have a one-night stand with a man; a man she loved and then deal with any fallout afterwards. She wanted him and he said he wanted her. What more was there to think about? She could do this. It was just one night of passionate sex, with no strings attached.

Her mind made up, she began to undo the buttons of her blouse, watching herself in the glass as the fabric slipped away from her shoulders, revealing her secret; the sapphire bustier underneath. A strange impulse had made her wear the underwear, tonight. Had she sub-consciously known something was going happen between them?

Well, regardless, he was about to get one hell of a shock when she walked out of here!

Her jeans discarded, Izzy gave herself a final once-over in the glass. She swallowed at her reflection, those panties were barely decent, but the bustier showed off her curvy figure to perfection.

This was it. It was time to face him.

You can do this!

There was a gentle tap on the door, followed by a discreet cough. 'Izzy, is everything okay in there?'

Her heart gave another extra loud thump. She must have been in here longer than she'd anticipated.

Keep calm. Own the moment. Walk out of here with your head held high Izzy Anderson.

Who was she trying to kid? Her stomach had been invaded by ten somersaulting Olga Korbuts.

'Yes, all good. I'll be right out in a sec.'

Undoing the lock and taking a steadying breath, she opened the door. Rick was standing there in his robe, and for a split second he squinted, before his eyes widened in disbelief.

'Fuck, Izzy! What the hell…?'

His voice disappeared to a hoarse whisper as his eyes swept over her several times, his jaw slackening and warmth pooled between her legs. It all made sense now. She'd seen that look on his face before; in Macy's fitting room when she'd stepped out wearing the dress.

'You like?' Izzy glanced up at him, feeling strangely shy under such smouldering scrutiny.

'Jeez, Izzy, I more than like... I've fantasised about seeing you like this, but....' The heat of his stare was scorching her skin. 'I don't understand...'

'I wanted to wear it for your birthday,' she explained. 'I know it sounds silly. After all, you were never supposed to see me in it, but...' She gave a tentative smile, 'Happy Birthday, Rick.'

'You look like a goddess stepped out of my dreams,' he held out his hand towards her, 'only so much better!' His dark eyes had turned black with wanting, just as she'd always dreamed. 'Come to bed with me, Izzy.'

With a smile and nod of quiet assent, Izzy placed her hand in his, her fingers trembling slightly as he pulled her into his arms.

As if sensing her nervousness, Rick lowered his head and kissed her fingertips, the tender gesture making her breath catch, before leading her towards the bed.

He quickly dispensed with his robe before pulling her down beside him, both of them on their sides, face to face. 'You're sure you want to do this?' he asked.

'More than anything,' she answered, before reaching up to pull his lips to hers.

His mouth was urgent now, his hands bold as they stroked down the length of her spine, before sliding inside the panties and cupping her bottom, drawing her hard against his very evident arousal, letting her know how much he wanted her.

Izzy's head spun. This was her. This was what she did to him. The power she had over him. How could she not have known?

With a little sigh of contentment, she gave in to her own need to touch him, running her hands over his shoulders and down across his chest, allowing her fingers to roam everywhere; stroking, teasing, savouring…

At length, Rick caught both her hands between his, stilling her progress of going any lower, his breathing ragged.

'No, pretty lady, no more, not yet, unless you want this to be all over before it's begun.' He gave a sheepish grin. 'I've dreamt about this for so long, Izzy. But now you're actually here, I almost don't know what to do with you. I still can't quite believe it.'

'Believe it,' she breathed. 'I'm all yours. Un-wrap me, if you dare, Rick Hambro.'

His fingers went to the little hooks that held the bustier together, and, with some difficulty, he slipped the first one open, a little gasp escaping her lips at the light brush of his fingers against the curve of her breast.

But the hooks and eyes on the bustier were proving to be fiddly, Izzy finding it hard to hold back her giggles at the pained expression on Rick's face as he wrestled with each one.

'Shit, Madeleine never mentioned how difficult this was to get off in the heat of the moment…' He muttered crossly, pressing a frustrated kiss to her mouth as—at last—the final hook popped free, and he was able to pull the material away from her body, dumping it onto the floor beside the bed.

Turning back, he feasted his eyes on her body for what felt like ages, making Izzy blush to the roots of her hair at the intensity of his gaze.

'Don't be shy with me, Izzy. You've no idea how beautiful you are.' he told her softly.

A breath caught in her throat at the unmistakeable look of fierce adoration on his face. No one had ever looked at her like that before, *ever.*

'And, tonight, you're all mine.' He winked, drawing her to him.

'Yes,' she echoed, smiling back.

Leaning over, he trailed a line of hot kisses from her lips, down her throat, to her breasts, taking one engorged tip into his mouth and tugging on it gently with his teeth, his tongue dancing over the nipple, making her cry out.

All the time, his eyes were trained on her face, and she could see he was savouring her reaction to each touch.

'Rick… I… Ohhhhhh,' Izzy moaned, unable to stop her back arching up off the bed as she pressed her body into him, searching for more contact, needed more pressure.

In answer, his mouth moved to her other breast, repeating what he'd just done.

Izzy buried her hands in his dark curls, holding him against her, loving the feel of his insistent mouth against her breast, luxuriating in the waves of pure pleasure washing over her body; not wanting to let him go.

'Told you I was a nipple man,' he murmured, his teeth lightly grazing her skin, and Izzy couldn't stop her laughter bubbling over.

She wanted him so badly, needed him to address that heavy pulsing ache building between her thighs. Her hips lifted from the bed and rubbed against his restlessly, enticing him.

Her silent invitation worked. His hand moved to the waistband of the panties, undoing the bows and pulling the material aside, cupping her gently, brushing his thumb against that pulsing part of her in a slow circular rhythm, the sensation sending her into overdrive.

No, she'd definitely never experienced anything like this.

'Izzy, you've no idea what you've been doing to me.' Rick lifted his head, his eyes locking onto hers. 'I've had more cold showers and hand jobs in the last four months that I've probably had since I was a teenager. All I can think about is touching you like this, over and over again.'

'Yes,' she breathed in answer.

She'd had those same thoughts. But her brain was finding it harder and harder to concentrate. Make sense of anything but the amazing touch of his fingers. How could she when those lips had started to travel from her breasts, lower, down over her stomach to press his mouth to the centre of her body, his lips replacing those stroking fingers; sucking, licking, teasing a response; all the time pushing her closer and closer to some kind of precipice.

For the briefest of moments, she was poised, teetering on some kind of brink, and then with another masterful stroke of that tongue, pulses of pure ecstasy began rippling through her body, making her cry out; her orgasm taking hold.

It was a deliciously slow float back to reality.

'I don't want to stop yet...' she murmured, when words would finally form, still needing to feel him deep inside her, her hands reaching out to pull him back towards her, her mouth reaching up to press feather light little kisses against his throat and chest.

'I've no intention of stopping, but we need the condom remember. Keep my pretty lady safe.'

In seconds, he'd retrieved and dealt with the necessary protection, and then she was back in his arms, his body pinning her down, his kisses—if anything—harder and more intense; Izzy's own just as fervent, suddenly re-energised for what was still to come.

Rick rolled her beneath him, Izzy wrapping her legs up around his waist as he brought them together, easing his way inside her, oh-so-slowly, letting her get used to the sensation of him filling her full. And all the time, Izzy heard herself recite his name like a prayer on her lips.

'Open your eyes, Izzy.'

They were forehead to forehead. Their bodies joined. Rick's hips rocking gently against hers, and already that wonderful tight feeling was building within her again. His forearms were braced on either side of her head, cocooning her.

It was just as she'd imagined; the two of them locked in their own little world.

'I know it was never great with James,' he told her, 'but, tonight, I want this to be perfect for my pretty lady.' He dropped a kiss on her nose. 'Do you trust me?'

'You know I do.' Izzy replied, her eyes never leaving his.

'Then keep talking to me while we do this. Don't be afraid to say what you're thinking, what you're feeling, what you need. I don't believe in silent sex,' His fingers tangled into her curls, 'because I'll certainly be letting you know….'

1.57 AM

Rick's body collapsed over hers. His dark head buried into the pillow beside hers. His mouth was at her ear, telling her—between tortured gasps—how incredible she'd made him feel in those final moments as their bodies had come together.

Izzy only had the energy to nod in response, a smile playing on her lips. Her eyes closed and completely incapable of stringing a meaningful sentence together herself, her body still reacting to the volcanic aftershocks of her second and more powerful orgasm. Every part of her felt so gloriously heavy, as though she could just melt into the mattress and disappear entirely.

So, this was the real deal; proper grown-up orgasmic sex, she thought hazily. The earth-shattering feeling all her friends raved about, what she'd read about in books and magazines, but had never really experienced with Alex. It was though Rick had blown their bodies apart in those final few seconds, only for them to be put back together again—piece by glorious piece—just as perfectly as before. Another forceful pulse shot down to her feet making her whole body spasm, her fingers and toes curling into the sheet below her.

With what little strength she had left, she reached up to run her fingers down his cheek. Rick stirred and lifted his head, their eyes meeting and holding. Neither of them spoke. They didn't need to.

God, she adored this man with every fibre of her being. If only this could be her forever; spending every day and night safe in these reassuring arms.

'I knew we'd be good together,' Rick broke the silence, pushing her sweat-dampened hair back from her brow, and placing a gentle kiss at its centre, 'although the word 'good' is a bit understatement after what just happened' That grin was decidedly cheeky.

'You said it!' her fingertips caressed the scruff at his jaw.

He rolled onto his side, gathering her up into his arms. 'Don't ask me how, but I knew we'd end up here one day. Why do you think I was so keen on giving you swimming lessons? I had to find a way to get to know this pretty lady with the mesmerising eyes.' He pressed another kiss to her temple. 'I was going out of my mind wondering how to get close to you. And at the same time, I was fighting it every step of the way, telling myself to hold back, not fuck up both our lives. And then you revealed that seriously hot red swimsuit. And that was it, I was lost.'

'You liked me in it?' she asked in genuine surprise. 'You never said. As I recall, it got barely a glance that night.'

Rick let out a laugh, 'Not true. It took all my time to keep myself under control. You have no idea how much I liked it. How much I've fantasised about it?' He winked at her. 'What I've wanted to do to you, both in and out of it!'

'I've been fighting myself too,' she agreed with a giggle, 'especially all those times you insisted on prancing around me wearing nothing but a towel or those obscenely tight swimming trunks that left very little to the imagination. Don't ask me how I've managed to keep it together to give you the massages. I've learnt a girl only has so much self-control.'

'I knew for sure you were attracted to me that day in Tokyo. Those eyes gave you away, instantly,' he told her. 'If Airi hadn't been there, would you have pushed me down on the bed and had your wicked way with me, I wonder?' He dropped another kiss to her brow. 'And, hand on heart, if you had, I wouldn't have stopped you.'

Izzy laughed.

'I've not been able to think about anyone else but you,' Rick went on. 'You've heard the jokes. I know the guys are convinced there's something seriously wrong with me downstairs.'

'Nope, definitely nothing wrong down there.' Izzy snuggled her face into his chest. 'And, in case you're in any doubt, you made the old earth move for me tonight—twice.'

'Don't want to sound conceited, but I was in no doubt, whatsoever.' He made a show of polishing his nails. 'It's good to know you're not the only one with the magic touch. And don't worry. We'll be going for the hat-trick, once this old guy gets his breath back.'

He tightened his arms about her, as Izzy sunk her fingertips into the matting of chest hair, giving it a playful little tug, before slowly and sinuously rubbing her breasts against it, unable to stop a contented little purr. The reality was even better than her imagination.

'I've always wanted to do that.' She admitted.

'Then, you've my full permission to do it—as often as you like!' He waggled his eyebrows. 'Now, give me a sec, I'll be right back.' He deposited a kiss on her nose before pushing the coverlet back and rolled out of bed, heading for the bathroom to dispose of the used condom.

Once back lying beside her, Rick spoke. 'Look, Izzy, I don't want this—tonight—to be a one-off between us.'

Izzy propped herself up on an elbow. 'You don't?' Her brow wrinkled. He wanted more than this? But how could they? This was a one-night stand; could only be a one-night stand—surely?

'Do you?' he prompted, brushing his fingers into her hair, when she didn't answer straightaway.

'I…' she paused, wondering what to say.

Yes, she wanted so much more, but she had to be realistic. This wasn't going anywhere. They both knew it. It was only sex—for him—and for her……

'Talk to me Izzy. Tell me what you're thinking. Was it just a one-off for you?'

'Rick, I care about you, so very much,' she stressed, her eyes holding his for a long moment. 'But, neither of us as in the market for anything serious are we? I know I'm not.'

Izzy hated that she could never be completely honest with him. 'You're engaged, about to be married.' As if she really had to remind him. 'And I'm still finding my feet again after A… James.'

Shit! In this state of post-coital bliss, she'd nearly used the wrong name.

'But yes, if I'm honest, I'd really like this to happen again—very much! But how can it? Francesca arrives in a matter of days.' She bit her lip. 'And I won't play second fiddle to anybody, Rick,' she stressed. 'I'm not about to become your bit on the side, sneaking around behind your fiancée's back, like some dirty little secret. If anything else happens between us, it follows band rules, and stops the moment Francesca arrives. Do you understand?'

'Izzy, I'd never…I want—'

Izzy placed a finger on his lips, silencing him. 'No, I mean it, Rick. Those are my terms. Take it or leave it.'

He exhaled a long breath before he spoke. 'Then, I guess I'll take it. I'd never want to treat you as a dirty little secret, Izzy. You're much too special for that. You deserve an open and honest relationship with the right guy. And you're right, I can't give you that. Not now.'

So, he saw the sense to her words. It made Izzy feel relieved and unbearably sad in the same breath.

'You'd be happy for us to spend time together—like this—until New York?' he asked.

She nodded as those wonderfully long fingers began to stroke her body again, making her skin tingle. Coherent thought was heading back out of that window again. They could have the next ten days together, and no more. She could handle that. Enjoy a brief fling with him and then, somehow, find the strength to walk away.

Rick had rolled onto his back, settling her on top of him. She could feel how ready he was for her.

'I think it's about time we tried for that hat-trick. Don't you? And this time, I want to see you on top, taking control of the situation, Miss Stevenson. Kinky or what?' he teased, cupping her bottom and giving it a leisurely squeeze.

'Mmmmm, I thought you'd never ask, Mr Hambro.'

Reaching over, she picked up a condom from the pile he'd left on the nightstand and waved it in his face, before placing the wrapper between her teeth and ripping it open.

5.33 AM

Izzy awoke to a deliciously warm male body wrapped all around her, Rick's arm settled across her rib-cage, pinning her back against the heated wall of his chest.

Had she died and gone to Heaven? She must have. She'd never felt so blissful or so cherished in anyone's embrace. Alex had liked his own space in bed. Not keen on cuddles, even after sex. She'd get a perfunctory hug—only if she asked for it—and then shoved back to where she belonged, on the cold side of the bed.

But Rick was different. Cuddling appeared to be something he actively enjoyed, and Izzy wasn't complaining. She was an unashamed snuggler, wanted him to hold her; hold her and never let go.

However, now that she was awake, her brain started to race, unwelcome thoughts beginning to intrude on the moment. They only had a limited time together; an agreed end-date. Was she a good enough actress to maintain the pretence until then? Not betray her real feelings?

There was only one answer to that question—she had to be! He was unavailable for anything long-term, and as for her, she'd spent the last five months lying to his face over her real identity. He could never get to know the real Izzy. Not now. Not ever.

She snuggled closer. She loved him so much, but sex and love meant different things to men and women. Men could compartmentalise their feelings, split off emotions. The members of Eclectic Deviation were past masters at that game, given the rules they lived by on the road. But for Izzy, this was love; the forever kind. Rick had spoiled her for anyone else.

A hand had begun to slowly caress her upper thigh; fingers drawing infinity circles against her skin, making tiny goosebumps appear.

She let out a low groan, loving his touch.

'Good morning, pretty lady!' Warm breath tickled against her earlobe, flowed by the touch of his lips. 'I was terrified I'd wake up and find you'd disappeared on me.'

'Nope, still here. You don't get rid of me that easy,' she replied, twisting her head to meet his gaze.

She was rewarded with a slow, lingering kiss on the mouth.

'Have I told you, you've got perfect thighs?' His fingertips were still working their spell-binding magic. 'And that I love having them wrapped around my waist when I'm deep inside you?'

'I think you mentioned that quite a few times during the night.'

He'd been very vocal about her body. How much he loved it, how beautiful she was and all the things he wanted to do to her. In fact, some of things he'd described had made her blush, but his words had also turned her on no-end, and that had been a complete surprise.

His hand moved to cup her behind. 'And the most exquisite bum. Just a nice wee handful, as you Scots would say.'

'That's a truly terrible Scottish accent, Richard Hambro, I'm offended,' Izzy lamented, then sucked in a breath as his marauding hand skimmed up over her hip, across her stomach to rest against her breast, his fingers capturing and rolling the rosy tip to aching hardness. A jolt of desire shot down through the centre of her body.

'Not to mention my personal favourites, two totally awesome nipples.' He murmured; his mouth nuzzling that sensitive spot behind her ear, while his hand switched to her other breast, applying the same sweet torture.

Izzy squirmed, unable to stop another little yelp of pleasure escaping her lips.

'So, Miss Stevenson,' he turned her in his arms, their faces inches apart, 'are you ready for a proper good morning?'

She nodded in eager anticipation, his next words making her laugh out loud.

'As a member of the band, I have exclusive access to all areas around here, remember,' he murmured, 'and that includes my beautiful PA.'

'Izzy?'

A fully dressed Izzy raised her head, doing up the zips on her over-the-knee boots. She watched as Rick hauled himself up onto his elbows, blinking several times in the early morning gloom of the hotel room, before shoving his fringe back from his forehead, his lips creasing into a relieved smile as their eyes finally met.

'Where are you going?' he asked.

'Good morning.' Her answering smile was upbeat, but inside, she wondered how best to play this. Maybe, he'd change his mind on what they'd agreed just a few hours previously. Allow morning-after awkwardness to set in and make him back peddle into one-night stand territory? Or worse, say it had all been a terrible mistake?

But from his contented expression, it didn't look like it. Rick had settled back against the headboard, one arm tucked behind his head, those eyes watching her intently as she stood up.

'I thought you agreed we should enjoy a shower together. Or had you forgotten?' He delivered a sexy wink.

No, he definitely didn't appear to be regretting it. Her heart leapt.

'I haven't forgotten,' she answered truthfully, remembering every spine-tingling word he'd whispered to her about that shower and the fun they could have beneath its spray, 'but tempting as it is, I really need to get back downstairs.'

She gave him an easy smile as she tucked her denim shirt into her jeans. 'We don't want anyone seeing me sneaking out your room. It might be difficult to explain.'

Although that excuse sounded a bit like shutting the stable door after the horse had decided to head off into the wide blue yonder for a quick canter.

'I guess so.' he answered, reaching out a hand, and Izzy moved over to sit by his side. 'Do you have any regrets about last night, pretty lady?'

He laced those warm fingers through hers, but the look she received was decidedly pensive now, those beautiful eyes guarded and a definite tension in that firm, but gorgeously stubbly, jaw.

Jeez, you don't know how gorgeous you are, Rick Hambro.

'No,' she replied, 'do you?'

Her breathe held. She'd give him the get-out if he should need it.

'Nope; it was the best night of my life, Miss Stevenson.'

Somehow, she doubted that statement, but let it pass.

As though sensing her scepticism, Rick placed a finger under her chin, tilting her head up to look him in the eye.

'I mean it, Izzy. I won't lie to you.' Brown eyes blazed into blue. 'Last night was beyond what I'd ever dreamed. And believe me; I've developed a very fertile imagination where you're concerned.' His grin was incorrigible, making her tremble in remembrance at everything they'd done over the last few hours. 'You still want to do this?'

'Yes. But only until New York,' she reminded him. 'And it has to be private. No one can suspect anything.'

And she definitely wouldn't be spilling the beans to Kathy. This was way too personal to share with anybody.

'Okay, whatever you want.' He pushed his fingers through her hair, cupping the back of her head, drawing her towards him for another temperature-rocketing kiss.

'It's still early. Can't you stay a little longer?' he wheedled, attempting a sneaky move to undo the top buttons of her shirt, steal a peek down her cleavage.

'Behave! You know I can't.' She slapped his hand away, laughing out loud at his disappointed pout. 'I'll see you at breakfast. And don't be late.'

47

PORTLAND, MAINE

'So, remind me, what have you organised for the happy couple?' Jonny had ground to a halt; bent double, his hands on his knees while trying to catch his breath, and refusing Izzy's entreaties to go another step.

They'd been heading towards the stage, tonight's concert scheduled to start in less five minutes; Jonny late as he'd been playing *Space Invaders* on the arcade game in the Dressing Room. A late addition to their tour rider.

'Unfortunately, a bit of a situation has developed around that,' she answered, knowing he wasn't going to like the latest news. 'Your parents' anniversary dinner is now clashing with the *RTV Rock Awards* ceremony in New York.'

'We're going to a fucking awards ceremony, since when? Is this your idea of some kind of belated *April fool?*' Jonny straightened; his light blue eyes had turned decidedly chilly.

This was going to take some careful handling. John and Kate's Anniversary dinner was a three-line whip for their only son.

'Nope, it's not an *April fool.* And since about 7.43pm this evening, to be precise,' Izzy went on. 'According to Lindsay, as tour sponsor, *RTV* have suddenly demanded the band's presence on the night, rather than you doing a pre-recorded link-up as previously mooted. They

397

won't entertain a no-show. It's been hinted that voting figures could be massaged with the awards going to *Metallica* and *Bon Jovi* instead.'

'The bastards; they wouldn't dare!' Jonny levelled a kick at the wall. Thankfully he didn't do much damage, except leave scuff marks.

'But you do realise my beloved mother is going to go fucking nuts. I'm still in the dog house after Uncle Stan popped his clogs and I missed *his* funeral, remember!' He rolled his eyes heavenwards, and the wall received another hefty blow. 'Jeez, this will be another nail in *my* bloody coffin as far as "Kate" is concerned.'

The 'mother/son' bond between Jonny and Kate was somewhat strained. In many ways, it explained a lot about his relationships with women. Freud would have had a field day unpicking those two.

'Don't worry. We're trying to think of something,' she replied, reaching to grab his arm, urging him on once more. They didn't have the luxury of debating the pros and cons now.

'Yeah, you'd better. Or you'll be arranging *my* frigging funeral. She's going to bloody kill me.'

They'd finally reached the stage, Jonny taking the steps, two at a time; Izzy hurrying after him. He was still grumbling as he retrieved his guitar from the outstretched hand of his roadie and slipped the leather strap over his head.

'Just find some way to fix it, Izzy, and fast,' he muttered, beginning to run his fingers over the strings.

Giving him a nod of assent, Izzy swung away to find Rick grinning at her, safely perched on his stool behind the drum kit, drumsticks in hand, and ready to go as usual. She couldn't help but find her lips titling upwards at him.

'Okay?' He received her usual thumbs-up sign. 'Do you need me to do anything for you?' She delivered her own suggestive little wink.

'Nope,' he replied, before mouthing, 'I will later.'

Izzy's stomach gave a clench of anticipation. Another swimming lesson was pencilled in for after the show. What did this wonderfully sexy man have in store for her, tonight? She couldn't wait to find out.

48

PORTLAND, MAINE

'Rick! You awake, mate?'

It was Jonny hollering through the bedroom door. 'Open the fucking door and let me in!'

Izzy sat bolt upright, her eyes zeroing in on the travel clock on the nightstand. The fluorescent digits read three minutes past four.

Reaching out, she snapped on the bedside lamp, her heart settling in her mouth. Apart from Davey and Terry, no one else had caught them. Was their luck about to run out?

'What the hell does he want?' Rick groaned, attempting to cuddle closer, his fingers closing around her hip bone, trying to tug her back beneath the covers.

Izzy didn't answer, just swiped his hand away, and scuttled naked from the bed, collecting up discarded clothing from the floor as she went.

'You need to get rid of him; fast,' she hissed, heading towards the bathroom, evidence of her presence clasped tightly to her chest.

Not to be denied, Jonny called out again.

'Rick, will you open up and let me in?'

Closing the bathroom door, and securing the lock, Izzy now pressed her ear to the wood, trying to discern what was taking place outside in the bedroom.

She heard the suite door being opened.

'Hey, man, how's it going?'

Then there was a muffled sound, Izzy interpreting it as Jonny swamping Rick in one of his over-enthusiastic embraces.

'I'm here to make you an offer you can't refuse.'

'Let go of me, you daft bastard.'

She'd been right.

There was a pause before Rick continued, 'And as to the offer. Yeah, I probably can. What the hell do you want? Some of us are trying to get some sleep.'

Izzy heard footsteps. It sounded as though Jonny had entered the room.

'Just back with two gorgeous babes,' the lead guitarist explained, 'a blonde and a fire cracker of a brunette—her best mate—stacked just the way you like them. And as we speak, both are relaxing in my room, totally up for some fun. If you know what I mean?'

There was a pause then Jonny spoke again, 'Said I wouldn't be long, so, are you game or what?'

'Nope; count me out.' It sounded as though Rick was stifling a large yawn.

'I don't think you appreciate the wonderful opportunity I'm giving you here, Ricky boy,' Jonny went on. 'Wait till you see her. She's fucking gorgeous. Long brown hair, big brown eyes, a pair of tits to die for and legs all the way up to her armpits. She has Rick Hambro running through her like a stick of *Blackpool Rock*. It's a no-brainer.'

'Read my lips, Jonny. I said *NO*.'

Izzy couldn't help but smile at Rick's flat refusal.

'Come on, its way past time little Ricky came put to play. I'm getting really worried here, man. What the hell has got into you? It's been weeks since you've seen any action. Plus, this vow of chastity you've taken is bad for the band's reputation. Eclectic Deviation doesn't do fucking celibacy on tour. You wimped out on me with Lynette, and she was supposed to be your bloody birthday present. What gives? Can't get it up these days? Is that it?'

'Do you want a crack in the jaw, little cousin?'

'You need to see a fucking doctor and fast! Make sure downstairs is in full working order before you get hitched. '

There was silence for a few seconds and Izzy listened closer, wondering what was happening now.

'Or maybe I'm worrying, unnecessarily.' Jonny's voice had risen, and from his tone, he sounded distinctly amused by something. 'If that's what I think it is, lying on the floor over there?'

Izzy looked down at the bundle of clothing in her arms, her mouth falling open in shocked disbelief. Shit! No red swimsuit. How could she have missed it? It had to be still out there for the all world and Jonathan Hambro to see.

She'd done an extremely provocative little striptease for Rick after they'd come back from the pool, which had ended with them having unbelievably intense sex pressed up against the bedroom door; another first for Izzy.

But how the hell was Rick going to explain away the presence of her swimsuit?

'Ahhhh, now I get it! You've got someone here, haven't you?'

'I'll take that, if you don't mind, Jonathan.'

But Izzy could tell by Jonny's voice his interest had been well and truly piqued.

'So, when did this happen? And, more to the point, who's the lucky lady receiving Ricky's full—and long overdue—attentions? I didn't see you talking to anybody after the show, except Izzy. And we both know it's not Miss Goody Two Shoes.'

Jonny let out a loud belly laugh, making Izzy bridle with indignation. If only he knew the truth!

'No one you'll ever *know* in the biblical sense.' Rick snapped back. 'We met in the pool downstairs and got talking. Don't think I need to explain, further. Do you?'

Izzy liked Rick's play on words. Jonny would certainly never know her in the biblical sense.

'Yeah, well I'm glad to hear it. I was beginning to think you'd lost the old lead in your pencil—permanently!'

Izzy pressed her hand to her mouth, stifling the urge to giggle. They were like rabbits; at it every spare minute they could get.

'If you want a belt in the mouth, keep talking, you're heading in the right direction? Now shouldn't you be getting back to your guests?' was Rick's grumpy reply.

'I suppose so.'

Another pause, then Izzy heard footsteps, moving towards the bathroom door.

What was happening now? Was Jonny expecting an introduction to Rick's mystery woman?

'I take it she's in there.'

Damn! Jonny was right outside the bloody door.

Izzy rechecked the lock but it was firmly bolted. There was no chance of him barging in.

'Yep, and she'll be out any minute, so if you don't mind leaving…'

'You mean you're not going to introduce me?'

Jonny rattled the door handle. 'Hey, it's Jonny! Are you coming out to say hi?'

Izzy was glad she'd had the foresight to lock the door. Knowing Jonny, he'd have walked straight in and introduced himself. And, she asked herself, who'd have got the bigger shock?

'Okay, be like that!'

Another pause, and then she heard Jonny's footsteps retreat. The main door of the suite was reopened with a long squeak.

'Hey, Rick, how about I send the brunette along here. Make things twice as interesting for you? Make up for lost time?'

'No thanks Jonny! Here's the door. Use it!'

'Well, don't say I didn't offer.' Jonny then slipped into a very bad John Wayne impersonation, 'I guess it's down to me, then. A man's got to do what a man's got to do. Have a good one, cuz.'

The door was slammed, and she heard Rick curse under his breath, before calling out to her.

'You can come out, now.'

Undoing the lock, Izzy opened the door and peeked out, her eyes wary.

Seeing her, Rick fished out the scrap of red material from his robe pocket, and shook it at her, the sexiest of smirks lighting up his face.

'Think you forgot something, Miss Stevenson?'

49

BOSTON, MASSACHUSETTS

'Well, if it isn't Rick's little bit on the side?'

Damn! She was trapped.

On cue, her flesh began to crawl at the unwelcome sight of Terry, slipping through the lift doors just they were closing, imprisoning them both inside.

Instinctively, Izzy tried to put as much distance between them in the confined space, all the time hoping he'd alight at a lower floor. But no such luck, his finger was already punching zero for the hotel lobby. He was going her way.

And she didn't have time to duck out at another floor either. Marc was already waiting— impatiently—for her in reception; he wanted her to deal with a complaint.

The lift creaked into life.

From Maine, they'd flown to New Hampshire before arriving here in Boston. After tonight's concert they'd be back in the air, travelling straight to the Tour's final destination, New York City and, in another six days, she'd be heading home.

'Cat got your tongue, Miss Stevenson?'

Izzy's skin prickled. Without looking at him, she could sense those snake-like eyes slithering all over her. The man was nothing if not predictable.

'Or are we too snotty, now we're a permanent fixture in Rick's bed?' he mused with a derisive shake of the head. 'You are remembering that Francesca arrives tomorrow?'

Izzy remained silent, only too well aware of that fact, and refusing to dignify Terry's comment with even a flicker of acknowledgement.

Instead, she kept her eyes glued to the descending floor numbers, counting down until she could get safely out of here.

What she didn't expect was Terry's arms suddenly shooting around her and— before she'd an opportunity to react— being bundled backwards into the far corner of the compartment; her head making painful contact with the mirrored surround.

Terror gripped Izzy. What the hell was he going to do to her? Had he decided to make good his repulsive threats right here in this lift? He wouldn't dare! Would he?

'Owww; get your hands off me, Terry!'

Ignoring her protests, Terry grabbed her wrists in one hand, and pinned them high above her head. With the other, he reached over and stabbed the lift's Emergency Stop button. The machinery above their heads coming to a grinding halt, and momentarily, the compartment's lights dipped.

His face was just inches from hers, so close she could see beads of sweat forming on his top lip. He was breathing hard, the smell of his breath, noxious. Nauseated, Izzy wrinkled her nose and recoiled backwards, bumping her head for a second time.

'Get your hands off me, Terry.' she repeated.

The man was like a bloody python, his body coiling around her, compressing the air in her lungs, and making her head spin. The weight of him was making it impossible to fight back.

'I've had enough of waiting around, Izzy. From now on, I'm calling the shots. Got that?'

A hand clamped onto her right breast, squeezing it hard through the wool of her sweater, his green eyes glittering with venom. 'And guess what? I going to have you screaming for more; you snotty little cow.'

She wanted to scream her head off now, but that wouldn't do any good; no one would hear her for a start.

'Get. Off. Me!'

She tried to kick out, free her legs—land a knee to his groin if she was lucky—but he was too strong, had her completely at his mercy, pinned against the wall. His great mitt of a hand moved to grope her other breast, his pinching fingers making her cry out in pain.

'Like that, do you?' Without waiting for an answer, he did it again, only harder this time. 'Thought so. Don't worry, there's plenty more where that comes from. Rick's way too much of a mummy's boy to please a feisty girl like you.'

Black dots danced before her eyes, and the ability to breathe was becoming virtually impossible, but she'd be damned if she'd give him the satisfaction of passing out.

'You're deranged.'

'Don't think so. I know exactly what I'm doing, and so do you. From the start, I got the feeling a bit of rough sex would be right up your street. Unleash all those repressed desires you keep buttoned up inside. Desires, our Ricky-boy, wouldn't have a fucking clue how to handle.'

With that he ground his pelvis against hers. From the evidence in his trousers, he was seriously getting off on this horrifying show of male machismo.

'You bastard!' Izzy bit out.

'Tut tut! Language, Izzy!' His laugh had turned ugly. 'Not like that pretty mouth to spout words from the gutter. Although by the time I'm finished with you, the gutter might be the only place you're fit for.'

Terry's face loomed closer, and in that horrible moment, Izzy knew he was going to try and kiss her.

'Don't even think about it!' she warned.

'It's time for your debt to be called in, Izzy.'

'What debt? I owe you absolutely nothing.'

What was the revolting animal raving on about now?

'You owe me a great deal, Izzy. You're the reason Ricky's stopped taking his medication like a good little boy.'

'If you mean did I stop him poisoning his body with those filthy pills, then you're damn right.'

So that was what this was *really* all about. He was blaming her for the loss of a valuable revenue stream.

'And that means after the last show in New York, you'll be settling that debt—in kind— and I intend to get my money's worth.' Those fingers bit harder into her wrists. 'And if you don't show me some enthusiasm on the night, then I'll just have to take what I want, with or without your co-operation.'

'You wouldn't dare!'

He was threatening to rape her. The blood roared in her ears as she fought for control.

'Wouldn't I? After all, it's my word against yours.' His grin became smug. 'And when it comes to a choice between their loyal Head of Security—the man who closely guards *all* their dirty little secrets—or a jumped-up little PA, in the door two-minutes, there's no contest.'

'I'll tell Rick.' A bubble of sickness burned the back of Izzy's throat.

'Don't think so.' Those eyes glinted dangerously. 'Once Francesca is back on the scene, he won't want to know you. None of them will. It'll be Angie all over again. You might get some money thrown at you to keep that smart mouth buttoned, but that's about it.'

An awful feeling of clarity was beginning to wash over Izzy.

'You raped Angie. That's why she left, wasn't it?' Her eyes widened in revulsion as the horrific realisation sunk in.

'No I fucking didn't.' He grabbed a handful of her hair, winding it around his fist and giving it a violent tug, as though punishing her for even suggesting such a thing. 'But that's the story she ran bleating to Jack with. It was all fully consensual—eventually—and she knows it.' He sneered. 'And what did Eclectic Deviation and our Jack do when they heard her pathetic little fairytale? Paid her off and sent the little slut packing. But not before she'd signed a gagging order to keep her trap shut. You won't be treated any different.'

More bile pooled in Izzy's throat. There was no way that was happening to her.

His hips thrust into her again, only harder this time. 'Anyway, everyone knows when a woman says no, it really means yes. And you'll be no different, Miss Stevenson.'

Izzy had heard enough, beginning to struggle against him. He had to let her go? She tried to twist her fingers from his grasp, dig her nails into him, but he barely flinched.

'Rick and his mates didn't get where they are today without trampling over people and not giving a toss, in the process.' His voice continued to rasp in her ear. 'They've got their rules they live by, and women like you and Angie don't matter. He might be fucking his "pretty lady's" brains out, but when push comes to shove, you won't be allowed to upset his nice little life. Now, why don't you give me a kiss; keep Uncle Terry sweet?'

'Drop dead, ars—'

Her words were swallowed by Terry's mouth swooping down on hers, flattening her lips back against her teeth; his eel-like tongue forcing its way inside.

Using every last ounce of strength she possessed, Izzy clamped her teeth down on the edge of the marauding invader, biting hard into its rubbery texture, aiming to hurt as much as possible.

With a howl of shocked pain, Terry released her hands instantly, slamming himself back against the opposite wall as though she'd just electrocuted him. The metallic taste of his blood filled her throat and she coughed it away in disgust, noting more trickling down the side of Terry's jaw. *Good!* He wouldn't forget that kiss in a hurry. And if he tried it again…

'You vicious little cow.'

He took a step towards her, raising his right hand and she braced herself for the blow, but then he seemed to think better of it, dragging a handkerchief from his pocket, instead.

'You're going to be sorry for that, bitch.'

Without waiting a second longer, Izzy dived for the lift's control panel, stamping her finger on zero and holding it there until the metal box responded, cranking itself back into life, and they were shooting downwards once more.

'No, Terry'—Izzy hoped she sounded braver than she felt—'you'll be the one who's going to be sorry.'

'Don't think so! Your time's up, bitch. I'll be coming for you on Tuesday night. That's a promise!'

10.32 AM

'I got something for you, Izzy,' Rick was frantically rummaging through the higgledy-piggledy contents of the suitcase lying open on their bed. 'Jeez, I better not have fucking lost it.'

'Sorry, what did you say?' Izzy looked up.

It was time to give him her full attention. For the last five minutes, she'd been gazing into space, her mind blank to everything but Terry's attack.

As soon as he'd vacated the lift at reception, she'd returned to her floor; Marc's complaint forgotten in her haste to get away. Somehow she'd held it together until she'd stumbled inside her own room, locking the door and heading straight for the bathroom, where she'd wretched violently.

After a long hot shower, trying to scrub off the repulsive stench of Terry, together with a complete change of clothing—the sweater he'd touched had been consigned to the bin—she'd managed to restore some outward composure. But inside, she remained in total meltdown.

What the hell did she do? Tuesday! He'd said he'd come for her on Tuesday. She wanted to leave now. Get away now as fast as possible. But she couldn't. She had to be there when Betty and Jim arrived in New York. Terry had her entangled at the centre of his grotesque web with no means of escape.

'Fuck, I'm sure it's in here, somewhere!' Rick had finally upended his case in frustration, clothes going in all directions.

Izzy watched on helplessly, wanting to tell him what had just happened, but somehow her lips wouldn't cooperate. All she could hear in her head was Terry's sneering tone, *'Once Francesca is back, Rick won't want to know you'*.

And that would probably be true. Rick would be only too glad to be reunited with the love of his life. Much as he said he cared for her, Izzy knew she wouldn't get a second thought once Francesca was back on the scene.

'Here it is.' Rick gave a sigh of relief, holding up a small blue velvet pouch. 'As soon as I saw it, I knew my pretty lady would love it.'

Izzy's brow wrinkled. He'd bought her another present. And why did she get the feeling he'd just spent an obscene amount of money into the bargain?

'Rick, I keep telling you, I don't need any presents.' She tried to keep the exasperation from her voice.

'But I wanted to.' He tucked a loop of chestnut hair behind her ear and, reaching over, pressed a tender kiss to her forehead.

'What is it?'

'Well, the idea is that you open it and find out,' he teased back.

Izzy poked out her tongue, but she knew her show of childish petulance couldn't put off the moment much longer.

Reluctantly, she took the bag from him, and undid the drawstring, before tipping its contents into the centre of her palm. Her eyes widened in stunned disbelief as she took in the solid gold bangle with its delicate heart-shaped drop. Embedded at the heart's centre was what looked to be a real sapphire?

'Oh God, it's beautiful, Rick.'

Her mouth went dry. It really was the most exquisite piece of jewellery she'd even seen. And he was right, she loved it on sight. Somehow, he'd got her taste to a tee. But much as she adored the bangle, there was no way she could accept it. Not something as expensive as this. Her guilty conscience wouldn't let her.

Taking a deep breath and telling herself it was for the best, she replaced the bangle inside its pouch, doing up the drawstring into a bow.

'Please take it back, Rick.' She held it out to him, not making eye contact.

'But you love bracelets!'

She'd totally flummoxed him by her reaction.

'You wear a different one every day.' He pointed at the multi-strand pearl one currently adorning her wrist.

Izzy's eyes alighted on it briefly and gave a shiver, remembering the angry red marks it covered; marks that had been left by the hungry bite of Terry's fingers.

'See, I'm getting to know all your likes and dislikes, and not just between the sheets.' He winked at her. 'Like how much you enjoy me—'

'Yes, I do love bracelets,' she interjected sharply, 'but that's beside the point. This one is way too expensive. You've already bought me a gorgeous set of underwear. I really don't need anything else.'

Reaching over, she cupped his cheek, letting her thumb rest against the plumpness of his lower lip, her tone softening. 'You are a wonderful, kind, and extremely generous man, Richard Hambro, and I have loved every minute of our time together. What I'm not is some grasping little gold digger out for all she can get along the way.' she reiterated, 'being here with you is enough.'

Leaning over, she kissed him briefly on the mouth.

'Shit, Izzy, give me some credit. I know you're not.' A vee had appeared between his brows. He looked hurt by her choice of words. 'It's just a bracelet. No big deal.'

She shook her head stubbornly. It was to her.

'Izzy, surely we're not going to fall out over a piece of fucking jewellery?'

'A very expensive piece of jewellery,' she corrected him, refusing to back down. 'And don't tell me it wasn't. I'm not stupid.'

'I know you're not stupid.' He huffed. 'Okay, so it cost a fair bit. But so what? I can afford it. And I want you to have it. It reflects what you mean to me, Izzy; how much I care about you.' His face softened into a half-smile. 'This is our last full day together. Don't spoil it by arguing. Please!'

Izzy's shoulders slumped in defeat. He'd deployed the "puppy dog eyes" as back up. They got to her every time. 'I don't want to fight with you, either.'

'Good girl.' Rick had the bangle out of the pouch and onto her wrist in seconds; the facets of the sapphire glinted in the sunlight filtering through the open bedroom curtains.

'I chose the sapphire because of those sexy eyes.' He brushed his lips against the heart. 'Never forget, pretty lady, you occupy a very special place right here.' He pressed her hand to his beating heart. 'And you always will.'

4.36 PM

From Izzy and Kathy's vantage point out, sitting out in the Auditorium, today's sound check had deteriorated to nothing short of farcical. Steve's microphone was on the blink, reducing him to nothing more than an incoherent railway announcer, while Jonny's guitar appeared to have developed its own gremlins, regardless of the endless attempts to rectify it by his Roadie. The concert was just over three hours away.

Worse, Davey and Marc were grabbing every opportunity to butt heads over an incident that had occurred earlier in the afternoon.

'Nice to see normal service has resumed.' Kathy removed the wrapper from her bagel and nodded towards Marc and Davey, who were now involved in a face-off over Marc's bank of keyboards. 'Fisticuffs don't look far away.'

His voice raised, Davey's index finger was being stabbed forcefully into the front of Marc's T-shirt. .

'Yes, they've been like that since they left the radio station.' Izzy didn't waste any energy looking up. Marc and Davey's most recent

414

blow-up was old news. 'Davey accused Marc of talking over him in the interview—which he did repeatedly— and Marc—who's conveniently forgotten that fact— has spent the entire afternoon denying it to anyone who'll listen.'

'You'd think they'd manage at least one day without bayonets drawn.' Kathy bit into her food, an ecstatic smile spreading across her face. 'Yum, these are seriously good. Try yours,' she urged.

Not wishing to disappoint her friend, a very reluctant Izzy forced herself to take a bite of the bagel in her hand. Her stomach still hadn't settled since this morning; eating was the last thing on her mind.

'Gosh, yes,' she fibbed, her stomach heaving in protest. 'Where did you get them?'

'From a smashing little deli across the street; the girl was ever so nice. I told her exactly what we were looking for and she made them up, no quibbles.' She winked. 'Also I did a bit of name-dropping; said they were for Jonny's lunch. Result—they didn't cost me a cent.'

Miss Davies was nothing, if not enterprising.

'And what did you think of Sabrina stirring things in the dressing room,' Kathy went on. 'Since when has she become the world authority on shooting music videos? You'd think she'd have learned her lesson by now, but no, she has to keep poking her nose in where it doesn't belong.'

'And it's always "accidently on purpose" too?' Izzy wiped away some stray mayonnaise from her top lip with a serviette. 'Then we get the "butter wouldn't melt" look as if to say "Oh dear, have I put my little size-eights in it again?".'

'And Marc's so bloody besotted he just nods and says "you're so right, darling". That one needs to get back on the cat-walk. If not, she'll be Eclectic Deviation's answer to Yoko Ono!'

Izzy nodded, wondering how much more of the salad-filled bagel she could actually stomach. In all honesty, one bite had been more than enough.

'And another thing…' Kathy went on. 'Marc can't afford to subsidise her "resting" for much longer. With all the shopping she does, she'll bankrupt him before the year is out. How much excess luggage will you have to pay for now?'

'Too bloody much!' Izzy rolled her eyes.

Another string of oaths emanated from the stage. This time from Jonny, who'd had it with his guitar. He dumped the six-string into the arms of his perplexed Roadie and stomped off towards the backstage curtain, kicking one of the amplifiers on route.

As if by magic, Terry appeared in his path, Izzy's eyes narrowing as he and Jonny exchanged a few terse words, before a conciliatory arm was slung around the guitarist's shoulders and Terry led Jonny away.

'Don't worry,' Kathy continued to demolish her bagel, 'a bit of medication's about to be administered and the smile will be back on Jonny's face before you know it.'

'Correction, you mean he'll be wired to the bloody moon and impossible to work with.' Izzy muttered, replacing her half-eaten bagel back in its paper bag. That was it. Terry's appearance had been responsible for her throat closing over completely.

'What's wrong?' Kathy asked, quirking an eyebrow.

'It's lovely, really, but I'm just not very hungry at the moment. I'll finish it, later.'

But Kathy didn't appear to be fooled by her answer, immediately placing a supportive hand on Izzy's knee.

'I'm not just talking about the food,' Kathy prompted. 'You've been really off all day. What's wrong, Izzy?'

Izzy's chest deflated, knowing she'd have to update Kathy on her white-knuckle lift-ride with Terry; she'd held off long enough.

'Just something that happened earlier. My nerves haven't settled yet.' Her voice faltering, Izzy went on to disclose what had taken place that morning.

'Fuck, Izzy!' Kathy's eyes had grown to the size of saucers. 'The guy's a rapist. He's as good as admitted it.'

'Will you keep your voice down?' Izzy shushed her; terrified anyone—especially the man himself—might somehow overhear their conversation.

'He's practically told you the date and time he'll do it to you,' Kathy retorted, her voice lowering. 'You can't just sit back and wait for it to happen. You need to fight back. Tell Jack.'

'I can't,' Izzy answered. 'It wouldn't do any good. When Angie finally went to Jack, he didn't believe her. Didn't do a thing, except throw money at her; make her sign some kind of gagging agreement and show her the door. He won't believe me either. Terry's too powerful, and you didn't see him this morning, heard the threats he made. God knows what he'd do to me if he knew I'd spoken to Jack. And don't say go to the police, either.' Izzy gave a helpless little shrug. 'Think of the publicity…'

Plus, she'd have to disclose her real name in any police report, and then the whole story would come out about who she really was. Rick would get to know everything and that would blow his relationship with his parents' sky high.

'Believe me, I'm not sitting back. I'm considering all my options.'

She hadn't stopped since her altercation with Terry. For a second, Izzy contemplated telling Kathy about her plans for an early departure after the last gig, but decided against it. She'd brief her nearer the time. There were still too many last-minute details to iron out.

'Izzy, this isn't a joke. Regardless of what happened with Angie, you still need to tell Jack, as soon as we get to New York.'

'No. It wouldn't do any good,' Izzy emphasised. 'Think about it. Terry's too important around here. He knows where the bodies are buried. That's his get out of jail card. Jack and the band will do anything to keep his mouth shut. You know—as well as I do—Jonny's 'kiss and tells' are just the tip of a very large and extremely sordid iceberg. Now, can we talk about something else, please…?'

50

NEW YORK CITY, NEW YORK

She'd have to be downstairs soon. Back in her room before anyone was up and about and could potentially witness today's final walk of shame.

A quick side-eye confirmed that Rick appeared to be still asleep, his face relaxed, a faint smile playing on his lips. Was he dreaming of Francesca?

She'd be here in another six hours.

Trying to put that depressing thought from her mind, Izzy snuggled in closer. She really couldn't bear the thought of moving—not yet. She didn't want to face the reality of this being over; back to them just being two friends, and nothing more. And once she walked out his bedroom door, that's exactly what was set to happen. The magical spell they'd woven with their frantic lovemaking over the last few hours would be gone forever; the little matter of her broken heart, just—as they say—collateral damage. No, she needed to savour these final minutes, commit them to memory. Enjoy the security of being cradled in Rick's arms one last time.

With a sad smile, she allowed her mind to drift back over the last ten magical days. The time had flown by. She could hardly believe they were here in New York already. A line from an Elton John hit kept repeating in her brain. For every one of those days, they'd been "laughing like children, living like lovers and rolling like thunder under the covers".

They were so perfect together—and not just in the physical sense either, although that was pretty damn incredible—but emotionally and intellectually too. In fact, it was scary how deep the connection between them had become. In every sense, the man lying beside her was her soul mate; the other half of herself. They just worked—on every level; worked in ways that she'd never even imagined with Alex. Rick made her feel safe… special….complete… loved?

No. Not loved. That was the one component that was missing. He wasn't in love with her. Not the way she was in love with him. He cared about her; she knew that by his protective actions and his words, but his heart would always belong to Francesca.

Letting out a slow breath, she gave her watch a cursory glance. Those bloody hands had shot forward. She'd have to get up now. She was due to meet the bands' parents, fiancées and Jack off the noon flight at *JFK*, and she'd a lot to accomplish before then.

'Where did you get that cute little scar?' Rick's voice unexpectedly broke the silence as he slid his index finger against the white scar that zigzagged down Izzy's left kneecap.

'What?' Izzy glanced up to find Rick was now very much awake. 'I thought you were still dead to the world.'

'Nope, I'm just lying here savouring these moments with my pretty lady.' He grinned back, letting his hand wander up her thigh. 'So, tell me; how did you get it?'

She caught those mischievous fingers in her own, pressing a kiss to their tips. 'Fell off my bloody bike. Hit a stone and next thing, I'm splat in the middle of the road with blood everywhere.' She giggled at the memory. 'Don't you remember?'

Shit! The laughter died in her throat and she sobered instantly. Had she just given the game away as to who she was?

You total idiot, Izzy!

Rick had been there that day. She and Michelle doing their best to catch him as he'd streaked miles ahead on his brand new *Chopper* bicycle, Buster barking madly at their side, enjoying the fun.

After her accident, Rick had sat with her, an arm awkwardly placed around her shoulders, Izzy sobbing her heart out into his teenage chest while Michelle had run for help, Buster's head resting in her lap; whining.

Rick had been so kind; treating her just like his little sister, holding a tissue to the wound in her leg to stem the ridiculous amount of blood flowing. All the time, he'd told her not to worry, that he'd look after her. She'd needed several stitches to the wound and been on the receiving end of a furious tongue lashing from her father about acting so recklessly while cycling. Now, the thin white scar was the only reminder of that day. But, by his actions, Richard Hambro had been cemented as her hero.

He still was.

'Don't you remember?' She repeated. 'You've asked me about it before—in the shower.' She gave him a hopeful smile. Had she managed to cover up the slip?

'Did I? I don't recall....' he began, frowning.

She had to distract him with something else.

'I'm sure you had lots of accidents when you were little?' she went on hurriedly.

Rick's face relaxed into a grin. 'Jeez, I'd too many to count. I was always getting into scrapes.' He reached over to nuzzle his lips against her temple. 'A week didn't pass by but mum would have me up at Reading General. Said I had a season ticket for the A&E Department. Got so bad, she was worried they'd send the Social Services round.'

Izzy gave a mental sigh of relief. Disaster had been successfully averted.

'So do you have any distinguishing marks, I should know about?' she teased.

'Given how intimate we've been, pretty lady, you mean you haven't found them all by now?'

She was treated to a cheeky eyebrow wiggle, before lifting up his left arm, indicating a small raised bump on the side of his wrist.

'That was our Jonny. The little bastard whacked me with one of those sodding great Tonka trucks at his fourth birthday party. Broke a tiny bone and for some reason it never healed properly, despite the cast being on for bloody weeks.'

'Nice to know he's always had a violent streak.' Izzy commented as Rick shifted in the bed, moving to snuggle his head against her breasts.

She wrapped her arms about him, hugging him tightly to her.

'This has been so much fun, Izzy.' He said.

'Yes, it has.' She agreed, trying to ignore the sinking sensation in her stomach; fun that was now—most definitely—at an end.

'If only we'd had a few more days…' His voice had taken on a strangely wistful note.

'But we don't, Rick.' she reminded him, tousling her fingers through his hair. 'Just until New York, then back to being friends. Anyway…' Somehow, she forced brightness into her tone. 'Francesca will be here this afternoon. You must be looking forward to seeing her.…'

'I suppose ….' He expelled a long breath, the air making her sensitive nipples tingle, before he continued. 'It's just I like how I'm able to be myself when I'm around you. Not feel as though I have to put on a front…'

'I know. But it won't be long, now. Then you can explain everything to her.…'

'Maybe.…'

He caught her hand in his, pressing her palm against his own, their fingers lacing together. 'I'd like you to be at the meeting on Wednesday. Be my piece of Dutch courage when I drop the bombshell…'

'Don't be silly. You won't need me there.'

It was time to be encouraging. She'd be gone by then, anyway. 'The band will understand, Rick. I know they will….'

Izzy brushed her lips against his forehead.

'And then once those conversations are over, we need to talk…' he looked up, his eyes capturing hers, his expression intense.

What would they need to talk about? And then she remembered. He still expected an answer to his job offer.

3.27 PM

'Hi, I'm just checking in. Making sure you've settled in, okay?' Izzy beamed as Jim Hambro, Rick's father, opened the hotel room door.

Jim's face relaxed into an answering grin, ushering Izzy inside.

At fifty-two, he was an extremely handsome man, and a fleeting thought struck Izzy; his son would probably look much the same at that age.

'Everything's great, love. Thanks. We've just been looking over the schedule you left. It looks fun, if somewhat hectic. But Betty warned me about how organised you are.'

His blue eyes twinkled with amusement. 'Betty, it's Isabelle,' he called out, then as if realising the glaring mistake, his cheeks flushed guiltily. 'Ooops, sorry, I can't get used to referring to you as Izzy.'

Betty bustled out of the bedroom, her brows drawn together and lips pursed, eyeing her husband with undisguised annoyance.

'Please try to remember, Jim,' she tsked, before holding her arms out to Izzy. 'Come here, my love, I want to say hello, properly?'

When Izzy had met them at the airport—over two hours previously—they'd maintained, for appearances' sake, an appropriate distance as though strangers, but now Izzy found herself enveloped in a wonderfully warm bear hug, which she returned with interest. In truth, she'd never felt so glad to see someone in her life.

'And how are you?' Betty stood back, holding Izzy at arm's length and giving her a critical once-over. 'You look as though you've lost weight since Christmas. Mary and Andrew won't be happy about that.'

'Betty, I'm great— honestly,' Izzy answered with a smile and dismissive wave of the hand. 'It's been so manic; food always seems to be the last thing on everyone's list.'

But she'd a feeling Betty's comment was spot on. Her appetite had taken a nosedive since her encounter with Terry; the waistband of her skinny jeans slackening. And now they were here in New York, things were only likely to get worse.

From the moment the band's fleet of limos had drawn away from their Manhattan hotel at nine-thirty this morning, heading out to their first engagement of the day, the pace had gone up another gear. Every minute of their next seven days accounted for in mind-boggling detail on Izzy's schedule. Given all the unfinished business she still had to address, a knot of nerves had taken up permanent residence in her gut, meaning eating had become the last thing she felt like doing.

'After all, this is what everyone has been working towards, three sell-out nights at Madison Square Garden.' She forced a cheerful smile to her lips. 'But more importantly, how are you both? How was the flight on *Concorde*, Jim?'

'It was phenomenal, love! And you'll never guess; we were invited up to meet the Captain.' He gave Izzy a boyish grin. 'First-class supersonic is definitely the way to travel.'

'Yes,' Izzy agreed, pleased he'd enjoyed the little surprise she'd arranged for him and his two younger brothers. 'You can get used to it, can't you?'

Name-dropping Eclectic Deviation opened a lot of doors, including the one to *Concorde's* flight deck.

'Izzy, before I forget, I must thank you for the delphiniums.' Betty indicated the large vase of fresh blue blooms sitting on the table by the window. 'But how did you know they're my favourite flower? They're supposed to be out of season at this time of year.'

'A girl has her ways.' Izzy tapped her nose.

The delphiniums had taken a bit of time to track down and get flown in specially. But Betty was so worth it.

'Well, they were a wonderful surprise! The always remind me of our wedding day,' Betty's expression had taken on a distinctly dreamy look, 'which will be thirty years ago, this coming July. Where have all the years gone? And more to the point, Izzy, how have I've managed to put up with him for so long?' She jerked a thumb towards her husband.

'Yeah, and hopefully, we'll make it to that milestone,' Jim quipped back, giving Izzy a conspiratorial wink, 'if I don't murder her first. It's been a close-run thing, I can tell you, Izzy.' He cast a sly glance at his wife. 'While I was up in the cockpit, I sounded out the captain about the possibility of pushing her out at sixty thousand feet, but he wasn't receptive to my idea.'

More laughter, Jim receiving a light tap on the cheek from his wife, but Izzy could see the love shining in both faces, belying the harsh words.

'Don't listen to him, love. My dear husband doesn't know he's born.'

'True.' Jim's grin was suitably chastened.

'Oh, and thank you for the champagne and chocolates, too.' Betty went on. 'We'll be making a large dent in those later. We feel totally spoilt already, and we've only just arrived.'

'It's a pleasure. Rick mentioned you'd a soft spot for chocolate truffles. But remember you need to thank him—not me—for the all the pressies.'

And it wasn't just Betty who'd received her favourite chocolates and flowers; Izzy had made sure that all their mums' favourite blooms had been waiting in their rooms, together with a gift basket containing handmade chocolates, champagne and other luxury goodies.

'And now, give me an update on Richard?'

Betty had made herself comfortable on the sofa, patting the space next to her, indicating Izzy should come and sit down.

'Exhausted and longing to go home and put his feet up, but so much better,' Izzy answered truthfully, flopping into the cushions at her side.

'And definitely no more tablets?'

'Nope, and he's finally promised to see a real doctor. Obtain a proper diagnosis for his sleep problems.'

That promise had been wrung from him during their final steamy encounter in the shower this morning.

'Oh, Izzy, you've no idea how good it is to hear that.' Relief was written all over Betty's plump face. 'And has he mentioned anything more about leaving the band?'

'He'll be speaking to everyone on Wednesday; you and Francesca included. It's all pretty much what I told you, he'll outline what he's been thinking and discuss what happens next. I'm sure there will be a lot of legal formalities to put in place. You know royalties, publishing rights, ownership of the band's name; that sort of thing. Understandably, he's nervous about reactions, but he's made peace with himself, which is the important thing.'

'And no doubt we'll witness the fireworks once Francesca's let in on the secret,' Betty speculated, giving a little shake of her head and glancing over at Jim. 'Not quite the start to married life she envisaged, eh Jim?'

'Please don't worry, Isabelle…' Jim rested a hand on his wife's shoulder. 'I mean Izzy…. we're not about to say anything, are we, Betty?'

Izzy caught the warning look Jim directed at his wife.

'Of course not,' Betty agreed. 'Once you told us about him leaving the band, it all fell into place. Francesca will just have to like it or lump it.'

Out of nowhere, tears pricked Izzy's eyelids at the mention of Rick, Francesca and their forthcoming wedding. Suddenly it all felt so real and so final. This was really the end for her and Rick.

She blinked them away, hoping neither Betty not Jim had noticed. It was time to get on with some work, not start sobbing her heart out over something she could never change. There would be time for more tears, later.

'Right,' she said, injecting as much breeziness as she could muster into her tone, 'they're leaving for the sound check at quarter past, I'd better go—'

She was interrupted by a sharp knock on the door.

It was Rick and Francesca; Rick grinning as soon as he saw Izzy standing beside his parents, but Francesca's expression remained frosty.

No change there. Francesca had had a face carved from the polar ice cap from the moment she'd laid eyes on Izzy at *JFK*. And, Izzy noted, Francesca's hand was clamped possessively around Rick's. The message being sent was clear: *Rick's mine now. Keep your thieving hands to yourself, Izzy.*

She cleared her throat, trying desperately to remove the ball of emotion that had settled there. She couldn't show how seeing them together, affected her. She had to be strong, pretend it didn't feel as though someone had just rammed a rusty knife into her gut.

'Well, Mr and Mrs Hambro, everything on the schedule should be self-explanatory. Please be down in reception by four-thirty. I'll be waiting for you. Make sure you get away to the *Waldorf Astoria* okay. And remember; if you need anything don't hesitate to lift the telephone, day or night. My room number and telephone extension are printed at the top of the schedule. I'm entirely at your disposal for the duration of your stay. Just don't tell Marc, I said that.'

Everyone laughed with the exception of Francesca who merely barred her teeth.

Izzy turned to leave. 'I understand the food is amazing at the *Astoria*. Let me know how many 'stars' you decide to award the chef', she grimaced, 'because given tonight's workload, I'll be lucky if I've time to swallow one of those *Hershey* chocolate bars the Americans rave about.'

'Then, why don't we sneak you out a doggy bag?' Betty joked.

More laughter ensued, Izzy catching Rick's gaze momentarily. 'Sorry to rush you, Rick, but you've only got five minutes with mum and dad and no longer. Then you need to be downstairs for the press conference.'

She was rewarded with a wink and a salute.

'Yes, boss.'

'Right, I'd better go and chase up your nephew.' Izzy rolled her eyes at Betty. 'Knowing Marc, he'll be wandering around in his underpants, claiming he's got nothing suitable to wear.'

In all her time with the band, Izzy had only ever watched a full show twice. The first and last fifteen minutes was generally all she had time for. But given the importance of these final dates for Rick, she'd been determined to sneak out front; soak in the atmosphere one last time.

And forty-five minutes in, standing out here in the auditorium, the band's adoring fans pressing in on all sides, she had to hand it to them; Eclectic Deviation knew how to entertain an audience. The lights, the dry ice, and pyrotechnics were mind-blowing, as was the atmosphere in the auditorium, the enthusiasm the band generated for their craft totally infectious; everyone in the audience having the time of their lives.

After five years at the top of their game, Steve, Jonny and Davey were seasoned pros at working a crowd up into frenzy. Every little 'rock'n'roll' swagger across the stage or 'little boy lost' look—dutifully supplied by Jonny into camera at regular intervals—was answered by louder and louder screams.

But Izzy couldn't bear to drag her eyes away from Rick, situated up on his plinth at the rear of the stage. His head down, earphones on and focused entirely on the job at hand, keeping a steady beat to each track on tonight's playlist.

She cast a surreptitious glance over to the VIP area, easily making out the swaying figures of Francesca, Caron, Caroline and Sabrina. She-Bitch-from-Hell was back in her rightful position, and it hurt like hell.

Reaching up, she wiped away another stray tear from her cheek. Images from this morning filtering through her mind, the ballad the band was playing now a fitting backdrop to her thoughts.

After they'd finally dragged themselves out of the shower, Izzy had hurriedly dressed— both of them strangely quiet. What did people said to each other at the end of this type of relationship? In the end, neither of them had said anything of consequence, just sharing one last lingering kiss before Izzy had rushed off—citing a fictitious meeting with Lindsay—before departing for the airport.

Back in the sanctuary of her own room, she'd given into her misery, sobbing until her throat had been raw, before she'd—somehow—pulled herself together and painted on the mask she'd worn all day.

As the old adage went, "the show must go on". But she'd never felt so bloody miserable in all her life. When she'd split from Alex, she'd been sad. Sad that things hadn't worked out, but the overwhelming feeling had been one of relief.

This was so different. It was like slow torture; losing Rick an actual physical pain, ripping her inside out and—worse—there was absolutely nothing that she could do about it. She'd no choice but to hide her emotions behind a fake smile and carry on.

The band had come to the final song of the set. They'd be heading off for a three-minute breather before the encore began. It was time for her to get back stage too; make sure they were all okay. Then she'd need to put through a last-minute telephone call to the nightclub in lower Manhattan, check that everything was in place for the band's estimated time of arrival—traffic permitting—of around ten-thirty pm.

Climbing the narrow wrought-iron staircase to the upper VIP Lounge of the nightclub, Izzy scrutinised the sea of anonymous faces before her, trying to spot Kathy. Searching for a needle in the old haystack sprung to mind.

She'd never seen anywhere so jam-packed with sweaty bodies. Before her was an ocean of humanity, all gyrating to a thumping bass line, delivered courtesy of the sound system's massive speakers.

At that moment, strobe lighting illuminated a far corner of the club, causing Izzy to do a double take. And some of the revellers appeared to be indulging in more than just dancing by the look of it! She hastily averted her eyes and scanned about herself once more. Where on earth had Kathy disappeared to? They'd agreed to meet up here, barely forty-five minutes ago.

Her eyes fell on an empty table off to her left and she let out a hiss of annoyance.

Shit! Finding her AWOL best friend would have to be put on hold. A bigger problem had just landed in her lap. It looked as though she'd succeeded in losing the band's parents, too! None of them were sitting at their designated table.

Trying not to panic, she deliberated on her next course of action. She'd waved them off in the limos, issued Lee with clear instructions as to where they had to be deposited i.e. right here. What on earth had gone wrong?

Then, in answer to her silent plea for divine intervention, the crowd parted like the *Red Sea*, and a smiling Betty appeared, waving frantically to attract her attention.

'Izzy, you've made it at last,' she called out, walking forward to meet her, 'I've been watching out for you.'

Betty pointed over her shoulder towards a dark archway, surrounded by pulsating red and green light bulbs. 'I know you expected to find us here, but our Kate *insisted* on being moved to a quieter spot. You know what she's like. Lee managed to find us a home through there. It's quieter—but only just!' She giggled. 'As we're all in our fifties, it's no fun spending your evening trying to have a decent conversation, when all you end up doing is yelling yourself hoarse!'

She signalled that Izzy should follow her. 'Come on through, love and have a glass of champagne. You look as though you could do with one.'

Deciding that Betty was absolutely right, she did deserve a spot of bubbly, Izzy fell into step behind the retreating figure of Rick's mother. Catching up with Kathy would have to wait.

11.34 PM

Kate, Jonny's hard-to-please mother, lifted her empty champagne glass and shook it meaningfully towards her husband. Picking up on her unspoken request, John Hambro dutifully reached for the bottle nestling in its ice bucket, and topped up his wife's glass.

'Thank-you, darling,' Kate acknowledged with blown kiss, before turning back to Izzy. 'Well, from what you've just been telling us, Izzy, it sounds as though you're a mixture of PA, nursemaid and general dogsbody around here. I don't know how you put up with it. I really don't.' Kate gave a little shudder, before managing to expertly dispose of her replenished drink in one swallow.

Izzy caught Betty's eye roll. Kate Hambro wasn't known for her diplomacy skills.

'I certainly don't run after Jonny whenever he deigns to come home, and nor will I be starting either. He's a grown man.' That comment was accompanied with a loud sniff. 'Not that he acts like one. As demanding today, as he was in nappies, isn't he, John?'

John Hambro, clearly used to his wife after twenty-five years together, merely nodded but made no reply.

'Well, thank God, I don't have to change any nappies, Mrs Hambro. That's where I definitely draw the line,' Izzy replied with a smile.

Kate laughed. 'Please call me Kate, Izzy?' she invited.

'My job is really to make life a little easier for them, Kate,' Izzy went on. 'After all, their day jobs are extremely stressful—playing the shows, dealing with the media and the never-ending hysteria from the fans. They really don't have the time to worry about all the mundane stuff life throws up. That's my job. I wave the magic wand and make it all go away.'

'Well, Izzy,' Kate continued, 'knowing Jonathan, your magic wand will be constantly in use. My son seems determined to jump from one embarrashing escapade to another. Some weeks, it's impossible to face people in the supermarket, especially when his sex life is spread across the front pages—'

'Oh, stop moaning, Kate,' Betty cut in with a grin, 'you're as proud of Jonathan as I am of Richard.'

'Of course I'm proud of him, and all he's achieved,' Kate replied, her tone suggesting she took umbrage at the very idea of anyone saying otherwise, especially her sister-in-law. 'But I just wish he'd find a nice girl and settle down; just like your Richard has with Francesca. John and I were married by his age, as were you and Jim.'

She failed to clock the fleeting grimace that flashed across Betty's face at the mention of Francesca's name, but Izzy picked up on it straightaway. 'Nice' wasn't a word Betty ever used in connection with her future daughter-in-law.

'Every week Jonathan's name is linked to some new floozie,' Kate continued, 'I can't keep up. At least he's finally ditched that empty-headed glamour model.'

Kate placed a hand on Izzy's arm, and leant in close. 'Jilly Fletcher was not my idea of a suitable daughter-in-law, with those breasts permanently on show.'

Her comment prompted an awkward silence all round, which was finally broken by Betty.

'Well, here's my boy, now.'

Izzy turned, her breath catching in her throat. Rick was striding towards their table and he'd never looked sexier in that black silk shirt and super tight leather trousers, both items of clothing clinging to his incredible body like a second skin. A body she'd known every inch of…..

With hungry eyes, she watched as he crouched down between his parents, all three chatting animatedly for several minutes, before he looked over at her.

'So, are you up for it, Miss Stevenson?'

'Up for what?' she asked, taking in the amused faces of his parents.

'Mum wants to know if you're brave enough to hit the dance floor with me,' Rick explained. 'I told her, I've still never had the pleasure of dancing with my lovely PA. We always seem to get interrupted. So how about it—third time lucky?'

Not quite true, they'd danced together—naked—one night in the privacy of Rick's hotel room, but it hadn't lasted long, not when hands and mouths had started seeking out intimate places…

Izzy bit her lip. There was nothing she wanted more. But could she trust herself? Pretend they were nothing but friends? Or would those bloody tears overtake her again? Maybe, it was better to err on the safe side, and sit this one out.

'Much as I'd love to, Rick'—she put down her half-touched glass of champagne and picked up her clutch bag—'I should be getting back to work. No doubt, Marc will be sending out a search party, any second now. I still haven't checked in with him.'

The corners of Rick's mouth had turned down and, catching his expression, Izzy was consumed with guilt.

'Come on, Rick, you know what he's like,' she appealed, desperate for a flash of his smile. 'Anyway, Betty was telling me earlier that you're a bit of a liability on the dance floor? You never told me that.'

'What on earth have you been saying, Mum?'

Betty received a stern look from her son.

'Just that Izzy's lovely pink boots would need steel-toe caps,' Betty chuckled, pointing down at Izzy's suede-clad feet. 'Because you're size nines require a *Government Health Warning*.'

'And as I've told *you*—numerous times—that was an accident.' Rick turned back to Izzy. 'I suppose she's told you the story of our Cheryl's wedding?' He rolled his eyes at Betty. 'But she's been economical with the whole truth, if I know Mum. I was fourteen, mortified at having to dance with my mother. She was becoming too enthusiastic with her moves in platform heels—too much *Cinzano Bianco*, and not enough lemonade—that was your excuse.'

A playful slap connected with his left shoulder in answer to his cheeky remark.

'Mum overbalanced and I *accidently*,' Rick emphasised the word, 'trod on her foot and next thing I know, we're down and I'm sprawled on top of her. Unfortunately, she broke her ankle in the process. We spent the rest of the night in A&E. I've been blamed ever since. Nothing to do with her unsuitable footwear or inebriated state, you understand.'

'Oh, darling, I wasn't inebriated!' Betty giggled, reaching over to give her son an affectionate hug.

'Believe me, Izzy,' Rick went on, finally disentangling himself from his mother's embrace, 'these days I reckon I could teach John Travolta a thing or two!'

He reached out, catching Izzy's hand, his eyes pinned on her. 'Anyway, Izzy knows me well enough to know she'll be quite safe in my arms.'

His face wore that same tender expression she'd seen so many times, the double meaning behind those words making her heart lurch. It was time to capitulate; feel those arms around her, one last time.

'Oh, okay then. I suppose I can risk it.' Telling herself she could do this, Izzy allowed him to pull her up beside him. 'But one wrong move, Mr Hambro and you're on your own,' she reminded him.

'Rick! Where on earth are you going, *now*?'

At the sound of that voice, Izzy hastily pulled her hand from the security of Rick's warm fingers.

Bloody Francesca! Worse, given the furious glower on Francesca's face, Izzy knew she hadn't been quick enough to remove her hand from Rick's. Miss Reiss had clocked it.

'You'd better not be sneaking off onto the dance floor without me, Rick?' Francesca's gaze had switched back to her fiancé, her voice accusing. 'Honestly, one minute you were there chatting to Jack, and then you vanished into thin air.'

A bland smile was now directed at her future in-laws. 'You might have told me you were checking in on your Mum and Dad, *again*.'

With that she leant over and gave Betty a perfunctory kiss on the cheek.

Betty's eyebrows shot upwards, practically disappearing into her hairline, clearly stunned by the kiss, as well as being addressed as '*Mum*'.

'See what I mean, Betty,' Kate chimed in, reaching over to pat Betty's knee, clearly taken in by Francesca's perfect daughter-in-law-to-be routine.

'Izzy, Marc's on the warpath.' Francesca had now looped her hand through Rick's. He wants to know where you've disappeared to.' The chill in her voice had bottomed out at absolute zero. 'Apparently, you've made a monumental balls-up of tomorrow's schedule and he wants it fixed. So, I wouldn't keep him waiting any longer!'

Marc had dispatched the search party, and it would have to be in the shape of her number one fan!

'Where is he?'Izzy asked, retrieving her clutch bag from the table.

'He's taken up residence through there.' Francesca waved a hand vaguely over her shoulder towards yet another archway surrounded by pulsating red and green lights.

Instructions given, Francesca's attention had reverted back to her fiancé. 'Now, come on, darling, *I* was promised the first dance, remember.'

With that, she began tugging him towards another set of steps, which led to the private VIP dance floor. 'You're not usually this reluctant; I must have really exhausted you in the bedroom, earlier.'

Izzy knew that not-so-subtle little dig had been delivered entirely for her benefit. She turned away, biting her lip and blinking hard to regain control. Francesca had pierced her intended target first time; dead centre of Izzy's heart.

51

NEW YORK CITY, NEW YORK

The following morning, the newspapers and Breakfast TV shows were awash with admiration on Eclectic Deviation's sell-out first night at Madison Square Garden.

'According to the New York Times, not since the days of *Beatlemania* had New York seen such wild scenes of hysteria. They gave us five stars,' Steve read out triumphantly to the rest of the band—minus Marc, who was still lounging in bed. His excuse being he needed to catch-up on *all* the Breakfast TV reports.

Unfortunately, the early press releases, filtering back across the pond from several British newspapers, weren't quite so fulsome with their praise.

'Well, wait till you hear this.' Jonny's disgruntled voice piped up from behind his *Daily Mirror.* 'Once more, New York was treated to a mediocre show, performed by a mediocre band, sadly still oblivious to their mediocrity.'

'Arseholes! They've obviously forgotten the six *Brit Awards* we pocketed last year, as well as the arse-licking article they trotted out afterwards.' Davey fumed back. 'And if you believe this pile of shite'—he rapped his copy of *The Sun* in disgust—'we're nothing more than a bunch of has-beens, who can't hold a torch to bloody *Bon Jovi!*

He glowered over at Izzy. 'Tell Lindsay, we're not offering *The Sun* any more exclusives from now on. Got it?'

Izzy nodded, taking a sip of her coffee. There would be tears before bedtime when Marc read that one.

9.23 PM

A final slash of pink lip gloss sealed the deal, and Izzy hurriedly replaced the tube within her clutch bag. She'd need to head back to their table; the night wasn't over yet.

They were at the *RockTV Rock Awards* Ceremony, held within the Banqueting Hall of the New York *Hilton*. Given *Rock TV's* intransigence over the clash with the Silver Wedding celebration, Jack had threatened a last-minute no-show, if the bands' parents' weren't accommodated at an adjacent table and given the full five-star treatment. In the face of Jack playing hard ball, *Rock TV* Executives had finally caved to his demands, even managing to rustle up a celebratory cake for John and Kate.

Izzy allowed herself a final once-over in the mirror opposite. She looked passable, but that was about all that could be said about the despondent girl staring back at her. She leaned in closer, noticing faint traces of bags beneath sad sapphire blue eyes. Her lack of sleep was starting to show. As well as a loss of appetite, she was the one suffering from insomnia, now. Back in her lonely bed and missing being snuggled up against Rick's warm body every night. Then she stopped herself.

Don't go there, Izzy. Don't think about Rick. Don't think about him making love to Francesca. Concentrate on your appearance. The dress looks great…

But her mood plummeted again. She'd never be able to compete with Francesca in the fashion stakes, either. Francesca looked breathtaking tonight—every inch the rock star wife-to-be, dazzling from head to toe in silver sequins—playing up to the paparazzo's instructions on how to pose, their flashbulbs popping as soon as she'd stepped from the limo.

Izzy let out a heavy sigh.

If only the last ten days with Rick had meant more to him than just sex. If only he wasn't spoken for, and she—Izzy—hadn't been passing herself off as the fictitious Miss Stevenson. If only, he was in love with her...

Forcing a smile, and giving her fringe a final flick, she turned to leave, only to find her path unexpectedly blocked by both Reiss sisters, and neither looked like budging any time soon.

Izzy froze, immediately sensing danger. So far, she'd managed to avoid any face-to-face confrontation with Rick's fiancée.

'Well, Caron.' Francesca flashed her sister a sideways smile. 'Look who it is, my fiancé's *personal* assistant.'

Caron drew Izzy a suitably disparaging once-over, but for once kept her opinions to herself. Little sister was clearly in charge here.

'I think you and I need another of our chats, don't you?' Francesca told Izzy in a low voice. 'Why don't we move over there?' She gestured towards a small out-of-the-way alcove that boasted its own vanity unit. 'It's much more private. I'm sure you won't want the entire room to overhear what I've got to say.'

Izzy's eyes darted about herself, desperate to sidestep any kind of altercation and make a quick escape.

'I'm sorry, Miss Reiss, Mrs Eastman,' she fought hard to keep her voice level, 'but I really need to check in with the band's parents. Make sure everyone is okay. So, unless this is really important…, you'll have to excuse me…'

She left the comment hanging, and meeting with no immediate challenge to her words, tried to step around the other woman.

'Not so fast, bitch!' Francesca latched a restraining hand onto Izzy's arm, her scarlet nails digging into her skin, deep enough to make Izzy wince. 'Or maybe I should address you by *your* real name, Miss Anderson; Mary Isabelle Anderson.'

Izzy's head snapped back instantly, the blood draining from her face, hating the triumph which had dawned in Francesca's amber eyes at her unchecked reaction.

How the hell did Francesca know her real name?

Realising she'd no choice now but to hear Francesca out, Izzy turned and stalked over to the vanity unit indicated.

'Well, you've definitely got her attention now, little sis,' Caron drawled, placing her bag down on its marble surface and retrieving her lipstick.

'Yeah, I bet the lads don't realise they've got their very own "super sleuth" hiding in plain sight?' Francesca agreed with a humourless laugh.

An icy shiver ran down Izzy's spine at the words "super sleuth". It sounded as though Francesca had some kind of knowledge as to why she might be here, but how?

'I don't know what you're talking about.' It was better to deny for the moment until she worked out what was going on.

'Always playing Miss Goody Two Shoes, Izzy, except we both know you're anything but...' Francesca had begun searching inside her own silver clutch bag.

What she drew out next made Izzy shrink back against the wall in horror. Clasped in Francesca's right hand was Izzy's passport.

'But you must recognise this?' Francesca smiled. 'Or are we still suffering from that sudden burst of amnesia?' She flipped open the document and thrust it in Izzy's face. 'Say's it all here; in black and white. Miss Mary Isabelle Anderson. No mention of any alias. So, who is the fictitious Miss Izzy Stevenson, I wonder?' Francesca pretended to think for a moment. 'Oh yes, I remember. You've conveniently decided to adopt your mother's name around here.'

Shit, Francesca knew all about the identity swap.

'Where did you get that?' Izzy croaked; her throat so dry she could barely get the words out. Her passport should be back in the hotel, safely tucked into her nightstand, not here clasped in a gloating Francesca's hand.

'Let's just say a very accommodating laundry maid let me inside your room,' Francesca explained. 'Amazing how security goes out the window when you wave a fifty dollar bill in a girl's face. It proved money well spent.'

'You went through my belongings?'

Izzy chose to ignore the fact she'd resorted to doing pretty much that herself. This was a nightmare. How did she get out of this?

Francesca cocked her head to the side, her smile decidedly smug. 'Of course I did. How else could I get the final proof I needed before confronting Betty's little Private Eye?'

Izzy's pulse pounded in her temple, and the Cordon Bleu dinner she'd picked at shifted uncomfortably in her stomach.

'Yep, I heard the whole story straight from the horse's mouth.' Francesca went on. 'Not that Betty knows I was listening in. I just happened to be in the right place at the right time and overheard an eye-opening row between her and that hen-pecked husband. All about the lovely Miss Anderson and the real reason she's been parachuted in here as the band's new PA.'

Yes, it looked like the game was up, but maybe Francesca was still on a scouting mission, trying to fish for more information. Well, she wasn't about to help her out.

'I know all about your mother being Betty's pen friend from way back. I know they hatched this idiotic little scheme between them, because Betty's got some bee in her bonnet that Rick's going round the fucking bend. That sound about right to you?' Francesca returned Izzy's passport to the safety of her bag. 'How you were asked take on the job, keep tabs on Rick and report back his every move to "mummy dearest". How you had to use an assumed name, just in case Rick might recognise you?'

Francesca shook her head incredulously. 'And it's all such fucking nonsense! I think I'd know if there was anything wrong with my fiancé up there, don't you?' She tapped her fingers to her forehead.

'If you think Rick's really okay, then you're blind as well as stupid?'

The words flew out Izzy's mouth before she could check herself. How could Francesca be so dismissive of Rick's very obvious unhappiness and his way of dealing with it? The woman was supposed to love and support him.

'You're too busy concentrating on the "Wedding of the Year" to notice—let alone care—about what he might be going through.'

'You really are an irritating little bitch, aren't you, Izzy?' Francesca's eyes blazed with temper, and her hand had balled into a fist by her side.

Izzy swallowed, catching the subtle movement. Was Francesca about to let rip with a left hook? She took a step out of firing range just in case.

'Do you seriously think you know my fiancé better than me?' Francesca went on. 'He's been fucking you for what—five bloody minutes at most—and suddenly you're the expert on all his inner feelings. Don't think so, darling!'

Izzy let out a sigh. Maybe it was time to admit defeat.

'Ok, you're right, I'm Mary Isabelle Anderson. As to the rest, think what you like. I'm saying nothing else.'

'You're so bloody sure of yourself, standing there with your degree and stuck-up accent. Think you're better than me. Just like Betty and that snotty family of hers.'

Francesca pressed her face up close to Izzy's. Spitting mad like a feral wildcat, Rick's fiancée was anything but attractive.

'And was whoring yourself part of the deal, too? Did Betty ask you to drop your knickers in the interests of pumping him for more information?'

No, getting romantically involved, and having her heart shot to pieces in the process, had never been part of the deal. Betty would be shocked if she was made privy to that part of the story.

'Well, Caron?' Francesca gave the side-eye to her sister. 'I think it's about time Rick found out about Miss Anderson's little game, don't you?'

Caron's head nodded vigorously as she continued to touch up her make-up.

'You're going to tell him?' Izzy bit her lip. This was what she'd always dreaded most, Rick finding out.

'Of course I'm going to tell him, I've just been biding my time since I arrived here. In fact, they should all bloody know what you've been up to.'

'You can't do that?'

'And why the hell not, answer me that?' Francesca's eyebrows rose at Izzy's fearful expression.

'Because… because… it's cruel and completely unnecessary. For a start, it would destroy Rick's relationship with Betty and Jim.'

'You think I'm seriously bothered about his bloody parents in this mess?' Francesca replied. 'No, Izzy, I've just learnt what Saint Betty is fucking capable of. I certainly don't want her keeping tabs on me for the rest of my married life, thanks very much. The sooner she's out the picture, the better.'

'But you can't.' Izzy realised she'd have to try to get Francesca on side. 'If you love Rick, you wouldn't do this to him. They're his parents. He adores them.'

It was time to come clean. There was nothing else for it. 'Not when Betty only sent me here with the very best of intentions. There was never any malice intended, and certainly not towards you. That was the last thing on Betty's mind. She was just worried sick about her son.'

'Crap, I've waited years to get that interfering bitch off my back, and now she's played right into my hands. Betty destroyed her relationship with Rick the moment she involved you in her nasty little plan, and you were stupid enough to help her. Probably still had some stupid school-girl crush on him and thought it would be a good opportunity to get up close and personal again.'

Izzy shifted uncomfortably at the truth in Francesca's words, before carrying on, 'Betty was desperate. She'd found out he'd started taking sleeping tablets to deal with his insomnia. She was worried he'd become addicted, maybe move onto harder drugs. And he'd been acting strangely, distancing himself. He'd stopped talking to her and Jim. Betty only asked me to keep an eye on him, let her know if he was okay. If he'd started taking anything else…'

Hopefully she hadn't said too much? Francesca didn't know anything about the underlying reason for Rick's insomnia battle.

'And the ever-helpful Miss Anderson was only too happy to oblige.' Francesca rolled her eyes. 'Rick's not some stupid kid. He knows what he's doing, unlike that idiot cousin of his shoving cocaine up his nose, and frying his brains in the process.'

'And how would you know?' Izzy flared back. 'When the original tablets stopped working, Terry got him started on something called *Teraxapen*. Made it sound like some miraculous cure. According to Betty, they're potentially lethal. Doctors want them banned…'

'Stop being so fucking melodramatic, you're as bad as Betty. So, Rick took stronger sleeping pills, so bloody what? I know all about his insomnia. He's had it for years. It comes and goes. It's nothing to worry about!'

'If someone can't sleep over a prolonged period it's serious, especially at the pace Rick has been living lately. Can't you see he's burning out before your very eyes? Anything could have happened with those tablets?' Izzy retorted.

Anger had started to surge through her veins at Francesca's continued inability to see what was staring her in the face. 'Betty asked me to—'

She stopped short. She'd nearly put her foot in it again!

'But then you decided it'd be a nice perk of the job to jump into his bed,' Francesca arched an eyebrow, 'and soothe his fevered brow. And, given what a bloody tom-cat he is on tour that suited Rick down to the ground. Sex on tap from the band's lovesick little PA. Wait till he hears that the treacherous little bitch runs off to Mummy with weekly reports.'

'It wasn't like that,' Izzy argued, knowing it kind of was. 'If you really love Rick, please don't tell him. My contract finishes on Mo… very soon.'

She bit down on her lip hard. Her temper was making her say things she shouldn't. She had to calm down, and fast. 'And then he'll never see me again. You have my word. He doesn't need to know anything about the real reason I was here.'

Izzy gave both Francesca and Caron a beseeching look, but neither of the Reiss sisters replied.

The silence stretched for what felt like hours, Rick's fiancée continuing to eye her up and down, before a calculating smile slowly formed on Francesca's crimson lips.

'Okay, you win, Izzy,' she said, 'I won't tell him.'

Izzy's heart leapt with relief.

'You'll tell him, instead.'

Instantly, it plummeted back to her toes. Out the corner of her eye, she caught Caron beginning to nod, clearly liking her little sister's nifty bit of on-the-spot improvisation.

'Me,' Izzy let out a gasp of dismay. 'But I can't. I can't betray Betty's trust.'

'Oh yes, you can,' Francesca reiterated, 'and you'll do it before we leave New York.' She paused, letting that caveat sink in.

'But—' Izzy began only for Francesca cut her off instantly.

'It all boils down to a simple choice.' Francesca patted her immaculate up-do in the mirror. 'Either you do it, or I will? He can't remain in blissful ignorance, forever.' Her lips now stretched into a satisfied smile. 'And you're forgetting that I have just the bit of leverage I need. No passport; until he knows everything.'

Izzy was on the ropes now; Francesca had her exactly where she wanted her.

'And I want to be there to witness it, Izzy. Make sure you don't wriggle out of it.'

'But—' Izzy closed her mouth. She'd just been placed in an impossible situation. Then she realised. It wasn't Francesca who'd done that. She'd done it to herself the moment she'd said "yes" to Betty's scheme.

'You and Betty are about to learn that no one fucks with me, or mine,' Francesca continued. 'And when Rick finds out about the little plot you and his precious mother have concocted between you, he'll go fucking ballistic. As you've probably realised, he takes the invasion of his privacy, seriously—very seriously indeed.'

52

NEW YORK CITY, NEW YORK

'I'm so sorry, Betty.' Izzy clutched her head in her hands, finally giving way to the tears that had been threatening for the last few hours.

Somehow she'd managed to make her way back to the band's table, sitting through the rest of the evening, pretending to the outside world that she was having the time of her life, when inside she'd sunk into her own private hell, her whole life imploding at her feet.

She'd clapped mechanically, smiling and voicing her congratulations, as the band took to the stage an unprecedented five times to collect awards, but all the time she was replaying her conversation with Francesca; trying to ignore the meaningful glances that both Rick's fiancée and her sister were firing in her direction.

Back at the hotel, and unable to put off the moment any longer, she'd called in on the Hambros and brought them up to date, explaining how her cover had been blown following Jim and Betty's argument; how Francesca had got her hands on Izzy's passport; and the ultimatum she'd delivered about telling Rick the truth.

Wordlessly, Betty had wrapped Izzy in her arms, rocking her gently back and forth, stroking a hand through her hair.

'It's my fault, Betty,' Izzy sobbed into the curve of Betty's shoulder, 'I've made things so much worse. Francesca's really got it in for me.'

'What do you mean, my love?' Betty replied. 'It was Jim and I that Francesca overheard; our stupid bloody argument.'

Izzy sniffed, pulling back and pressing a tissue to each eye. It was time to admit to her own part in derailing Betty's plans.

'But there's something else. Something I haven't told you. Something I hoped you'd never find out.'

Taking a steadying breath, Izzy tried to compose herself. 'I told you Rick and I had become close friends, but that's not strictly true.' She looked away, unable to look either of them in the eye. 'We've also been sleeping together.'

'Oh, Izzy….' Betty squeezed Izzy's shoulder, and Jim gave an awkward cough.

Getting to his feet, he nodded towards his wife. 'Time to make myself scarce, I think; leave you two girls to it.'

Then, very tactfully, he withdrew to the adjacent bedroom, closing the door quietly behind him.

'I'm so sorry, Betty. That wasn't what I was here for, but it just sort of happened and it shouldn't have.'

'Well, my son's an extremely handsome boy, even if I'm a little bit biased.' Betty's lips twitched into a smile. For some reason, she didn't appear to be shocked by Izzy's admission. 'I imagine he was very easy to fall for.'

'Yes,' Izzy bit her lip, 'but it still shouldn't have happened. I let my feelings override my better judgement, and now I've made things so much worse.' She sighed. 'Terry found out about our swimming lessons. Then he saw me leaving Rick's room after a massage session. He jumped to conclusions; told Davey we were involved in some kind of affair; even though Rick and I getting together didn't happen until much later. We were just friends at the beginning. You have to believe that.'

Betty brushed Izzy's hair back from her brow affectionately. 'I do, love. And Davey— being the big mouth he is—told Caron.' Betty was filling in the blanks. 'Izzy, it really doesn't surprise me. In my book, those four are utter poison.'

'Please don't tell Mum,' Izzy's voice shook. Her parents would hit the roof if they were made aware of her less-than-platonic relationship with Rick. 'She and Dad would be furious. Say I'd let you down, which I have but…'

She was rewarded by another bone-crushing hug.

'Don't be silly, Izzy. You haven't let anyone down; far from it. Jim and I owe you everything. And you're a grown woman. Your relationship with Richard is no one else's business but your own. Not mine and certainly not your parents.'

Betty took Izzy's hands into hers, clasping them tightly; her look shrewd. 'And something tells me you've fallen in love with Richard.'

'Yes.' Izzy nodded. 'But Rick doesn't feel the same. It's only ever been…sex …for him' Heat suffused her cheeks. 'Yes, he considers me a friend, someone he trusts, someone he… cares for a great deal,' she rolled her eyes at the irony, 'but that's all. It's not the kind of relationship he has with Francesca. He's not "in love" with me, Betty.'

'Oh, Izzy…' Betty squeezed her hands.

'And even if—by some miracle—he did suddenly feel the same,' Izzy's smile wavered, 'it couldn't go anywhere. Because it would require me to confess who I really am and why I'm here, and I can't do that to him… or you.'

'You're such a good girl. You put everyone before yourself,' Betty cupped Izzy's cheek in her right hand, 'but I'm the one who should be apologising here.'

'Why?' Izzy replied. 'I went into this whole business with my eyes open. It was me who knowingly stepped over the line. I knew sleeping with him was a stupid idea, given the circumstances. But I did it anyway and now we're paying the price. If I don't tell Rick, she says she will. And she's got hold of my passport as leverage. She won't give it back to me, until Rick knows everything.'

'She really is a little bitch!' Betty shook her head in disbelief. 'Well, in that case, we need to get in first.' Her brown eyes—so like her son's—held Izzy's steadily. 'Call her bluff, and try and salvage this situation before it's too late.'

'But Rick will be furious. I don't want him blaming you—.'

'But it was my idea, Izzy. I must take the blame. You only agreed to help out. Jim warned me at the onset of the repercussions if Rick got wind of it, but…' Betty gave a resigned sigh, 'Richard's sensible. I think, once he hears my reasons, he'll come round.'

'Okay, but we tell him together, Betty.' Izzy squeezed Betty's hand, and gave her a watery smile. 'I won't let you do this on your own.'

53

NEW YORK

The hotel foyer was a hive of activity as everyone prepared to depart for another day, and all to an unrelenting soundtrack of screaming teenagers, crowded ten deep on the sidewalk outside, desperate to catch a glimpse of their idols.

The band was scheduled—within the next fifteen minutes—to zoom off to a photo shoot at *Radio City Music Hall.* And so far so good; timings remained on track.

Izzy had just waved off four sets of parents on the trip to the *Statue of Liberty.* She only had Betty and Jim to settle into the final car, which was purring to a standstill now.

Hotel Security and a large host of NYPD officers were doing their best to keep the hordes in check, the band's parents having received as much hysterical adulation as their sons when they'd broken cover. One girl had almost fainted when John Hambro had agreed to pose for a photograph. Given his flirtatious antics while the photograph was being taken, Izzy had the feeling Jonny was a chip off the old block.

Not so, his brother Jim. Izzy held the door wide, allowing him and Betty to scramble inside the limo. Both Hambros exchanging anxious glances and looking slightly shell-shocked at the cacophony of sound surrounding their stretch Lincoln.

'I don't think I'll ever get used to this.' Jim flinched, as an especially loud shriek of 'Steve, I love you' pierced the morning air; eagle-eyed fans having spotted the lead singer giving them a sly wave from the hotel's entrance. 'How the hell does Rick put up with it every day?'

Izzy gave Jim a reassuring smile. She could appreciate how overwhelming all the screaming could be. 'Funnily enough, you get used to it after a while,' she observed, 'learn to tune out…'

'Can you imagine enduring this every time we pop out to Tesco, Jim?' Betty glanced at their rear window in panic.

Some of the fans had started their regular practice of beating fists on the glass.

'It doesn't bear thinking about, love. I just hope that bloody window holds up and isn't smashed to smithereens.'

'Don't worry, its presidential security thickness,' Izzy was quick to supply, 'not even a bullet would get through it. Anyway, you're in good hands. Lee's on duty this morning, he won't let anything happen.'

She nodded towards their minder sitting beyond the privacy partition, conversing with the car's driver.

Betty leaned over, catching hold of Izzy's hand and dropping her voice. 'I've finally managed to speak to Rick; three-thirty pm in our room, Izzy. Would that be okay with you?'

Izzy's stomach flipped. Would it? Somehow, she doubted anything in her life would ever be okay again once Rick knew the truth.

'Yes, that's fine,' she heard herself agreeing.

'Don't worry, love.' Betty gave her hand a reassuring squeeze. 'This will take the wind out of you-know-who's sails. You'll see.'

Izzy sat perched on the edge of sofa, her fingers twisting restlessly in her lap, nerves currently treating her stomach like a makeshift trampoline.

She glanced at the clock on the wall for what felt like the hundredth time, but the hands had barely moved. This must be what Anne Boleyn felt like waiting for the chopping block.

Then, as if those thoughts had been read, her executioner decided to put in an appearance, announcing their arrival with a sharp staccato knock.

Both Betty and Izzy reacted instantly, two sets of haunted eyes seeking out the other while Jim, who'd been hovering by the window, hurried over to answer the door.

Betty let out an audible sigh as her son and fiancée were ushered inside; Francesca clinging onto Rick's arm, a triumphant smile on her face. With a tight nod, Betty indicated Rick and his fiancée should take a seat on the sofa opposite her and Izzy.

Izzy caught Rick's brow furrowing as soon as he sat down. He'd be wondering why she was here. Well, he'd know soon enough.

As he tried to catch her eye, Izzy very deliberately averted her gaze, staring straight ahead, willing herself to remain composed.

'Betty, I hope this won't take long.' Francesca had settled herself back into the cushions, crossing long slender legs encased in a tight, black leather mini, a possessive hand resting on Rick's thigh 'I've a hair appointment at four downstairs in the Hotel's Salon...'

Izzy swallowed. Francesca was enjoying every last second of her and Betty's discomfiture.

'Yeah, what's up, Mum?' Rick asked; his handsome face growing more and more puzzled as the seconds continued to tick by.

Izzy glanced across at Betty.

With an answering smile, Betty patted Izzy's knee. 'We'll try not to keep you too long, son. Now, love, I need to tell you something…'

Betty glanced towards her husband, and Jim sent back a reassuring nod and tight smile.

'Shit, you're not ill are you, Mum?' Rick burst out.

Izzy's gaze darted back in his direction. He'd obviously caught those uneasy looks passing between his parents.

'Because, if you are, I'll pay for you to go private.' he went on. 'You know it's a given.'

Betty shook her head. 'No, love, I know you would, but I'm not ill and neither is your dad.'

'Then, is it Michelle? Jeez, she's not got herself fucking pregnant, has she? After all the times she's lectured me about practising safe sex…'

'No, love, Michelle is fine, too.' Betty took a deep breath. 'Richard… Rick,' she amended.

That was a first. Izzy had never heard Betty call her son Rick before. More to the point, Rick looked to be a little stunned too, his eyes widening as he gazed at his mother.

'Do you remember when you were about thirteen, and we all went on holiday to Scotland.'

'Vaguely,' he answered, wrinkling his nose. 'Wasn't that the summer we met up with your pen pal's family?'

'Yes, the Andersons.'

'Yeah,' Rick gave his chin an absent scratch, 'didn't you say something about them coming to the wedding?'

'Over my dead body,' Francesca muttered to no one in particular, inspecting her immaculate French manicure.

'Yes I did. Mary happens to be one of my oldest friends.'

Izzy heard the razor sharp edge to Betty's tone.

'And didn't they have a daughter?' Rick continued.

Izzy shifted in her seat. Rick's brain had obviously started to whir. What would he remember about the Anderson's daughter?

Then he appeared to answer his own question, a grin spreading across his face.

'Yeah, they did, didn't they? She was a fat dumpy little thing,' he let out a chuckle, 'with one of those awful page-boy haircuts and hideous black NHS spectacles.'

'So, she wasn't terribly attractive.' Francesca let out a laugh.

Hurt flashed inside Izzy at his derogatory—but painfully accurate—description of her eight-year-old self. Thank God, she didn't look like that anymore

'Jeez, I didn't get a minute's peace that holiday.' Rick went on. 'Both her and Michelle were always pestering the life out of me. Kept following me round all the time, ganging up together and begging me to play their games. She was always gazing at me from behind her spectacles as though I was some kind of superhero. She had these really intense… sapphire blue… eyes….'

Rick ground to a standstill.

Without looking up, Izzy knew he was now staring at her, hard. The eye colour was clearly triggering more memories…

'Isabelle was a lovely little girl,' Betty interjected into the heavy silence, 'and I know for a fact, she's blossomed into a very caring and beautiful young woman.'

Her eyes met Izzy's, her expression full of apology for her son's tactlessness.

'So, Betty,' Francesca made a play of checking her state-of-the-art digital watch, 'while this meander down memory lane is riveting stuff, is there any actual point to it? I really need to get going. We're heading out for dinner later.' She turned to Izzy. 'That is, if Izzy remembered book the table?'

'Of course, seven forty-five pm at *Luigi's* as requested.' Izzy's tone was clipped.

'Izzy doesn't forget to book things,' Rick answered, but he still sounded strangely distracted as he dragged his puzzled gaze away from Izzy towards his mother. 'Look, Mum, Francesca's right, I think it's time you told us why we've received the royal summons? What's it got to do with some holiday fifteen years ago?'

Betty pulled Izzy's hands into hers and squeezed them tightly.

The moment had arrived.

'Rick, this is Isabelle Anderson, Andrew and Mary's daughter; or Izzy, as she likes to be known these days.'

Rick's jaw dropped open; completely pole-axed by the unexpected introduction.

'What the fuck…' he began, getting to his feet.

Izzy let out a shuddering breath, knowing he was seeing her for the first time. Not as she looked today, but how she'd been at eight years old. The pesky little girl who'd hero-worshipped him with her eyes.

'It *is* you.' Recognition had dawned completely for Rick. 'But …?'

A lump of tears pressed into the back of Izzy's throat. This was a nightmare. She wanted to run; run away from that hurt bewildered look on his face.

'But your name is Stevenson?' He was half talking to himself, as he slumped back down onto the sofa. 'I don't understand. If we already know each other, why didn't you say something?'

'I couldn't.' Izzy hung her head.

'I asked her not to, Rick,' Betty explained. 'Izzy's only here because of me.'

'But she can't be.' Rick shook his head; his eyes ping-ponging between Betty and Izzy. 'She answered our advert. We selected her from two applicants….'

'Yes I know, love,' Betty soothed, 'but I'd briefed her about the job beforehand, given her some inside knowledge on what to say in the application, hoped it might help swing things in her favour. Thankfully, it did.'

'What sort of inside knowledge?' Rick's Adam's apple bobbed. 'Mum, what the hell is going on here?'

Betty gave her husband a beseeching look, and Jim moved to sit on the edge of arm of the sofa, looping a comforting arm around his wife's shoulders, pulling her in close.

'There's something else you need to know, son.' He kissed the top of his wife's head.

Tension radiated from both Betty and Jim, mingling with Izzy's own. The second bombshell was about to be detonated.

'And you're not going to like it, love,' Betty continued, picking up her husband's cue, 'but you must understand, we only did it with the best of intentions. Your father and I felt we'd no choice left. You were never meant to find out who Izzy really was, or find out why I sent her here.'

'Sent her here?' Rick exploded. 'What do you mean?'

Francesca had sat up a little straighter. Izzy could almost hear the bitch purring in satisfaction at the scene unfolding before her eyes. The final act of Izzy's execution had come. The axe was being swung for that final fatal blow.

'What wasn't I meant to find out, mum?' Rick was now looking directly at Izzy, and he was beginning to nod. More memories of that holiday were clearly coming thick and fast.

'That scar on your knee.' He screwed up his face. 'Shit, I *was* there that day. I helped clean you up, stayed with you when Michelle ran to get help.'

'Yes, you did,' Izzy nodded, 'and you were great. I never forgot. When Betty asked me to help…'

She stopped, unable to say anymore, sending a silent plea for help towards Betty.

'Look, it's like this, Rick…' Letting out a breath, Izzy's back-up arrived, Betty launching into the whole story, explaining how she'd found the sleeping pills in his suitcase, their presence fuelling her nagging worries over his strange closed-off behaviour. She went on to outline her idea of keeping a closer eye on him, before moving onto her discussions with Mary, and how they'd roped Izzy into replacing Angie. Finally, Betty explained the deception around Izzy's surname, and what she'd asked Izzy to do.

'You sent her to spy on me.' Rick's nostrils flared.

During Betty's revelations, the shock and puzzlement on his face had slowly been replaced by fury, as the unvarnished truth had tumbled from his mother's lips.

'It really wasn't "spying", love,' Betty reasoned, 'not really. It was just to keep an eye on you, make sure you were okay. When I found those sleeping tablets, I didn't know what to think. I waited for you to say something, but you never did. You'd put up this wall between us. Shut us out, just like Jonny has with Kate and John. You'd always promised you'd never get into hard drugs, and yet I had the evidence of sleeping pills here in my hands. It was starting to happen as I'd feared. I know how addictive sleeping pills can be; the road they can lead you down. I guessed your insomnia had come back, and you were desperate. Every time we saw you, you looked so tired and unhappy, but you kept reassuring us everything was fine; that life was great. I couldn't let you go down the same path as Jonny…' Betty took a breath. 'Mary had mentioned Izzy was working part-time until she obtained a permanent job. We asked her to apply, and if she was successful try and find out what was going on. You'd stopped talking to us. We didn't know what else to do.'

'So, you decided to invade my fucking privacy instead. Get her to nose into my life.' Those eyes, always been so warm before, had grown cold, hard, and accusatory as they met Izzy's. 'You lying bitch, how could you do that to me?'

She shrank back against the sofa, quaking under his look of utter contempt, but knowing he had every right to be angry with her.

'Richard,' Jim warned in a low voice. 'Please keep a civil tongue in your head.'

'Fuck! This is some kind of bad dream. So, what did she tell you, Mother?'

Izzy knew it was time to speak up. 'I told her everything, Rick…. everything you'd confided in me.' She chewed her lip. 'I know it was betraying your trust, and I'm desperately sorry for that. You'll never know quite how much. But my first loyalty was to Betty. And when Terry gave you the *Teraxapen*, we knew we had to act. Get you to open up, talk to me about what you were feeling. Find out why the insomnia had returned. We couldn't let you carry on taking those tablets.'

'Everything I told you. Every fucking detail I trusted you with, you just blabbed it straight back to my mother?'

'Yes, and I'm so sorry.' Izzy's voice cracked.

Rick was back on his feet, his hands bunching into tight fists at his side. 'Is that what the swimming lessons and massage sessions were for?' He came to stand over her. 'All instigated to worm your way into my confidence. Soften me up. Get me to spill my guts?'

'Massage sessions?' Francesca was sitting forward now, her expression a picture of righteous innocence and indignation. 'What the hell have you been doing with my fiancé, Izzy?'

'Shut up, Francesca,' Rick waved his fiancée silent, his eyes still on Izzy. 'Stop pretending that you don't know what happens when we're on tour.'

Chastened, Francesca closed her mouth, but if looks could kill, Izzy knew she'd be six feet under this very second.

'You offered to teach me to swim first, remember?' Izzy felt bound to point out. 'But yes, when I told Betty, we agreed it might be a good way to get closer to you. That if we became friends, you'd maybe relax and feel able to confide in me.'

'But it was all a set-up; engineered to manipulate me.' He stated. 'You knew exactly what to say, how to lead me on. And now I learn it's all been a fucking act, from the very start.'

'It was never an act.' Izzy insisted, wiping her eyes, tears beginning to leak out. 'Everything I told you about being unable to swim and why I learned massage was true. I'd have done anything to stop you taking those tablets.'

'You certainly did that. And what did you get out of this?' Rick had begun to pace about. 'Did it give you some kind of sick little kick that you were taking care of Mummy's baby?'

'No, of course not,' she answered truthfully. 'From the moment we met again, I liked you, Rick. I *really* liked you. I've never faked my feelings, ever. The friendship that grew up between us was totally real. You have to believe that.'

'Sorry, but I don't buy it. You played me for a bloody fool, that's what you did, and now the shit's hit the fan, you'll say anything to paint yourself in a better light. And, mug that I am I fell for it.'

Izzy's shoulders slumped. 'Okay, at the start, I'll admit, I took on the PA's job—in part— because I was looking for a bit of excitement. Working with the band sounded like fun. But I also wanted to meet you again. See if you were still as lovely as the boy I remembered.'

'You don't know how fucking pathetic that sounds.'

Izzy ignored his snide put-down. 'Plus, it promised to be a diversion after Alex, something different before I settled down to a career in teaching.'

'And who the hell is Alex?' Rick's pacing ground to a halt, his hands resting on hips.

'My ex-fiancé,' Izzy explained. 'I told you his name was James, but that's his middle name. Betty and I agreed that I couldn't risk giving you any clue—however small—as to who I really was, just in case you might put two and two together and came up with Isabelle Anderson; the pen friend's daughter. I altered the facts.'

'Yeah, you've been good at altering facts. You've spent the last six months telling everyone bare-faced lies, Izzy. Jeez, it all makes sense now. All your evasiveness about home, I thought it was because you didn't get on with your parents; that the situation was much worse than you made out.' He slapped his thigh in frustration. 'And I thought James… No, Alex was a complete arsehole for letting a girl like you slip through his fingers. Shit, I was totally deluded, wasn't I? The poor bastard dodged a bullet—.'

'Richard, I won't tell you again,' Jim interjected. 'Watch your mouth and your manners when speaking to Izzy and your mother.'

'Like hell, Dad!'

'As Betty said,' Izzy began to fiddle with the hem of her miniskirt, sniffing more tears away, 'you were never supposed to find out anything about the real me. Izzy Stevenson was supposed to just be your PA—a fleeting friend you'd take into your confidence—and then disappear at the end of her contract.' She sighed, 'But then it all started to get a bit complicated.'

'Too fucking right, it got complicated.' The pacing had started up again, Rick roaming the room like a caged tiger. 'And when we ended up in bed… was that part of Mum's master plan, too?'

He looked back over his shoulder, his hurt and disillusionment all-too evident in those brown eyes. 'Did Mum ask you to take one for the team? Lie back and think of "Betty" in the hope you'd get more out of me with some pillow talk?'

'Of course not,' Izzy replied, momentarily pressing a hand to her mouth, eyes turning ceiling-wards and blinking hard. 'I slept with you because I wanted to, because I was attracted to you. I was—'

'Rick, please stop taking your anger out on Izzy. I'm to blame here, not her,' Betty interrupted. 'Your dad and I were worried. You were bottling things up, just like you always do.' She reached out a hand towards him. 'I didn't know what else to do.'

Ignoring his mother's entreaty, Rick flung up his hands in disgust and stalked towards the door. 'So, it's my fault. Typical, mum! I need to get out of here, or I'll say something I really regret.'

'Richard, wait…' Jim struggled to his feet, lunging forward to snag his son's arm before he could attempt to leave. 'We love you, son. We only wanted to know what was going on. Then offer our help, if we could.'

'Love me. Help me!' Rick shoved his father off, Jim stumbling backwards as Betty let out an agonised cry, reaching to steady her husband.

'Jeez, Dad, you've got a funny way of showing it. How dare you interfere in my life, and use that bitch'—he jerked a thumb towards Izzy—'to do it.'

'But it's not Izzy's fault. Please don't speak to her like that.' Tears had started cascading down Betty's cheeks.

'I'll speak to her any way I fucking want, Mum. She's my employee. Someone, you managed to foist onto me six months ago.'

The words 'employee' and 'foist' were like daggers being rammed into Izzy's already shredded heart.

'Davey had you summed up on Day One, Izzy,' Rick shook his head derisively, 'but I didn't see it. He said you were trouble, and shit, the little bastard wasn't wrong!'

'I guess not.' Izzy swallowed, looking down.

'So have you told anyone else what I told you?' Rick demanded. 'Got some sleazy little tabloid deal lined upon the side that Mum doesn't know about. Are you going to spill the beans on what I like to do in bed? I'm sure I've given you enough fodder for a *'Sun'* Exclusive over the last few weeks. I can see the headline "Rick likes doing it under the shower". Going to give me marks out of ten for my sexual prowess?'

'Rick, I'd never tell anyone about what happened between us,' Izzy burst out 'or your reasons for leaving the band.'

Shit! Her big mouth; she'd let the cat out the bag—good and proper.

For a beat, there was a horrified silence all round before all hell let loose, courtesy of Francesca.

'You're leaving the band?' She was at Rick's side in an instant. 'What the fuck is she talking about, Rick?' Her fists were pummelled into his chest. 'And why the hell don't I know anything about it? I'm your fucking fiancée. First, I have to sit here and listen to you admitting to sleeping with that little slut, and now this. Why did you confide in her and not me?'

Before Rick could reply, Francesca's palm made a resounding thwack against his cheek.

'I'm sorry, Rick. I didn't mean to—' Izzy gulped, knowing she'd just made everything a hundred times worse, if that were possible.

'Save it, Izzy,' Rick spat back, rubbing his cheek. 'I'm sorry, Francesca. Yeah, you're right. I deserved that slap. I should have told you first, but I wanted to break the news face to face, not over the telephone. And as for sleeping with her...'

Izzy watched as he closed his eyes momentarily, his expression bleak, 'that's the biggest mistake I've ever made in my life.'

He shook his head, and his eyes snapped back at Izzy. 'I hope earning your thirty pieces of silver was worth it, Izzy.'

'Rick, please. I'm so sorry. You have to believe me—.' Izzy began.

'You're sorry!'His laugh was bitter. 'Jeez, you're not the only one, sweetheart!'

Cold eyes slid to his parents and Francesca. 'And I'm warning the rest of you. None of this afternoon's shitshow goes beyond these four walls. Do you hear me? I don't want the others knowing anything about what's been said, or who that bitch really is. I think I've been humiliated enough, don't you?'

5.35 PM

Izzy set down her pen, carefully re-reading the letter she'd just composed. But for some reason, it still didn't sound quite right, her usual way with words deserting her completely this afternoon. The letter's contents still failing to convey everything she wanted to say, especially the over-whelming guilt eating her away inside.

Her eyes dropped to the paragraph where she'd written about falling in love with him. Should she leave that bit out? That was probably the very last thing Rick wanted to hear. But, surely, he had a right to know. Maybe she'd leave it in and take another look with fresh eyes later.

She expelled a breath. Somehow, she'd a feeling that no matter what she said—or indeed how she said it—he'd still hate her; still believe the worst of her. In fact, knowing it came from her, there was a good chance he'd just consign the letter straight to the bin, without a backward glance.

Fishing out an envelope from the drawer, she popped the sheet of writing paper inside. Once she'd given it more thought, settled on the final wording, she'd write it out again and then ask Betty to pass it on.

But what did she do for now? It wasn't as if she could just disappear. She had to honour Rick's wishes. It was the least she could do. He'd asked they all carry on as normal and she didn't want to draw attention to herself. Make sure the rest of the band didn't get a whiff of what had passed within Betty and Jim's suite and, when the time came and she did leave, the situation with Terry would be emphasised as her reason for departing.

Nerves twisted in her stomach at the thought. She just had another twenty-four hours to kill before tomorrow night's flight. Terry was now the final hurdle for her to overcome.

Someone rapped on her bedroom door, and for a split second, she hoped—prayed—it might be Rick.

'Izzy, are you in there?' It was Kathy. 'It's time to go, Miss Stevenson. We need to leave now if we want to grab food before the start of the film.'

Too caught up in her own misery, she'd forgotten about their plans to check out the new Harrison Ford movie across town. Kathy had been bubbling with excitement all day.

Grabbing another tissue, Izzy wiped her eyes and placed the letter into her handbag, out of sight; definitely not for Miss Davies's eyes.

It was time to pretend again; put on her best attempt at a brave face.

She headed for the door and opened it a crack, peering out.

'Izzy, what on earth has happened?' Kathy's mouth dropped open in a silent 'o'.

Great! She'd spotted the swollen red eyes, as well as the remnants of mascara streaked down her cheeks. Izzy tried to smile but the corners of her lips just weren't playing ball.

'It's Terry isn't it? Shit, he's done something to you, hasn't he?'

Not waiting for Izzy to answer, Kathy barged her way inside. 'Right, we're going to Jack now. No excuses.'

She made a grab for Izzy's arm and began tugging, but Izzy pushed her off.

'No, it's not Terry,' she assured Kathy, trying desperately to hold back the floodgates.

Those bloody tears were threatening to make another appearance.

'Then, for God's sake, what is it?'Kathy demanded. 'Tell me.'

At the determined set of Kathy's jaw, Izzy's resolve broke and a sob escaped from her throat.

5.52 PM

'I've been such an idiot,' Izzy admitted.

Both of them had their backs resting against the bed, Izzy's head propped on Kathy's shoulder. She wiped her eyes with yet another tissue. She'd lost count of the number she'd used over the last few days. She'd have to buy shares in *Kleenex* at this rate.

'What are you talking about, now?'

For the last five minutes, Izzy knew she'd been totally incoherent; Kathy patiently allowing her to sob her heart out until there was nothing left, not seeking any explanation, just offering the comfort of a reassuring arm, and a steady stream of tissues.

'I've not been entirely straight with you,' Izzy confessed, wondering how much she could actually divulge even now. 'You see…' She paused, 'I've been involved in a relationship with Rick.'

'You have?' Kathy pulled away from Izzy, her eyes narrowing. 'Have you been sleeping with him?' she demanded. 'And more to the point, why didn't you tell me? You insisted he wasn't remotely interested in you?'

She had. No wonder Kathy was hurt by Izzy's late-in-the-day confession. She flushed guiltily.

'I know. I should have come clean to you before now.' Izzy agreed, reaching out to place her hand over Kathy's. 'But it all started out quite innocently, you have to believe that. He's been giving me swimming lessons for the last few months.'

'He's been giving you "swimming lessons"?' A loud snort of derisive laughter erupted from Kathy. 'Well, Miss Stevenson, that's a new name for it!'

'No, it's the truth. That's all it was at the start,' Izzy explained.

Better to leave out the out the massage; that would just open a whole can of worms.

'We'd been chatting over breakfast one morning. He'd just been for a swim, and was teasing me about joining him. The others weren't around and I confessed I'd never learned to swim; had a phobia about water. Before I knew it, he'd offered to give me lessons.' She sighed. 'And feeling the way I did about him, I foolishly thought, why not? But we agreed to keep it quiet. We didn't want any leg-pulling from Davey and Jonny.'

Kathy's expression still looked unforgiving. 'And before you knew it, he'd got himself inside the old swimming costume.' She shook her head. 'So much for his supposed vow of celibacy!'

'Yes,' Izzy agreed, 'but us sleeping together only happened for the first time on the night of his birthday. That's the truth. Before that, I'd no idea he was even interested in me. He'd never given any indication during those lessons. He'd been the perfect gentleman…'

A blush settled on Izzy's cheeks. 'But our relationship—such as it was—ended when we arrived in New York.'

Kathy goggled. 'So you're telling me you've been at it for nearly a fortnight?'

Izzy nodded. 'Well ten days,' she corrected, 'and I was stupid, I fell hook line and sinker for him, didn't I?'

'Started seeing Happy-Ever-Afters, which explains the tears,' Kathy guessed with a perceptive smile. 'Oh, Izzy, I did warn you. We'll never be suitable "wife" material with that lot, and you definitely don't mention the 'L' word. Is that what you did? Blurted out how you really felt about him?'

You could say that.' Izzy's cheeks grew even warmer at the lie.

'And now he's pissed with you for getting too involved; not playing by their stupid rules.'

Izzy ran a hand down her face. 'I really am sorry I didn't say anything, Kathy, but we couldn't risk anyone finding out.'

This was horrible, but she couldn't say any more. It wasn't her story to tell.

Kathy blew her cheeks, before her lips creased into a half smile. 'Don't worry, I'll forgive you. A mate doesn't kick a girl when she's so obviously down. But this is real life, Izzy, or rather Eclectic Deviation's fucked-up version of it. Not some lovey-dovey *Mills & Boon* romance.'

'I know. I realise that now.' It was time to let Kathy in on her plans to disappear. 'That's why I've decided get myself out of here—as soon as possible. I can't see out the final three weeks of my contract. My feelings for Rick ....well, it hurts too much to stick around. In fact, I'm planning to go straight after tomorrow night's show.' She wiped her nose. 'It has to be then, if I want to avoid Terry and what he's got in store for me.'

But only if she managed to prise her passport out of Francesca's grasp, first.

'That goes without saying.' Kathy nodded. 'And you know I'll keep schtum; help any way I can.'

Izzy was enveloped in a warm hug.

'I'm sorry you got your heart broken, Izzy!'

'Yes, you and me, both,' Izzy pulled away, 'I'm leaving Jack a letter, apologising. Explaining to him about the situation with Terry, but not about what happened with Rick. Jack will probably go nuts that I've walked out on them, too.' She gave Kathy a pleading look. 'Please, you can't say anything about what I've just told you; not to anybody, Kathy?'

'Don't worry, these lips are zipped'

'All I ask is that you cover for me later tomorrow night,' Izzy went on. 'Deny all knowledge of my whereabouts, if anyone who asks. Now, this is how I'm planning to do it…'

7.15 PM

'I've come to collect my passport.'

It was time to confront the witch in her lair. Izzy jutted out her chin, trying to feign defiance in the face of a still jubilant Francesca. 'Betty and I have done what you asked. So, I think it's payback time, don't you?'

Francesca smoothed down the labels of her black tuxedo jacket, her smile morphing into a definite self-satisfied smirk, and Izzy felt the centre of her palms tingle.

'I still think Rick's making a mistake,' Francesca commented as she retreated back inside her room, leaving Izzy with no option but to follow suit, 'the others have a right to know about you and what you did. You fooled everyone with your "butter wouldn't melt act." I'm sure they'd all love to know what a lying deceitful little bitch you really are.

Francesca arched one perfectly plucked eyebrow at Izzy. 'For all we know, you could be spying on them too.'

'Don't be so ridiculous! Anyway, you heard what Rick said. No one can know about what I did.'

Izzy glanced about herself. The suite was empty, Rick obviously absent.

'And if you really love him, as much as you claim to, you'll respect his wishes and keep your mouth shut. If Rick wants to tell them about…' Izzy hesitated, 'about me—or his future—then that's his prerogative. No one else has the right; not even you.'

'Huh, we'll see about that. And I suppose you're still carrying a torch for him?'

Izzy's cheeks burned at Francesca's perceptive comment.

'As ever, Izzy, you're so fucking hilarious.' Francesca gave a derisive chuckle. 'For the record, he now equates his "Pretty Lady" with "Public Enemy Number One". Quite a fall from grace, don't you think?'

Francesca had moved to the dressing table. Selecting a bottle of perfume, she gave her wrists, neck and cleavage a liberal spray, its clawing scent catching the back of Izzy's throat.

'Chalk this down to experience,' she told Izzy, still checking herself out in the mirror, and making a couple of final adjustments to her diamond necklace and earrings, 'spying on men, at the behest of their interfering mothers, is never going to end well.'

With a last tweak, this time to her glossy brown bangs, Francesca stood back to admire her reflection. 'And tell that mother of yours not to hold her breath. Her invitation to the wedding will be permanently lost in the post.'

'Believe me; my mother wouldn't come to your wedding if her life depended on it.'

The thought of her parents being in the same room as She-Bitch-from-Hell made Izzy want to gag.

'Good, because I'm going to make sure Betty doesn't spoil our wedding photographs, either!'

Somehow Francesca's latest admission didn't surprise Izzy.

'You really are a nasty piece of work, Francesca.' Izzy retorted.

Francesca could go to hell if she expected Izzy to use the respectful "Miss Reiss" now. 'I just hope Rick finally wakes up to the fact—before it's too late.'

'You've the *gall* to call me a nasty piece of work?' Francesca checked out a side view of her outfit. 'Sorry, but the expression "pot, kettle and black" fits here, Izzy. So, before you start enjoying the view up there on the moral high ground, remember your part in this fiasco.'

As if Izzy could ever forget.

'I just made sure he found out the ugly truth about you and his mother.' Her posing session in front of the mirror at an end, Francesca stalked back to the bed, and picked up her handbag. She drew out the passport, holding it out to Izzy between thumb and forefinger, as though it might contaminate her.

'Now take it and fuck off out of our lives, Izzy. You won't be missed.' She tossed the little booklet at her.

Izzy caught it with ease, and for several precious seconds, she savoured the feeling of having her means of escape back in her possession. Just the 'Terry' bridge to negotiate and then she'd be out of here.

'Not going to thank me?' Francesca snapped the catch on her bag, slipping the strap over her shoulder. 'Really, Izzy—'

'What the fuck are you doing in here?' Rick's voice cut Francesca off mid-sentence. 'I thought I told you to stay away from me.'

Izzy's throat constricted, as she spun on her heel to look up at him. He was standing in the open door, jaw clenched, a pulse visible in his cheek, and for the briefest moment, genuine sadness appeared in those beautiful brown eyes, before the shutters went down.

'I was just…' Izzy trailed off, not sure how to explain her presence. Uncertain if he knew that Francesca had confiscated her passport.

'Are you ready to leave, darling?' Francesca had crossed to Rick's side, placing her hand on his arm. 'After Izzy's little bombshell earlier, you and I have a lot to talk about. Don't we?'

But Rick didn't appear to be listening. His gaze had zeroed in on what Izzy held in her hands. His Adam's apple bobbed twice in quick succession before he spoke, his voice gruff.

'Francesca's filled me in on her own bit of detective work.' He nodded towards the passport. 'What was it you said to me? Oh yeah, I really don't like people seeing my photograph. Well, we know why now, don't we?' He gave a bitter laugh 'You must have been shitting yourself that night. If I'd looked inside, your cover would have been blown straight out the water.'

He held out his hand. 'Show it to me, Izzy.'

Izzy licked her lips, reluctant to give him the final humiliating confirmation of her true identity.

'I said, fucking show it to me, Izzy!'

Letting out a breath, she placed the passport in his outstretched hand, watching as he scanned its contents.

'Yep, it's all there in black and white, Miss Mary Isabelle Anderson.' That pulse flexed in his cheek, again.

'Should have treacherous little bitch tagged on at the end, don't you think, darling?' Francesca sneered.

The passport slipped from Rick's fingers onto the carpet at Izzy's feet.

'How could I have been so wrong about you, Izzy? I was such a fucking idiot, wasn't I?' his voice sounded pained.

'I'm so sorry, Rick.' Dropping to her knees, Izzy hurriedly collected up the passport in trembling hands and stuffed it into the pocket of her jeans, trying hard to avoid looking into those hurt-filled eyes. 'If you'd just let me explain—'

'Explain?' he cut her off sharply 'No, I don't think so. You've done enough talking. And that job offer we discussed, consider it off the table, permanently!'

54

NEW YORK CITY, NEW YORK

'You were late coming in at least six times during the sound check.' Marc poured himself a glass of mineral water, popping in a couple of ice cubes and then taking a sip. 'I hope you get your bloody act together for tonight. What the hell is wrong with you today? You've been like a bear with a fucking migraine since breakfast.'

Izzy hovered in the doorway to her office, on tenterhooks as to what might unfold now. Her final day had started badly; Rick had been in a foul temper from the moment he'd dropped into the seat opposite her at breakfast, snapping at her over last minute changes to the schedule. His out-of-character rudeness shocking everyone around the table; Izzy quick to pick up on the disbelieving glances being exchanged between the rest of the band, while Davey's gloating smile only got wider and wider. It was obvious the little git knew something had transpired between her and Rick, but clearly Caron hadn't been made privy to all the gory details—yet.

As ever, Marc was completely unaware he was treading on thin ice. All eyes had swung back to Rick. Rick never had issues with timing, but during the sound check there had seen a whole string of them.

'So, go ahead. Sack me, Marc,' Rick retorted, peeling off his sweat-dampened T-shirt, and tossing it across to Kathy. 'I know you'd like to.'

He took the towel she proffered, and began to dry off the perspiration from his hair and chest.

'Don't be so bloody stupid.' Marc rolled his eyes. 'I only pointed out you were late. There's no need to go off the fucking deep end.'

'Come on, Marc, we're all knackered. It's the last night,' Steve interceded, his concerned eyes not leaving their drummer. 'And since when have you been so fucking perfect, anyway?'

'I was only saying—' Marc began.

'Well, for a change, don't.' Davey selected an apple from the bowl on the buffet table and rubbed it clean against his shirt.

'And I wish you'd stop biting my head off too.' Marc swung away from Rick to face Davey. 'Your constant sniping is getting on my fucking nerves.'

'I will, but only once you start giving Rick and the rest of us a bloody break.' Taking a large bite, Davey leaned close to Marc's face, chewing it loudly with his mouth open.

'Just fuck off and die, Eastman,' Marc retorted.

'Thank God tonight's the final show,' Davey continued, making an exaggerated play of licking his lips, 'then Boy Wonder will be off our fucking backs.'

'And stop calling me that,' Marc seethed. 'Isn't it about bloody time you grew up?'

'And turn into a boring old fart like you; permanently up my own backside. No bloody fear, mate!'

'What did you say to me?' Marc took a step towards Davey, his hands up ready to push him away. 'If you don't get out of my fucking face—'

'You'll do what, Boy Wonder?' Davey taunted, chucking away the apple, and squaring up to him.

Jonny stepped between them. 'Just as well we're having one hell of a party later,' he commented, placing a restraining hand on Davey's arm, 'perfect opportunity for everyone to let off a bit of steam. It's been a tough few months, don't you agree, Steve?'

'Yeah, let's all have a bloody party.' Marc retorted before Steve had an opportunity to answer. 'That seems to be your default setting these days, Jonny. There are more important things in life than getting off your face every five minutes, or have you forgotten?'

Jonny's nostrils flared; his attempt at peace-making coming to an abrupt end. 'You know what Marc? Davey's absolutely right! You *are* a fucking bore!'

He looked across at Rick, now wearing a clean T-shirt. 'You up for getting seriously pissed tonight, Ricky? Show this boring arsehole, how to party!'

Rick's eyes momentarily collided with Izzy's across the room, before he pointedly looked away. 'Yeah,' he agreed, 'I plan to get so fucking hammered I'll forget these seven months of hell ever happened.'

Izzy felt as though she'd been stabbed through the heart. That comment had been for her.

Rick addressed his next words to Marc. 'And, Marc, if you think the drumming isn't up to scratch, go ahead and replace me with a fucking drum machine, for all I care. I've just about had it with you and your constant criticism.'

With that final comment delivered, he flipped his middle finger towards his cousin and stormed out of the dressing room, slamming the door hard behind him.

Backstage was mobbed as usual—girlfriends, parents, the band's manager, personal guests, VIPs, and representatives from *Virgin* and *Rock TV*, as well as the music media—all jostling to get close to the band, add their congratulations on the completion of a successful tour.

And the band looked exhausted, but delighted, as the enormity of what they'd achieved slowly sunk in. Their final night at Madison Square Garden had been a triumph—with absolutely no mistakes whatsoever—and another fifteen thousand ecstatic fans were now pouring back onto the city streets.

Izzy slipped into her office with Betty, closing the door against the mayhem of the dressing room.

'Betty, would you give this to Rick, please?'

Izzy retrieved the letter from her handbag—she'd re-written it three times—and pressed it into Betty's hand. As well as the letter, the envelope also contained the sapphire bracelet.

'What's this, love?' A puzzled Betty looked down at the lumpy envelope, Rick's name printed in Izzy's neat handwriting.

'I wanted to apologise to him, properly.' Izzy explained, unable to stop the catch in her voice. 'Give my side of the story. Not that it'll do much good. He probably won't read it. I'm also returning something he bought me. In the circumstances, it wouldn't feel right to keep it.'

It would only make him believe she really *was* a gold-digger, on top of everything else. Her birthday gift to *him* had disappeared off his wrist, overnight.

Betty took Izzy into her arms. 'Why not try to talk to him again?' she pressed, giving Izzy a pleading look.

Izzy shook her head, her smile decidedly watery. 'No. It's too late. He won't even look at me, Betty. He's made it very clear how he feels. He hates me. I betrayed his trust. He'll never forgive that.'

'I'm sure he doesn't hate you.'

But Izzy wasn't convinced. 'No, Betty, I can see it in his eyes every time he looks at me. My letter's just the last throw of the dice.'

Betty let out a deep sigh. 'Hindsight is a wonderful thing, Izzy. I wish I'd done things differently. Listened to Jim and come up with some other way to find out what was going on in Rick's head. Yes, he's off the sleeping pills now, as well as making a firm decision about his future, but at what cost?'

Betty cupped Izzy's face in her hands, searching her face. 'I've hurt my son, and I've hurt you too, Izzy. And that was the last thing I ever wanted. We're trying to maintain appearances, but you've seen how strained it is with Rick.'

She kissed Izzy's forehead, her face full of concern and regret. 'God knows where we go from here, but I won't give up trying to make him understand.'

'I know, Betty,' Izzy sympathised, glancing briefly at her watch. She'd need to get a move on.

'And you still intend to go through with the plan?' Betty asked.

'Yes. Terry expects me to meet him at my room at midnight. We agreed the details at lunchtime.' She swallowed, remembering her stomach-churning last interview with Terry. He'd told her exactly what expected of her tonight; his violent threats—if she didn't comply— chilling her to the marrow. Somehow, she'd steeled herself to play along, acquiesce to all his nauseating wishes and agreed to meet him back at the hotel, once the band was settled at the nightclub. He'd been gloating at her seeming capitulation; the git confident he'd finally got her within his grasp.

Izzy gave a little shiver, knowing she was playing a very dangerous game and praying nothing would go wrong; giving herself up to Terry's disgusting demands just wasn't an option.

Betty removed her room key from her handbag and pressed it into Izzy's hands. 'Then, please be careful. I'm so glad you decided to take me into your confidence; told me what was going on with that animal. You should have told me, sooner. But please don't take any unnecessary risks back at the hotel. I'd feel so much better if either Jim or I accompanied you. Then I'd know for certain you'll be safe.'

'You know you can't. We agreed. No one can suspect what I'm doing, and certainly not Terry. I'll be fine.' Izzy smiled. 'Telling you was my final piece of back-up, just in case things go pear-shaped. Thank you for suggesting I stash my luggage in your room.'

Betty waved away her thanks. 'That's the very least I can do. It made more sense than you having to go anywhere near your own room, even for a minute. Now are you sure, I can't—'

'No,' Izzy was firm. 'You have to go to the party as arranged. We have to maintain my cover for Rick's sake. That means you can't do anything to show we already know each other. Plus Terry has to think I'm doing exactly what he wants. Nothing can arouse his suspicions.'

She threw her final few bits and pieces haphazardly into her bag. 'I've told everyone I'm going straight to the club now to check the party is set up as instructed. Terry and the band are scheduled to leave here by ten thirty-five pm at the latest. And it takes about ten to fifteen minutes to get downtown, traffic permitting.'

Izzy checked her watch. For her own timings to go like clockwork, she'd need to be out of here in the next five minutes, no later.

'Once I've picked up my luggage, I'll return your room key to reception and jump in a cab. I'll be in and out the hotel in no time. Nothing should go wrong.'

The lift doors slid apart, and Izzy stepped out into the foyer. Clasping her suitcase determinedly in her right hand, she headed towards the lone receptionist on duty behind the mahogany desk.

Her cab had been ready and waiting in the Garden's loading bay, allowing her to sneak back to the hotel, and uplift her luggage from Betty's suite. Now she just had to formally check out of the hotel and then she'd be on her way to *JFK*.

The foyer was quiet, although she could hear the noise from the ever-present fans camped outside. One of the band's No1 hits *'Time to disappear from the game'* was being sung with gusto in high-pitched teenage voices. Hopefully its words would prove to be a good omen, mean she'd successfully given that Neanderthal the slip—for good.

The receptionist looked up at the approach of Izzy's footsteps, giving her a welcoming smile. 'Good evening, Miss Stevenson, what can I do for you?'

'Hi, I'd like to check out, please.' Izzy placed her suitcase at her feet, resting her handbag on the countertop. 'And this is Mr and Mrs James Hambro's key. They forgot to hand it in, earlier.' She deposited both sets of room keys in the receptionist's hand.

'So, you're leaving us early?' The receptionist asked once the keys had been returned to their respective pigeon holes.

'Yes. Unfortunately, I need to go home tonight.' Izzy glanced at her watch. Her no-show at the nightclub should have been noticed by now. 'Would you be able to order me a taxi to the airport, please?'

'Of course, just one second, please.' The blonde receptionist turned to her computer, quickly calling up Izzy's details. 'There's an additional fifty dollars on top of the room charge. Room service,' she explained.

Nodding in quiet acknowledgement, Izzy took out her wallet and handed over the required cash without quibble. As she awaited her receipt, she glanced idly behind herself, hoping the girl wouldn't be much longer. She couldn't begin to relax until she was out of here, and in that taxicab. Time was of the essence.

But, in that moment, time decided to come to a grinding halt, Izzy's breath catching in her throat.

Shit! So much for the band's song being a good omen! Sweat broke out on her brow and she blinked several times, unable to quite believe what her eyes were telling her. Terry Costello was strutting towards her from the direction of the lift bank, large as life, and with that oh-so-familiar, stomach-churning leer spreading across his face, his eyes sweeping over her from top to toe. Where had he materialised from?

Shit! Shit! Shit! He should still be at the club!

Something must have gone decidedly awry in her plan, but what? And, more to the point, what on earth was she going to do about it?

Think Izzy!

'So here you are, Miss Stevenson.' Terry's tone was decidedly conversational as he flashed a toothy grin in the receptionist's general direction. 'Stopped by your room a few minutes ago, but I appeared to be too late.'

He drew level, his eyes glinting malevolently as they rested on Izzy's suitcase for a second too long, and her heart began to hammer painfully.

He knows I'm making a run for it.

'If you'll excuse us, for a second,' Terry addressed the receptionist, reaching out to grasp Izzy's elbow. 'Need a quick word with Miss Stevenson. There's something she forgot to update me on.'

It was as plain as the nose on her bloody face. Terry knew exactly what she'd failed to run past him. She should have known better than to underestimate that rattle-snake.

Terry latched onto her arm and tugged her away from the desk, well out with the receptionist's hearing.

'Heard you telling all and sundry you were off to the club,' he hissed in her ear. 'But, somehow, you were laying it on a bit too thick for my liking. My gut was telling me not to trust our resourceful Miss Stevenson, so I followed you to the loading bay. And what did I see; only that silly bitch, Kathy, hugging you as if her life depended on it. Looked very much like a final farewell.'

He'd seen her and Kathy making their goodbyes. No wonder he'd smelt a rat. Kathy had been utterly distraught.

'But of course, it all fell into place once I'd turned up at the nightclub and found Miss Stevenson nowhere in sight; had never set foot in the bloody place. But had still managed to find time to contact the manager; advised him that Miss Davies would be in charge of tonight's party. He said something about you having just resigned?'

He treated Izzy to a decidedly fake smile. 'Given all the puzzled faces I've just left, you clearly omitted to tell Jack and the lads that little piece of pertinent information. An intentional oversight, was it?' He gave a short bark of laughter 'That's when I decided to get back here, stop you taking matters into your own hands. After all, your contract doesn't officially expire for another three weeks. Jack's already talking about suing...'

'Let him sue. He'll find out soon enough the reason why I'm leaving.' Izzy's voice was clipped.

She'd posted her letter to Jack's London office earlier in the day.

'But more to the point, we've got a date tonight, Izzy.' Terry cocked his head to the side. 'A date you agreed to just this afternoon.

Although, thinking back, you agreed to it a bit too easily, given all your previous protests?'

'Did you really think I'd seriously go through with it?' Izzy's lip curled in disgust.

Instantly, Terry's genial mask slipped. 'You owe me, Izzy.'

'No, I don't.' Izzy flashed back. 'So take your filthy hands off me.' She tried—unsuccessfully—to twist her elbow out of his grasp.

'Too late, bitch. The sand's run out the timer. Time to tell that snotty cow behind the desk to look after your bags, you'll be back down to collect them later—if I let you.' He dropped his voice. 'Or maybe, I might just arrange to have your body dumped in the East River to swim with the fishes, given how much you enjoy "swimming" these days!'

Did he think she'd go *anywhere* with him willingly after that chilling threat? No, this ended here. She'd scream the place down first.

'Drop dead, Terry!'

'Or do I need to use force to get you up there?' The nauseating stench from his mouth was threatening to overpower her. 'I could break your little arm now; snap that bone clean in two.' His grip tightened to emphasise the point, and an unbelievably sharp pain shot up through her elbow, making Izzy gasp out loud. She didn't doubt his claim. But she still wasn't going down without a fight.

'Is everything alright, Miss Stevenson?' The receptionist looked up, her expression curious.

Izzy was given a meaningful little push back towards the desk. 'Tell her!' he rasped against her ear.

Concerned grey eyes met Izzy's. 'Miss Stevenson?' the receptionist prompted once more.

'Yes…' Izzy's voice was unnaturally high.

What did she do?

Think, Izzy, think.

Those vice-like fingers treated Izzy to another burst of excruciating pain.

'The sooner we get this over with, the sooner you can be on your way,' Terry reminded her.

Izzy darted a surreptitious glance at her suitcase resting by her right foot, then at the still questioning face of the Receptionist, and lastly back at Terry.

All at once an idea flashed into her mind. It was time to wipe that dirty great smirk of his face, but could she get away with it?

'Em, could you possibly keep an eye on my luggage for a little while longer? I need to have a quick meeting upstairs with Mr Costello; bring him up to speed on a few *points.*' Izzy addressed the receptionist, lifting her suitcase in her right hand.

Out of the corner of her eye, she could make out an answering grin spreading across Terry's features. The idiot actually thought she was going to hand over her luggage, and then go upstairs with him.

No chance! It's time to fight fire with fire.

At the last possible second, she turned, giving an unexpected little jerk to the right, pretending to over-balance with the suitcase's weight, before twisting back on herself, all the while swinging her weapon as hard as she could, taking direct aim for Terry's crotch.

There was a sickening thump, as she made contact.

First point covered, Izzy.

For a split second, Terry looked at her with an altogether bemused expression, his mouth forming a silent 'o', and then his body concertinaed in on itself as he let out a howl of pain.

Dropping Izzy's elbow, he staggered backwards, both hands clasped between his legs. With grim satisfaction, Izzy watched him fall onto his knees, swaying backwards and forwards, tears of fury appearing in his eyes.

'What the fuck…' he managed to grind out just as Izzy swung the suitcase for a second time.

Her second blow proved equally successful.

Second point successfully covered

Squealing like a farrowing pig, Terry collapsed backwards onto the terrazzo flooring, writhing in genuine agony.

'And don't you ever come near me again, Terry!' Izzy brandished the suitcase above his head. 'Don't like it when the boot's on the other foot, do you? Well, consider this a parting gift from me, Angie and every other female who's had the misfortune to cross your path over the years.'

'You fucking bitch. You'll be sorry for this.' Terry wheezed, his head snapping towards the stunned face of the receptionist. 'Don't just stand gawping, you stupid cow. Call the fucking police! I want that bitch arrested.'

Shit! Arrested? Izzy's face fell. She hadn't figured on that outcome. Were NYPD's finest now about to descend on the hotel and frogmarch her down to the nearest police precinct? Charge her with GBH?

She flashed a hurried look in the other woman's direction, hoping she'd read the desperation in her eyes.

'I think Mr Costello must have tripped and fallen over when the suitcase slipped from your hand, Miss Stevenson?' the receptionist prompted, holding out Izzy's receipt as though nothing untoward had just occurred. 'And please don't worry; I'll call security to assist you...'

Picking up the telephone receiver, the receptionist glanced towards Terry. 'Please rest assured; they'll make sure this gentleman doesn't harass you any further.'

Izzy let go the breath she'd been holding. Somehow, against all odds, she was home and dry.

'Thank you.' Her face broke into a grateful smile.

'What the fuck did you just say to her?' Terry remained prone on the foyer floor, clearly still suffering from his close encounter of the "suitcase" kind. 'Are you fucking deaf, woman? I told you I want her arrested. Get the god-damn police, *NOW!*'

At that moment, two of the hotel's security team appeared at the receptionist's shoulder.

'Could you escort Miss Stevenson to her taxi, please? It should be outside.' she explained, before nodding towards Terry. 'And make sure she's not bothered by this gentleman. He also requires removal from the premise.'

'You can't do that.' Terry made a half-hearted attempt to pull himself up to a sitting position, wincing as he did so. 'I'm a fucking guest here, remember!'

'I think you'll find we can, sir. We don't tolerate threatening behaviour towards any of our guests.'

'What the Fuck? *She* was the one who fucking clobbered me with her suitcase. *TWICE!* I think that constitutes threatening behaviour!' Terry had made it onto his knees, hands resting on his thighs, breathing heavily from the exertion.

'Nor members of our night reception staff,' the receptionist went on, 'or have you forgotten about that little incident, which necessitated the Manager's intervention?'

So, Terry had been trying it on with the hotel staff? Izzy smiled to herself. Good, hopefully they'd throw the book at him.

'Would like to come with me, ma'am?' an altogether comforting male voice said in Izzy's ear.

Looking up, Izzy received a reassuring smile from a giant bear of a man, before he reached forward and took the case out of her hand, indicating she should follow him.

'Not so fast, bitch, I've not finished—' Terry was on his feet now, and attempting a few tottering steps towards Izzy.

'Oh yes you are,' Jim Hambro's determined voice cut in, behind them.

Izzy swung around to be confronted by Rick's anxious parents racing towards her.

'Are you alright, my love?' Betty's arms were outstretched. 'I'm sorry, but we couldn't leave you here,' she explained, as Izzy allowed herself to be enveloped into a tight hug. 'I'd never have forgiven myself if something had happened.'

'Don't worry.' Izzy pulled back, giving them both a relieved smile; glad they were there. 'I'm fine. Everything's good. But I have to go, my taxi's waiting outside.'

'And we're coming with you, love. Make sure you get away, okay.' Jim gave her a reassuring wink.

That's where Rick gets it from.

'Thanks Jim, I'd like that very much.'

'If you take one step out that door, we'll see you in court, Izzy. Do you hear me?' Terry called out, but his progress had been barred by the hulking figure of Security Guard Number Two, who had a restraining hand pressed—very firmly—to the smaller man's chest.

'Please leave the lady alone, Sir.'

'Get you fucking hands off me?' But Terry had met his match; his attempt to push past Security Guard Number Two failing miserably.

'Do you hear what I'm saying, Izzy?'

With Betty's arm tight about her shoulders, steering her towards the hotel exit, Izzy allowed herself one final withering glance in Terry's direction, before walking away.

She was going home.

55

OVER THE ATLANTIC OCEAN

The 'Please fasten your seatbelt' sign clicked off, and Izzy released her belt with a sigh of relief. The flight had left on time and they were now airborne. Even better, according to the cheery voice of their captain up on the flight deck, barring any unforeseen circumstances, they'd be landing back at London Heathrow in approximately seven hours, just in time for a full English breakfast.

She settled back, stealing a quick look out of the window, the blazing lights of New York City were receding, being swallowed up by the enveloping darkness of the night sky.

Well, she'd made it, back in Economy class amongst the ordinary mortals and no longer rubbing shoulders with the international jet set, but at least she'd got to the airport safely— thanks to Betty and Jim. And, in just a matter of hours, she'd be back with her parents. She could afford to relax. Izzy Stevenson had shed her skin and Izzy Anderson had made a welcome reappearance.

Before she'd been forced to leave the Hambros behind, Betty had confirmed that she'd passed her letter over to Rick at the nightclub. With that news, Izzy had briefly hoped Rick might race to the airport and—like all good romantic novels—stop her boarding the flight, declaring his undying love on bended knee. But of course, that hadn't happened; he wouldn't have made it through security for a start. This wasn't a soppy romance novel.

Reaching down to her handbag, she dug out the copy of *Harper's Bazaar* magazine she'd bought at the newsstand, the sole reason for its purchase, an article it boasted on the band. She flicked to the relevant pages, pausing to stare down at Rick's picture; his eyes staring moodily back at her. She traced the contours of his face with her index finger, her heart contracting. She'd never being able to talk to him or kiss those lips ever again. How would she learn to cope without him in her life?

'I'll always love you, Rick,' she whispered to the photograph.

Taking a deep breath, she flicked back to the previous page, ready to start reading. She paused momentarily to take in the image displayed there.

A hung-over Jonny was being hustled towards a waiting limo by a grim-faced Terry, girls pressing forward on all sides, trying to make a grab for any part of the guitarist's anatomy within reach. Her lips twitched. Hopefully, a certain part of Terry's anatomy was still feeling tender, after its close encounter with her suitcase.

A stewardess appeared at her elbow with the refreshments trolley, and Izzy selected a *Pepsi*.

'I was lucky enough to catch them on Thursday night at Madison Square Garden,' the stewardess commented, nodding towards the open magazine, as she handed over an open bottle, together with a glass, and fresh napkin.

'Me too,' Izzy answered. 'Did you enjoy the show?'

'Sure did!' The stewardess had an attractive southern drawl. 'They're all such gorgeous guys, especially their drummer, Rick. Boy, I wouldn't mind spending a few hours with him—just one to one?' She giggled. 'With that sexy smile, he sure knows how to send a woman's pulse rate skyrocketing.'

'Yes, he certainly does.' Izzy agreed.

With a final knowing look, the stewardess moved on to assist the next passenger, leaving Izzy alone with her thoughts. Tears prickled inside her eyelids, and she blinked them away, determined not to cry any more. She had to hold it together just a little longer; just until she was safely back within Mum's arms, her Dad's comforting 'I told you so, Izzy', ringing in her ears. Only once she was there, could she give in to the pain of her broken heart.

56

PORTREATH, CORNWALL

Izzy rested her chin on her knees; arms wrapped about her legs as she gazed out towards the far horizon, her unread book open but face down, at her side. The mid-day sunlight was sparkling onto the water, and out in the bay, white horses were playing merrily under the direction of a gentle Cornish breeze. She might be a world away from Avalon Beach, but here was just as picturesque.

She allowed herself a small smile at some toddlers paddling with their parents in the crystal clear water, nearby; their squeals of joy making her feel wistful. The beach was crowded with locals and tourists alike, taking advantage of the unseasonably scorching June weather. Portreath itself was truly breathtaking—a real chocolate-box of a village perched on rocks surrounding a horseshoe harbour—but she was finding it hard to appreciate its sunny delights. Not when her mind and heart were currently miles away in Portugal.

She looked down at her watch, the hands touching noon and, on cue, those damn tears dampened her pale cheeks. They'd be at the Registry Office, and any minute now, he'd be married; married to Francesca.

She fished out a damp tissue from her shorts. She was a total mess; all she did was cry. It was her default setting. From the moment she'd stepped off the plane at Glasgow and ran into her mother's arms at Domestic Arrivals, hardly twenty-four hours had passed without her breaking down. She'd completely fallen apart, and it was all so un-Izzy-like.

She sniffed, pushing up her dark glasses, and wiping the moistness from the rims of her eyes. Her parents were worried sick. She'd lost so much weight over the last few months; her clothes were hanging on her. And while they knew part of the story, they didn't know all the gory details; her dad growing increasingly unsympathetic, telling her she needed to snap out of it and fast, men like Rick Hambro were no good. There were plenty—and far more appropriate—fish in the sea for his beloved daughter. A rapprochement with Alex had even been mentioned, as a way to heal her shattered heart, but Alex was the last thing she needed.

Not when all she craved was Rick, and this gut-wrenching grief wasn't showing signs of disappearing any time soon. Whoever said time was a great healer was— in her opinion—an out-and-out liar. All time had done was brought what she'd lost into even sharper focus. She loved him; she'd never stop loving him. She missed that smile, his husky voice whispering 'pretty lady' in her ear as they made love, and those melted chocolate eyes. Eyes that had made her feel like she'd been the centre of his universe over those ten magical days.

But the sensible part of her, knew her Dad was right. She had to try and pull herself together; accept Rick was never coming back to her. That was why, with the wedding day rapidly approaching, she'd decided to take herself off on holiday. Her mother had begged to be included on her trip, only too aware of the significant date looming, but Izzy had been adamant. She needed this time alone; time to get her head straight. Make a concerted effort to pick up the pieces, but so far, Cornwall hadn't worked any of its magic.

A seagull let out a piercing scream, making her flinch as it soared low overhead. Watching, as the bird disappeared off into the horizon,

Izzy wished—with all her heart— she was that bird and could fly away from all her problems, just as easily.

'Stunning view, isn't it?'

Rick's voice cut into her thoughts, and Izzy jumped for a second time, looking upwards at the dark shadow looming over her, her breath catching in her throat, blinking behind her sunglasses.

Wordlessly, she watched as the man she'd been dreaming about collapsed down onto the sand at her side.

'Wha…Wha…What are you doing here?'

Was she suffering from the effects of heat stroke? After all, she'd been out in the sun since just after breakfast, or was she having some kind of spontaneous hallucination, her mind so fixated on Rick and the wedding?

But this Rick looked real—drop-dead-gorgeous real—in his trusty *Levi 501s* and white shirt, sleeves pushed up over those strong forearms, aviator sunglasses shielding those beautiful eyes from view.

Izzy blinked again and pushed her own sunglasses onto her head.

'Mum told me you were visiting Cornwall, so I thought it was time to take a trip along the coast to see you.'

Yes, it was his voice. She was treated to a flash of that bone-melting smile, as he slipped off his sunglasses, hooking them into his shirt pocket.

Izzy's brow crinkled in confusion. The last she'd heard, Rick and his parents weren't on speaking terms. Francesca had banned them from the wedding.

'But you're supposed to be in Lisbon,' she blurted out, checking her watch again. It was now heading for ten past twelve. 'You're supposed to be saying "I do" at this very minute.'

'True, that was always Francesca's plan,' Rick agreed, 'but it was never mine. I was never getting married, today.'

He reached out to gently stroke her cheek, his touch warmer than the mid-day sun up above. 'I couldn't marry Francesca, or anyone else for that matter. Not when the girl I'm madly in love with is sitting on this beach looking so bloody sad, and knowing I'm the bastard who's broken her heart.'

'Me…' Izzy's throat dried as she stared back at him.

Had she heard properly? He wasn't marrying Francesca and—somehow—he'd just declared he was in love with her.

He gave a rueful grimace. 'Yes you, pretty lady. It's always been you. Didn't you guess, after everything that happened between us in the States?'

One hand continued to cup her cheek, while the other fished out a piece of well-read paper from the pocket of his jeans. It was held together with strips of cellotape; her letter.

'It's been you from the moment we met, Izzy,' he went on, replacing the letter carefully back in his pocket. 'But, knowing what a stubborn, ignorant dickhead I've been, I've probably succeeded in losing you for good. I should have come here sooner; come as soon as I read the letter, but things have been crazy. I'd a load to sort out legally, between the sabbatical, and ending things with Francesca.'

Reaching over, he tried to plant a kiss on her forehead, but Izzy pulled away, instantly wary.

'Please don't.' She held up a hand against him, and Rick pulled back.

He couldn't let him touch her. Not yet. She was too raw, too vulnerable. Not ready to let her guard down until she knew what was going on? Looking up, she could see Rick's expression was resigned, as though he'd expected that kind of reaction.

She was also aware that people were beginning to stare at them; her unexpected visitor being recognised.

'Izzy, do you think we could go somewhere and talk?' Rick was clearly picking up those same vibes. 'I've got so much I need to say to you, but...' He gave another uncomfortable side glance at the beach's occupants. 'It's not very private around here. Will you hear me out? At least, give me the chance to apologise for treating you so badly?'

Izzy gave a brief nod. 'Okay.'

Still feeling stunned at his unexpected appearance, she struggled onto her sandal-clad feet, brushing the sand away from the seat of her denim shorts. 'We can go back to the cottage if you want?'

He stood up too, giving a rueful smile. 'I've already been there; met your neighbour. She told me where I could find you.'

'My neighbour?'

'The woman who lives in the house next door; said she was your landlady.' He raked a hand through his hair. 'She told me you're a lovely girl, but with terribly sad eyes.'

'Yeah, Mrs Trevelyan,' Izzy realised, 'she's really nice, but a wee bit of a nosey parker. Wanted to know all about me and why I was here. Told her I needed a break. That I'd just split up with someone.'

Rick reached for her hand, raising her fingers to his lips and when she didn't pull away this time, he kissed their tips tenderly. 'That's what I told her, too. Told her I'd lost the love of my life, but I was here to win her back; if she'll have me?'

His look was questioning. 'Come on, let's go. We really need to talk. Sort out this mess.'

They sat side by side on the sofa, Izzy having made them both some coffee. They'd covered the two-minute walk back to the cottage in silence. Izzy's hand held firmly within Rick's grasp, as though he was frightened she'd disappear if he let go—even for a minute. A black, top-of the-range Mercedes—brand new, and obviously Rick's—was parked up in front of the cottage door.

But how had he known where to find her?

So many questions were churning inside Izzy's mind, but she didn't know where to begin. He'd called her the love of his life. Said he was madly in love with her. But what did it really mean? Could she dare to hope?

'Thanks.' Rick put down the half-drunk mug of coffee onto the table. 'I needed that. I'd a bit of an early start this morning.'

'How's Southampton?' she asked, for something to say, fiddling with the pendant at her neck. According to his mother, he'd moved down there at the beginning of May. Izzy had presumed it was with Francesca, but clearly, not.

'Great,' he answered with a smile, 'the views over the Solent are magnificent. Just the kind of place I need to do my thinking, but…,' he sighed, 'it's a bit lonely with just Barney for company. He's not one of life's great conservationists.'

'Barney?' Izzy's eyebrows knotted together in a frown.

'My golden retriever puppy; I told you I was buying a dog. Picked up the little monster last week; Michelle and her boyfriend are dog-sitting him for me, today. He chews everything in bloody sight. He's already had a go at the leather sofa. I'd love for you to meet him. I've a feeling he'll love you just as much as I do.'

He took her hand in his, his long fingers linking snugly around hers, resting them on his thigh. 'Izzy, I finished it with Francesca a few weeks after you left. As I've said already, there was never going to be any wedding.' He gave her a tentative smile. 'She knows everything, including how I feel about you. She agreed to keep her mouth shut. Maintain the pretence that the wedding was still happening, until I'd formally announced my sabbatical. Even her family didn't know it was all off, until a few days ago. But it's cost me—big time,' he went on. 'She's now the sole owner of the London flat, together with all its contents, including Marc's awful painting'—he winked—'and she should be jetting off tomorrow to the Bahamas, to spend our honeymoon with Davey and Caron. She's also received a very generous cash settlement on condition she doesn't sell her story to the newspapers. Jack's issuing a press release later this afternoon, stating we've gone our separate ways.

News on Rick's sabbatical from the band had hit the mainstream press a week ago, confirming—in part—wild rumours that had been swirling within the music industry over the band's future. The *Live Aid* Concert in July would be Rick's last official outing with Eclectic Deviation—for the time being.

'But I've spoken to your mum; she never said a word about you splitting up with Francesca. Just that she was wasn't going to the wedding.'

'She was sworn to secrecy,' Rick clarified. 'I needed everything kept hush-hush, until I could get here. Talk this through with you face to face. Your mum's in on it too. Mum asked for her help; begged her—on my behalf—for your address. '

'She did?' Izzy's eyes widened incredulously at that piece of news. 'But you were so angry after what I did. You looked like you hated me. And now, suddenly you're here, telling me you love me. That you've split from Francesca...' she trailed off.

'First, let's get one thing straight,' Rick answered. 'I've never hated you, Izzy. I could never do that.' He gave her hand another gentle squeeze. 'But I won't deny it hurt like hell when I found out about what you'd both done. I lashed out without really thinking it all through.'

Without letting go of her hand, he pulled her letter from his jeans pocket again. 'I have read and re-read your letter— torn it up and stuck it back together. And no surprise, the insomnia's back. But I've talked it through with Michelle—who gave me such a bloody bollocking over the way I've treated you—and I understand everyone's reasons. Mum was right. I did cut her and dad out; distanced myself. I should have opened up more, but I was too proud. I'm working on that now.' He sighed. 'But more importantly, I'm not prepared to lose you. You are the one person who's been in my corner from day one. That's why I'm here to fight for you, fight for us and some kind of future together, but only if you'll have me, Izzy?'

Izzy's breath hitched at the sincerity reflected in the depths of those pleading brown eyes. He meant every single word of his impassioned speech.

'Because, when I met you again last November, something really weird happened, Izzy.'

'It did?' Their eyes were locked together now.

'I knew I'd met the person I wanted to spend the rest of my life with. I hadn't just met my new PA. The love of my life was sitting before me with the most beautiful sapphire eyes.' His smile became wry. 'Believe me, those aren't the kind of thoughts I usually have within ten seconds of meeting a pretty girl. I'm not a mushy love-at-first-sight kind of guy. That's Marc's bag. But then, sexy beautiful you took my breath away. When you walked through the door, holding out your hand to me and saying, "Hi, I'm Izzy Stevenson", I was hooked.'

He shook his head. 'But the sensible part of me was still dubious. How could I fall for someone just like that? Initially, I thought it must be lust, some kind of weird crush, but as the interview progressed, all I could think about was finding a way to persuade the others to hire you. I could tell Davey and Steve weren't keen, but I just knew I needed to get to know you. Thank God Jack listened to Marc and I.'

He sighed. 'And I've been keeping another secret too. I was going to talk to you about all this after I'd spoken to the band and Francesca. What I've never told you is that things hadn't been good between Francesca and me for a good six months before you even walked into my life. I wasn't in love with her, anymore. I was seeing too many glimmers of the real her, and didn't like it.

'Then last April, we had an almighty row over something she'd said about my parents and I ended it, for good—or so I thought. I had a meaningless fling with Kathy, but then Francesca turned up, begging for another chance; guilt-tripped me into going back. Before I knew it, I'd proposed to her. Even though I knew it was an almighty mistake. But I was in so much turmoil about the band...

Izzy stroked her fingers through his hair. So many things about their time together, conversations they'd had, were finally dropping into place.

'Making the last album had been hell on earth,' Rick went on, 'and the thought of the forthcoming tour was scaring the crap out of me. I just ended up going through the motions; buried my head in the sand as far as she was concerned. Even let her begin to organise a wedding I knew I'd have to cancel at some point.'

He let out a deep sigh, his eyes meeting Izzy's. 'And the feelings I had for you only got stronger and stronger the more time I spent with you. Your smile, that fantastic body and those mesmerising eyes; you pretty lady were enslaving me more and more, and I couldn't keep away. Jeez, I became so calculating. Always thinking up more ways to get your attention; get close to you without you suspecting.'

He winked, and Izzy flushed with pleasure, but one thing still niggled at her.

'But the paperwork for the wedding, why did you ask me to fix things so urgently, if it was all going to be called off anyway?'

'I couldn't break up with Francesca over the telephone. It wouldn't have been fair.' He answered. 'I didn't love her, but she still deserved an honest face-to-face conversation. We were so bloody busy, and I was so knackered, I didn't have time to throw the distraction of a break-up into the mix. It was just another plate I had to keep spinning until I'd time to take a breath and deal with it. It was easier getting you to sort the paperwork, than come clean to Francesca. But it was always my intention to end it with her in New York; once I'd spoken to the band.'

Izzy gave a little nod, seeing the logic of his argument.

'Plus, getting you to do things for me was just another excuse to be near you. With all the crap going on, I decided to use the old 'you remind me of my sister' routine. Big mistake, I was hopeless. I couldn't keep up the pretence.' He shook his head. 'When we finally got together on the night of my birthday, it was so fucking amazing. And I could tell you felt something for me too, even though you were trying to hide it. I knew I was going to talk to you at the end of the tour, beg you to make a go of it with me. But then I found out what you and Mum had done, and that made me question all my decisions— the band; my future; Francesca—all over again.'

Izzy looked down sadly, hating how much she'd hurt him with her deception.

'But underneath it all, you were still the only one I wanted, Izzy. Not Francesca. Not anybody else; just you.' He placed a finger under her chin, tilting her head upwards. 'Can you forgive me for being a total bastard? For all the horrible things I said? Put this behind us and maybe move forward? Allow me to spend the rest of our lives making it up to you? Please don't say it's too late for us?'

He bit his lip, looking so uncertain that Izzy had to restrain herself from jumping into his lap. Instead, she allowed herself a full beat, before putting him out of his misery, her face breaking into a wide smile.

'Nope, it's not too late, Rick. That's what I want too, more than anything.'

Reaching up, she pressed her lips to his. 'I love you too, and I'm so sorry for doing what I did,' she confessed, as they pulled apart. 'I'd been in love with you for so long, Rick, but I couldn't see any future. You seemed so settled with Francesca, and I was lying to you practically every time I opened my mouth. I knew if you found out about me—about what I'd agreed to do—it could destroy your relationship with your mum and dad. I didn't want that on my conscience.'

'I know. And that's one of the reasons why I love you so much, because you're selfless, prepared to walk away to protect me and my family. God, I hate myself for all the cruel, hurtful things I said. If I could take them back…'

He reached over, and they kissed again.

'I was an arrogant, spiteful shit.' He let out an impatient sigh. 'I wanted to hurt you the way I was hurting inside. Deny my feelings; hoping they'd go away, but they wouldn't. They just got harder to ignore, especially when you admitted to loving me in your letter.'

Rick felt in the pocket of his jeans and drew out a tiny black box. 'I bought this for you last week,' he explained, flipping the catch on the lid. 'I hope you like it. If not, we can go shopping again; I'll buy whatever you want…'

Izzy let out a gasp at the sight of the ring nestled in red velvet pad. An oval sapphire flanked by three smaller diamond chips on either side.

'No need; it's perfect,' she said, blinking up at him through her lashes.

'I know this might be way too soon, but I have to ask.' He slid off the sofa to kneel at her feet, and Izzy's heart leapt. He was about to propose to her; actually propose to her.

'Will you marry me, pretty lady?'

His eyes still held a degree of uncertainty. 'I know it's crazy. You might feel we need more time to get to know each other. Take it slower. And if you do, that's fine. I'll wait. I'll wait for however long it takes.'

'Nope, it's not too soon. I love you too,' she answered, before flinging her arms around his neck, kissing him now as though her life depended on it.

The sound of a car backfiring outside in the street, finally made them come up for air. Taking her left hand in his, Rick slid the engagement ring onto its rightful place.

'My pretty lady, I've learnt there is no way I can live without you. Because when cupid's arrow fired last year, it lodged so deep in my heart, it's never coming out.' He grinned. 'Or maybe he just realised fifteen years ago there could be something pretty special between us. Pulled a few strings to get us back together again.'

'Yep, Cupid's definitely one clever guy,' she agreed with a chuckle.

'And this ring is never coming off.' He vowed, planting another lingering kiss to her brow.

'You said it.' Izzy agreed, loving how snugly the ring fitted around her finger. 'It looks like you've got me for keeps.'

'That's all I want to hear.'

He fumbled in his pocket a third time, this time drawing out her bracelet.

'You actually kept it!' she squealed, taking it from him and slipping it onto her right wrist.

It was then she noticed that her birthday gift to him was also back in its rightful place.

'Of course I kept it. It will always be yours. But I wanted to give you the ring first. You mean the whole world to me, Izzy Ste… Anderson,' he corrected with a grin, pulling her to her feet. 'Sorry, I'm still getting used to saying Anderson, but I can't wait for you to become Izzy Hambro.'

'Me neither.'

A tingle shot down to her toes at the intense look they exchanged, and they kissed again. This time when he drew back, he pretended to stifle yawn.

'Jeez, I'm suddenly feeling really tired. And my neck and shoulders have stiffened up.' There was a definite sexy twinkle in the depths of those chocolate eyes. 'Had to get up so bloody early this morning to drive over and find you. Took me hours; got lost—twice. Map reading's clearly not my thing. Not surprising given I failed my Geography O-level.' He linked his arms about her waist. 'I could really do with a massage?'

Izzy was unable to contain her laughter at the expectant look she received. 'You want a massage, Mr Hambro?' She arched an eyebrow.

'I sure do. Rob, my physio's great. He's six foot six, an ex-rugby player, who beats the crap out of me every chance he gets,' he went on, 'but he's not a patch on a certain pretty lady.'

Izzy couldn't help but fall in with his teasing. 'Well, I suppose I'd better see what I can do. Given you're *so* tired and stiff. Purely for old times' sake, of course.'

She caught his lingering glance down the front of her cotton vest and felt that wonderfully familiar pool of heat in the pit of her stomach.

'We could make it a full body one?' She offered. 'Take up where we left off?'

He was already tugging her towards the narrow staircase that led off the lounge. 'Lead me to your consulting room, Miss Anderson?'

A long time later, they lay snuggled together in the rather cramped double divan the Cottage's master bedroom boasted, Izzy's head resting contentedly against Rick's chest.

'I wonder if my neighbour has noticed my bedroom curtains are suddenly closed?' she commented, glancing up and treating him to a saucy wink.

'Just hope she didn't catch an eyeful when I finally remembered to do the actual closing. I'm sure I saw her lurking out there on her doorstep.' Rick commented, leisurely stroking his thumb up and down the skin on Izzy's arm.

He'd been naked at the time, crawling on all fours towards the window, while Izzy lay back in bed, laughing hysterically at the floorshow.

'Lucky her, if she did.' Izzy snuggled closer. 'Seeing you in all your glory would make any woman's day.'

'Is that so?' Rick replied, his lips brushing against her brow. 'Well, next time she sees you, she'll see I've managed to put a smile back on that gorgeous face.'

'You certainly have. Especially as you claimed I was never your type in the first place.'

This comment immediately earned her a mystified look from Rick.

'What do you mean by that? When have I ever said you aren't my type?'

A giggling Izzy recounted what she'd overheard outside the band's hotel room the previous November. 'And you emphasised that my knickers would always be perfectly safe whenever you were around.'

With dawning realisation, he gave her one of his breathtaking smiles. 'Okay, I suppose, technically, you weren't the type of girl I'd ever gone out within the past.' He gave a little shrug. 'Nor was I about to admit to my bandmates, the thoroughly indecent thoughts I'd been having about our new PA. But believe me, Izzy; your knickers were anything but safe.'

Reaching over, he caught her chin between his thumb and forefinger. 'There will never be anyone else but you, Izzy. No more fucked-up one-night stands and idiotic band rules about what we can do on tour. You're the only one I want to wake up with. Make love with. Have kids with. Live my life with; nobody else, Izzy.'

Izzy shivered with anticipation at the thought of them having children; their children.

'But there's still something we need to discuss.'

'What's that?' Izzy had rolled onto her stomach to gain a better look at him.

'Why didn't you tell me about Terry? He tangled his fingers in her curls, his expression suddenly grim. 'And especially after I'd offered to help. You should have told me, Izzy.'

'I know, but I couldn't.' She flushed guiltily, pressing a soft kiss to his chest in apology. 'I felt you'd enough on your plate without me bothering you. And given why I was there, I didn't want to draw too attention to myself, just in case my cover was blown. So, I decided early on, Terry had to be *my* problem.'

'But the bastard was going to rape you. Mum told me everything.' Temper flashed in his eyes, his jaw clenching. 'Jeez, Izzy, I wanted to kill him when I heard. You'll be glad to know Jack has sacked him.'

'Sacked him?'

'Yep, he was out on the spot. As soon as Jack read the letter you'd sent.' Rick frowned. 'If he'd touched you, Izzy…?'

'But he didn't… well not really. It *was* horrible what he did do, but I dealt with it,' Izzy reassured him, twisting her fingers into the hair on his chest, her little tug teasing a reluctant smile out of him. 'But aren't you more concerned about what he could do now? He knows so much, Rick. He could do real harm if he goes to the press.'

'He can try.' Rick's mouth remained in a grim line. 'But remember, we know plenty of stuff about him, and not just the Angie incident. She isn't the first one we've had to pay off. There were others….' He blew out his cheeks. 'I'm not proud of what we did, Izzy. I'll never be proud of brushing his repulsive behaviour under the carpet. It will always be on my conscience. But in those days, we were young and stupid with our careers before us, fame beckoning. Only with hindsight do you realise how crazy and fucked up it was.' He paused before carrying on, 'If Terry decides to retaliate, he'll find himself tied up in so much legal shit that he'll wish he'd kept his mouth shut. '

She was finally treated to a long overdue smile. 'We're a team, Izzy. It's you and me from now on. Promise, you'll never keep something like that from me again.'

'I promise.' Izzy was glad that there were no more secrets between them.

'And by the way, we also need to talk about your interview?'

'What interview?'

'Well, I still need a PA, remember,' he went on. 'Although, Mum said you've just taken a job at your local university…'

The penny dropped. 'I'm sure, if someone else made me a better offer, I'd reconsider it,' she said, airily.

'Good answer, pretty lady. And you might have two additional bosses in future? Would you be able to handle that?' He winked.

'Depends who they are?'

But somehow she could make a pretty good guess.

'Let's just say, they'll be silent partners at first. Although I don't know how long Marc will manage that feat. Less than ten bloody seconds, if I know him.' Rick rolled his eyes. 'Marc and Jonny are coming in with me. The band will continue as a foursome until the end of my sabbatical and I'll make my final decision, then. But they're both interested in the studio idea, long-term. Steve's been approached about a couple of acting jobs, which he's seriously considering, and Davey and Marc are still at loggerheads. To be honest, I don't think it will be long before Davey jumps ship. After all, I'm not his favourite person, either.' He stole another kiss. 'But the studio will go ahead in some guise, and I'm in charge of getting it off the ground.'

Izzy's brow wrinkled. 'But are Marc and Jonny happy to work with *me* again? Have you told them about what I did; who I really am?'

'Of course I have, and they're more than happy to be on board with my choice of future wife—and PA.'

'I recall you said the job of PA was off the table, permanently.' Izzy teased, wanting nothing more than to work alongside him, make both their dreams come true.

'Well, it's very much back on, but you'll need a very thorough debriefing on my terms.'

'Shouldn't that be "briefing"?' Izzy couldn't resist correcting his English with an impish grin, feeling his hand slip down her body to caress her bottom.

'Don't tell me you're contradicting your new boss already, Miss Anderson?' he asked, giving it a playful slap. 'No, *debriefing* is much more appropriate. Make sure you know exactly what I expect of you—at all times! Think you can handle my terms, Izzy?'

Her bottom received a second light, but extremely pleasurable, smack.

'Yep, I think I can.' Her eyes blazed down at him as brightly as the sapphire ring on her finger.

'Then let's start now, pretty lady. No time like the present'

Within seconds, a giggling Izzy was on her back, the wonderful heat of Rick's body covering hers.

'Mmmm, a debriefing from my new boss sounds an idyllic way to spend a Friday afternoon.' She mused, before brushing her lips against his. 'And don't worry, as always, you'll be permitted access to *all* areas, Mr Hambro.'

The End

ACKNOWLEDGEMENTS

Firstly, I would like to say thank-you, reader, for taking the time to read my book. You don't know how much this means to me.

The premise of 'Access all Areas' was first written forty years ago when I was only fifteen. I was a true child of the 1980's, totally immersed in all the music, fashions and glamour of those times, and my first version very much reflected the 'teenage' me and my massive crushes on the pop stars of the day. The second version - an extension of the first - with certain themes developed, was created in my early-twenties.

This final version evolved during lockdown, when many of us had time on our hands. It was during those strange days that I decided to see if I could actually get the romance between Izzy and Rick (the final names I'd chosen for my two protagonists) published.

The support of, and friendship given, by the following people has been integral to me continuing this project to fruition. They know who they are on this list: - Anne, Cheryl, Maja, Maureen, Christine, Mairi, Joan, Maria, Carole, Arlene, Caroline, Elaine, and Moira.

I must also give a special mention to some local published authors - Colin Campbell, Ivor Campbell and Lindsay Littleson for their invaluable advice and answers to my many questions - thank-you.

I also have to say massive 'thank-yous' to my Editor, Sarah Smeaton - you have taught me loads and I could never have done this without you - and to Ashley Santoro for your amazing art work. You brought my characters and book so beautifully, and colourfully to life.

And lastly to my cat, Kimi, who has sat beside me - under the desk - as every word was typed - and retyped - onto the page. Love you loads.

Again, thank-you all,
Joanna
Xxx